SHE OWNS THE KNIGHT

(A KNIGHT'S TALE BOOK 1)

DIANE DARCY

DEDICATION

To Grandma Murphy, with love.

And also for Brent, my own knight in shining armor, who is just as wonderful and clueless as Kellen.

ACKNOWLEDGMENTS

A great big thank you to Heather Horrocks and Bruce Simpson for the fun plotting day. Draining the dragon didn't end up in the story, but it sure was hilarious at the time!

Also, Melody, Heather, Lesli, Kristin and Sandra. Thank you so much for taking the time to read and refine. You ladies are awesome!

PROLOGUE

ENGLAND, 1260

"*I*s aught amiss?" Brows drawn together, Lord Kellen Marshall reached a hand to steady his wife. "Is it the babe?"

Catherine set her goblet on the sideboard, but seemed unable to take her gaze from it. "You switched the cups?"

"Aye. To give you the less cloudy, more pleasing drink. I'll not have you drinking the dregs." He gave her a smile, hoping, *aching* to receive one in return.

Her face turned ashen.

Kellen quickly set his drink aside, lifted her slight weight, and carried her swiftly to the bed to set her among quilts and pillows. He ran to the heavy wood door, threw it open, bellowed for help, then hurried back to where Catherine lay sweating, clutching her swollen belly. In the distance, people scrambled and orders thundered as Kellen lowered himself to her bedside.

"'Tis Cowbane," she whispered to him.

"What?" Mouth gaping, he shook his head. "No. That cannot

be." Who would do such a thing? Who would dare to poison his wife?

"You have ruined everything." She turned away from him, pressing her face into the pillows, gagging and shuddering before rolling back to grip his surcoat, her face taut with fear. "Please. You must save me. Please." She put a hand to her stomach. "The babe."

Several knights appeared in the doorway, *"Find the midwife! Bring the healer!"* Kellen roared the words.

A wide-eyed servant rushed out of the chamber as others filled the entrance.

Kellen gripped his wife's cold hand as her breathing quickened and resignation set her face. "You cannot save me," she said, tears filling her eyes. "'Tis not possible."

Her breathing became labored, her throat violently clenched, and her entire body tightened, head thrown back.

Kellen, every muscle in his body constricting with panic, shook her shoulders. "Catherine!"

She took a loud, gasping breath, then relaxed for a moment. Kellen wiped sweat from her brow with shaking fingers. "Catherine, you must be well." His voice broke. "Perchance the babe comes early?"

"The drink was meant for you." She breathed heavily, drawing breath an effort.

"What are you saying?"

"My daughter is not of your seed." Again, she convulsed violently, foam gathering at the corners of her mouth, then relaxed once more, placing a hand to her belly. "Nor is the one in my womb."

Kellen studied her face, the swelling of her body. He swallowed and gripped her hand. "You are out of your head." His voice roughened, low, deep, and pleading. "A devil has overtaken your mind."

"I despise you."

He tried to convince himself she was not herself, yet saw in her clear eyes she spoke true. And he was well aware the poisoned drink had been meant for him as he'd switched them himself. Why would she dishonor herself this way? It was senseless. "Why?"

"You sicken me." Her face twisted. "I hate your disgusting, overlarge body. Your vile face. My lover is wonderful, slim and beautiful as a knight should be. Handsome and without scars." She smiled, her face relaxing. She laughed once, then stopped breathing.

His wife, eyes open and staring, lay dead in his arms. He shook her, rage and despair welling within him. *"No!"* He clutched her to him. *"No!"* She'd swallowed poison meant for him? She'd meant to kill him? Surely, he'd misunderstood. She was no poisoner. She could not be.

Kellen's eyes filled with hot tears and he gently shook his wife once more. "Live. Live, curse you. *Live!"*

She didn't move.

His wife was dead. His son, as well. *His* son.

Kellen's head pounded. He lay his wife gently on the bed, stood, and backed away. His head, suddenly heavy, bobbed up and down as dizziness overtook him.

Air finally filled his lungs and he threw his head back, and howled like a madman. He clenched his hands in his hair and, heart pounding, every muscle constricting to the point of pain, Kellen turned and grabbed the long bench from against the wall.

With a yell, he heaved it into the fireplace and watched as pieces of heavy wood, ashes, and smoke burst into the air.

Next, he gripped a chair and dashed it against the stone wall, once, twice, until the heavy wood shattered. He ripped a tapestry Catherine had fashioned from the wall. He smashed her writing table with his fists. Threw a basket of knitted baby clothes into the fire. Tore and pulled the linen hangings from the great bed and cast them to the floor.

Breathing hard, searching for something else to destroy, Kellen stood still in the middle of the chamber. He looked to the doorway, where only a few of his knights remained, and a few more beyond, out in the hall. The servants had run off.

Only the midwife, Catherine's old nurse, the one come from Corbett Castle, had dared enter the bedchamber. She covered Catherine's body with a fur coverlet, knelt on the stairs beside the bed, crossed herself, and wailed.

Kellen watched her wipe foam from Catherine's mouth, and turned away.

His dream had died with Catherine. With the babe. His marriage, the chance to continue his line, to build a family, was the one thing that had kept him alive through all the petty wars, the politics, the tournaments, and his dangerous allegiance to King Henry.

Who provided her the poison? Who turned her against him? He knew she could not have done this on her own.

Her lover, no doubt.

Kellen's teeth ground together, and a guttural sound escaped his mouth. The babe was not his? The girl child not of his seed? There lived a man who did not have long for this world.

"Mamma?"

Kellen turned to see his three-year-old daughter lingering in the passageway with her nurse, and pain twisted his guts. She should not be there, and he did not want to look on her. He waved his hand in a dismissive gesture. "Take the girl away from here."

He would not be cheated this way. His eyes narrowed. He would marry again. He would petition the king and remind him of his loyalty and—

No. That could take years and numerous favors. At a score and ten, Kellen could not wait. Would not. He sucked air into his lungs. Corbett owed him an honorable daughter. He had seven. Six, now. He would demand another, the youngest, and most trainable, or Corbett would pay the price for his daughter's treachery with a war. Any betrothment on the girl's part would needs be broken. He would show no mercy. He'd have his heir within the year, or else.

He grabbed the nurse still kneeling beside Catherine, startling her, and hauled her to her feet. "Give me the name of her lover."

Rigid with terror, the woman gaped. "My lord?"

"Catherine's lover. His name?"

The woman trembled, shook her head, and her head-cover slid to reveal gray hair as fear widened her eyes. "Nay, my lord. She would never play you false."

Kellen forced himself to release the woman before he gave into the desire to shake her. "She admitted such. Doubt not that I will find and kill him."

Teeth clenching, he nodded toward Catherine. "Finish this. After, go home to Corbett. Tell him of his daughter's infidelity, of her attempt to murder her lord. I want another daughter in reparation, or there will be war. You will leave directly after the burial."

He would have a wife and heir. But he would never make the mistake of trusting another woman. With one last glance at Catherine's white face, he turned and strode from the chamber.

CHAPTER 1

*T*he slam of a car door alerted Gillian Corbett to the fact that she was no longer alone. She had a hard time pulling her gaze from the sketchpad and the castle ruin she drew but finally glanced up to see three men getting out of a Volkswagen.

They'd parked beside her rental car, and a tingling at the back of Gillian's neck suddenly made her aware of the remoteness of the location.

Her mouth went dry, and her stomach hollow.

She glanced around. Thanks to her lousy, cheating, money-grubbing, narcissistic ex-fiancé, she was spending what was supposed to be her honeymoon sitting on a big gray rock, in the middle of a big green field, in the heart of a foreign country. Alone.

It had seemed like a good idea at the time.

Her car sat parked off the side of the road, about a football field's length away. The rolling grass in front of her, leading to the picturesque graveyard and castle ruin in the distance, didn't calm her sudden unease. What had seemed so beautiful and interesting only moments ago, now appeared desolate, threatening and . . . stupid.

What had Ryan said that last day? *'You're like a throwback to another time, babe. It's like you live in La La Land. Going to England to do genealogy? What are you going to do, anyway? Take pictures of head-stones? That's just wrong, Gillian. Disturbed. And drawing castles? Look at yourself. You're only twenty-four years old and even your clothes are old-fashioned, with your skirts and blouses. You need to loosen up a bit. Unbutton and show some skin. Stop being so frigid and prudish. Cut your hair or something. It's like you're an old-timer in a babe's body.'*

Again, the distant slam of a car door seemed loud in the silence, and brought her out of her reverie. There were now four of them.

And one of her.

Gillian swallowed as they headed in her direction. They didn't talk amongst themselves, and Gillian tried to convince herself nothing was wrong. They were probably just friendly locals who'd spotted her, and wanted to chat. Maybe even flirt.

But her heart hammered in her chest. None of them glanced at her, or each other. They just steadily moved her way and Gillian felt a sense of menace. She hadn't seen another soul until the men showed up, or noticed any cars driving by. She was staying in the town of Marshall about six miles away, but the river, hills, and trees isolated the area.

She'd been a single woman living on her own in a big city for too long to ignore the caution she felt. She'd taken a self-defense class once, and the instructor taught to always go with her instincts. Hers were screaming to run.

One of the men finally looked up and waved at her, a jerky pointing of fingers, but the friendly gesture didn't make her feel safe. It had the opposite effect. She felt marked. Hunted.

Her heart pounded against the sketchpad she clutched to her

chest. She slipped her pencil inside the pink backpack and fumbled for her cell phone.

It wasn't there.

She had candy bars, a light jacket, a change of clothes, her wallet, keys, some extra pencils, and pepper spray, but no cell phone.

She suddenly remembered taking it out and sticking it in the convenient car cubby, in case any of her friends or coworkers called to see how her trip to England was going.

It wasn't going so well at the moment.

She quickly studied the area. Nothing but fields, trees, the graveyard, castle, and river in the distance. Not a soul in sight to help her.

The men moved steadily closer.

Was she being foolish? Paranoid? All she knew for certain, was she couldn't wait around like an easy target. She'd rather avoid them, and look like a fool in front of strangers and be safe, than stand there like an idiot and get robbed. Or worse.

She quickly stuffed her sketchpad in her backpack, put on her jacket, dug out her pepper spray, pulled the zipper, hoisted her pack, tightened it, and headed quickly for the castle. Away from the men, but also away from her car.

If she were mistaken about their intentions, they'd realize they'd scared her and leave her alone. If she wasn't, then they'd come after her. Either way, she'd know for sure.

With her heart hammering, she was almost too scared and embarrassed to look back. Would they follow? Leave? Head toward the cluster of rocks and hang out?

The fine hairs on her neck stood on end and she considered running, but was already breathing so hard she was afraid she'd hyperventilate if she tried. Heat suddenly flooded her face.

What if the guys were simply trying to help? Maybe her rental car had a flat, and they were going to offer to fix it? Or perhaps these were their favorite stomping grounds and they simply wanted to say hello? She could be making a total and complete idiot of herself.

Ha, ha! Look at the foolish and paranoid American. What a tourist!

She felt like an idiot. A scared one. She hoped they'd get the hint, realize they'd frightened her, act like gentlemen, and leave. She reminded herself that even if she were wrong, she'd never see these men again, so if she completely humiliated herself, it didn't matter. Better safe than sorry.

Gillian let her jacket sleeve fall down over the pepper spray in her hand, and finally chanced a glance over a shoulder. The men were still walking toward the boulders, but only talking and checking in her direction, not following.

Relief flooded her but, still uneasy, she didn't break stride. Maybe they'd just think she was hiking to the castle and leave her alone. They were more than welcome to climb, picnic, or play king of the mountain on the rock, just as long as they left her to go her own way.

Gillian rose over the slight hill, getting a better view of the graveyard in the process. Her stomach sank. She'd hoped to find someone there, but it was completely deserted. Why wouldn't it be? Old and decrepit, with weathered headstones, and grasses grown up around everything. The surrounding fields were dotted with wildflowers and clusters of trees. Earlier, she'd planned to explore it, now she just wanted to get through it as soon as possible.

She checked out the castle. Didn't people hang out in ruins all the time? Maybe she'd find someone there. A tour group would be nice. Perhaps visitors came at the castle from the back side. Maybe the castle even had a gift shop, and she could bum a ride to her car.

She glanced at the men again. They'd veered in her direction, and walked toward her, fast. Gillian gasped, and her heart seemed to stop for a moment, before thudding painfully in her chest.

"Hey, wait up there, pretty lady," one of the men called out to her.

She didn't answer, only shook her head. Every one of them gazed straight at her now, and fear trilled through her. Forget about embarrassment. She ran.

She glanced over a shoulder to see them chasing her! They laughed and panic and fear flooded her. Her heart pounded so hard it hurt, her feet slipped on the grassy slope. Could she make it to the castle? Surely, she'd find help there. For all she knew, there was a city or something on the other side. Or an archeology dig setting up camp.

Or there could be absolutely nothing at all.

Her anxiety level spiked as she rushed through the graveyard. There were headstones, trees, bushes, the road curving up to the castle in the distance. But nothing and no one seemed to offer shelter.

She continued forward, passing markers, flying across the bumpy ground, the castle her only likely goal. *Please, someone be there. Please, someone see what is happening and help.* If only it weren't so far away.

The hills and grass gently rose and fell and, not knowing what else to do, Gillian flat out ran for the castle. She glanced over her shoulder and stifled a scream.

She wasn't going to make it.

Pushing herself, Gillian ran faster, fear overwhelming her to the point of numbness, an unexpected blessing.

Her strides evened out and became almost effortless, and visually, everything sharpened into focus—each clump of grass jumped over, each headstone rounded, each random flower or weed crushed beneath her shoes—every step a dreamlike, measured movement.

Exhilaration surged through her veins, and her mind sharpened to the narrow focus of a straight line to the castle. She could do this. She could make it.

She pumped her arms to increase speed. She couldn't hear anything other than her own harsh breathing and the dry slash of grass as it buzzed her shoes. She dared to believe she was outdistancing the men.

Or perhaps they'd given up the chase?

Ignoring the sharp pain growing in her side, she finally chanced a glance over her shoulder.

They'd gained on her.

One man, his strides even and his face set with determination, easily jumped a slab and kept right on running, his pace deliberate and eating the distance between them.

Disbelief had her half-tripping on a weed, her body lunging forward, her backpack slipping to one side, knocking her slightly off balance.

Fear came rushing back.

She pulled herself forward by clutching at grass until she regained her pace, but her gait was now frantic, clumsy.

How could this be happening?

She scrambled up a small hill and ran the few steps down the slope, nearing the far side of the cemetery. She could hardly breathe as laughter sounded behind her, close, and a scream rose in her throat.

They were enjoying this! How could they be enjoying this?

She was suddenly shoved forward, and the scream escaped as she failed to regain her balance in time, and fell hard to her knees. She quickly scrambled up and turned to face them, backing away, but toward the other two coming up behind her.

The men, breathing hard, faces filled with triumph, smiled as she halted against a headstone, her heart hammering, her eyes darting for escape. "What do you want? Why are you doing this?" She could hardly get the words out. Gillian pressed a hand to her chest and sucked in air.

The men, younger than she'd assumed, slowly surrounded her, one on either side, one directly in front of her, and another behind the marker where she couldn't see him. He chuckled and the hair rose on the back of her neck.

She latched onto the idea that they were young, perhaps even teenagers of eighteen or nineteen. Maybe this was just a game to them. Maybe they were simply out for a good time and just wanted to scare her.

If so, it was working beautifully.

Looking into the dark eyes of the young man in front of her, hope slipped away. Those eyes, the color of coffee, were pitiless, ruthless, and mocking. She was in deep trouble.

Her hand tightened to the point of pain on the vial of pepper spray, hidden by the long sleeve of her jacket. Could it disable all four of them? She was afraid if she tried to use it, it would only anger them and have unwelcome consequences for herself.

She swallowed audibly. "What do you want?" she asked again.

The boy took a swaggering step forward, his dark hair half-covering one eye, a smirk spreading on his face. Tall and lean, he wasn't bad looking, but his intense stare, sharp-boned features, and black wardrobe intimidated.

"That there is an interesting question, isn't it, lads?" his deep voice, lyrically charming, struck her as incongruous in the awful situation. His smile widened. "What do we want?" His face bent toward hers and the smile disappeared. "Well, what are you offering?"

His friends laughed again, low and ugly.

Gillian choked back a sob and lifted a trembling hand to ward him off. "What are you going to do?" She glanced at the others, hoping for compassion, a hint of pity or disquiet, but could see in their eyes they meant to hurt her.

The sweat on her body chilled, her heart continued its relentless thumping, and her throat tightened. She couldn't seem to get enough air into her lungs, but her chin lifted defiantly and she straightened.

Come what may, she'd go down fighting, not cowering. If they planned to hurt her, they weren't going to come away unscathed. Her hand tightened on the pepper spray. She could hurt them. She could leave DNA under her fingernails to convict these men later.

Of course, if they were searching for DNA under her nails, chances were she'd be dead, so it wouldn't personally do her much good. She'd watched too many *Cold Case Files* not to be kicking herself right now. Why had she isolated herself? Stupid, stupid, stupid! She knew better. One minute she'd been peacefully enjoying the countryside, and the next, hunted and afraid this might be her last day on earth. Her last hour. And it was her own fault!

"What do you want?" She asked the question again, more calmly this time. "Why are you chasing me?"

The young men snickered, obviously loving the power they held over her. The power of life and death. The man in front, obviously their leader, lifted a hand. "Well, for a start, pretty girl, we want that gold ring hanging from your neck. Why don't you give us a look-see then, and, after, we'll talk about anything else you may have that we might be wanting." As the men laughed, their leader's gaze dropped briefly to her chest, and there was no mistaking the lascivious intent.

Her hand flew to the ring. "It was my father's ring. An heir-loom. I treasure it because it was his. I-it's engraved and every-thing," she stuttered. "Y-you can't have it."

"Bad luck that, because actually, I can." So quickly she didn't have time to flinch, he knocked her hand away and grabbed the ring in his fist, scratching her chest with a long, hard fingernail.

Gillian shrieked, sucked in a breath, and sprayed him full in the face with a red stream of pepper spray.

He screamed and her chain pinched the back of her neck as it stretched taut and broke. He dropped to his knees yelling, holding his face, and gasping.

Through squinted, burning eyes, Gillian saw the ring fly

through the air, the gold flashing, before it landed on a patch of matted grass behind the man writhing on the ground.

"Get her!" screamed the downed man. She jumped over him, made a dive for the ring, snatched it up, and ran. She shoved the ring onto her middle finger, scraping the skin and cutting herself in the process.

With blood dripping onto the grass, she ran, expecting to feel a hand or two quickly dragging her down. Gillian's eyes burned and dizziness overwhelmed her. She didn't remember tripping on anything, but fell for what seemed a long distance. Her knee landed hard on a rock, the pain so intense her vision blacked for a moment.

Fighting the darkness, she crawled, scrambled against a headstone, and tried to pull herself up. She finally stood, and forced her body into a limping run toward the other side of the cemetery where the graves seemed newer, better tended, and mounded with the recently deceased.

Strange she hadn't noticed those before.

The men hadn't grabbed her yet, and she didn't dare waste a second to look back. Blinded by tears, her chest and knee aching, she limped out of the graveyard only to be faced by men on horseback.

A sob escaped her as she stopped, stunned. *Where had they come from?*

She pivoted to look for the men chasing her, but no one was there. She turned around to see a good-looking blond maneuver his horse to get a better look at her. He leaned forward in his saddle and smiled. "Well, well, what have we here?"

Her face slack with confusion, Gillian whipped her head around again, looking for the men who'd been on the verge of attacking. There was nothing but . . .

Gillian gasped as a village, and the well-fortified castle beyond, came into focus.

Where was she?

She slowly turned to the men on horseback. They'd completely surrounded her now, every one of them dressed in medieval knight's garb.

Had these men scared the others off? Had she hit her head? Was she unconscious and dreaming? She looked at a nearby headstone. *Was she dead?*

"Excuse me, sir. But can you tell me what just happened?"

The blond man's smile turned into a leer. "With a surety, I can tell you what is soon to pass."

Gillian swallowed and tried to move away. She glanced at the faces of the men surrounding her, and each sneering, sly, suggestive grin made her wonder if she'd escaped a bad situation, only to land herself in a worse one. *What was going on?*

CHAPTER 2

"*Y*ou goatish, idle-headed, footlicker—"

Kellen's sword clashed with Sir Tristan's, cutting off his friend's familiar insults, and he tried not to laugh as Tristan attempted to force a retreat. Kellen welcomed both the effort and the exuberance displayed.

Sir Owen, as well as most of the other men, stopped training to watch. "Come, Tristan, press forward! You can defeat him! He's been in a foul mood for months now, and this is your chance to pay him in kind!"

Tristan continued to strain, his face red and damp. As he was one of the few with enough experience and muscle, and therefore a slim chance of beating him, Kellen was having more sport than he'd had in months.

"*Aaaahhhhh!*" Tristan managed to shove Kellen off, only to fall forward. Tristan's face went from triumphant to angry as he realized Kellen had moved apurpose, and Kellen laughed aloud at Tristan's wild expression, reminiscent of battles past.

On the sidelines, Sir Owen's cheeks reddened and he shook a fist. "Come, Tristan, fight harder. 'Tis not our fault his bride is late in coming. Defeat him!"

Off to the side, three young boys commenced cheering for Kellen, and Sir Owen turned to chase them away. Shrieking, they ran out of reach.

Kellen's smile widened. It was the first time he'd felt alive in months. The first his spirits had lifted since his wife's death. Tristan, breathing hard, ran at him and they took up the fight again, swords clashing, metal sliding, muscles straining. Kellen snickered at Tristan's obvious frustration. "Tired?"

"Nay, curse you, you puny, beslubbering wretch." Tristan hacked like a novice with his sword. "You infectious bunched-backed haggard. You cold-hearted miscreant."

Swords clashed a few more times, then Kellen slid his sword around Tristan's, metal slipping against metal, disarming the man. Kellen kicked Tristan's feet out from under him, and set the tip of his sword against his throat.

Breathing hard, Tristan pounded the dirt with a fist, gulped in air, and finally smiled his usual gamine grin. "Have I mentioned I admire such qualities in you?"

Kellen laughed again and backed away. "Many times."

Sir Owen groaned, threw up his arms, and turned away. The men moved back to their training.

Tristan threw Kellen a dark look as he surged to his feet and quickly retrieved his sword. "Not so many times as all that."

"Again?"

Tristan took up his stance and Kellen circled.

Kellen understood the point his men were trying to make. He'd been irritable, bad-tempered, and impossible to live with. Mayhap they'd all needed a good tussle to clear the air, and if it had the added benefit of keeping him from brooding, so much the better.

It had been almost eight months since his wife's death, and he had yet to wait another five weeks for his new bride to arrive. Corbett had already moved the date back twice. Would Kellen declare war on the Corbetts if they didn't bring their daughter this time? He was considering it, but wasn't sure he had the stomach for the deed. But he needed an heir and, to his mind, they owed him one.

Two of his foster boys came running, breathing hard, excited. "My lord, someone is on our property. We can see them from the top of the gatehouse."

Kellen and Tristan both stepped back, checking their swords. Kellen ignored the fact that the boys had been where they should not. Their fascination with the murder hole was understandable, but dangerous just the same. "Scottish?"

One of the boys, Lord Marlowe's son, eyes gleaming, shrugged and shook his head. "I do not know, my lord. 'Tis too far away."

Grimly pleased, Kellen smiled. A real fight was exactly what he needed to take his mind off his problems. He turned to his men still training on the field. "Mount up."

Excited whoops were followed by a quick scramble toward the stables and, minutes later, Kellen rode out, his men behind him. They quickly made their way through the village, across a vast, wet field, and closed in on the cemetery where a group of riders huddled together. Kellen was disappointed to see it was just his neighbor, Sir Robert Royce, and some of his men.

Tristan, now riding beside Kellen, remarked, "It's that poxmarked, fly-bitten, eye-offending lout, Royce."

"I can see that."

But there was nothing offensive about Royce's looks other than he'd been born pretty enough to be female. As lads, they'd been companions, taking their training together, fostering with Lord Wallington. But Kellen's fighting ability caused awe and admiration among their lord, others, and finally the king. That, in turn, caused jealousy on Royce's part. No doubt it hadn't helped that Kellen and the other boys had once forced Royce into a gown.

Eventually all had been forgiven and they'd fought side by side in several battles, at home and across the ocean. Afterward, Royce tried his hand in beating Kellen at several tournaments, but of course, had as little luck as any other against him. They'd grown distant in the last few years, and even more so when Lord Wallington died on Royce's watch, something Kellen could never quite forgive.

"Does this mean we don't get to fight?" Tristan asked.

Kellen considered. Mayhap they should take this opportunity to rile Royce. Lax as ever, the idiot did not even see them coming, as he and his men looked at something on the ground. They were laughing and Royce appeared vastly amused. Kellen, curious, signaled for his men to spread out.

Royce and his followers finally turned at their approach, and Kellen saw a girl in their midst. She was in a state of partial undress, wearing short breeches that formed to her figure, and in no way, hid a beautiful set of legs, and a tunic so tight, it concealed nothing of her body.

If she'd been trying to pass for a lad, she'd failed miserably. She was attractive, curvy, and blonde as his wife had been. Her long hair tumbled about her shoulders.

Fear was evident in the girl's face, but the beauty's fists clenched and unclenched and she looked ready to fight. One of the villagers? Kellen hadn't seen her before and would have surely remembered if he had.

Royce's men quieted as Kellen moved in, looking between Royce and the girl. "What is happening here?" Kellen asked, his mild tone apparently not putting anyone at ease as their expressions remained wary.

The girl answered before Royce had the chance. "These men are scaring me. They won't back off. I just want to get back to my car. Could you please help me?"

Not a villager, then. Her speech was strange, but Kellen was able to sort through her words and understand most of them.

He looked around for a nearby carriage, but was unsurprised when he didn't see one. With spring barely over, flooding had washed the road out in several places, and it wasn't yet dry enough for cart nor carriage to travel on.

He addressed Royce. "Why are you and your men on my property? Who is this girl?"

Royce lifted his chin. "Some of my livestock went missing, and we were searching out the thieves when we came across the chit."

"You were thinking to find your cattle on my land?" Kellen's words were smooth as silk. "Are you making an accusation?"

Royce went still for a moment, then smiled slowly, that smirky lifting of lips that always made Kellen want to punch him in the mouth. Or stick him in a dress. "Of course not. I simply think the thieves used this route. Scottish, no doubt."

Tristan and Sir Owen moved forward to get a better look at the girl. "She does not look Scottish," said Sir Owen. "But you never know. As weedy as your cattle are, perhaps she's hidden the beasts behind her back?"

Kellen's men laughed. Royce's did not.

The girl raised a hand to her forehead as if dizzy, and Kellen froze. As impossible as it seemed, the ring she wore looked to possess the Corbett emblem.

Off his horse in an instant, Kellen quickly covered the ground between them, grabbed her arm and lifted her hand. She hit him in the chest with her free fist, but he barely noticed as he studied the ring.

There could be no doubt. The Corbett coat-of-arms, a raven in flight, glinted bright and clear in the sun. Kellen would know it anywhere, having endured Corbett's insulting missives of excuse in past months, the raven seal always seeming to mock him.

He quickly looked about, but saw no other knights, near nor in the distance, only Royce's. Could Corbett's men be hiding? He turned to Sir Owen. "Search the trees."

Had Corbett simply dumped her here? Was he afraid to face Kellen? Did he truly fear Kellen's wrath enough to leave his daughter to make her own way to the castle? To leave her vulnerable to attack? It was cowardly and insulting to them both. Kellen had always respected the man in the past, but no more.

Kellen studied his bride's face. Edith was her name, if he remembered aright. She was lovely, with blue eyes exotically tilted at the corners and fringed with lashes as dark and thick as any he'd seen before. At least her features were nothing like those of her sister. She was even more beautiful, but in a completely different way. "Come."

"Where are we going?" Her eyes widened when he tugged a blanket off his horse and wrapped her in it, noting the cut at her chest and knee, as well as the way her finger was bleeding as if someone had tried to steal the ring from her.

His anger rose a notch. She'd obviously been abused. It was yet to be determined to what extent. He grabbed her up and lifted her onto his horse before hoisting himself behind her.

"Do you have a phone I could use?"

Ignoring her strange request, he wondered just when Royce's men had arrived. Had they taken her clothes? Defiled her? He could feel his skin heating at the thought.

He turned to Royce. "If my betrothed has been injured in any way by you, or your men, you will pray for death before I am done. I vow it."

In the stunned silence that followed, Kellen turned his horse toward the castle. He ignored Royce's stammered protests that he'd only just come upon the girl, and took comfort in the realization that the men had all been seated on horses. Only the girl had been upon the ground. With a rising sense of protectiveness and satisfaction, he pressed her stiff body closer to his own. He would guard and defend what was his. And she was his. Indeed, he held his future in his arms.

CHAPTER 3

*W*hat the heck was going on?

Gillian, stiff, chilled, and clutching her back-pack, sat in front of the knight, silently scared out of her wits. She wasn't sure what had just happened, and trying to make sense of everything was giving her a headache.

First, she'd been chased by hoodlums.

Then they'd suddenly disappeared and she'd been faced by a bunch of different men on horseback. *Medieval hoodlums.*

Now she was on a huge horse, sitting across hard muscled thighs, wrapped tight in a knight's strong arms and . . . and what? He'd saved her? Or claimed her for himself? She wasn't sure. But if she'd gotten it right, he was the good guy here. Or was that simply wishful thinking on her part?

Now they were headed toward a village that she knew darn good and well hadn't been there a moment ago. Was she going crazy?

Huts with thatched roofs, close and in the distance, dotted the countryside. The buildings hadn't been there before. She would have seen them, and certainly she would have noticed all the people milling about. There was no way she could have missed them.

Gillian shivered as the knight's heat penetrated her back, and he held her a bit tighter like she was a prized possession. She felt claimed and couldn't help another shiver. She had to stop letting her imagination run away with her. She was going to ask for an explanation, in just a minute, after she wasn't so intimidated by the scary guy at her back.

Gillian stared up at the castle beyond the village. Strong and rugged, it looked a whole heck of a lot like the one she'd been drawing except for the teeny-tiny little fact that it wasn't a ruin in any way, shape, or form.

Perhaps there was another castle close by and she'd been taken there? Had she gotten turned around and somehow been moved to another location? Had she passed out? She had no memory of any of that. None of this made any sense. One minute she'd been standing near a deserted ruin, prepared to fight for her life, the next . . . here. That fast.

She couldn't help but notice the guy holding her in his arms was also dressed as a knight. Could she have fallen in with some sort of medieval reenactment group? Had they started ad-libbing when she'd shown up? Was this some sort of joke at her expense? Or was it a dream? As they rode on she looked back, searching for her car.

Nothing.

Was it over the hill where she couldn't see it? Had it been stolen by one of the guys who'd been chasing her?

Taking a breath, Gillian gulped back impending hysteria. This was all going to make sense in a moment. She finally allowed herself to look up at the knight and promptly lost what was left of her breath as she exhaled in a rush.

He'd pushed back his chain mail coif allowing her to clearly see his fierce expression as he returned her gaze. She swallowed and forced herself to breathe again. He wasn't exactly handsome, as his nose was slightly crooked and had obviously been broken at some point. He also sported scars on his forehead and cheek. But he was striking, heart-poundingly sexy, and very masculine. In a word, magnificent.

She resisted the impulse to reach up and touch his tanned face, his high cheekbones, or his thick black hair, just to make sure he was real.

His gaze was intense, his eyes the warm color of amber, and the contrast to his hard features was startling. Her glance lowered to his massive shoulders, thick with muscle, and she swallowed again and cleared her throat.

"Do you think you could you take me back to my car?" Her voice came out breathless, and she cleared her throat again and laughed nervously. "I'm still kind of shaky after what happened, so I'd appreciate a ride."

The knight stared down at her for a long moment. "You have no need of a carriage." His deep voice rumbled, his harsh accent wrapping itself around her in the cool afternoon air. "I am keeping you."

Gillian laughed shakily.

The knight didn't so much as crack a smile.

"Ah, okay. I can walk." Gillian looked down. She was in some sort of trouble here. She knew it but just didn't know what it was. She didn't know much of anything at the moment.

"You will stay."

Okay, the guy was scary, but that comment irritated. "Like a dog? I don't think so."

"You will."

Should she try and slip off the horse and make a break for it?

As if reading her intentions, or perhaps the way her body had tensed at the thought of jumping off the huge animal, the knight's arm tightened again holding her in place effortlessly. Perhaps that was for the best. She could break a leg or two jumping from that distance.

Turning her head, her gaze slid to the men who'd surrounded her earlier, now riding in the opposite direction, and then to the graveyard. The location and layout were the same as the one she'd run to earlier: but everything else was different and new—pristine headstones and wooden crosses where there'd been none before.

The knight's large hand reached out and pulled her head back against his chest, forcing her to face forward again. Okay then. Sitting stiffly, and not looking up at him, she tried her best to ignore the guy. She tried to ignore his heat as it burned though his chain mail, tunic, the blanket at her back, and beneath her legs. She had to think.

"Do you have a phone?"

She could feel the knight studying her for a long moment, could feel that she was trying his patience even before he let out a long sigh. "Nay."

She'd find one up at the castle. She'd call the police and they could try and make sense out of everything that had happened to her. Maybe they'd have a laugh at her expense as she tried to explain the wild things that had occurred. Maybe everyone in the area knew what was going on here and she'd look like an idiot. But surely, they'd escort her back to her car? Or find it, if it had been stolen?

Relaxing a little now that she had a plan, she swayed with the horse as they went through the small village full of busy adults and playing children. Simply built cottages lined the streets. Some looked to be businesses displaying wares. Animal pens clustered between dwellings were filled with noisy, smelly pigs, goats, cows, and sheared sheep. Plowed fields and pastures with people working them surrounded the village, but Gillian couldn't see any farm equipment.

She spied a river, a pond, and what looked to be a mill. A man pounded metal in one of the buildings, and smoke poured from a chimney in the middle of the structure. Several paths led from the village to the castle.

As Gillian and the knight passed, everyone stopped what they were doing to stare. She looked back wondering if she should call out for help, wondering if she needed help, only most of these people didn't look as if they would, since they were bowing and dipping as the entourage moved by.

Every person was dressed in medieval clothing. The women in loose dresses with their hair covered, the men in belted tunics and tight pants. Most of the children were barefoot. Could this simply be a new style in England?

She gazed up at the castle dominating the landscape, again searching for differences, but nothing had changed since the last time she'd looked. She'd stared at the ruin for hours while she'd sketched. There was the turret in the correct location, the parapets, the bay windows, and the tower. Did they make identical castles back in medieval times? Sort of like medieval tract housing without the subdivisions? Cheaper to make the same type over and over again? Had she been moved to a restored version?

The gatehouse, with its twin towers jutting skyward, caught her attention. According to the brochure, they were completely unique, with no other in England or anywhere else like them. This had to be the same castle, only now it stood in its full glory, strong and rugged, not a crumbing stone in sight.

She shook her head. How could that be? What was going on? Had she fallen into a fairy ring? Moved through a worm hole and into the past? Entered a time machine without noticing?

She looked for electric lines, anything that would establish this as the twenty-first century, but found nothing.

She closed her eyes. She was a logical person; she could figure this out. If she took away all the illogical things she believed she was seeing and remembered back to the last thing she remembered for sure, it was obvious that none of this was even happening to her. That only left one explanation.

She was dreaming, delusional, or out of her mind. And was

there anything that had happened to her that could cause her to be in that state of mind?

She felt the blood rush out of her face. Of course, there was an explanation. The hoodlums who'd chased her toward the castle ruins were assaulting her right this minute; she was lying in the graveyard and her mind was taking her to this far-off place, so she could escape the trauma.

Her heart pounded in her chest, and her breathing escalated.

She'd turned the hoodlums into medieval hoodlums in her mind and then conjured up a Knight in Shining Armor to defend her, complete with sword, shield, and strength. She patted her knight's arm, grateful for his reassuring presence, but ready to let go now and face reality.

Because this was unacceptable. How was she going to fight the violence if she didn't show up for the event? Had she hit her head? Had her attackers hit her head? Was she unconscious? In a coma? Would she wake at any moment? Or would they kill her when they'd finished, with no resistance whatsoever from her?

Anger built in her chest, sharp and stinging. She had to wake up. She wouldn't let them kill her. She would survive this. She'd come to her senses and defend herself. She was strong and could handle this.

She had to fight!

She had to live!

She definitely had to wake up.

Gillian tried to will herself back to the scene of her assault and attempted murder. She needed to defend herself before she actually *was* murdered.

She closed her eyes. Wake up . . . wake up now . . . wakey wakey time . . .

Nothing.

She opened her eyes. All she could hear, see, and smell were the knight, his horse, and the village.

Anger and heat emanated off the knight, as it should. He

should be very angry at the way she was being attacked back in the real world. Like any good imaginary knight worth his salt would be.

She glanced up at him, impressed all over again at what a really great imagination she had. Sure, he was a little rough around the edges. His face was hard, all angles and planes, his jaw as rugged as any Hollywood hero's.

But the possessive way his gaze roamed her face and blanket-wrapped body, lingering on the skin above her tee-shirt, sent a little thrill through her. Her feminine side couldn't be more pleased with him. He really was her perfect dream knight.

His long, thick, and dark hair stuck to his thickly muscled neck. His chest was hard and seemed to simply bulge with power. She shivered. The better to protect her.

She reached out to lightly touch his chest, wondering if it was the chain mail that made him seem so big; but under a thin layer of chain, it was warm muscle flexing.

Their eyes met, and she barely resisted a fan-girl sigh. His gaze was bright against his tanned face, his lashes and brows as dark as his hair, and the combination was startling. She could feel a sappy smile forming on her lips.

He was really a good-looking guy in a rough-and-tumble sort of fashion. And the possessive way he held her, the way he looked at her, made her feel incredibly beautiful and feminine. Not bad for an illusion. Maybe she shouldn't be in such a hurry to leave.

As they started to cross the drawbridge, the horses' hooves struck hollow notes against the wood distracting her, and she looked down into a stream of murky water. "Are you serious? There's an actual moat around the castle?" The detail in her hallucination was amazing.

"Aye. All my fortifications are strong."

Strong like him. Feeling very safe, she laid her cheek against her knight's chest and when his arms tightened around her, melted into him.

Why not feel the comfort he could offer before returning to the nightmare her life had become? She hadn't had a man's arms wrapped around her like this since . . . well, she never had. Certainly, not like this, and not with a man like him.

Another feminine trill of excitement caught her off guard and she shivered. He was everything he should be. Everything a knight and hero ought to be. And for the moment, he was hers.

THEY TRAVELED under the rusted spikes of the raised portcullis; its dangerous teeth pointed menacingly downward. Seconds later they were fully enclosed in the darkened, walled passageway of the gatehouse, and Gillian glanced at the ceiling and spotted a murder hole.

She knew from artistic research it was used to drop boiling water or rocks onto the trapped and unsuspecting. There was a balcony, slits in the walls to fire arrows through, and a well-protected stairwell to maneuver weapons from above. In other words, the place was a death trap to invaders.

One of these days she was going to depict the inside of a gate-house and make it spooky, dark, and exciting. She was sure the paintings would sell.

If she were still alive.

The sound of the horses' hooves rang loud in the enclosed space as they moved single file through the enclosure, finally coming out into the huge bustling inner courtyard.

She gazed at what looked like a small city enclosed within the walls. The huge keep in the middle dominated, and buildings were set around the outer edges: barracks, stables, and other outbuild-ings. People were busy, some carrying trays, others pulling horses behind them, some children playing, but most stopped what they were doing to stare at Gillian.

This was just so amazing. She'd had no idea her imagination was so rich.

Her knight rode his destrier up to the keep; and in one smooth move, dismounted with her still in his arms and easily carried her up a few stairs, through the open doorway, and inside the keep.

Gillian, limp as a wet noodle, enjoyed every moment of it. She laid her cheek against him again, soaking up the tingling, melting, and thrilling sensations he inspired in her.

The muscles in his arms and chest shifted as he moved; and when he came to a stop, he wasn't even the least out of breath. She, on the other hand, was losing her own.

Wow. Just wow.

Once inside the castle her knight bellowed something, and it took a moment for Gillian to decipher his words.

He was calling for someone and his accent! Fabulous! She wanted to squeal. This was simply the best dream she'd ever had, bar none, in her entire life.

An older woman, dressed in medieval garb, came running; her head covered with a white sheet, a set of keys dangling at her waist. "Yes, my lord?"

The knight set Gillian on her feet and when she stumbled a bit, placed a big, warm hand on her shoulder until she steadied herself.

He didn't remove the hand as he gave the other woman instructions. He turned Gillian and grabbed her cheeks with one hand; she wondered if he was going to kiss her, right there, in front of all the people who'd started to gather around.

She couldn't think of a reason why she shouldn't let him. It was just a dream, after all. Her gaze dropped to his full lips, curved in an inviting smile. She might wake at any moment. This could be her only chance. She wasn't going to protest and miss out.

His hand firm on her cheeks, he squeezed them together,

forcing her mouth to gape open and looked inside. "Well-formed teeth," he proclaimed and looked up at their audience.

The servants leaned in for a look, murmuring and nodding their approval; Gillian shrieked as anger, outrage, and embarrassment boiled up inside her. "What are you doing?"

She jerked away and slapped the knight's hand. "What am I, a horse?" So much for her dream man.

Her response visibly surprised him.

Making sounds of disapproval, the woman with the keys took Gillian's hand and led her toward stone steps going up the side of one wall. "Come with me, lass. I'll see you settled soon enough."

Gillian glanced back at the knight, sending him a dirty look to let him see how disappointed she was in him; but at his bewildered expression, her anger dissipated.

Okay, the guy was sort of a clod. But she was willing to give him a second chance; because the man, as well as the place, was making her romance buttons hum on high alert.

Since she'd no doubt wake to a nightmare, she didn't want to waste even one tiny moment of this experience.

Anyway, what was the harm in taking a look around the place before she woke up? After all, it seemed real enough that she might be able to use something she saw in her paintings. Imagined or not, the place felt so authentic she considered patting herself on the back for having such a great imagination.

Of course, she was assuming she'd eventually snap out of it and wake up in the real world. But what if she wasn't able to? Was she simply unconscious? Or was it possible she was dead and her version of heaven included castles and knights?

Uneasily, she acknowledged that this particular fantasy could be tailor-made for her. She shrugged off the prickly sensation tickling her shoulder blades. If she saw her parents or brother, she'd know for sure and deal with it then.

As much as she liked the thought of seeing her family again, she liked the version where she was simply unconscious, dreaming, and had a full life ahead of her still. Did people in comas resist waking because they were somewhere nice and didn't want to leave?

Something else to think about later. Right now, there were tons of much more pleasant things to focus on. The place was amazing. Gillian ran her hand on one section of the wall as she walked up the stairs admiring the rough, mismatched stonework and the way the staircase curved around to form an arch above a window.

She tripped on the uneven steps, not a good idea as she could fall off to the side and to the floor below if she wasn't careful, so she pulled the blanket from her shoulders and hung it over one arm so she'd have a better view of the steps.

Key Woman, jangling with every step, shrieked, and spilled words so fast Gillian couldn't catch what she was saying; but the woman was obviously in some sort of distress, her face panicky and screwed up like a lemon.

The woman lunged forward, pulled at the blanket around Gillian's arm, and tried to cover her legs with it; but the bulk of the material tightened around her arm when Gillian pressed herself against the wall to keep from tumbling over the side.

Eyes wide, heart pounding, Gillian gripped the stones. Was the woman trying to kill her?

When tugging didn't work, the woman held out her skirts as if to hide Gillian from view. The woman called out to others, serving girls by the looks of them, and they rushed up to push Gillian up the stairs and into a hallway. Gillian, getting the hint, hurried on her own and finally rounded the corner; Key Woman shrieking behind her all the way.

Once in the hallway, the woman calmed down and Gillian, still unsettled by the shrieking and pushing, tried to ignore her and the others.

Spying a colorful wall hanging, flickering wall sconces, and a couple of handcrafted tables; Gillian turned her attention to her surroundings, pausing to study an aqua and white vase, but was firmly pushed down the hallway and into a room where they shut the door behind them.

She hardly had time to glance at the large bed with its heavy wooden frame, comfortable bedding, and linen hangings before the women circled her.

Gillian took a breath and crossed her arms. This was the third time she'd been circled in less than an hour. What was it with this place? Was her subconscious acknowledging that she was still in danger? Couldn't she simply enjoy this hallucination into another time and place without constantly feeling threatened?

The women talked amongst themselves, reached out, and though Gillian's instinct was to batt their curious hands away, she refrained.

They felt her clothes, rubbing the material of her shirt and jacket. Gillian nodded. "Old Navy."

They fingered her cotton shorts. "Macy's. And I got the belt at a yard sale when I was in college." One woman ran her hands down one of Gillian's legs, and Gillian was glad she'd shaved that morning.

Another pushed a finger into an athletic shoe then plucked at the laces. "Adidas." Gillian finally squirmed away. "May I ask what you're doing?"

Key Woman gestured at her clothes. "Disrobe, please."

The woman finally spoke slowly enough that Gillian understood, and she wanted her to strip? Gillian narrowed her eyes. Was this a mental representation of her fear of the assault she was worried about? She shook her head. "No way. That is not going to happen."

Key Woman crossed to a large chest against the wall and opened it. She took something out, shook it, turned, and lifted a beautiful blue gown for Gillian to inspect. It was similar to the one Key Woman wore only smaller, finer in quality, a better cut, and a prettier color.

Gillian wavered. The dress really was gorgeous, and Gillian loved the color blue. And it would be fun to wear while she was in this medieval castle.

The women noted her expression and nodded to each other. Another walked forward to spread the bottom of the dress and another girl dug a thin gold belt out of the trunk and held it up for Gillian's inspection.

Again, she wavered. The outfit was gorgeous. "Why do you want me to wear the dress?"

They took a moment to decipher her words, then Key Woman answered. "The master desires it."

The master being her dream knight? "Why would he want that?"

They didn't respond but simply looked at each other as if trying to understand her words, and then Key Woman shrugged.

Gillian shook her head. It didn't make sense, but then dreams never did. Why not go with the flow for a while? It might turn out to be fun. A great adventure to remember if and when she woke up.

She held out her hand for the dress and all the women smiled and voiced their approval. Again, they wanted her to take off her clothes.

"I'd like some privacy, please."

They discussed it then finally all turned their backs.

Good enough. Gillian moved to the bed and laid out the dress, slipped off her athletic shoes, took a shaky breath, and removed her clothes. She ignored the obvious peeking. It was all among women, right?

She was down to her bra and underwear and reaching for the dress when the women turned as one and grabbed her.

Shocked, Gillian tried to wrench her arms free but couldn't. "What are you doing?" Gillian tugged again trying to free herself from the hands imprisoning her; but collectively, the women were too strong and easily pulled her across the mattress, flipped her onto her back, and held her there.

Gillian screamed with rage, and one of the women quickly cupped a hand over her mouth. Gillian bucked, twisted, writhed, and screamed against the hand.

It didn't matter. The women relentlessly pulled Gillian's legs together and yanked her underwear down her legs and all the way off.

Anger, embarrassment, and disbelief heated her entire body, overriding any fear she might have felt.

Key Woman went to the door and admitted another woman, old and hunched, who shuffled toward the bed to look at Gillian.

Gillian stilled. What was going on? What could possibly be happening?

The old woman scooted a young servant to the left with her hip, dipped her hand into a bowl that Key Woman provided, rubbed her hands with what looked to be grease, leaned forward, and reached out a hand toward Gillian's privates.

What in the name of all that was holy?

Gillian wrenched her mouth free and screamed her rage and disgust.

That was it.

She was done here.

Now would be a very good time to wake up.

CHAPTER 4

*A*nother scream—long, loud, and peppered with words no lady should know—drifted down the stairs.

Kellen winced, and his brows rose, as he exchanged a glance with his open-mouthed friend, Sir Tristan of Alnwick.

Kellen looked to a flushed Sir Owen de Burgess, standing straight at attention, fiddling with his sword hilt, something he did when nervous or upset. "Has the girl been raised in the barracks with the foulest of knights?" Owen asked between stiff lips.

Kellen flushed and felt the need to defend her. "Lady Corbett, Edith, is obviously not herself. She has been frightened out of her wits and will recover her delicate nature soon." At least Kellen hoped for that result.

Tristan took a breath and turned from the stairs. "Er . . . as I was saying. This is a most unusual situation. Perhaps the girl needs a chaperone until the wedding?"

Kellen was glad to latch onto the subject, to have something to think on, and a decision to make. "A good notion." He spoke the words too loudly and attempted to lower his voice to a more moderate pitch. "Since her own mother was not sent to prepare

for the wedding, I will send for my father's wife and some of her
ladies."

"Good, good." Sir Owen stared at the opening to the hallway at
the top of the stairs, his cheeks flushed.

Kellen turned away. The girl *would* be a virgin. She must needs
be. He did not want any further delays; and if he refused to wed
the girl, he might have a long wait until another bride was granted
him. Kellen sank onto a long bench, then moments later was up
pacing again, much to the amusement of Tristan.

"Perhaps if you simply went upstairs, you could wait outside
the door and receive the news that much the sooner?"

Kellen shot him a narrow-eyed glare. He was trying not to feel
disappointed in the girl. He had waited long for an heir and a
mending to his alliance with Lord Corbett. And this foul-
mouthed girl was the reward for his patience?

Kellen stifled a wince as more language drifted down the
stairs; and servants, going about their work in the great hall; and
his men, studiously cleaning their weapons at a far table; kept
their eyes on their tasks, but no doubt listened intently.

Kellen rubbed a hand over his face and thought on the
immodest clothing the girl had worn. She had not spoken overmuch to him on the way to the castle. And now this foul language?
With all of Corbett's daughters, surely he did not send a defective
for a bride? Surely, he would not dare?

No. Not after Catherine dishonored the family so. He glanced
up the stairs as his fury roared to life once more. Fury at himself
and at the situation. First, he could not protect his wife from
being influenced by a villain, then he could not discover who the
villain was, and now his new affianced had been robbed, and
perhaps worse?

All on his own property!

His pacing resumed. Pure or not, his wife or not, he would
avenge the girl. And protect her reputation. But would he
marry her?

Needing to do something, Kellen called one of his men to him. "Leave immediately for my father's keep, and fetch his wife and her ladies. Ride as fast as possible."

"Yes, my lord." With a nod, the man was gone.

It felt good to be doing something. He would also assign a maid to follow the girl about. To keep an eye on her, aid her, but most especially to report back to him. There would be no hint of impropriety with *this* bride.

Not as there had been with his first.

If he was to even consider this alliance, he would make sure of that from the beginning, starting with proof that she had not been defiled.

Tristan sat and leaned against one table. "She is very fair to look upon. Getting heirs off her would not be a hardship."

Kellen waved a hand. "One healthy woman is as good as the next." He ignored Tristan's laughter. Of course, her body and her mind must be fit. He wanted strong sons. If this bride was not satisfactory, he would demand another of Corbett's daughters.

But with his goal finally within his grasp, did he care to wait any longer?

Kellen wanted to go outside to train, to work off some of his anger, but must needs wait for the midwife. Spying the pack the girl had brought with her on one of the tables, Kellen grabbed it up.

It possessed a drawstring with an impossibly thin and silky rope, and Kellen opened and shut the pack a few times.

Ingenious.

And the material itself was fine, yet sturdy, the bright color unique and one he'd only ever seen at sunset, or at the edges of a rainbow. He studied the pockets on the outside, filled with an assortment of oddly formed orange sticks, then dug inside the pack.

First, he pulled out a square, silver box and studied the circular markings on the piece. A chunk of fine metal? Perhaps it could be melted into a sword hilt. Could it be a gift from his bride?

Kellen set the piece aside and plucked out a tiny book, finely made. He opened it and gasped. His bride's picture, so finely drawn it should have been impossible, stared back at him.

The artist was skilled indeed.

His bride was smiling and beautiful in the tiny square, not a hint of insanity in the clear blue eyes that stared back at him. He didn't understand the writing on the paper, but perhaps the priest would.

Tristan leaned in to look. "The work is amazing."

"Aye."

"The artist would not have come cheap. Why have the likeness set on paper in such a way? Why not embed it within gold?"

Kellen could not fathom it.

Owen, finally curious, moved stiffly forward.

Kellen gave the book to Tristan and reached into the bag again, this time pulling out a smaller bag made of paper so fine he could see through it as if it were not even there. It was filled with colorful objects. He pulled one small piece out and studied it. He lifted it to his nose, widened his eyes, and held the object out to his friends. "Smell!"

Tristan took the piece, sniffed once, let out a breath, and smelled again. "Amazing! A spice?"

Kellen shrugged.

Owen snared it, sniffed once, grunted, and placed the object on the table.

Next Kellen lifted out a small metal rectangle, so bright a color as to confound the eye. He had never before seen the color. The object had a white cord even longer and finer than the one that closed the pack but made of a stiffer material. A finely wrought belt perhaps? The colored box would make a pretty accessory against a gown. He'd never seen the like. He needed to travel to London more often.

He dug out a small packet with what looked to be clear gauzy material inside; then a tube of stiffer material with a tie around it came next. Kellen plucked at the tie and the material gaped open; and when Kellen gave the object a shake, the thing shot longer and blew itself wide, as would a bullfrog's throat.

Startled, Kellen dropped it and it rolled off the table and onto the floor.

"What is it?" Tristan asked.

Kellen shook his head, leaned forward, and plucked the thing off the ground by the stick protruding from its top and lifted it high. "A hat?"

All three men shook their heads in mute horror as Kellen set the thing on the table and they all watched it rock and finally settle.

Tristan let out a long whistle. "Let us hope it does not become the fashion, else there will be no room to sit next to the ladies at supper."

"Aye." Kellen nodded his agreement, and reached into the pack and removed a long tube of blue metal that mushroomed at the top. A man could easily grip it in his hand but what of its use? As a bludgeon, it was shorter and much inferior to the one he already possessed.

Setting it aside, he reached into the pack once more. Finally, something he recognized. Paper. But the paper was unbelievably fine.

Tristan looked over his shoulder. "Corbett must travel often to find such treasures. And to send them with the girl, as part of her dowry, must be a message of the esteem in which he holds you."

Kellen nodded. He couldn't help but agree and regardless of the unexplained way of his bride's arrival, couldn't help but feel relieved.

He opened the binding of paper and found a sketch. It was his castle, but it looked to be a ruin, hundreds of years old.

Owen sucked in a breath. "An insult? A threat?"

Kellen could not imagine what purpose there could be in drawing his castle old and decrepit. A shiver raced down his spine; he threw the papers down to the table, stood, and started to pace again. He did not understand any of this. Did Lord Corbett wish to incur his favor or his wrath?

"My lord." Sir Owen followed close behind. "If it is an insult, we should go to war to defend your honor."

Frustrated, Kellen shook his head. "I will get answers from the girl before making any decisions."

"But, my lord—"

Kellen sliced a hand through the air. "We will wait and see."

Kellen had plans. Big plans. And war would interfere with them all. He needed an heir, an alliance, and prosperity for his land and people. Honor and building his family name were all important. He could overlook a slight or two in favor of his goals. Mayhap it was simply a joke in poor taste?

Kellen glanced up the stairs again, the unanswered questions giving him a headache. Did they think to send her unchaperoned so she would be compromised? So he would feel honor bound to marry her? Or so he would not?

Or perhaps she had been ruined before they had even sent her out? Did her knights strip her and dump her at the cemetery so he would find her thus? Was she being punished by her father? Or did Royce attack her then mount his horse again before Kellen's arrival?

There was no sense in any of it.

Kellen thought of Corbett's ring on the girl's finger and of the bag of beautiful treasures. It must needs be a message from Corbett. He was just not sure if it was a welcome one.

He could still hear an occasional rant in the background. Finally, the midwife came down the stairs toward him.

At last.

He strode toward the stairs to meet up with her at the bottom.

"Well?" he asked, when she stopped level with him a few steps up, her hand on the wall for balance.

The old woman's face cracked into a smile, showing missing teeth. "She is a virgin still."

Kellen's breath left him.

The midwife came the rest of the way down the stairs and held out a strange article of clothing Kellen recognized as the short breeches the girl had worn.

The old woman pulled on a metal sliver and the front of the short breeches magically sealed themselves.

The hair rose on Kellen's arms and a nearby servant gasped and crossed herself. Kellen took the clothing and examined it.

"'Tis a chastity belt." The midwife stated.

Kellen pulled the clasp down and up once more. "Ingenious."

Owen and Tristan moved forward and Kellen pulled the tab up and down a few times to demonstrate.

Owen was visibly impressed. "A fine trick indeed."

Tristan was grinning and excited. "And clever. Very clever to my thinking. If one did not know how to work the seam, it would be impossible to peel the garment off without a knife."

Kellen remembered how tightly the breeches had formed to the girl's body. Mayhap even a knife would not fit between her and the skin. "One might have to kill her before ravishing her. Very cunning."

Elation filled him.

She was a virgin.

He would have his bride.

Kellen nodded once to dismiss the midwife. He allowed himself to feel relief and hope as he looked down at the tiny garment in his hand.

Tristan slapped him on the back. "Congratulations."

"'Tis good news, my lord," Owen concurred.

Tristan's grin widened. "She is a comely thing."

Sir Owen nodded. "And she seemed to like you well enough."

"That is true," said Tristan. "She lay her head on your chest. To my way of thinking that showed a level of trust and gratitude for your rescue."

Owen looked as if he might actually smile. "A fine beginning."

Kellen did smile. "Yes, it is." It was good they had started their marriage with his rescue of her. She seemed to have a limited understanding of things, even for a woman; and her speech was strange, but surely she would appreciate having a strong lord. Of course, he would have to break her of her foul language. But perhaps the fault lay with another.

He wondered if her mind were simply damaged by a recent attack, by her father's knights, Royce and his men, or others he did not know of. He had many questions in need of answers.

Kellen took a deep breath and let it out with a smile. "Better a virago than a weakling to my way of thinking."

Tristan agreed. "A strong mother produces strong sons."

"Yes. That is true," said Owen.

The girl in question came to a halt at the top of the stairs. As her gaze settled on him, she lifted a finger and pointed.

"You!"

She stormed down the stairs dressed in a proper gown that swirled about her in agitation as she moved downward. His bride looked beautiful. And very, very angry.

Kellen guessed he was about to get the chance to voice his questions.

CHAPTER 5

here he was! The man she blamed for this entire debacle was standing near the bottom of the stairs! Gillian, her face burning hot and her temper flaring hotter, stopped halfway down to wrestle her skirt free of her shoes; as she jerked the caught material, she stopped long enough to point a finger again.

"You despicable, loathsome, creep!"

She was torn between letting him have it and fetching a police officer or two to let him have it. She'd relish seeing the big jerk handcuffed and face down in the dirt . . . er . . . was that straw on the floor?

But her heart pounded and her hands fisted to keep them from shaking. She wasn't sure she could wait long enough to find an officer; and so finally freeing the hem of her skirt, she headed toward him, the material of her sleeves fluttering, and her shoes slapping against stone.

She'd let him have it, and *then* an officer could let him have it.

She no longer had any doubt that she was wide awake. This wasn't a dream, and she wasn't in a coma. There was nothing like a good gynecological exam to snap a girl out of a delusion. She still wasn't sure where she was. In fact, the day was starting to blur together.

How did she get here? No idea. Someone along the way had probably drugged her somehow. Why did they give her an exam? Why was she wearing a medieval dress? Again, no idea.

Apparently, just because Americans and English people spoke the same language, it did *not* mean they understood each other's cultures. She was definitely joining up with a tour group for the rest of her trip. One run by Americans. No more touring foreign countries on her own. What had she been thinking?

As Gillian finally came to a stop in front of the knight she'd trusted her throat constricted and tears burned her eyes. Yes, he was big. Yes, he was fearsome. And yes, he was still mind-numbingly gorgeous even with the confused look on his face.

But she hated him like poison now and wouldn't be sidetracked. Righteous indignation was on her side. He was going to get it, and she was going to be the one to give it to him.

Gillian lifted her arm and slapped his face as hard as she could, stinging her fingers.

His mouth dropped and he lifted a hand to his cheek.

The other men, and the servants in the cavernous room, gasped.

"Just *who*," she poked the knight's chest hard enough that it hurt her finger which ramped her anger even higher, "do *you*," poke, "think you *are?*"

The guy captured her hand with his and she jerked away, angry that the big, warm calloused hand engulfing hers had reminded her of the ride to the castle and the security she'd felt.

She sucked in a breath. "At your request, I've been violated by a group of women. *Violated!* By *women!*" Her face burned with remembered humiliation and she swallowed. "Granted, it's been a very strange day, but who could have expected I'd be given an exam against my will?"

Gillian's hand flew wildly in the air and the guy jerked back a step, caution and watchfulness in his expression.

"And by a woman with extremely dubious sanitary practices, I might add." Gillian's entire body flushed again at the memory. "And not only that, but except for my athletic shoes, my clothes have been stolen; and I've been stuffed into a hot, heavy, itchy gown." Beautiful too, though she'd never admit it now.

"I want out of this loony bin. I'm going to sue every person here. My trip to England, and probably my next vacation, and maybe even my next *house* is going to be paid for, gratis, by *you*. And by those women, too. How dare they . . . they . . . they . . . well how dare they!"

The guy continued to look wary and confused, but that was all. She didn't see a smidgeon of repentance, and he didn't look intimidated in the least. And darn it, she was still attracted to the guy! Tears sprang to her eyes. When he was down on his knees in the dirt, he wouldn't be quite so attractive, would he?

Unable to help herself, Gillian gave him a hard shove. He didn't move and just continued to stare down at her, that slightly baffled expression on his face.

"Oooh!" She hit him in his large chest with both fists. Again, other than his eyebrows raising, no real reaction on his part. The guy didn't so much as step back. With a scream of frustration, she shoved past him.

She gulped in air. Her face reheated every time she thought about what had just happened. Granted she hadn't been hurt, but the humiliation kept replaying itself in her mind; and she wanted out of there. She gasped in another breath.

Two men stepped forward and one bowed at the waist. "Lady Corbett, please allow me to introduce myself, I am—"

Gillian looked beyond them and disbelief had her jaw dropping. "You've been in my backpack! You've looked at my passport! You guys are *so dead!*" Feeling lightheaded, she strode over, grabbed up her pack, and started stuffing her things inside it. "This is my stuff. *Mine.* My pencils, my camera, my candy, my iPod, my umbrella, and my pepper spray. Snoopy, invasive, nosy, prying, weird. . ." She glanced at the knight again—cute, confused—Gillian groaned. Could a person get Stockholm Syndrome in less than an hour?

She finished loading her pack, then slung it over one shoulder. She needed to get out of there. Apparently, she was just not equipped to handle this situation. She needed to find an officer to deal with these cretins. And since she still found the guy attractive, she obviously needed to find a therapist, too.

Spotting a few of the maids peering down at her from above had fresh mortification heating her face; unable to help the pressure building up within her, she turned back to the knight and started to rant. Again.

KELLEN TRIED to hide his bewilderment. She'd pushed him. Struck him. Some might even say she'd thought to attack him. Without a doubt, the girl was in no wise like her sister. And her speech was odd, but leastways she was talking to him. Shrieking, mayhap, but communicating nonetheless.

He had questions he wanted answered. He needed to find how she came to be there, and what her father's purpose in sending her in such a way might be.

But she babbled on, and Kellen was having a difficult time understanding her words. She talked very fast, alternately pacing, and pointing her finger at him, at his men, and at the servants peering down from above. He did not understand her meaning, and some of her words were strange to him.

Had she been hit on the head? Had she been injured in some way? She was a beauty, no doubt, her cheeks warmed with color and her eyes flashing with anger. Even the shorter hair fluttering about her face was attractive, but her speech was very odd.

Kellen reached out a hand to pat the top of her head to feel for bumps and search for bruises, but the girl knocked his hand away and continued to blather.

Kellen tried not to feel disappointed. First an unfaithful wife and now a violent and broken one? Was he to have no luck in begetting a healthy heir?

He would take this up with Corbett. The man had seven daughters. Their original agreement promised his best, and instead they'd sent him a murderer. And now a mental deficient? Kellen would hold Corbett to his promise.

But perchance *all* Corbett's daughters were so afflicted? Mayhap Kellen *was* given the best of the lot. Again, he wondered why her father sent her to him in such a manner. Was Corbett really so afraid of him? Perhaps afraid that when Kellen met this daughter he'd be angered by her deficiencies?

Kellen moved toward the girl and tried to keep his tone gentle so as not to upset her further. "Mayhap I could take your father's ring into safekeeping until your family arrives?"

The girl jerked her hand away as if he were a thief.

Kellen's impatience grew. "Where are your guards? Your ladies? Your personal maid? Why do you arrive five weeks early?"

She did not answer, did not seem to understand. He was saddened that such a beauty was so damaged.

"You are a jerk!" The girl took a deep breath, swallowed, and spoke in a much slower vein. "You ordered those women to . . . to . . . grope me. You are going to pay for the humiliation that's been inflicted on me. Do you honestly think a pat on the head and a pretty dress are going to pacify me?"

He finally understood that the girl was angry with him about the violation of her privacy. Confounded at her ire, Kellen said, "I own you. You are mine to do with as I will."

"What?" The girl looked amazed. "How do you figure?"

Kellen's puzzlement grew. No one ever questioned him, and

for this tiny girl to do so was as astounding as the blow she'd dealt him. "We are betrothed."

The girl's face reflected surprise, then she glanced quickly around. Kellen looked too but could not fathom for what or whom she searched.

"What is this?" The girl's eyes narrowed in suspicion. "The English version of Punked? An improv play? A medieval weekend in the country complete with command performance?"

Now that she spoke more slowly, Kellen understood her words better but still not their meaning. He tried to explain again, speaking more slowly himself. "You are my betrothed."

Her face took on a haughty expression, much like the one her sister had always worn. "I see." She glanced around again, her gaze taking in his knights and the servants staring at her. "As in engaged to be married? To you?"

"Yes, matrimony." He saw a glimmer of understanding on her face and so tried to explain further. "Your father has paid a dowry, the contract is signed, and we are to be married in five weeks' time."

Her mouth tightened. "And this is your excuse for ordering those . . . those . . . women to violate me?"

"I need no excuse to establish your virginity."

The girl gaped at him for a moment, her face losing its color before flooding with red once more. Then she took a step forward, sucked in a breath, and poked a finger in his chest. Again.

"Now you listen here, *bucko*. Even if we were engaged, *which we are not*, do you think engaged means owned? Because I don't think so!"

She walked away, took several audible breaths, then came back, shaking her head. "So, let me just make sure I have this straight. You're saying we're engaged, right? Isn't that what this ad-libbing is about?"

Kellen was getting more befuddled. "What?"

"Betrothed." She spoke slower. "Are we betrothed, you idiot?"

Kellen stiffened. He did not like her tone nor her name calling, but as they seemed to be making progress, such things could be discussed at a later time. He nodded his agreement.

She smiled, but it did not reach her eyes. "So, my *father* paid a dowry? Making it all right and tight?"

"Aye. That is true."

Her smile thinned. "Well, in that case, I am the one who owns *you! You* are *mine.*" She lifted her nose in the air and gave him a condescending look. "Not only have you been paid for, but as the woman I am your superior in almost every way." She held up a fist. "I am the only one who can ask for directions, have children, and cry in public." Three fingers went up, one at a time.

"And women live longer! Women are smarter!" Holding up five fingers, she lifted her other hand and continued the count. "And they have better peripheral vision and can load the dishwasher without acting like they've been asked to eat horse droppings!"

She shot him a look filled with triumph. "And didn't the girl's . . . *my* father, give you money? A transaction was made, was it not? My family paid for you. I own you. Money is power. The only thing men are better at is peeing standing up! So, count them." She lifted both hands higher to hold up eight fingers. "Eight reasons, and that's just to start with, so I am the winner; therefore, I own *you!*"

Kellen could not help the big smile that spread on his face.

"You agree?" she asked.

Kellen nodded slowly, very pleased by the show of intelligence. She could count? Reason? "What about strength? Am I not bigger and stronger?"

Her tight smile was presented once more. "Who do you use that strength for? If we are engaged, that would be me. I guess I win again, don't I? That makes nine."

Kellen laughed, startling many. He was incredibly amused at her reasoning. Also, relieved that while she might be angry, and

her talk strange, she not only seemed sane, but intelligent. His
first impression of her was obviously wrong. Her way of speaking
was still odd, but charming, now that she'd slowed her speech and
he understood her. "How came you to be here?"

The girl's shoulders drooped and for the first time she
appeared lost. "I was drawing a castle and some men started
chasing me."

She looked so dejected that Kellen softened his tone. "Yes. This
I already know. But how did you make the journey from your
father's keep?"

"What do you mean? How did I get to England? I flew here."

Kellen glanced around. He did not want any accusing her of
witchery. Obviously, she was being sarcastic and did not wish to
answer him, a trait he would soon break her of. He knew she
could not have made the journey by herself and suspected her
father sent her out for reasons of his own. Her temper? Perhaps
she was in love with another? Did she seek to escape the match?
Corbett's reasons were unimportant now.

If her family did not know how to care for her, he would
gladly do so.

She might think she owned him, but she belonged to him now.

And he was keeping her.

CHAPTER 6

This was going absolutely nowhere. With an exclamation of disgust, Gillian turned to leave. She didn't have to stand around while this bozo questioned her.

She gave the knight one last, long look before heading for the door. The guy obviously wasn't even the *least* bit sorry, so now would be a *really* great time for her to find a police officer to *make* him sorry!

Feeling uncertain, wondering if she'd be stopped, she left through the open front doors. When no one tried to intercept her, she breathed a sigh of relief and headed down the steps and into the courtyard. She spotted a couple of men nearby dressed as peasants.

Gillian approached, hoping she wasn't jumping from the frying pan and into the fire by asking a favor from complete strangers. "Excuse me." She sounded a little breathless and cleared her throat, not wanting to sound like anyone's victim. "I need to get a ride back into the town of Marshall. Do you think you could help me out? Or at least lend me a cell phone?"

The men looked at each other, at her, then as one they shook their heads, bowed slightly, turned, and walked away whispering and casting glances over their shoulders.

With a sigh, Gillian watched them go.

She was really starting to hate this place.

She looked around, hoping for someone more sympathetic. Everyone was busy. She could see a stable with several men at work, what looked like barracks being fixed by a couple more guys, and some buildings that could be storehouses with some kids playing in the dirt nearby.

There were a couple of workshops, doors open wide, with men inside. Herbs, plants, and roots hung from the rafters of one building; and in the other, what looked to be pieces of wood in various shapes and sizes. What she didn't see were any friendly faces. People were casting wary glances in her direction or flat out ignoring her.

She looked at some men digging in the dirt on the side of one stone wall. Not one of them would meet her gaze, so no help there. Further on, a cart was being loaded by several men; and beyond them, a tall, rounded structure with a cross over the doorway looked to be a chapel; but its doors were shut tight.

Another building, from what she could see and hear, was a kitchen filled with energetic women coming and going.

She started in that direction when a woman with an armful of material bustled across the courtyard. Feeling a one-on-one conversation might be less intimidating, Gillian hurried to intercept her. As she approached, the woman's eyes widened, she stopped, and dipped a quick curtsy.

"Excuse me." Gillian halted in front of her. "I'm looking for a ride into town? Could you help me out?"

"My lady." The woman stared at the ground then bobbed another curtsy.

Impatient, Gillian said, "Could you at least point me in the right direction for some help?"

The woman pointed toward the keep and Gillian turned to see

That Man in the doorway, watching her. She suddenly found it difficult to breathe. She swallowed, turned away, and walked in the opposite direction feeling very much on display as everyone stared as she passed. She was positive she could *feel* the knight watching her.

She went around to the back wall looking for the parking lot. If someone had left keys or a cell phone in a car, she *might* not even ask for permission to borrow one or both items.

She came to a stop. There was no parking lot inside the inner walls, which made sense. Spotting a spiral staircase situated at the bottom of a corner tower, she quickly climbed the rough stone stairs getting her second or third workout of the day. Panting, her skirt pulled up to her knees, she finally reached the top and looked over the edge.

There was a huge outer courtyard enclosed within a high stone wall. More stables, a stream, an orchard, and a garden. Some men were fighting with swords in the far corner. Beyond the outer wall, she could see nothing but more fields and trees. Not a car, or anything else for that matter, in sight.

From her high position on the wall, she turned and looked over the castle and its inner courtyard. She had to admit it was beautiful with its imposing exterior and fairy tale flavor.

She noticed three little boys watching her from below. They pretended indifference when she looked their way, and it made her smile. And that, in turn, made them run away.

There were no movie cameras, no overt drama. It looked as if people were simply going about their daily business. No one was wearing modern clothing, and there was nothing to indicate this was the twenty-first century.

She didn't see any phone wires, electric lines, or anything like that, and she was getting more than a little freaked out. It was almost as if she'd tumbled into the past.

That thought jarred her memory.

Gillian's college roommate, Sophia, had honeymooned on a

western cattle drive with her husband. It had been touted as a 'heading back in time' experience and had sounded to Gillian like a very odd way to start a marriage.

Gillian wondered if she'd inadvertently stumbled on a similar vacation package. To the extreme. It would explain why everyone stayed in character. It wouldn't really explain what had been done to her, but . . . maybe they truly were die-hard fanatics? What would they have done if she hadn't been a virgin? Burned her at the stake? Gillian couldn't help a shiver. She had to get out of there.

She climbed back down and a girl hurried toward her. Breathless, she stopped and gave Gillian a slight curtsy. "I am Beatrice. I am to be my lady's maid, assigned by his lordship." The girl actually looked excited at the prospect.

"Oh. Okay. A maid, huh? You'd think that if your parents are paying for this vacation you'd get a better part, but you probably weren't given a choice." Gillian waited for the girl to comment, but she simply stared, uncomprehending.

Impatient, Gillian decided to try the straightforward approach. "Look, honey, can we step out of character for just a moment? I need a phone. Do you have a cell?"

The girl looked confused. "I sleep with the other girls and have no chamber of my own."

"Ah . . . okay . . . look, I just need to know if you have a phone I could use to make a local call. I need to call a cab or something. Also, where exactly are we? I'm lost and don't know where to direct the driver."

The girl smiled. "I will take you to his lordship, and he will answer your questions."

Gillian's mouth twisted. "You're what, fourteen, fifteen?"

"I am all of fourteen summers."

"You're fourteen and you're telling me you don't have a cell phone glued to your hip? Come on, just let me borrow it. I promise to make the call really quick. No one has to know."

Beatrice looked around as if seeking help.

"Cross my heart," Gillian made a crossing motion over her chest and smiled reassuringly. "I won't tell a soul."

The girl looked scared. "Perhaps if her ladyship would like to lie abed for a time? Her ladyship's bedchamber is most comfortable."

"Yeah, I laid on that bed earlier; and let me tell you, it was *not* a restful experience."

The girl looked at the ground and clasped her hands in front of her.

In frustration, Gillian turned. "Fine, if you're not going to help me, I'm out of here."

A couple of hours later, with the girl still on her heels, Gillian sighed. She'd studied every inch of the place from the buttery to the barracks, to the blacksmith's and the brew house, to the dovecote and the garderobes—which Gillian had unwillingly made use of. No one was giving up a phone, and most ignored her.

Even more worrisome, she couldn't find anything that indicated she was in the twenty-first century. Not so much as a light switch or a pair of athletic shoes. And as far as she could tell, not one single woman wore makeup. Not even mascara. Surely that went beyond fanatic?

Unless she really was in the past?

Again, she went over what had happened before she'd arrived at the castle. She'd been running. She'd almost fallen a few times, but she didn't remember actually hitting her head or anything. And she wasn't in any pain.

She'd only sipped from her water bottle and didn't remember being stuck with any needles. So how had she been drugged and brought to this place?

She tried to think, to remember every single detail. Right after she'd shoved her father's ring on her finger, the hooligans had disappeared and the medieval guys had shown up. Suddenly, it was as if she were in a different place.

A frisson of fear chased up her spine. *Was* she in a different place? In a different time? Had she somehow managed to *travel through time?*

She studied the ring and thought about the engravings on the inside. She knew her father had hired someone to translate the markings, but she couldn't remember what they meant. She let out a breath. If it had caused the problem, then she could remedy the situation quickly enough. She grasped the ring and pulled.

The ring stuck to her finger.

She spit on it, rubbed the moisture around, and tried to twist it off again. It didn't budge. Panic bubbled in her chest. She didn't remember the ring being so small when her father had worn it. Tugging at the ring was making her finger swell and she gave up.

Later she'd find some cold water to soak her hand in. What she was thinking couldn't be the truth, anyway. "Beatrice. What is the date today?"

Beatrice curtsied, and smiled. "The first day of June, my lady."

Gillian sucked in air as goosebumps ran up her arms. As far as she knew, it was April the eighteenth. With a shiver she asked, "What year?"

The maid looked confused. "The year of our Lord, 1260."

Chills ran up Gillian's back, and the hair on her nape stood straight. But disbelief had her scoffing. "The real date, if you please."

The girl's face showed absolutely no understanding. Either she was an incredible actress, or she really was more than seven hundred years old. "Are you telling the truth?" asked Gillian, trying to sound stern.

The girl looked scared. "Of course, my lady. I would never lie to you. If I did so, Father Elliot would serve up bread and water for a sennight!" The sincerity in the other girl's face sent an icy chill through Gillian.

"What is the name of this castle?"

"Marshall Keep, my lady."

Suddenly dizzy, Gillian placed a hand to her forehead. When she'd been drawing Marshall Keep, it certainly hadn't looked anything like this.

She looked toward the keep. It looked like she needed to have another talk with *That Man*, after all.

And this time she intended to get some answers.

KELLEN, seated at the head table and going over accounts with his steward, was very pleased when Edith finally sought him out. He had marked her whereabouts throughout the day and had waited patiently while Edith explored her new home. He had kept himself busy by performing his duties in the hall on the chance she might need him.

He was proud of his home and wished her to be happy there. He hoped his keep, stalwart and affluent, would sway her into accepting their marriage more readily.

Edith moved toward him and Kellen stood, struck anew at how beautiful he found her. Her gown didn't hide her curves, and her slight form walked with purpose and allure. She looked to be refreshed and radiant from her afternoon outside. Obligation and duty aside, he found himself glad she belonged to him.

Edith stopped in front of him. "What is the date today?"

Kellen's brows rose at her abrupt and demanding tone. As his betrothed, she must needs work on her address; but he would let it pass for the moment.

He wondered if she were worried about attending mass. Her sister, Catherine, had been quite devout. It was unfortunate the priest had not the influence to check her murderous inclinations.

But he would not think on that. This was a new girl and a new beginning. Kellen did his best to keep his expression pleasant as he answered with a slight bow. "It is Tuesday, my lady."

She gifted him a look he did not appreciate. Like he was the idiot she had named him earlier. "The full date, if you please, as in month, day, and year."

Kellen's brows rose, and he tried to hide his disgruntlement. Did she now question his wits? "It is the first day of June, 1260."

Edith's expression was disbelieving. "Are you sure it isn't April eighteenth? Are you sure I haven't simply been kidnapped by a weird medievalist cult or something? I saw the movie *The Village*. They had all those people holed up in an isolated location thinking they were living in the past."

Kellen knew not what she referred to, and fearing to look a dolt, he remained silent.

Edith placed her hand on her hips, momentarily drawing his gaze there. "Or perhaps I really did travel through time?"

Again, Kellen was not sure what she referred to but could clearly hear censure in her tone. This she must work on also. He narrowed his eyes in warning but again did not respond.

Edith sighed, and the tension drained from her body. "What exactly is it you want from me?" The belligerence evaporated and she sounded weary and confused.

Ah. This was good. His patience had finally yielded profits. Kellen relaxed a bit, pleased at her inclination to learn her role here. Her distress in coming to him in such a manner had likely frazzled her nerves and made her awkward. Now they could discuss their betrothal in a reasonable manner.

Kellen reached to take her hand, to reassure her. She did not resist, only appeared bewildered as she gazed down at his larger hand engulfing her smaller one, and this pleased him also. She would soon learn to lean on his strength and to trust him in all matters. The softness of her skin made him smile, and the quiver of awareness prickling throughout his body had him looking forward to their wedding night.

Perhaps after they had known one another better she would not make him wait the five weeks until they wed to consummate the marriage? If she carried his heir on their wedding day, he would be doubly pleased.

"You may call me Kellen. May I call you Edith?"

She jerked her hand from his. "Why would you?" Her words were sharp again.

Kellen was taken aback, his pride stung, and he straightened. "That is your name, is it not? Lady Edith Corbett? We are betrothed, so formalities between us can surely be dropped?"

Lady Edith sucked in a breath. "I might not know much about what is going on here, but I am *positive* we are not engaged and that I am *not* Edith."

Kellen struggled to hold his temper, but it was obvious she tried to escape the marriage. She did not like her new home? She did not like him? That was unfortunate, because she would find him unyielding on this subject. They *would* marry.

Anger hardened his heart. "You are not Lady Edith Corbett?"

Edith folded her arms. "No, I am not."

Kellen gave her one final chance. "You are not Lady Edith and are not my betrothed?"

"I already said no on both counts, didn't I?" Again, her tone held the sharpness he was beginning to detest.

Kellen sucked in a breath and tried to control his temper. Obviously, his betrothed needed instruction on the way of things. "Then how came you to be here? Who are you? If you are not Lady Corbett, you must be a thief and a spy and therefore must be hanged immediately."

Shock and fear were plain in Edith's face as she swallowed and stepped back. "I'm not a thief or a spy."

Kellen did not want her afraid. He wanted his wife to want him. To yield to him. This display of neediness on his part, the fragile hope for a companion in marriage, made him angrier still. When would he learn?

He hit out harshly. "You wear the Corbett ring. If you are not his daughter then you must have stolen it."

Edith hid the ring under her hand. *"No! This was my father's ring!"* Fear laced her expression and voice.

"Then once more, I will ask for your name."

She studied him for a long moment, and he was well aware of the visage she beheld. Brutal, grim, harsh. Her unwanted future.

She gulped. "I am Lady Edith Corbett, your betrothed." She grabbed her bag, turned, and ran out the door again.

Kellen let out a breath and tamped back the pain and anger. It was not as he had hoped. But there would be no games played between them. He would not allow it. She would learn her place and keep to it. The marriage would be one of duty, and any tender feelings he felt toward her he would keep to himself.

Eventually those sentiments would expire.

Just as they had in his first marriage.

CHAPTER 7

*T*he guy was a . . . a . . . *a big, scary jerk!* Gillian ran outside, finally slowed, and came to a stop. Breathing hard, she looked around.

So, the year was 1260, huh? These guys were good. Everything pointed to this being medieval England: the castle, the way everyone dressed, their speech, the way they occupied themselves, everything. There was not one little clue that this was the twenty-first century.

But, of course, that was impossible. Time travel via a grave-yard? The idea was ridiculous. She had to look at this logically. Take away the time travel idea and what was she left with?

A fraud of some sort. A trick. And probably drugs and a kidnapping to boot. But for what purpose?

Perhaps this was some sort of English Candid Camera type show that had gone way too far. A give a girl a gynecological exam, then threaten to kill her, type show. It was hard to believe anyone would arrange something this elaborate, but it made more sense than time travel.

They were probably going to feature her on YouTube or some-thing along with a bunch of other idiot tourists who fell for their ploy and were molested by them. British humor? Somehow watching Monty Python would never be the same.

But shouldn't they have jumped out by now and admitted it was all a joke? Surprise, surprise, we got you. Ha, ha, ha.

Or did they realize they'd gone too far and now didn't know what to do? Didn't know how to get out of it? Were they afraid of being sued? Gillian's mouth tightened. If not, they should be.

She headed toward the front gate. She'd climb to the top of the wall and take a good look at the view from the front of the castle this time. See if she could spot a road or perhaps even her rental car if they'd brought it along.

She still had her keys in her pack, so she could hike out to it and drive away without a backward glance. If she didn't see the rental, well, at this point she was even willing to take her chances and hitchhike to the town of Marshall. As long as the driver wasn't an obviously drooling psychopath or dressed in medieval garb, or both.

Ignoring the way everyone continued to stare, she walked to the imposing front gate, located the circular staircase, and started to climb.

When she'd almost reached the top, two men rushed forward blocking her way. Guards from the looks of them, one taller with a bigger nose, one shorter with worried brown eyes. Strong men, stocky with muscle. Both looked uncomfortable.

Big Nose glanced at his friend then ordered. "My lady, you must turn back. 'Tis not allowable for you to be up here."

Gillian stopped a few steps down and glared as she tried to catch her breath. "Just get out of my way, okay? I've about had it with this place, and I don't need any more men telling me how it's going to be; so back off, buster."

Surprise registered on both faces and the brown-eyed worrier positioned himself more firmly in her path but glanced between his friend and Gillian as if unsure which side to take. His voice was gentle. "We cannot let you by, your ladyship. 'Tis high off the ground. Turn back lest you be frightened by the view."

Gillian smiled tightly. "I was just looking at the view from the back side of the keep a while ago. This isn't that much higher and I promise it won't scare me. Just get out of the way, will you?"

Big Nose placed a fist on one hip. "'Tis not allowable." Arrogance oozed down the steps.

Sudden suspicion had Gillian's eyes narrowing. "Why not? Is there something you don't want me to see? A parking lot, perhaps? Or a nearby town? Policemen on patrol? A telephone?"

The men exchanged a confused glance, or was that a guilty one? Big Nose's brows rose. "Er . . . no, miss."

The worrier looked visibly distressed but didn't move out of her way. "Please miss, this is no place for a lady such as yourself."

Gillian gave a fake smile. "What's a girl like me doing in a place like this, huh? I'm asking myself that same question. Now, move it."

Gillian surged up the few steps and tried to squeeze around the shorter guy. She pushed but couldn't get much of a foothold from her position on the stairs, and the guy didn't budge at all. Gillian, hands and head pushing against the man's stomach, said, "Nothing you can say is going to stop me. Get out of my way!"

Neither guy moved.

Gillian sighed and let up. She moved down a step so she could glare up at them. "Look. The jig is up. I surrender." She lifted both hands. "You got me. Ha. Ha. Ha. You can show me your tiny little cameras, and we can all laugh together. Okay?"

Both men looked at each other then back at her again. She made another dive, and this time the taller man blocked her way grabbing at her arms as she tried to go around him.

Off balance, upset, and on the verge of tears, Gillian shrank back. "What are you trying to do? Push me down the stairs? If you touch me, if anyone dares to touch me again, you are both going to be in so much trouble!"

The guards looked anxious and uncomfortable, but both held their positions. The worrier looked around as if seeking more help. "Miss. Please. You must not come up here. The height will only upset your sensibilities."

"Turn back." Big Nose's arrogance reared its ugly head again.

Gillian looked down, shook her head, and sighed. Fine. They wanted her to play damsel in distress? She'd play it their way. She tried to look scared as she peeked up at them. "The view is truly frightening?" Gillian tried for fear, but wondered if she'd over-played when her voice wavered. "I guess you're right. I'd better go now."

Brown Eyes looked relieved. "Thank you, miss. That is for the best."

Big Nose smiled in a superior way. "There's a good lass. And don't be coming back up here." Under his breath he muttered, "Meddlesome female."

Gillian twisted her body to look down the spiral staircase. "I should just go back this way? I'm not sure how to get down. It's so steep."

Gillian's dress hid her firmly planted feet as she pretended to lose her footing. "Oh . . . oh, dear . . . oh, no!" She started to wind-mill her arms and let out a real scream as her pack pulled her backward. "Help me! I'm falling!"

The shorter guy grabbed her by the arm and pulled her up the few steps.

Gillian clung to him as she looked down the staircase. "I . . . I can't. Oh, thank you . . . I almost . . . I'm so scared. I could . . . I could have died!"

The man's grip tightened protectively. "Fret not. I have you."

Both men pulled her the rest of the way up the stairs and she collapsed on the stone floor, her heart pounding. She started to laugh as she scooted away, then stood and brushed off her skirt. "Thanks, guys. Now that I'm here, I might as well look around."

Big Nose's mouth fell open then his face tightened into an angry mask. "Now, see here." He reached for her.

Gillian backed away. "I wouldn't if I were you. I'll scream the castle down if you so much as lay one finger on me."

Brown Eyes made frantic motions toward the staircase.

"Mistress, please."

Gillian skipped a few feet backward out of their reach. "Back off. I'm just going to take a look around, and then I'll be on my way. Okay?"

Gillian turned, walked to the edge and clung to a stone parapet in case they tried to use force. She looked over the village and the surrounding countryside.

Within moments, her shoulders sagged in disappointment. No car, no sign of a paved road, no sign of civilization at all. She'd expected to see something to convince her she wasn't in the thirteenth century. If not a car, at least a satellite dish on the side of a hut or a telephone wire. Something.

"Now, miss," said the worrier. "I told you ye'd feel faint. And now look, you've gone pale as parchment. Shall I carry you down, then?"

Gillian waved a hand at them. "No. I'm fine."

The man nodded reluctantly and the two walked a few feet away to confer. Big Nose's voice rose as he talked about trickery, women, and guile all in the same sentence.

And then Gillian spotted the cemetery. Could it be the same graveyard she'd run through before? How could she possibly know? She looked beyond it and saw something that made her spine stiffen. In the distance sat a cluster of rocks, one bigger than the rest, in the middle of a field.

Gillian's heart started to pound. Could it be the same rock she'd been sitting on a couple of hours ago as she'd sketched the ruin? As she'd drawn the castle with the exact same arch as this one had?

At a guess, the rock was located in exactly the position it should be in relation to the castle.

Was she being ridiculous? Was it simply coincidence?

She looked to the left of it, to where the road should be. There was no road in that direction and no car. But there wouldn't be if she were in the thirteenth century, would there?

She brushed the thought away. She refused to buy into that madness. The rock simply had to be a fluke. Of course, it would be easy enough to put her mind at ease. Her rock had been unique.

Turning away from the men, Gillian dug into her pack, pulled out her camera, turned it on and scrolled through the pictures she'd taken of the ruin until she came to the rock.

She checked it against the one on the outskirts. It did look like the same rock. But from that distance and angle, she couldn't be sure.

Gillian scoffed at herself. Surely rocks like that were scattered throughout England? But they wouldn't be exactly the same, would they? It had been unusual with its dips and curves. And up close she could check it against the picture to be sure.

She sprang into action, shoved her camera in her pack, and shrugged it onto her shoulders. She headed for the stairs and pulled the strings tight on her backpack.

"Do you need help going down the stairs, mistress?" asked Brown Eyes.

"Hardly!"

Big Nose sniffed. "A good riddance to ye, then. And don't come back."

Gillian's mouth twisted. "Don't worry. If I have anything to say about it, I won't." Scrambling down the staircase, she hurried to the bottom and then around the corner. She was relieved when no one stopped her from leaving through the huge front gate. She'd go and get a look at that rock and settle her doubts once and for all. And when she was done, she'd just keep on walking.

CHAPTER 8

Wearing a dress, and moving across the harsh terrain, it took Gillian about thirty minutes to go through the village, past the cemetery, up the rise, and over the field to the rock formations.

Breathing hard as she neared them, fear constricted her chest. Because the closer she got, the more convinced she became that they were *the same group of rocks.*

The gray stone, interspersed with green and black markings, the different shapes of the boulders, the way they were positioned, all looked remarkably familiar.

Chills climbed the middle of her back, spread across her body, and had the hair on her arms standing on end. The rock she'd climbed before had vaguely resembled a mushroom, *and there it was.* Even from the ground she could see the dip in the front that looked suspiciously like the depression she'd been sitting in.

Could a rock remain unchanged over a period of seven hundred years? Was that even possible?

Gillian took off her backpack, retrieved the camera, and scrolled through the pictures until she found the rock. She skirted the boulder until she found the exact location from which she'd snapped the shot.

Shivers raced up her spine as she compared the past and the present. Unless they had lookalike rocks strewn across England, then yes, this had to be the same rock. The shallow depression was there, even the ledge on which she'd set her pencils was right where it was supposed to be. She could even see the other rock formations in the background, both in the photo and in the present.

Could this really be happening?

Encumbered by her dress, she bunched the material in one fist, climbed the backside of the rock, and lowered herself into the hollow.

Sitting in the exact indentation she'd occupied earlier, she looked toward the castle, took a few deep breaths to stave off dizziness, and scrolled through the pictures on her camera.

Looking between the castle ruin on her camera, and the now pristine version of the castle with the village set out in front of it, Gillian's breath caught. The same arch, towers, arrow slits, everything. Even the graveyard was in the correct location. There could be no doubt.

Gillian felt the blood drain from her face and a whirling sensation had her dropping the camera in her lap and clutching at the rock as she took a few deep breaths, trying to get enough air into her lungs.

This was unbelievable. How could this have happened? Why would this have happened? Somehow, she'd actually traveled through time? Had she stumbled through a wormhole without noticing? Or been snatched up by the hand of God and moved to prevent her murder by those boys?

Did things like that happen?

Gillian rubbed her fingers against the scratchy surface of the rock, making sure it was really there. That *she* was really there.

She wasn't unconscious or dreaming and this wasn't some sort of elaborate set-up to trick her.

Unsurprised, she watched as Lord Kellen Marshall crossed the field on horseback, a few of his men following. She stuffed her camera into her pack, closed it, and waited.

He was without helmet or shield, and his black hair gleamed with shots of mahogany and gold in the sunlight, his tanned face hard and unyielding. He still wore chain, armor, and sword, and his loose tunic sported a coat of arms in red and green, depicting a black bird of prey, claws extended.

As she was feeling slightly hunted at the moment, his crest seemed appropriate.

His men stopped; but Kellen, eyes intelligent, perceptive, and without an ounce of guile, maneuvered his horse around the rock, never taking his gaze from hers.

Her own gaze dropped when he moved behind her, until finally he finished rounding the rock and stopped in front of her. He instructed one of his men to search the other rocks.

"What do you do here?"

Slowly she raised her head and met his dark gaze again. She shivered. A real, live, medieval warrior, and he was looking at her as if he owned her, as if she were his possession. His amber eyes took in every part of her, making the blood rush back into her face. A medieval warrior who believed she belonged to him and who believed he had the right to establish and then claim her virginity.

Gillian swallowed, then pulled her knees to her chest and hugged them. Breathless, and still even a bit dizzy, she thought it was a good thing she was sitting. She tried a smile. "Sightseeing?"

He didn't smile in return. "Sightseeing?"

Gillian nodded. "Yes. I enjoy sightseeing. I saw these rocks from the top of the castle and wanted a closer look."

Kellen glanced around. "You were not meeting with anyone in this place?"

Her brows rose. Was that why he'd rounded the rock? Why his man was, even now, searching around the others? Was he looking for someone? "No. How could I? I don't know anyone here."

Kellen nodded again, then maneuvered his horse closer and held out a hand. "Might I assist you back to the keep?"

Looking at the large, calloused hand, Gillian thought about going with him, thought about sitting on his lap again with his warmth and solid muscle at her back. She remembered the way his arms had held her tight and how she'd melted into him, trying to absorb his strength.

A part of her wanted to fall into those arms again for comfort; but now that she knew he was real, she was pretty sure it wasn't such a good idea. He either wanted to marry her or kill her. Since he wasn't joking about either option, she could really use a bit of time to adjust.

Especially since, if and when he found out she wasn't Edith Corbett, he might take option number two and hang her as a spy.

She smiled weakly at him. "How about a walk?"

Gillian watched with relief as Kellen gave a brief nod and dismounted. He threw the reins of his horse to a grinning knight, crossed the distance quickly, and held out his arms.

Gillian hesitated. She realized she'd either have to accept his help or turn around and scoot down with her butt in the air. She looked into Kellen's upturned face, to the four knights at his back, all grinning now, and realized that was *not* going to happen.

She moved to the edge, took a breath, and fell into Kellen's outstretched arms. Her hands landed on his shoulders and he caught her under her arms and lifted. She could feel the hardness of chain mail and bunching muscles as he easily hoisted her up and around, then slowly lowered her to the ground. She couldn't help the way her heart thumped at this effortless show of strength.

The romantic dress she wore, her hands slipping to his chest, the predatory way he looked at her, all combined to make her knees weak. The attraction she felt was stronger than ever and left her breathless.

Realizing her feet were on the ground, that she still gripped him and stared into his eyes like an enraptured groupie, she dropped her hands and turned away. She needed to think, and it was better if she didn't touch him while she did so.

She cleared her throat. "Shall we go?" Her voice was breathless and, embarrassed, she didn't wait for an answer.

Keeping her distance, she skirted the men and their horses, then started toward the small village. Kellen fell into step, his long stride enabling him to take one step for every two of hers, his chain mail making a soft clinking sound as they walked. His men fell back, leaving them a bit of privacy; and out of the corner of her eye, Gillian could see Kellen studying her. When she glanced up, the possessive look in his eyes startled her and she quickly dropped her gaze.

And why wouldn't he look at her that way? He thought he owned her, body and soul. He believed them to be engaged. Betrothed. Whatever. She shivered. She was going to be in deep trouble when the truth came out.

She remembered the hard look in his eyes earlier when he'd threatened to hang her. Would he actually kill her if he knew she wasn't really his fiancé? She swallowed. Maybe not. Probably not. Did they even hang women? She didn't know for sure, but this was a harsh time and he was a harsh man.

The bottom line was, if she didn't want to die, or end up cleaning medieval bathrooms or something, she was going to be Edith Corbett until she figured out what was going on and found a way back to her own time. And she would find a way. If she could get here, surely she could get back again.

Gillian thought about the physical exam she'd been subjected to and her cheeks heated. What if she hadn't been a virgin? What if she'd given in to Ryan's overtures as she'd considered? Would they have thrown her out and pulled up the drawbridge? Poor Edith. What a time to live.

Gillian considered the fact that Edith's last name was the same as her own. A relative? One of the ancestors she'd come to England to find? She had no way of knowing, but found it funny and stifled a laugh. She'd meant to find their headstones, not meet them in person.

"What amuses you?"

Gillian lifted a shoulder. "Life is just funny sometimes, you know?"

"How so?"

She decided to be as honest as possible. She had no way of knowing anything about Edith, anyway, so couldn't answer as she would. "One minute I'm alone, and the next," she shrugged, "on the verge of being married."

Which reminded her. Earlier, he'd said her arrival was sooner than expected. That meant the wedding party hadn't arrived and she wondered how long she had. "Let's talk about the wedding," she said brightly. "When is it to be, exactly?"

"You were supposed to arrive five weeks hence." Kellen's face was unreadable as he glanced her way. "Why are you early?"

"Why do you think I'm early?" she hedged.

"Your father fears my anger. That you wear his ring bespeaks a message from him. If your father has sent such, state it now."

Gillian sighed. "All right. I'll bite. Why would my father be afraid of you?"

"Your sister tried to poison me before dying herself, marking her death suspicious. He fears my anger." He sounded as if he'd hated his wife and she'd obviously despised him.

"You didn't kill her, did you?" Remembering the way he'd threatened to hang her, Gillian was only half-joking.

"Nay!" Kellen turned her toward him, his expression affronted. "Have you heard such?"

Gillian swallowed. "No." Kellen's hands were warm on her

shoulders. "I . . . just the way you worded it. It made me wonder. So, she killed herself?"

He nodded once. "In trying to poison me, she mischanced to poison herself, though rumors spread that suicide was her goal."

Good grief. And this psycho was supposed to be Edith's sister? And he wanted to marry *her*? How very awkward. Gillian lifted her face to the sunlight. "It certainly is a nice day, isn't it?"

Kellen grunted, and she supposed that was all the response her change of subject deserved. Gillian turned away and they started walking again. So, perhaps she had as long as five weeks before the bride and her parents showed. "Why do you want to marry me, anyway?"

"You bring more land and—"

"What!" Instant anger fired Gillian's temper. She stopped and turned toward him again, glaring into his face. "Oh, that's nice. Really nice." Gillian threw up her arms. "First my loser boyfriend turns out to be a user and now you only want what you can get from me. Don't men think women have feelings?"

Kellen looked surprised. "It is the way of things."

Looking into his confused face, she sighed, the anger draining away as suddenly as it flashed to life. They weren't really engaged, anyway, so what did it matter? She turned to walk again.

"Well, at least you aren't making any bones about it. At least you aren't sly. But why is it men only want me for what I can give them? Why can't someone just want me because they like me? Why can't someone just be attracted to me in the normal *boy meets girl, likes girl, and wants to marry girl* sort of way?"

Kellen laughed. "I must disabuse you of the notion that money and lands are the only reason I wish to marry you."

Gillian stopped, her face turning upward.

"I also want an heir." Kellen looked at her, a masculine smile spreading across his face. "And I plan to be very diligent in the endeavor. It will be my first priority. I look forward to the task and plan to spend much time in the pursuit."

Gillian didn't say anything for a moment as she stared into his eyes. Slowly she smiled, then laughed. Which, in turn, surprised a pleased expression from Kellen, which made her laugh all the more.

Strangely enough, the thought that he might want her for her body didn't offend nearly as much as him wanting her for financial gain. Kellen smiled, looking at her as if she were some sort of temptress. She liked it, and said, "Okay, then. It's good that we understand each other."

She started forward again and they soon reached the outskirts of the village. She was accepting this, wasn't she? Somehow, she'd been hurled through time and into the past. This *was* the castle she'd been sketching, and this knight *was* born in the thirteenth century. She'd time traveled, and was now engaged to a gorgeous guy who'd rescued her and looked at her like she was dessert. Not a bad setup.

Granted, his real fiancé was scheduled to arrive in five weeks; and when she did, Gillian would be exposed as an imposter and put to death, but why dwell on the negatives? Hopefully Gillian would be long gone by then.

In the meantime, she'd just go with the flow. She'd pretend to be Edith, have an adventure, enjoy the English countryside, and find a way home. She slid a glance up at Kellen and had to admit, his obvious admiration was a much-needed ego boost. When his real fiancé arrived, he'd no doubt forget all about Gillian, but maybe she could have a few great memories out of the deal?

She held out her hand and, looking pleased, Kellen took it, his large, warm grip dwarfing hers and sending tingles up her arm. She smiled again. Nice. Very nice. Who didn't hope for a holiday romance? And how many people got a chance to visit medieval England?

Gillian was going to buy into the whole fairytale for now, castle, knight, and all, and enjoy the adventure. At least until she found a way to return home.

"You wanted a message from my father? Here it is. The rest of the party is coming as scheduled."

Kellen looked down at their linked hands and nodded. "That is fine. It will give us time to know one another before the wedding."

Gillian smiled. "Time indeed."

CHAPTER 9

"*H*e is a dim-witted, softheaded *imbecile!*" Sir Robert Royce threw a cup across the hall and sprayed wine over the dirty rushes. Next, he threw a platter, then a chunk of wood. 'Twas satisfying when three servants scrambled out of the way as the wood exploded against a wall.

"A brainless, half-wit, *moron!* Everything is his fault. I *hate him!* I want him *dead!*"

Robert's throat was raw from airing his justifiable grievances and he realized he was somewhat in his cups. He'd been steadily drinking since his return home and continued to throw things about as servants rushed out of the way. His own men stood back, wary.

Breathing heavily, Robert looked around the hall for more ammunition. His humiliation by Marshall demanded he do something. But what? Every year that passed saw Marshall with more and Robert with less.

Suddenly weary, he sank to his chair at the head table and picked up the cup of wine a servant rushed to place at hand. He took a healthy swallow.

His men slowly moved forward, righting benches so they

could sit. His complaints against Marshall were entirely defensible. Marshall promoted ill will wherever he went, yet somehow retained the king's ear and married at the highest level in the land, adding to his already vast wealth.

It was not fair!

A servant moved cautiously forward to pour more wine, and another set a trencher of food in front of Robert. 'Twas of poor quality, the bread gritty, the cheese hard and slightly moldy, the meat scarce. Anger welled again for he knew from past visits that Marshall set a much finer table.

An adolescent raced in and bent to one knee, his head bowed. "My lord."

His spy, ready to report. Robert straightened. "Well?"

The youth stood, breathing hard, his skinny chest rising and falling beneath dirty clothes. "The Lady Corbett has arrived early for the wedding, my lord."

"She is truly Marshall's betrothed?"

The young man nodded vigorously. "Aye, my lord."

"Daughter to Lord Corbett?"

"Aye, my lord."

So 'twas true. Robert could hardly credit the half-naked girl he'd seen as Marshall's betrothed. Why hadn't he noticed the ring? Why hadn't his men?

"Had she been attacked?" Robert smiled at the thought. The marriage might well be invalid.

"The midwife affirmed her virginity. 'Tis said she wore a chastity belt of such strength and cunning ten men could not have removed it. And there is more to tell. Marshall Keep was in an uproar, for only hours after her arrival, Lady Corbett tried to walk back to her father's stronghold, my lord."

Robert laughed. "By the saints, did she truly?" Perhaps he need not kill the girl. Mayhap he could find a way to turn the chit against Marshall as he'd done her sister.

The boy nodded again, looking pleased with himself. "But

Lord Marshall rode after and brought her back. They held hands and smiled upon one another and even laughed. I saw it with my own eyes. Some say 'tis a love match in the making."

Burning anger raced through Robert. Did the youth mean to try his patience? "Is that so?" Robert raised a fist to strike the impudence from the boy, but the youth was fast and darted away.

Robert motioned to his men. "Catch him."

Robert laughed, heartily amused as the young man eluded his men, jumping over fallen benches, running over tabletops, and leaping and slipping in the dirty rushes. The boy received a few blows to his back for his trouble before tripping and getting caught.

A female servant lunged forward. "Please, my lord." She threw herself to her knees in the dirt and filth, her head bent, exposing greasy hair. "Please, do not hurt Valeric."

Robert stared at the downbent head for a moment, then remembered the boy was his whelp by the servant girl. She used to be pretty but was now haggard and pinched.

Dissatisfied, he looked about. His keep was dirty, his servants begrimed, and his food lacking.

He had a cheerful moment as he recalled how much he'd enjoyed the food at Marshall's table and then enjoyed his wife even more. He laughed aloud. Feeling magnanimous toward the crying adolescent, he waved a hand. "Let him go."

He turned to the woman. "Clean yourself and hie to my bed." Perhaps he would prove his virility once again this night. Her obvious fear was like an aphrodisiac.

Just so long as Marshall didn't prove his virility any time soon. If he fathered an heir, Robert would have no chance at talking the king into giving Marshall Keep to him, even were Marshall to die.

This time Robert would put a stop to Marshall's plans *before* they came to pass. Robert would get another chance at killing the girl.

Or mayhap he should think it through. Impregnating

Marshall's last wife had been such a pleasurable experience. Knowing Marshall's heir had sprung from his own loins had been heady and exciting. If the child had lived, and been a boy, Robert's own son would have inherited Marshall Keep. And with Marshall dead, Robert had planned to marry the girl and have it all: the keep, the girl, the heir.

He'd been so happy for a while.

Too bad the stupid woman had killed herself instead of Marshall.

He considered the new girl. She'd been most attractive. But he could not risk it again. Not with Marshall living there continually. The girl wasn't worth his own life.

She would needs be killed before the wedding, not after. He only wished he might have realized her identity sooner. He could have taken her and bedded her at his leisure first, enjoyed her to the fullest, and then killed her.

No, it wasn't too late for vengeance. It would simply take a different twist this time about. This time he would ensure Marshall was without bride, heir, or property.

And, eventually, without life itself.

CHAPTER 10

*G*illian woke to a face peering down at her. She jerked backward into soft pillows. *"Aaahhh!"*

It was only then she recognized Beatrice, her new maid. The young girl grinned. "Sorry, my lady. I was just checking to see if you were awake yet. Did you sleep well, then?"

Heart pounding, Gillian glanced around, surprised to find herself still in medieval England. "You should know."

Beatrice giggled. "Lord Marshall insisted you sleep without interruption. He feared you were overtired from your journey and ordeal."

Two other young girls filled a wooden tub with steaming water near the fireplace.

"Is that for me?" Gillian indicated the tub. A bath sounded wonderful.

"Aye, my lady."

Gillian tossed off the covers and slid out of bed. She'd been so tired the night before she barely remembered slipping into the voluminous white nightgown. Her feet touched cold stone and she immediately hopped from one foot to the other. "Cold. The floor is cold!"

Beatrice handed her fur-lined slippers and Gillian slid them on. They were a little small, but she was grateful for their warmth as she headed down the hall to quickly use the garderobe, an experience she completed as quickly as possible. When she returned, Beatrice hurried forward.

"Ye've already missed the morning meal, my lady. 'Twill soon be suppertime. And look! His lordship sent a gift." She held it out.

Gillian took the beautiful silver comb and studied the pattern of roses and ivy. Touched, she ran a hand over the intricate design and felt herself soften toward the big guy. She couldn't remember the last time a man had given her a present. Her so-called fiancé certainly hadn't. He'd taken her for all he could get. "It's beautiful," she whispered.

Beatrice smiled. "Lord Marshall will be pleased if you wear it this day. He waits below. He paces the hall and is like to wear a path in the stones."

This set all three girls giggling and Gillian smiling.

He was anxious to see her again? That was certainly flattering. Gillian noticed a beautiful green dress laid on the end of the bed. "All right. If you girls will leave, I'll take a bath and get dressed."

"Nay, my lady. We are to assist you."

And why didn't that surprise her? "Like you did yesterday? No, thanks. I'm not getting naked until everyone is gone."

Reluctantly, almost peevishly, as if Gillian were being unfair, the girls left. Gillian checked, but there wasn't a lock on the door.

Watching the entry, Gillian undressed and, seconds after she sank into the tub, Beatrice glided back into the room.

"I don't need any help!"

Chin high, Beatrice threw a petulant, reproachful glance. "I will tidy the chamber."

"Get out!"

Beatrice acted like she didn't hear, and, a moment later, the two other girls filed back inside.

Disgusted, Gillian sank down and let her head drop back against the wooden rim. It they came near her, she'd flatten them.

Ignoring her, the girls chattered as they put things away, made the bed, dusted, swept, and straightened the pots and jars lining one table. One girl straightened the logs beside the fire.

Gillian sighed and quickly made use of soap and cloth.

Beatrice brushed out the bottom of the green dress and threw Gillian an arch look. "Everyone is talking about how gallant it was for Lord Kellen to follow and hold your hand last eve. And Lord Kellen has laughed several times this day, already. His mood is much improved since your arrival. The guards over the gatehouse declare to have shown to you the rocks in the distance, and thereby lay claim to the romance."

"Everyone's talking about us?" Usually no one cared to notice anything she did, and it felt strange to have a starring role in the castle gossip.

"Aye. Some think to rename the rocks as Lover's Peak or Rapture Ridge. I myself favor Passion's Precipice."

Gillian groaned, then slipped down into the water. She quickly finished washing and was soon ready to get out. If Gillian wasn't mistaken, the women were now trying to find things to do. Surely the walls didn't need dusting?

"Have you any tidings from London? With your father a powerful baron, you must have gone there often. Have you news of the king and queen?"

Gillian considered her knowledge of history and drew a blank. She had no idea who they even were. "Um. Well. It's said they have romantic names."

Beatrice turned, her brows drawn together. "Henry and Eleanor? Think ye?"

"Of course." She filed the names away. She wished she did have some juicy bit of gossip to share based on a broad knowledge of history, but didn't. "Uh. They're doing fine. The queen's gowns are as pretty as ever," she said cautiously.

Beatrice lit up. "Have you details? The queen is said to be very beautiful. Is that true?"

"Sure, and she always wears the latest fashions." Since the woman was a queen, and considered beautiful, Gillian felt safe making the assertion.

Beatrice, eyes shining, asked, "What is the latest fashion?"

Gillian floundered. She'd drawn people in a couple of her castle paintings, but had pretty much used her imagination rather than done any research on clothing. This was what she got for being lazy. "Puffed sleeves, pointed shoes, and feathers?"

The girl squealed. "I had not heard this!"

Gillian cringed. She should have kept her mouth shut. "I'm ready to get out now, if you'll just go?"

Beatrice rushed forward. "I will help."

Gillian quickly held the cloth over her chest. "No, I'm fine, really."

Beatrice clapped her hands and rushed the two other girls out, then came back and held up a large, dry cloth.

"Really, I can do it myself. I insist."

"'Tis my right and my duty."

Gillian sighed. She was pretty sure she'd heard that before. Recently. "Fine. But if you try anything, I'll annihilate you, understand?"

Beatrice giggled. "Aye, my lady."

She squeezed the moisture from her hair, then from the wash cloth, laying it over the edge. She stood and reached for the drying cloth, but Beatrice backed away until Gillian was out of the tub, completely exposed. Giving Beatrice a dirty look, Gillian snatched the cloth.

Beatrice stared, eyes wide. "Your toes!" she gaped in astonishment.

Gillian wrapped up in the cloth and looked at her toes. "You've never seen neon pink toenails before, huh? You didn't notice them yesterday when you stripped me?"

"My lady. I most sincerely apologize for treating you thus. Lord Marshall had need to know of your purity, and we had to obey."

"Whatever." Gillian lifted her chin at the dress. "I like the dress. It's very whimsical."

"Let me help you into it."

It turned out Gillian was actually glad for the assistance. Hoses gartered at the knees, a tight undertunic, and then the gown. She probably wouldn't have figured it out on her own. To Beatrice's disgust, Gillian wore her athletic shoes which would have probably spoiled the effect, except they couldn't be seen.

"Do you miss your family?"

Gillian thought of her parents and brother. "Yes, I do. Very much."

"I'm sure they will visit often, and that Lord Marshall will take you to see them also." Beatrice opened the door and clapped her hands. "Bring the ribbons, that her ladyship might choose."

Gillian stifled a smile. She wasn't sure she'd get used to the bowing and scraping, but Beatrice was certainly taking to her new role.

Beatrice hustled her onto a stool and Gillian sat as her hair was damp dried, coiled, entwined with green ribbons, and the silver comb inserted.

"Any idea what I'm supposed to do all day?"

"My lady?" Beatrice continued fussing, cursing the thickness of Gillian's hair under her breath.

"You know, how do I keep myself occupied. What's my role?"

"Ah. Your responsibilities? To have children, of course. We are all very excited about the prospect."

Gillian shivered as she remembered Kellen's promise to spend a lot of time at that particular occupation. "I meant right now. Today."

"Ah. Well, of course, you will want to plan the meals, talk to the cooks, make menus, and keep the kitchen accounts. Sewing is a pleasant pastime and Lord Marshall has much material. I imagine he will be most generous with ye. Do you hunt? There are the falcons, of course. And as the weather is warm, perhaps you will plan a field day?"

"A field day?"

"Fun, games, and food out of doors."

"Oh. A picnic." Gillian chuckled at Beatrice's hopeful tone.

"Also, you are to make sure everyone is working to your satisfaction. You have no ladies to train at present, for they all left when your sister died. But I am sure that will change once your family arrives and news of your marriage spreads. Then there are the spinners and weavers. And, of course, preparations for the wedding."

Gillian's head reeled. "Is that all?"

Beatrice giggled. "Of course, you will have many hands to help with all. Lord Marshall is quite wealthy, you know, with countless servants. His father has many manors, but Lord Marshall won this keep through his own merits. It was an award from the king for his strength and loyalty." Beatrice sounded proud.

"And, of course, many fear him and having him thus on the border is a deterrent against the Scots." Beatrice gave Gillian's hair one last pat.

"Everyone is aware you brought his lordship a large dowry and is laughing about your claim of ownership over him. Lord Marshall, as well. No one has seen him laugh in a long time."

The girls' eyes were shining with mirth. "The men are also excited as your dowry will allow more of them a place of their own." She looked down shyly. "Which means a chance of marriage for some of the women, as well."

Gillian was amused. "Thinking of getting married, are you?"

Beatrice shrugged, but she was smiling as she handed Gillian a piece of polished metal and Gillian realized it was supposed to be a mirror. As far as she could tell, she looked presentable. She'd check her compact later.

Beatrice lowered her voice. "All wonder if a betrothal was broken to give you to Lord Marshall?"

A betrothal? Gillian thought about the way that faker Ryan White had fooled her into believing he loved her and wanted to marry her. The way he'd humiliated her and left her self-esteem in the mud. Angry tears formed in her eyes. She'd been a fool, and over such a worthless jerk. She didn't answer, but only shook her head.

"Oh, my lady. I'm sorry to bring up a sore subject."

"It's okay."

"I vow you will be most happy here. I promise to help sew some new dresses for ye. Lord Marshall sent out men to hunt for the thieves who stole your clothing, but I doubt there is much chance of its return. There are your sister's clothes, of course, but you are much taller and with more bosom, so they won't fit well."

Gillian wiped tears away. "That would be great. I'm not much of a seamstress so I accept the offer."

"You look very fine today, my lady. Do you wish for supper in your chambers? Or in the solar? Your sister ate thus often, and you could as well; but I know for a surety Lord Marshall is waiting for you to appear below. Or you could send word that you are not coming."

Gillian, wondering why wife number one had eaten by herself, apparently took too long in answering because Beatrice rushed into speech.

"Father Elliot considers it a sin to eat food in chambers unless you are ill. He declares it a form of gluttony."

Gillian laughed at the not-so-subtle comment. Actually, she was surprised to realize she couldn't wait to see Kellen again. She probably ought to be making a list of possible ways to get back home, but right now all she wanted to do was enjoy being here.

Kellen was attractive, attentive, and made her feel feminine—a state Ryan had managed to make her question. And, for now, being the lady of the castle sounded like fun. Why not enjoy the experience while she could?

For all she knew, she'd be whisked back as unexpectedly as she'd arrived. If not, she could think about returning in a week or two. For now, she'd just enjoy every minute and consider it her vacation. Albeit a somewhat dangerous one.

Besides, she seemed to be one of the main stars in the local gossip mill, so she'd best show up to provide fodder.

Gillian stood and, feeling very maidenly and beautiful in full medieval garb, headed for the door. "I believe I'll eat downstairs."

Beatrice's squeal made Gillian chuckle and, smiling with anticipation, she went to find her knight.

WHEN EDITH finally appeared at the top of the stairs, Kellen stopped pacing to wait at the bottom. He wished Edith to settle and planned to do all he could to ease her way as she accustomed to her new situation.

With a bounce, she reached the last step and smiled at him. "Hello."

Kellen tried not to show his surprise at her happy greeting. She'd not curtsied, but Kellen gave a slight bow, regardless. "A good morrow." Kellen considered the way her green gown brightened the blue of her eyes, the way her coiled hair revealed the length and smoothness of her neck, and the fact that she was more beautiful than he'd remembered.

Her skin was dewy, her figure lush and attractive, and the wide smile she gave belied any shyness or upset she'd suffered the day before. She wore his gift, surely a good sign, and he was pleased and hoped she would comment upon it.

He'd not had much experience with ladies and feared his gallantry to be sadly lacking, but stiffly offered an arm. "My lady?"

She entwined both hers around it, startling him, heating his blood, and he was gratified she touched him of her own accord. As she looked curiously about, Kellen led the way to the head table, sat her beside him, and motioned the servants to come forward with water. Kellen helped Edith wash and dry her slender, delicate hands. Her smooth skin and easy acceptance of his touch caused a surprising breathlessness on his part.

Edith smiled teasingly. "I just had a bath, you know. But maybe you're using this as an excuse to hold my hand?"

Owen and Tristan both laughed as they joined them across the table. "Aye," said Tristan. "Kellen is a tricky sort and must be watched always."

Owen smiled. "'Tis true, my lady. He plans strategies that cannot be seen until too late, and his victim gripped tight within his coils."

Kellen shot both men a dark look that promised retribution later. "Listen not to the slander of fools."

Edith chuckled, a melodious, rich sound that stirred the hair on the back of Kellen's neck. A trencher and cup were placed between them, and he cut the bread in half.

"A piece of stale bread?" Edith teased again. "Is that all I get after missing breakfast?"

Kellen's mouth lifted. "Perhaps I can manage something more."

With the priest gone visiting, a prayer was said by one of his foster boys; and then wine, bread, and butter were brought forward.

Edith slathered a piece with enthusiasm. "Yummy. This bread looks wonderful. Fresh out of the oven, too. I can't remember the last time I had homemade bread." She took a bite. "Mm. This is so good!"

Kellen smiled at her enjoyment and moved aside as a platter laden with food was set between them, as well as bowls with broth and vegetables.

When Kellen set the choicest meats upon her trencher, he realized his hand shook and feared he truly was an idiot.

He wondered if her father sent her early to soften him. If so, Kellen had to admit it was not a bad strategy. Her charm and allure would have even the hardest of hearts yielding.

Edith leaned in, her head tucking neatly beneath his chin. "Why is everyone staring at me?"

He inhaled, her wondrous smell making him dizzy. "Lady Edith, your beauty dazzles them all," he said with complete sincerity, and was pleased by the ease with which the compliment arrived.

Owen and Tristan pretended not to listen to the conversation, but smiled encouragingly when Edith looked Kellen's way.

Edith laughed and elbowed him in the ribs. "Get out of here."

Stung, Kellen asked, "You wish me to leave?"

"What? Heavens, no. Then who would feed me?" She seemed to banter, her smile wide, and he was confused.

"By the way, if you don't mind, I prefer Gillian to Edith. Could you call me that instead?"

He was pleased that she shared her pet name with him and nodded at once. "Gillian, then." He liked it. "A very pretty name." And it boded well for their marriage if she accepted him into her life so easily.

Sitting beside her was making him tongue-tied and Kellen considered and rejected several conversational tidbits. Owen nodded and gestured toward Gillian, but Kellen could think of naught to say besides, "The food is to your liking?"

"Yes, thank you. It's great. I didn't realize how hungry I was."

Tristan circled his hand at Kellen and, panicked, Kellen shook his head.

Tristan sighed, then turning to Gillian, offered up a bright smile. "My lady, 'tis enchanting to have such a lovely lass to grace our humble table. Thy matchless beauty shines upon this lowly assemblage and brings to us the hope of summertime after a bleak winter."

Owen backhanded Tristan in the chest. "Nay, dolt, you insult her with such sparse praise." Owen smiled upon Gillian. "My lady, the grace of thy presence 'tis as a flame brandished on the darkest of midnights, as the sun coming after a moonless night, a brilliant, radiant beam shining through a clouded winter day."

Both men looked expectantly toward Gillian, awaiting her praise, and Kellen tried frantically to think of words to woo her, but none came to mind. He considered killing his men instead, a task he well knew how to perform.

Gillian laughed. "Is that so? Well, I don't like to doubt your sincerity or anything, but do I know either one of you? Have we been introduced?"

Her goad inspired a delighted glance exchanged between his men. "Sir Tristan de Aguilon, at your service, fair Gillian. And this knave is Sir Owen de Burgess. And my lady, you must believe, we are in earnest! 'Tis like an arrow through the heart of love for you to question the fervor of our words!"

Owen nodded. "Aye, a dagger, a lance. Your cruel disbelief 'tis as a javelin, straight and true, to pierce this worthless hide."

"Nay!" said Tristan. "A battering ram to invade the wretched recesses of this disconsolate heart."

Gillian chuckled and Kellen's mood darkened.

"Somehow, I suspect you'll both recover," Gillian said.

Tristan placed a hand over his afflicted heart. "My lady, I beg you—"

Kellen pounded a fist on the table. "Enough! Let the girl eat without threat of thy vomit-inducing sweetness."

Gillian chuckled again and the sound lightened the jealousy overpowering him because he had not the words to enchant her half so well.

Looking at her, Kellen felt a very lucky man. Gillian was vibrant and beautiful and didn't seem in the least repulsed by him. In fact, she smiled frequently and looked to him when amused as if inviting him to share her good humor.

He was proud she was his and also liked the way she formed

her words, finding it unique and charming. If any were to say differently, they would needs discuss the matter with him.

A second platter was brought out, and Kellen selected cheeses, nuts, and fruits, giving her the finest pieces.

"You know, guys," Gillian said. "If I'm not mistaken, you two are the miscreants I caught pawing through my pack yesterday."

Kellen laughed, glad she found fault with the flatterers.

Tristan lifted a hand. "Nay, my lady. We merely offered assistance when your pack spilled about the table. We were tidying your possessions to make sure naught was lost."

"Aye, my lady, 'tis true," said Owen.

"Hmm. If you say so." Gillian's blue eyes slanted upward. "Kellen, do you think I should believe them?"

Kellen could hardly credit that she used his name and teased him thus. He certainly wasn't going to mention he'd been the miscreant to open her pack and spill its contents.

"'Tis hopeful you will believe such, my lady, else both will frown and pout and be like to worthless on the training field as they nurse tender feelings."

Gillian sighed. "All right, then. I supposed I'll simply have to thank you both for saving my possessions."

"You are most welcome, my lady." Tristan bowed his head.

"Most welcome, indeed," said Owen.

His men, well aware he didn't want his own part in the escapade revealed, laughed at him. He would pay them later on the training field.

"Tell me about the area," Gillian said. "Is there anything nearby worth visiting?"

Kellen, glad to have a subject to discuss, waved a hand to stop Tristan from answering. "The nearest township is a few hours ride to the east, and we've near neighbors to the west at Royce Castle, though it barely merits the name as 'tis small and unkempt, and without the presence of a lady. There are several to the south, as well."

"Could we go see them? I want to visit Scotland, too. I've never been."

Kellen's lip curled upward. "For what purpose?"

"Sightseeing! It's supposed to be a romantic place."

Kellen shook his head. The girl had strange ideas about the seeing of sights. "Your wits flee you. 'Tis dark and cheerless and filled with all manner of beasties. Better you should go to London."

"Please?"

The girl batted her lashes and Kellen was hard pressed not to smile. Unlike his first wife who'd wanted nothing to do with him, this girl was forward and demanding of his time. So why did he wish to indulge her?

Perhaps because she did indeed seem to bring a ray of light into his gloomy world.

"And Beatrice mentioned that a picnic would be a good idea. What do you think? If we gathered some blankets and planned some games it could be a ton of fun! I'd also like to go and . . ."

As she continued to plan the seeing of sights, Kellen looked to Tristan and Owen, who seemed equally caught by her charm. "Whatever happened to quiet, unassuming women?"

Gillian laughed. "I don't know any of those. My friends are worse than me. Speaking of which, they'll want to hear about the marriage proposal. Can you give me the details from your point of view? How did you plan the proposal? How did you end up choosing . . . uh . . . me? Was it romantic? Did you write poetry? Sing songs? Play the lute or something?"

Kellen felt suddenly panicked. Had her father protected her from the truth? Kellen had done none of those things but simply demanded a bride. Any daughter would do. He didn't know much of women, but was sure this answer would offend. "Romance and marriage are not always side by side, my lady."

At her hurt expression, he immediately regretted his words. When she looked down, Tristan and Owen threw him disbelieving glares, shook their heads, and gestured for him to make peace.

Gillian sighed loudly. "In other words, you're completely lame?" She looked at him accusingly. "You didn't propose correctly and now you're trying to make excuses."

Tristan and Owen both laughed and Kellen was relieved she attacked rather than sulked.

"'Tis true," said Tristan. "You cannot defend yourself."

He could. He did not wish his bride to think him lacking. "I am not lame. I am sound in body and mind."

She waved her hand dismissively. "But you're a knight. You have to live to the code of chivalry! I'm entitled to a romantic proposal."

Kellen, suddenly feeling trapped within the walls of his own hall, wanted out. She was making him nervous. He stood. "I must needs train these idiots across from us. Perhaps we can speak of this after my men have been taught their desired lessons."

"Hold on just a minute," Gillian said. "Did you forget I'm the one in the driver's seat? I bought you. I own you. I expect you to come up with the best and most romantic proposal any girl has ever received in her entire life. One to write home about. I want you to . . . uh . . . pledge your troth. I'll be waiting."

Kellen strode a few feet away, then turned back. "This I did already! We were betrothed by proxy!" He was sweating, and she looked as cool as a spring morning.

His men, gathered at the many tables, paused to watch the drama, adding to his discomfort.

"Like I said. Lame. All I'm asking is that you do it right."

Confused by her, Kellen started away and she called out to him. "Wait. There's just one more thing."

"Now what!" he thundered, well aware that every eye was upon them.

She followed and he slowly turned. She crooked her finger at him and he hesitated, then slowly leaned down. Better that all did not hear her words of reproof.

Cupping one cheek, she kissed the other.

"Thank you for the present. It's truly beautiful." She touched the comb. "I've never had anything like it and will treasure it."

He could see sincerity in her steady gaze and, face heating, stunned into immobility, Kellen tried to answer rationally. "Ah. Aye, then."

Never in the whole of his life had a girl kissed him of her own accord. His wife had always turned her face away. Looking down at Gillian's soft lips, he wondered what she would do if he pressed his own to hers.

His emotions running high, his body alive with energy, he bent slightly forward and she didn't turn away.

Remembering that everyone stared, he didn't kiss her, but quickly straightened and threw out his chest. "Consider the gift your first touch of my chivalry, my lady. 'Tis certain there is more to come."

She chuckled, a sound he was starting to adore.

Kellen turned and continued walking, but couldn't hold back a grin.

She hadn't turned away.

CHAPTER 11

"What shall we do this afternoon?" Gillian, elbows on the windowsill of her bedroom, watched people mill about below but didn't spot Kellen's broad shoulders or confident stride.

"Do you wish to plan menus?" asked Beatrice. "Or mayhap we could retreat to the ladies' solar to sew or weave?" She paused. "If only we had feathers, we could recreate the queen's fashion. Perhaps we could pluck a chicken?" She sounded hopeful.

"Oh, uh . . ." Gillian glanced over her shoulder to see if the girl was serious. She was. Gillian's brows rose as she turned back to the view. "No, thanks. Anyway, I sincerely doubt the queen is decorating her attire with chicken feathers."

Gillian, realizing she was watching for Kellen again, sighed. "Besides, I want to do something fun. I'm not going to be depluming poultry, planning menus, or sewing, that's for sure. The castle has been running smoothly for a long time, right? It can continue to do so for a bit longer."

Like, until Edith showed up to take over.

"I suppose you might wish to explore your new home?"

Another quick glance showed Beatrice looking as downcast as

she sounded. "I did that yesterday." Gillian hesitated. Of course, yesterday she hadn't known it was authentic, so that might actually be fun.

In the distance, Gillian spotted a man leading a horse out of the stables. "Maybe we could ride horses?"

"Not without his lordship. He would not permit it."

About to protest, Gillian thought about Kellen's huge horse and wondered if he had a smaller, more malleable one. Her lips curled upward. A really old nag might work for her; one reserved for children. Other than with Kellen, Gillian had ridden only once before, a Shetland as a child, her father leading the pony in a large circle while her mother took pictures. Gillian chuckled at the memory and doubted Kellen would be impressed with her far-from-vast experience. She pushed away from the window. "Where is Kellen, anyway?"

"No doubt training with the men." Beatrice looked suddenly hopeful. "What about goose feathers? If you gave Cook permission to—"

"No! No feathers!" Gillian should never have lied to Beatrice about the queen's fashions. The girl was developing a feather fetish, and Gillian was starting to feel quite guilty about it. Grabbing her pack, Gillian said, "Come on."

She headed downstairs and Beatrice hurried to follow, insisting on carrying the pack. The minute Gillian stepped outside the keep people stared, pointed in her direction, and watched her every move; but she was getting used to it.

She passed the kitchen and was stopped short when a chubby woman with gray-streaked hair rushed to block her path. Two more followed, a thin, middle-aged woman with a ruddy complexion and a pretty, younger girl, both standing slightly in the background looking anxious.

The chubby woman nervously wiped her hands on a stained apron and bobbed up and down. Her two counterparts followed suit. "Pardon, my lady, but have you any instructions?"

Gillian looked around. "Instructions?"

"For the meals, my lady."

"Oh. Oh, right. The meals." Gillian waved a hand. "Er . . . no. Just carry on. The food has been excellent. I'm very impressed with the quality and quantity. I don't know how you do it all."

The three looked at each other, smiles replacing anxiety, and obviously pleased, the youngest ducked her head to hide a grin.

The cook nodded vigorously. "Thank ye, my lady."

Gillian felt a slight heat rising in her cheeks. They were grateful to her for enjoying their cooking? She was just glad she didn't have to do it. "No, thank *you*. Seriously, I appreciate all you're doing. I haven't eaten this well in a very long time." Roasted chicken, veggies, and homemade bread beat instant noodles any day of the week.

Their smiles grew and with a wave Gillian hurried off, uncomfortable with their gratitude.

She passed the well and the chapel and watched a few little girls drawing with sticks in the dirt and a couple of chickens pecking nearby. The sound of clanking metal alerted her to the blacksmith in the distance.

A man on a bench looked to be making a pair of shoes, while another tied a length of rope around an axe-head, and a third hauled a barrel over one shoulder. A couple of soldiers crossed the yard. The place was a miniature city.

She'd think of her time here as if it were a resort or cruise vacation where everything was all-inclusive. Maybe they had shuffleboard or a spa?

Gillian stifled a laugh. What she really needed was a lounger, some tanning oil, and a good romance novel. Or better yet, a real live shipboard romance complete with a gorgeous, slightly dangerous hunk.

She wouldn't mind if Kellen were to rub oil on her, or vice versa, and if he were wearing swim trunks while doing so, well, so much the better. Gillian shivered at the thought of all that hard, bare skin, hers for the touching. Where was he, anyway?

Rounding the inner wall, Gillian almost stumbled into the three boys she'd seen the day before. The youngest, a blond of about nine or so, sat on the ground, clutching his knee, sniffling and trying not to cry. Instantly concerned, Gillian surged forward and knelt beside him. "What's the matter, honey-bun?"

"I got hurt." The boy pulled his hand back far enough so Gillian could see the scrape on his knee. It wasn't bad and didn't look dirty, but she'd bet it stung like crazy.

"Ouchie. How did that happen?"

The slim, dark-haired boy of eleven or so shook his head in disgust. "He's always clumsy. He fell because he was following us." The scorn in the older boy's voice was apparent.

The younger boy, face screwing into an indignant scowl, sucked in a breath. *"You pushed me!"*

Both older boys laughed.

"Hmm." Gillian looked down at the boy. "What's your name, sweetie?"

He looked surprised, then hurt. "I'm Francis, my lady. Don't you know me?"

The boys laughed again and the stockier one sneered, "I'd forget that face, too, if I could."

What did that mean? She'd seen the little guys running around, but didn't remember being introduced. Gillian placed an arm around Francis's shoulder. "Of course, I remember you, Francis. And what are your friends' names?"

Francis pointed to the slim, dark-haired boy. "Peter." He pointed the stockier one. "And he's Ulrick."

"Nice to meet you, boys. Did you know I went to school with a boy who was frequently clumsy? He was always falling down and into scrapes like you wouldn't believe. It's so sad what happened to him." Gillian shook her head.

Francis looked worried. "What happened?"

"Are you sure you want to hear this?"

The boy nodded and the other two moved closer, grinning.

Gillian sighed. "Okay, but remember, you asked. Well, the guy, Derek, was always falling down, scraping his knees, tearing his clothes, and getting bruises. The other boys used to tease him." Gillian shot a narrowed-eyed glance at the older boys and they smirked in return.

"But it turned out the reason he was so clumsy was because he was going to grow so big! The guy ended up huge! All muscles and fighting ability. And completely graceful with a football . . . er . . . lance when he got older. All the girls were in love with him. All the boys wanted to be his friend."

She looked into Francis's deep blue eyes. "So, there it is. I'm sorry to be the one who has to tell you, honey. I surely wouldn't want muscles that huge. But chances are you'll be very big one day. Perhaps as big as Derek."

Tears drying on his face, the child looked at Gillian with awe. "Truly?"

"Yup."

"Is he as large as Lord Marshall?"

Gillian nodded and mentally crossed her fingers. "About that size exactly."

A smile spread across the boy's face.

The dark-haired boy lifted his chin. "You made that up! No one is as big as his lordship. Runt here is never going to be larger than a tadpole. And I've never heard of a Sir Derek. My father is *Lord Marlow* and he's never mentioned him." His arrogant tone amused Gillian.

"Really?"

His friend shrugged, not quite so indignant. "Nor has my father, Lord Stonor."

Gillian stared blankly. "Who are they, exactly?"

"Both of Oxfordshire, my lady," the stocky boy sounded shocked, while the other's mouth dropped open and he sputtered.

"Hmm. Well, maybe they don't know him. Anyway, that's exactly what happened. Cross my heart, hope to die, stick a needle in my eye." Gillian made a crossing motion over her heart.

All three boys recoiled slightly. "A needle in your eye?" Peter said in disbelief. "'Tis disgusting."

Francis wrapped skinny arms around her waist and hugged her, as if worried her feelings might be hurt. Gillian smiled down and gave him a squeeze, her heart melting.

"Beatrice, hand me my pack."

Beatrice handed it over and Gillian rummaged around for a moment before pulling out the last of her miniature candy bars. "I have something that will make you feel better." She didn't think it would be a good idea to let them have the wrappers, however, so she opened the bars one at a time, handed them around, and then popped one into her own mouth. "Mm."

Francis looked dubious but finally ate the candy. The boys and Beatrice quickly followed suit. Francis's eyes widened. "What is it?"

Gillian smiled. "Chocolate. It'll cure anything that ails you."

Ulrick quickly swallowed his. "Can I have another?"

Gillian smiled. "They're addicting, aren't they?"

"My lady," Beatrice cleared her throat.

Gillian glanced up to see Beatrice gesturing frantically.

Gillian turned her head as Kellen and a couple of his men came toward them. Ah, her shipboard romance, right on time. She felt a rush of blood through her veins and tingles of excitement just from looking at him, and she couldn't help the smile spreading over her face. Speaking of addictions. He might even be able to compete with chocolate. "I thought you were training?"

"I am." He wasn't returning her smile. "Gillian, I must object to your coddling the boys. As pages, they are yours to raise, but I don't want you ruining them for the squires they are to be."

Francis squirmed away.

"Mine to raise? I don't understand. Where are their parents?"

At Kellen's signal, the boys ran off.

Gillian lifted a hand. "Wait! We need to clean that scratch!" The boys rounded the corner and were gone.

Kellen sighed. "I am fostering the boys. I do my duty by them and will not have them softened. Your mothering must cease. What were you feeding them?"

Gillian arched a brow. She held out a hand and he easily lifted her to her feet, his warm touch and effortless strength making Gillian's knees weak. Cheeks heating, aware of their audience, Gillian removed her hand from his and brushed at her gown. "I was feeding them chocolate. I thought you just said they were mine to raise?"

Kellen sighed again. "Men are honored to send their sons to me for training because I make them strong. You are not to interfere with such. What is chocolate?"

Gillian smiled. "Being around me might make them soft?" she teased.

Kellen's gaze dropped to her chest, then he looked away and rubbed the back of his neck. "You are not to be too easy with them."

Gillian laughed. "But they're just little boys. They should still be with their mothers."

"Gillian. You will obey me in this."

"Fine. No hugs and kisses. I'll go get my whip." She dug into her pack and retrieved the last candy bar, opened it and placed it to his lips. "Here. This is chocolate."

He ate it, his eyes widening. "More?"

She laughed. "It was my last piece."

Kellen studied her face, lifted a hand as if to touch her, and then let it drop again. "I understand your gentleness with Francis. I beg you'd not believe me ungrateful Lord Corbett showed his support by refusing the return of his heir when Catherine died. I'm glad the alliance is still strong. While I understand you are happy to see your brother, no babying."

Gillian's mouth dropped slightly and she was suddenly lightheaded.

"Gillian?"

Her mouth snapped closed and she swallowed. Had she heard him correctly? Francis was her brother? Or rather, Edith's brother? No wonder the kid had looked hurt when she hadn't known his name.

"Are you all right?"

Gillian forced a smile. "Oh, yeah, I'm fine."

This wasn't good. Would the little twerp give her away? Expose her? Reveal her as the imposter she was? Get her killed? She swallowed again.

"I'd not meant to hurt thy tender feelings."

"Uh, huh." On the other hand, Francis had hugged her and seemed to think she should know him. Maybe he didn't remember his sister well? Maybe they weren't close? Still, she'd better stay away from the kid.

"Gillian?"

Gillian refocused on Kellen, waved a hand, and forced the smile back to her face. "I am, of course, happy to do your bidding."

His snort turned her smile into a real one.

She wouldn't borrow trouble. As always, what Kellen didn't know couldn't hurt her.

GILLIAN, although very pretty in the sunlight, didn't seem to know how to comport herself. She challenged him, surprised him, laughed at him, and was unlike any female he'd ever met. Facing ten men in battle made him less nervous than one look from her laughing blue eyes.

And yet, much as Kellen needed to get his thoughts back on work, he couldn't seem to force himself to leave. He tried to think of something to say, something that would keep her smile in place, but, as always, nothing came to mind.

Gillian's cheeks warmed under his scrutiny and she turned away, displaying her profile. "Kellen, I was wondering, which direction did you say the nearest town is?"

Kellen instantly went cold. "Why would you wish to know this?" he asked quietly. Could she hope to escape him still?

"I'm just trying to orient myself. Maybe I'm hoping to find a mall." Her lips quirked as her tone teased. At his blank stare her smile widened. "Some shops?"

"Ah." Kellen felt sudden relief. She was a covetous little thing, there was no doubt of that. He glanced at the ring she had yet to give him and considered all the treasures she hoarded in her pack. The pack that even now her maid carried. Gillian did like her trinkets. He glanced at the comb, still in her hair, then thought of his own stash of treasures. He'd have to see if he had something more she would like. "Nay. I'll not tell you the location."

Her mouth parted in surprise. "You won't tell me where the town is?"

Amused by her frustration, he slowly shook his head.

"You seriously won't tell me?"

"I will not."

Gillian crossed her arms, lifted her chin and narrowed her eyes. "Fine. Do you have a map?"

"Aye, but as a woman you would be unable to read it. It would only confuse your mind."

Gillian sighed at his attitude, threw up her hands, turned, and walked away.

Surprised at how easily he baited her, and at how much he enjoyed doing so, he fell into step beside her. She looped her arm through his and he couldn't help but grin, amazed at how freely she touched him. And at how quickly his body responded.

He was tempted to place his hand over her own or to kiss the top of her head but refrained, aware of their audience and wary of her reaction. He'd have to content himself with teasing. "Mayhap after you give me an heir or two, I'll take you traveling. It would please me to show you London, Italy, and France." It would be fun to show her everything, and see it again through her eyes.

She glanced up, her eyes alight at the prospect, but she simply lifted a shoulder. "That's your big plan? To keep your wife barefoot and pregnant until she's done her duty and then she can have some playtime?"

Kellen laughed. "I'd not thought to take your shoes, but 'tis a good idea. 'Twill keep you close to home." At her raised brow, he laughed again. "Mayhap your duty will feel as play?"

Gillian chuckled. "Oh yeah, childbirth without anesthesia should be a blast. Fun, fun."

"I referred to the making of children."

Though her cheeks colored once more, Gillian chuckled again. "As a man, you would."

Kellen couldn't help the grin that spread on his face. This girl was just so different. He'd never in his life teased a girl and been teased in return. Now he found it came easily, and that he enjoyed it.

Kellen tried to think of something else to say and wished he were better with women. He wanted her to settle and be happy. But how? She wore the green dress again. "Mayhap you would like some material? For a gown or two?"

Gillian stopped and faced him, her head tilting back. "Can you please tell me why everyone wants me to take up sewing so badly? What is it you're doing today? Maybe you should be sewing instead."

Kellen laughed and several of his men joined in, quickly stifling their mirth at a narrow-eyed glance from Gillian. "I've the training of my men to see to."

Gillian brushed her free hand over his upper arm as if feeling his muscles and testing their hardness. Kellen tensed, the blood in his veins seeming to heat. He barely refrained from bunching his muscles, so she could truly see how firm he was.

Seeming to realize what she did, she pulled her hand away and flushed. He immediately missed her touch and wished he knew how to set her at ease and assure her she was welcome to caress him at any time.

"Well, I was attacked recently, remember?" she said. "Maybe you should train me, too. You know, show me some self-defense techniques."

Kellen, immediately insulted that she believed she needed such, shook his head. "Nay. Now you are in my care, I will protect you at all times. You've no need for concern or training."

Gillian shrugged. "Fine. I have my own way to defend myself, anyway. Have you ever heard of mace?"

Kellen looked down at her. "Yes. I have several." And he very much doubted she could swing one above her head.

"Well, I guess it's actually pepper spray, but it'll do the job." Gillian dropped her arm from his and turned to retrieve her pack from Beatrice, leaving Kellen feeling a sense of loss. She dug about, finally pulled something out, and held it up triumphantly. "Check it out."

The object in her hand looked to be a long, smooth, rounded black stone, with yellow and red markings. It fit neatly into her palm. 'Twould be difficult to hurt anyone with it and the thrower would need good aim and much muscle behind the launch. Kellen couldn't help it. He laughed. She obviously didn't know what a mace was.

Gillian's eyes narrowed and she walked a few feet away, held her hand high, and a mist was released from the weapon. Kellen got sudden chills. He'd seen the like when a traveling magician had passed a few nights in his keep, and wondered how Gillian had learned the trick. She walked backward, away from the dissipating mist and gestured toward it. "Go ahead and walk through and then we'll see who's laughing."

Kellen hesitated, then fearing to look a coward before her, threw out his chest and strode through the clouded air.

Tristan, curious as always, followed.

Kellen's eyes started to sting, he sucked in a breath, and immediately coughed as his throat burned. "By the saints!"

Gillian looked suddenly worried. "Oh, dear. I should have told you. I didn't think—"

Kellen coughed again, then hurried forward and snatched the object out of her hands and looked at it. He was appalled as his eyes watered and his throat clenched.

A clever trick, but all the same, quite useless. It would be hard for her to get an enemy to stand still long enough for her to release the mist, and then harder still to get the enemy to walk through it. Besides, in the heat of battle, naught would care for stinging eyes when the sting of steel was ever imminent.

But Gillian looked worried, so he shrugged off the pain and gave her back the toy.

"Kellen, I'm really sorry. I shouldn't have—"

"'Tis naught." Kellen wiped at the tears running down his face. He coughed. "Go with a guard at all times." His voice was hoarse. "Stay with your maid. You will be safe enough."

She looked worried and guilty. He knew how to relieve her mind. Kellen gestured to one of his men. "If Lady Gillian tries to leave the keep, stop her and take her shoes. She's to stay within the walls."

Gillian was instantly indignant. "Maybe I wanted to take a walk to the river or the village?"

Kellen shook his head. "Not without me."

"Have you ever been told that you are infuriating, bossy, and stubborn?"

Kellen struggled not to laugh and cough at the same time. "I could accuse you of the same."

"And obtuse. You are definitely obtuse."

He didn't know the meaning of the word, but was loathe to

admit it. He threw out his chest. "I have much to see to this day and cannot stand about talking."

Gillian made a sweeping motion with her hand inviting him to leave. "Please, don't let me stop you."

But he didn't leave. He was enjoying her company too much and, even with watering eyes, wanted to linger.

"You realize that while you're off doing important knightly stuff, I'll probably be stuck plucking chickens?"

"If the task is unpleasant, perhaps you should spend the day humbling yourself as befits my wife."

Gillian huffed, shot him a disbelieving look, and then walked away.

He watched her go, suddenly worried he'd gone too far with his teasing and had truly angered her. He was about to start after her when, in a loud voice, she started to sing about the difficulties of being humble.

Even with his eyes and throat burning, Kellen couldn't help a grin. He wanted to go after her again, and it was hard to stop himself. Tristan, wiping at his eyes, came to stand beside him and they watched her head toward the inner wall. "You do realize you are the luckiest of swag-bellied miscreants? She's a beautiful and lively heiress. What I would not give for such."

Kellen felt for Tristan, who was not in much of a position to marry well; and who would never have Gillian, even if he were. She was Kellen's and he was still amazed by that realization. "Your time will come."

When she was out of sight, they raced to the horse trough and dipped their heads in the water.

CHAPTER 12

a few hours later, Gillian and Beatrice scouted for a place to sit with an excellent view. Kellen didn't want her to go anywhere? Fine. Then he could babysit her. She was going to sketch big brawny men hacking away at each other.

Utter bliss.

Beatrice, finally satisfied with a location under a blossoming apple tree, spread out the blanket. She offered Gillian a smaller one as a shawl, which she refused, and they both settled under the branches. Gillian fluffed her dress into a semicircle and couldn't help a smile. The dress made her feel like a fairy princess and she loved it. She had to admit that, as far as fantasy getaways went, this one topped any list she could have devised.

Kellen didn't see her, or was ignoring her, as he fought another man. Eyes wide, Gillian realized she was literally holding her breath as the men swung swords at each other. The yelling, the clanging of metal, the muscles straining, and then Kellen forcing the other man back, and finally into defeat. Wow.

"He's a fine warrior, do you not think?" asked Beatrice.

"The best." Gillian, breathless, couldn't help but agree. "Very impressive."

They watched as Kellen fought another, and then a third. Eventually, it dawned on Gillian that he was showing off for her, and a smile spread across her face.

Picking up her pad of paper, Gillian started to draw. He was a lot fiercer than she'd realized and so buff! The lines of muscles, bunching and shifting in his arms and legs were impressive in their sheer size and strength. She was used to guys getting their physiques at the gym, not on the battlefield, and now realized there was a vast difference. Watching a guy work out with weights couldn't touch watching a warrior train to defend what was his. She felt weak and fluttery just watching him. Wow, again.

It was a little cold and overcast, but Gillian felt overheated. Maybe it was just the excess material of the dress, but somehow, she didn't think so.

"My lady, I've brought dried fruit or some nuts, if you'd like such?"

"Mm. I'm okay." Gillian's mouth was watering, but not for food. She tried to keep track of Beatrice's chattering and answer appropriately, but all the while she kept an eye on Kellen, continuing to draw him.

He really was the ultimate eye candy. She was enjoying watching him so much it took a moment to realize he was coming toward her.

Her face tilted up when he finally reached her, and she quickly hugged the drawing to her chest. He wasn't even breathing hard and Gillian's heart fluttered again.

"What do you, Gillian?"

"Nothing, just hanging out, watching all the eye candy parading about."

"Eye candy?"

"Sweets for the eyes instead of for the mouth."

Kellen nodded, glanced away, and Gillian bit back a smile when she saw him blush.

It was so cute she couldn't resist heaping on more flattery.

"You know, Kellen, I've never seen a warrior quite like you before. You're very strong."

Kellen's chest puffed out. "Think you?"

Gillian nodded and let her gaze drift down his body and back to his face. "I really do."

To her delight, the red in Kellen's cheeks intensified as he cleared his throat. "I must needs be to protect you from all the trouble you draw upon yourself."

Gillian laughed, and when her sketchpad dropped forward onto her lap, Kellen was quick to look at the brawny warrior she'd started drawing.

"Is that me?"

Gillian smiled. "Maybe, maybe not. I've drawn the fiercest warrior on the field."

"Me then."

Gillian laughed. "No modesty there."

"Modesty is overrated as a virtue, good only for men without strength or skill." His heated gaze dropped to her lips, and it was Gillian's turn to blush. Was he thinking of kissing her? Trying out some of his other skills? Her lips parted and softened of their own accord. She'd be glad to help him test his aptitude in that area.

Kellen sucked in a breath, and then looked back at his men, many of whom watched the interplay. Kellen's brows rose and the men immediately moved back and set to work.

"Will you walk with me?"

Gillian glanced at Beatrice, who seemed intent on her mending.

He leaned closer and lowered his voice. "Alone."

The look Kellen gave Gillian raised her temperature again, and she scrambled to her feet. "Beatrice, I'll be back later."

"Aye, my lady. I'll take your things to your chamber."

Kellen leaned down to pick up a small blanket and draped it around Gillian's shoulders. He took her sketchpad, set it next to her pack, and held out his hand.

They walked through the orchard and to a flower garden on the other side. "Do you like gardening? By midsummer many flowers will be in bloom. If there is aught you have need of, you must plant whatever you like." His grip tightened, loosened, and then tightened again, a nervous gesture.

He released her hand, and Gillian flexed her abused fingers without pointing out to him he'd almost crushed them.

Pulling out a small knife, Kellen leaned down, cut a flower, and handed it to her. "I know not what kind it is."

Gillian smiled. "A rose?"

"Ah, aye, 'tis a rose."

His obvious embarrassment was touching and she carefully held the flower so the thorns didn't prick. She sniffed. "Mm. It's beautiful."

Kellen looked relieved. Did he think she would reject his offering? Gillian lowered the flower and tilted her face up. "Thank you."

Kellen stared down at her, his expression suddenly intense, heated. Gillian realized they were completely alone for the first time since she'd arrived and didn't move. He was going to kiss her, and she very badly wanted him to. He leaned down and Gillian flinched as a drop of rain hit her upturned face.

Kellen immediately jerked backward only to stare down at her with yearning, before taking a deep breath and a step back. He looked up at the sky. "I'm glad for the rain as we have all the crops planted." His voice sounded strained, tight.

"You sound like a farmer." Gillian tried to keep the conversation going, tried to get him to look at her again because she, for one, was not glad for the stupid rain. She'd wanted that kiss.

"Aye. That I am. I have many mouths to feed and much of the land has been seeded." Without looking at her, Kellen lifted the blanket to cover her head, tightened it around her shoulders, then grabbed her hand again, tugging her toward the keep.

Gillian sighed as disappointment swamped her. She wanted a

kiss before she had to go home, wanted his mouth on hers, his arms wrapped around her, and hers twined about his neck. She wanted that kiss before Edith showed up to claim him for herself.

Sudden jealousy, dark and biting, had her lips tightening and her heart pounding. If Edith were anything like her murderous sister, she didn't deserve Kellen. Feeling protective, Gillian tightened her grip on Kellen's hand; he gently squeezed her fingers in return, his warmth sending chills up her arm.

Kellen deserved a girl who would appreciate his finer qualities, understand his gruffness, and flirt with him. Someone like . . . someone like . . .

Gillian took a breath. If she wasn't careful, she'd lay her heart out on a platter and get it smashed to smithereens when she had to go home.

She needed to remember to keep her heart safe. She would not fall in love with the big guy. She needed to remember that this was just for fun. A brief holiday romance. She only had a few weeks and didn't plan on getting hurt again.

LATER THAT NIGHT, Gillian lay in bed warm, cozy and snuggled in the blankets and furs.

She couldn't wipe the sappy grin off her face. At dinner, she hadn't been able to, either.

She could hear the rain outside hitting the wooden shutters and hoped Kellen was warm and dry. He'd gone off after dinner to hunt down some miscreants and, as far as she knew, hadn't returned.

Gillian turned over. Kellen was just so . . . so . . . wonderful. What would it be like to have a man like Kellen truly belong to her? To see the possessive gaze and know that she really did belong to him?

She thought about Ryan and the smile left her face. They'd

dated for a good six months, and she'd been stressed and off kilter the entire time.

And okay, she cringed, sort of desperate, too. It was embarrassing to remember how she'd acted. When she'd found out the guy was looking for easy money, she'd been ashamed of herself for sticking it out. For being a doormat so he would love her. For being so lonely, she'd traded in her self-respect for companionship.

She should have trusted her instincts.

What were those instincts telling her about Kellen? All she felt was happy. But what did it really matter? She was being foolish. She couldn't compare the two. Her boyfriend had been real life; and Kellen, well, he was fantasy. Like a hologram from an episode of Star Trek. Fun, but not real.

It was just the romance of the time and place affecting her so much. The castle, the candle glowing beside her bed, the way he'd held her hand. The kiss that almost happened.

It was like she was in a fairy tale with the starring role as princess. She turned over again and plumped the pillow once more. She'd have this time as a happy memory in her heart, nothing else. No hurt or pain this time, just good memories.

She snuggled down to sleep, then quickly sat up, blew out the candle, and laid back down.

After a moment, she realized she was smiling again.

She was so getting that kiss before she left.

After lunch the next afternoon, it was still raining; so Gillian retrieved her pad of paper and headed downstairs, bumping into a boy at the bottom of the stairs. "Oh, sorry."

She reached out a hand to steady the boy, who cringed back. "Sorry, sweetie. Just me not paying attention to where I was going. Are you okay?"

The boy, a wide-eyed teen of about fifteen or so, nodded.

"What's your name? I don't think we've met before. I'm Gillian." She held out her hand.

The boy stared at her hand for a moment then looked up into her face. "Valeric, my lady."

Gillian dropped her hand when he made no move to take it. "Well, it's nice to meet you, Valeric. I'll try to pay better attention in future, so I don't run you down."

The boy backed away. "Yes, my lady." Then he was gone.

By the time she reached the great hall, the food had been cleared away; Kellen's three foster boys sat on the straw-covered floor at the foot of a young, brown-robed man who looked to be tutoring them.

A little girl, about three or four, stood off to the side in front of the fire and watched the boys as a woman, probably the child's mother, knitted in a nearby chair.

The yearning on the girl's face caught Gillian's attention. The scene would make a fantastic painting; a large one done in oils with light colors, dark shadows, rain buffeting wooden shutters, and the fire brightening the girl's face and illuminating her longing.

Genius if Gillian could pull it off.

The tutor turned the book on his lap so the boys could study it, and the little girl leaned forward, obviously wanting to see.

Quietly, not wanting to distract anyone, Gillian pulled her digital camera out of her pack, looked around, and snapped a quick photo. She didn't use the flash for fear of seriously freaking people out and risking the whole burn-the-witch-at-the-stake scenario. Still, she got the gist of the scene in case she needed to refer back to it later.

After stowing her camera, Gillian headed over to the table between the boys and the young girl. "Hi. What's going on?"

Everyone glanced up at her approach, the tutor raising one

brow. Gillian noted he wore a crucifix around his neck. "We are about our lessons. Please refrain from interrupting."

"Oh. Right," Gillian whispered. "Sorry." She quickly sat on a bench beside a nearby table.

The tutor sighed. "'Tis Lady Corbett, correct?"

"Yes, nice to meet you."

He ignored that. "As a female, you ought not to listen as Latin might tax your wits."

Gillian's mouth fell slightly open as she looked to see if the guy was serious. Stern-faced, arrogant, younger than she'd realized, not bad-looking in a boy-next-door sort of way, and completely serious. She grinned. "Yeah, that's okay. I'll chance it."

Gillian glanced around, wondering where Kellen was. He'd disappeared right after breakfast, and she considered hunting him down as that might be more fun, but didn't want to go out in the rain. She could find him later if he didn't show.

Anyway, medieval school might be interesting and would certainly make her painting more unique if she could pick up a feel for what was happening.

The tutor started up again, but Gillian got bored pretty quickly. The little girl was still interested, but probably because school and knitting were the only things to hold her attention.

Gillian opened her pad of drawing paper and tore a piece from the back end. She beckoned the little girl, and the child looked startled then wary but after a quick glance at the knitter, eventually walked over. "My lady?"

"What's your name, kiddo?"

"Amelia, my lady."

The tutor lifted his head to glare at them; Gillian put a finger to her lips, tilted her head toward the group of boys and, as the child watched, carefully folded the paper.

Amelia, chubby-cheeked and wide-eyed, observed as Gillian made a production of each fold, raising her brows, smiling and nodding. Gillian made the last crease, pinched the bottom between forefinger and thumb, aimed away from the boys, and threw the airplane across the hall.

Amelia shrieked with joy and raced across the room, following the flight, and eventually retrieving the plane from its landing spot among the straw.

The boys jumped up and raced after the girl, the knitter laboriously rose and yelled sharply for Amelia, the tutor clapped his hands and chastised the boys, and both adults glared at Gillian.

"Sorry," she said weakly.

The boys snatched the plane from Amelia, who let out an unholy screech, balled both fists, and started hitting the boy holding the paper airplane.

"Boys," the tutor clapped sharply. *"Boys!"*

Peter pushed Amelia away with one hand, palming her forehead, and she changed her strategy and tried to kick him. The adults looked livid.

Oh dear. Not good. She should have thought this out first.

Peter held up the plane to show Gillian. "'Tis the most wondrous toy!"

Shaking his head, the tutor stomped off.

"Amelia," Gillian addressed the howling child. "I'll make you another one."

"And me, as well?" asked Francis.

"And me?" asked Ulrick.

"Yes. One for each of you."

The boys took turns throwing the airplane, and Amelia was soon laughing and running after it as Gillian quickly made more.

The boys gathered around as she folded the last one. "Where did you learn such?" asked Francis. "From a wizard?"

Gillian grinned. "What do you know about wizards?"

"The stories say they'll snatch you away from your home and force the devil into you," Francis said.

"They will not!" Peter said. "They'll apprentice you and teach you magic." He turned to Gillian and raised the airplane. "How does it travel across the hall?"

"Well, its wings cut through the air to generate lift. And if you change the shape of the wings, it affects the travel time and . . ." Gillian, struck by the phrase, fell silent.

"And?"

"And with a larger wingspan the plane will stay in the air longer." She paused. "Boys, have you ever heard any stories about time travelers?"

They looked at each other. "No, my lady," Peter shook his head.

"You've never heard of a traveler from a distant time?"

"A man from Spain once came to sell his wares and he had a pointed beard," Francis said.

"Do you know of such a story, my lady?" asked Ulrick.

All eyes turned expectantly toward Gillian. "Tell us a story!"

"My lady." The knitter, her face pinched and disapproving, interrupted. "Thy daughter is overexcited. 'Tis time for her nap."

"My daughter? Is she fostering, too?"

The older lady gave her a strange look. "She is Lord Marshall's daughter, thy niece, and now thy daughter."

"What?" Gillian quickly looked at the girl, taking in her blonde hair and familiar amber eyes. "Why didn't anyone tell me Kellen had a daughter?"

The woman looked suddenly suspicious. "Why would you not know such?"

Oh. Right. As Amelia's supposed aunt, everyone probably thought she did. "Ah. I guess I forgot." Amelia, clutching the paper airplane, reluctantly allowed herself to be tugged away and Gillian watched until they were out of sight.

"Tell us a story with dragons!"

Gillian, curious, looked at the boys. "Do you believe in dragons?"

"Of course, my lady," Ulrick nodded. "My father saw one once."

Gillian's brows rose. "Really?"

"Well, dragon bones, anyway. Sticking out of the ground, with fierce teeth, black from fire. But as more dragons were surely about, most likely the one that killed it, he left quickly. Otherwise, 'twould likely have killed him for sure."

"Is that so?"

All the boys nodded and Gillian wondered if Ulrick's father had stumbled across dinosaur bones. Ulrick's brows drew together, his face pinched in sudden anger. "Aren't you afraid?"

Peter elbowed him. "Girls aren't wise enough to be afraid. Come on, let's go. She probably cannot tell good stories, anyway."

Ulrick laughed. "'Twould tax her wits were she to try."

"Oh, really?" Gillian straightened and smiled slowly. "I might know of a dragon tale or two." Jurassic Park routinely scared her out of her wits when she watched the DVD once a year or so. She thought she could probably do the story justice. "I do know a good dragon story actually, but it's so scary you kids might not be able to handle it."

The boys looked at each other uncertainly.

"Well? Can you handle it? If not, there's the door."

Eyes wide, the three boys sank down and Gillian sent out a silent apology to Michael Crichton and Stephen Spielberg for pilfering their story. She took a deep breath and began the tale as three little boys, huddling ever closer together, listened intently.

CHAPTER 13

*L*ater that night, Kellen walked toward the keep with Owen and Tristan, noted the glow coming from the edges of Gillian's shutters, picked up his pace, and tried to outdistance his friends. "I bid you both a good night," he said.

Sir Owen followed Kellen's gaze. "A good night, is it? Why? Do you have something more entertaining in mind than spending time with the likes of us? Is Lady Gillian the reason you used soap down by the river? 'Tis truly hurt I am. I thought you wanted to smell sweet for us on the morrow and save us the reek when you raised your sword arm."

Kellen tensed when Tristan clapped him on the back. "Don't tease him, Sir Owen. He's not seen the fair Lady Gillian since dinner. 'Tis been an hour at the very least. Perhaps more."

Sir Owen laughed, then ducked when Kellen aimed a fist at his mouth. "But I do not understand." Sir Owen skipped backward a few steps and lifted his hands in mock confusion. "'Tis late now and time to be abed. What is he hoping to see of her?"

Both his friends laughed and Kellen ignored the impulse to slam a fist into two faces. He didn't want to get dirty, sweaty, or bled on in a scuffle, else he'd teach the two imbeciles a lesson.

"Only a simpleton would be surprised at my desire to behold Lady Gillian's beauty over the ill-favored countenances before me." Kellen lengthened his stride in the vain hope of outdistancing additional comments.

His so-called friends laughed and jeered after him. "Be sure and keep the sheets!" Tristan said. "All will want proof she's taken your virginity."

"Shall we follow and stand you both up?" called Sir Owen.

"Aye, 'tis a good idea," yelled Tristan. "'Twill give her the chance to run when she sees what you want of her."

"Nay, she'll not run. She'll simply slip back into her chastity belt and await a call to the nunnery."

Their laughter followed Kellen and he turned, walking backward. "Quiet, fools! Else she'll hear you and leave me no choice but to kill the pair of ye."

With his back to them once more, Kellen allowed himself to smile in anticipation as he headed inside and up the stairs. He only wanted to see her, only wanted to wish her a good night. He could not hope for more.

He was surprised to find himself in front of her door so quickly and paused, suddenly hesitant, glad his friends weren't nearby to witness his indecision. That would set the idiots to howling. He listened, but heard nothing inside and wondered if she were already abed.

Out in the hall there were the normal sounds of the keep settling, servants doing last minute chores, their murmurings, and pallets being laid about. Kellen raised a fist, paused again, then knocked softly on Gillian's door.

A moment later Beatrice answered, smiled when she saw him, and dipped into a curtsy. "Pardon, my lord. I was just leaving."

Kellen stepped back and watched the maid go. He noted the way she glanced over her shoulder and smiled before disappearing from sight and felt his face warm. Was he obvious in his eagerness? Would Gillian think him so? He turned back to the door and took a breath.

Give him a dozen men to fight against and he'd not have any difficulty, but Gillian, a tiny slip of a girl, made his palms damp and his mouth dry. Kellen forced himself to enter the bedchamber before others spotted him loitering about and spread the tale.

Gillian, her hair brushed and hanging down her back, stared into the fire, her nightgown a long, flowing concoction of white that covered from neck to toe. It ought to hide her curves, but instead molded in a most provocative manner, offering him a glimpse of rounded chest and hip.

Or perhaps he just imagined such in the flickering firelight. "Gillian?"

She turned and offered a slight smile. "Hi." She didn't seem embarrassed or shy and didn't shriek or throw him out. A good sign, surely.

Feeling like an overwrought maiden, Kellen closed the door behind him and glanced at her feet, hoping to glimpse the colored toenails he'd heard tale of, but slippers thwarted his view.

"Where'd you go after dinner?" she asked.

"Ah . . ." Had she'd missed him? "Down to the river to bathe."

He was very aware of the bed off to the side, of the intimacy of the darkened chamber, of the fact that he'd like to lay her down, kiss her, and so much more. His heart started to pound and he cursed his men for the crude jests that placed thoughts of love play in his mind.

"Burr. That sounds cold."

He raised a hand to rub the back of his neck and, unable to help himself, glanced quickly at the bed. "Ye might think such, but somehow I feel over warm."

Gillian met his gaze for a long moment before glancing at the bed herself, ducking her head, and turning away to fiddle with a brush on a nearby table. "Uh . . . I'm not really all that tired yet. Do you want to play a game or something?"

Or something? Kellen swallowed, the sound loud in the quiet of the room. "Aye. A game is a fine idea."

Gillian looked up again. "The kids taught me how to play knucklebones earlier. It was fun. Or we could play chess?"

Children's games didn't interest him, and it seemed as if they already played a game of strategy. Kellen's eyes burned with the effort to not look at the bed again, so he almost missed the fact that Gillian was smiling at him.

At the acceptance on her face, something inside him, deep in his chest, seemed to unclench and Kellen was suddenly hopeful she would let him stay this night. Taking a breath, he smiled in return. "I know of a game I could teach ye." He moved forward, determined to get a kiss, to feel her soft lips yield to his, to taste her, and see where it might lead. But at the very least, to get a kiss.

She looked at him, and his thoughts must have shown in his face because her eyes widened and her lips parted. She darted another glance at the bed, lifted a fluttering hand to her chest, and swallowed. "I like new games." Her voice was breathy, feminine.

Encouraged, Kellen swallowed then stopped in front of her. He lifted a hand to cup her cheek and its softness amazed him. In contrast his own body hardened, his muscles clenched, and he found his hand shook slightly.

She didn't pull away but looked up at him, her eyes dark and mysterious in the firelight. Taking in a shuddering breath, he leaned down and amazingly, she lifted her lips to his. His heart pounded and he hoped to perform the task correctly. To kiss her gently, please her, and make her glad she'd yielded. He leaned down a bit further, breathed in the light scent that was Gillian, moved to press his lips to hers—and a child screamed in terror.

In disbelief Kellen jerked upright and moved away in an instant. "Stay here and bar the door."

Slipping a dirk into his hand, Kellen eased cautiously out of the chamber, pulled the door shut behind him, and took off running, searching for enemies and finding none.

He burst into the boys' chamber and glanced about but saw nothing amiss. Just three boys, each sitting up in bed, looking fearful. Kellen looked to the window, but it was firmly latched, the wooden shutters secured with iron bars. "What is it?"

Ulrick's breath came hard. *"The dragon t-rex is coming to get me."*

"And me, also!" wailed Francis.

"And me!" Peter sounded aggrieved, as if the words were forced from him.

While Kellen tried to make sense of their blather, Gillian, moved up behind him.

"Oh, dear."

∾

"Is everyone comfy cozy?"

Kellen glared at Gillian as she tugged and smoothed the blanket over four sets of legs and feet. He moved his shoulders to try and get more comfortable, and as Francis dug an elbow into his ribs, Kellen winced.

His bed had never been so crowded, and he would no doubt be pushed to the floor before dawn. He'd hoped to share a bed with Gillian, not three hysterical faint hearts. "You do understand I am exceedingly unhappy with you?" asked Kellen.

Gillian bent her head. Was that a giggle? "Yes, I know." She rounded the side of the bed and tucked the blanket about Peter's shoulders. When she finally met Kellen's gaze, she didn't quite smile but looked impish in the candlelight. "I plan to feel guilty all night long. I doubt I'll sleep much at all."

Kellen watched her expression closely, questioning her sincerity. Was she trying to bite back a smile? "I would hope not since I doubt I'll sleep myself. I'd not planned to share my bed this night with three whimpering boys."

Gillian nodded. "This is all my fault."

Kellen shifted again, unable to get comfortable on the very edge of the bed. "Indeed. I am gratified you realize such."

Gillian was obviously trying not to laugh and Kellen's frown deepened. "This amuses you?"

Gillian ducked her head. "No. Not at all. I'm sorry. Really. I was thinking of something else."

He snorted, and as Gillian leaned over Peter and Ulrick to tuck the blanket around Francis, Kellen reached out and grasped her soft hand, forcing Gillian to meet his gaze.

She pressed her lips together, then nodded. "Truly."

Kellen's lips twisted. "These dragons you told them of. Perhaps you should keep such tales to yourself in future?"

Gillian tugged her hand free and, with finger and thumb, made a motion across her lips. "Never again. I promise, no more scary stories."

The boys protested and Gillian shushed them.

Kellen sighed loudly so she'd understand how put out he was with her. "I'd not guessed you'd be such a troublemaker."

Gillian laughed and tucked the blanket around Ulrick. "You were hoping for sweet, demure, and silent?"

"As if the gods would thus smile upon me."

Gillian laughed softly once more as she knelt on the bed and leaned over Peter and Ulrick to kiss Francis on the forehead. "To chase away the bad dreams," she told him.

She kissed Ulrick next. "To guard against dragons."

She kissed Peter. "To ensure a good night's sleep."

Kellen quickly leaned up on one elbow. "What of me? Perhaps I will need a kiss to keep my dreams sweet."

Gillian rounded the bed and looked down at him. "I thought you weren't going to get any sleep tonight."

Kellen lay back. "Mayhap a kiss will soothe me."

Gillian raised a brow. "If my kisses soothe you then perhaps we should rethink our engagement."

Kellen growled, grabbed her shoulders, and gently drew her toward him, giving her the chance to pull away.

Chuckling, Gillian leaned down to kiss his cheek and he turned his head at the last second, hoping to capture her mouth with his. She chuckled again, shakily this time, turned his head, and kissed his cheek with soft lips as her sweetly scented hair fell across his face.

When she pulled away, he quickly grabbed her hand, kissed the backside, and then turning her hand over, pressed her palm to his mouth, groaning slightly at the contact. Staring into his eyes, Gillian shivered, drew a quick breath, and pulled her hand away.

"You are correct." Kellen's voice was low. "'Twas not soothing in the least."

Gillian swallowed. "I'm glad."

"As am I. I could walk you back to your bedchamber. I will slay any dragons that show themselves."

Gillian laughed. "I'll take my chances with the dragons." She pushed Kellen back and tucked the blanket around him. "Besides, the boys need you here with them."

As if unable to help herself, she gave him one more quick kiss on the cheek, straightened and moved away, leaving Kellen to breathe in the last of her scent. "You should stay, also," he insisted.

"There's no room." She picked up the candle from the bedside table and, as Kellen considered settling the boys on the floor, she looked back one last time. "Good night."

He sighed heavily. "If these sheets are wet on the morrow, I'll hold you responsible."

Gillian's laugh was cut off as she shut the door, and Kellen lay in the dark wondering why he smiled over such obvious insolence.

The boys, completely quiet, lay tense rather than relaxed.

"Go to sleep. But know this, I am indeed serious when I say that if any of you wets the bed, they will sleep in the moat."

Three boys giggled and Kellen couldn't help it. He laughed.

THE NEXT AFTERNOON Kellen trained with his men when one of the guards rushed toward him. "My lord. You bade me inform you of any new arrivals." Breathless from his run, his red face crumpled in distress, the guard came to a halt. "Sir Royce is inside with a few of his men, asking for Lady Corbett."

Kellen's chest tightened, his jaw clenched, and without a word to anyone, he sheathed his sword and left the training field. After what felt an eternity, he strode into the hall to see Gillian speaking with Royce. She turned at Kellen's approach, a smile lighting her face. For him? Or that puss-bucket Royce?

Kellen hurried forward, wrapped an arm around her shoulder, and pulled her against his chest, feeling an absurd need to assert his claim. Absurd because she was already his. "Sir Royce. How fortuitous of you to stop by exactly at the dinner hour."

Kellen picked up Gillian's hand and rubbed her palm with his thumb, exactly where he'd kissed it the night before. She looked at their hands, at him, and then glanced between Royce and Kellen, her brows knit.

As for Royce, he stared at their now entwined hands. "Ah, well . . ." Ignoring Kellen, he turned his intense gaze upon Gillian, managing to look both sincere and contrite. "Again, I must apologize for any upset I may have caused at our first meeting, Lady Corbett. I fear my men frightened you and most humbly beg your pardon. Do not concern yourself. The miscreants have been severely punished."

Gillian lifted her chin, her expression stern. "Tell me, Sir Royce. Have you been punished, as well?"

"Ah . . ." As the fawning grin fell from Royce's face, Kellen laughed.

Gillian elbowed him. "Because you know what? You did scare me. And it didn't seem like you were prepared to help. All I can say is that it's a good thing Kellen came along when he did, because who knows what might have happened otherwise." She leaned back into Kellen.

Pleased with the way this played out, Kellen nodded toward an open-mouthed Royce. "This is upsetting you, my dear. Would you like me to send Sir Royce and his men on their way?"

Royce straightened in obvious affront. A few of his men, having overheard, shifted uneasily. Gillian hesitated, then shook her head. "No. They're our closest neighbors, after all. And I appreciate that he was willing to apologize."

Kellen didn't see this as enough of a reason and considered throwing him out, anyway. He had looked forward to seeing Gillian all morning and to come back and find Royce drooling in her presence was more than should be expected. But she leaned against him, and Kellen didn't want her to think him ill-mannered or that he would keep her from company.

"Would you and your men like to join us for dinner, Sir Royce?" asked Gillian.

Royce, standing stiff, dipped his head. "Thank you, Lady Corbett. You are all that is kind and gracious. Your pardon only accentuates your inner beauty and makes me envious of Lord Marshall for having such a lovely and charming bride." Royce's slyly pleased gaze had Kellen's jaw clenching as he looked to see how Gillian took the flowery speech. She looked skeptical and Kellen smirked at Royce.

As Tristan and Owen joined them, Kellen nodded toward the head table, led Gillian there, and seated her. Tristan hurried to sit at her side, taking the place Royce so obviously wanted for himself.

Royce hurried around the table, but Owen quickly sat across from Gillian, forcing Royce to choose the next seat over, which offered Kellen some satisfaction.

"Lady Corbett," Royce spoke loudly so as to be heard over the hall now filling with knights. "May I say you are all beauty, grace, and comportment? Being in your presence is the high-point of my week."

Gillian didn't look at Royce as she spread a cloth across her lap. "Thank you."

Kellen, unable to think of better compliments, glared at Royce and after a quick prayer by one of the boys, took a healthy swallow of wine.

"How are you settling as the new mistress of such a large castle?" asked Royce.

Curious to hear the answer, Kellen glanced at Gillian.

She grinned. "It's great. I'm having the best vacation of my life."

Kellen was not sure of her meaning. "Vacation?"

"Yes, you know, like a holiday, or time off."

He wasn't sure how to take that. He was glad she enjoyed herself, but did she somehow see this as a temporary arrangement? Or did he misunderstand her meaning? "Gillian—"

She waved a hand. "I know, once the marriage takes place it'll be work, work, work. But for now, I'm just having fun."

Kellen paused, then took a breath. "Gillian, I hope that after the marriage, you will continue to feel as if you vacation still."

Gillian slowly set her roll down and turned to look at him with soft eyes. She smiled. "That is so sweet. You are going to make a really great husband, do you know that?"

Kellen's chest swelled at her praise.

"'Twould be easy to spoil one such as yourself, Lady Corbett," interrupted Royce. "One so lovely should enjoy each day to the fullest."

Kellen barely heard Royce's words as Gillian continued to smile, and only the platters of food arriving turned her gaze and broke the contact.

Tristan leaned close to Gillian to whisper to Kellen. "Is your stomach turning? Am I mistaken or doth the beslubbering, weather-bitten weasel try to shift thy lady's affection?"

Kellen barely glanced at Royce and instead enjoyed Gillian's embarrassment as she lowered her gaze and pressed a cloth to her lips. "Tristan, hush. He'll hear you."

Was she trying not to laugh? Kellen hoped so. And while he wished Royce *had* overheard, unfortunately the noise level was high thanks to the addition of Royce's men at the next table.

Gillian buttered a roll while Kellen, feeling better by the moment, reached for the chicken.

"'Tis a beautiful ring you wear, Lady Corbett. It looks to be of exceeding value."

Gillian glanced at it. "Oh. Thank you. It was my father's, and I'm having a heck of a time getting it off." She rubbed butter into the skin around the gold, then tugged, but the ring didn't budge. "See?"

Kellen smiled at the frustrated tone. "What think you, Tristan? Sir Owen? We may have to cut off her finger to get to the prize."

Gillian sent him a mock glare. "You just try it, buster, and see which of your own appendages goes missing."

Kellen choked on his wine as Tristan and Owen laughed aloud. Kellen wondered if she knew what she implied.

Royce ignored the entire interplay. "Do you miss your family, Lady Corbett?"

"I do."

"'Tis such a hard time when a woman leaves her home. It can be exceedingly lonely."

Kellen sent Royce a hard look. "She will see them often enough and has a new home here with additional family to call her own."

Gillian smiled at Kellen once more, calming his jealousy. Royce seemed to be courting her. Trying to romance her. Kellen knew it was an accepted mode of treating a lady but did not like it. Men should court their own wives, or if unwed, bother unattached maidens.

He ought to plant a fist in Royce's pretty face and bash it up a bit. A crooked nose and a few missing teeth might balance out the comeliness nature had bestowed upon him and keep him from romancing women not his own.

At one time, Kellen had even wondered if Royce could have seduced Catherine, but none had seen him at the keep when Kellen was away, and it had been rumored Royce was abroad himself. It still rankled that Kellen could not find his wife's seducer and mete out the justice the man deserved.

Again, Kellen considered the possibility that Catherine had lied. That the poison had warped her thoughts at the end.

Royce raised a hand to draw Gillian's attention. "You have a different way of forming your words, Lady Corbett."

Kellen glared at Royce. "She is all that is charming."

"Of course. I meant no insult. Her voice is most pleasing. And her face so beautiful. The stars no doubt vie to glow upon her skin as the sun takes pleasure in lighting her path."

Gillian smiled, and Kellen fumed. 'Twas obvious the lines were well-rehearsed and had no doubt been uttered to numerous women, but would Gillian realize such?

Tristan leaned forward. "How fares the planting, Sir Royce?"

Royce's eyes narrowed. "It goes well. But some of my livestock have been stolen recently."

"As have some of mine," Kellen said.

Royce studied him. "Any idea who raids us?"

"Nay, but I will catch the culprits and punish them."

"In the meantime, where will you hide and guard your cattle?"

Did Royce think him a fool? "The western parts of the estate."

Across from him, Owen's lips barely tilted as he reached for his goblet, well-aware Kellen was lying.

After a long silence Royce started up again, apparently unable to keep quiet. "Lady Corbett, have you been to London of late? What of the current fashions?"

Gillian shrugged. "It changes so often. It's hard to say."

"So true. But you would grace whatever you chose to wear."

"Thanks. So, what's your favorite fashion trend at the moment?"

As they spoke, Kellen glanced down at his clothing, feeling loutish and rough in comparison to Royce. Perhaps he should take an interest in such and have finer clothes made to please Gillian. He wondered if she would make him some. Her sister had not.

He gave her the best pieces of meat off their shared platter, but she did not seem to notice. He had a servant come forward to refill her goblet. Again, she continued to discuss fashion. Kellen glanced around and gestured toward his daughter's nurse, and she quickly brought Amelia forward.

His daughter held the ingenious flying toy Gillian made of paper, and Gillian's conversation with Royce finally came to an end as she scooped up the child and placed Amelia on Kellen's lap, which panicked them both.

Gillian smiled as she looked between them. "She's darling. She looks like you."

Kellen, staring down into the child's face did not see the likeness. Had never seen it. Amelia studied him as well, her expression slightly wary.

Gillian fussed over Amelia before she was called by her nurse and taken for a nap.

Royce watched the child walk away before turning back to Gillian. "Will there be entertainment for Lady Corbett's pleasure?"

There was none, making Kellen wish he had planned amusement for her. Did Gillian miss such from her father's keep? He would get some minstrels to entertain on the morrow. But for today it was better there were none, as Royce would linger if given the opportunity.

As soon as the meal ended, Kellen stood, as did Tristan and Owen. When Kellen helped Gillian to her feet, Royce was finally forced to stand and follow them out, his men trailing behind.

At the door, Royce tried to capture Gillian's hand; but Kellen snatched it first and held tight, giving Royce a fierce glare.

Royce's laugh was stilted and uneasy. "I thank you for the meal. A good day to you all."

Gillian smiled. "Thanks for stopping by."

She watched Royce leave and Kellen shifted uneasily on his feet wondering at her thoughts. Had she been taken in by his flattery?

Gillian sighed and Kellen went from uncertain to murderous. Did she sigh after the man? As soon as Gillian no longer looked, he would follow and kill the misbegotten cur and she could sigh over his grave.

Finally, with a shake of her head, Gillian turned to Kellen.

"I'm sorry, Kellen. I know Sir Royce is your closest neighbor, but we simply can't have him over too often. Not only do I question his sincerity, but he's so much prettier than I am that my vanity can't take it."

Intense relief swept through Kellen. She did not want the other man? She had seen through him? Then he might allow Royce to live, after all. "That is fine by me. But before I leave for the training field, I must correct you. *None* is prettier than you."

He gave her hand one last squeeze, dared a quick kiss on her forehead, and did not wait for her to respond as he headed out the door. Her stunned expression was reward enough.

CHAPTER 14

*T*he Scottish heathens melted out of the shadows, startling Sir Robert Royce. 'Twas the third night he'd waited, and he'd not been sure they would come. He urged his horse out of the dark copse of trees and into the moonlight, three of his men following, five others waiting and watchful for any signs of aggression.

They stopped, English facing Scots, and Robert's horse moved under him in nervous reaction to the huge animal the Scottish Laird rode. Robert fought the same feeling of intimidation.

The full moon shone on MacGregor, casting half his face in shadow, seeming to highlight a beast, feral and savage.

Not unlike Lord Marshall himself, if it came to that, only dressed even worse. The savage actually wore animal skins. Robert suppressed a shudder and tried to hide his distaste.

MacGregor smiled, if it could be called that. He seemed amused, but at the same time his expression expressed contempt.

Robert straightened in the saddle, his mouth tightening. He was English, and therefore superior. How dare this dirty heathen show disdain? He was fortunate Robert had sent for him. The savage was obviously not bright enough to know better.

Robert lifted his chin. 'Twas Robert who was wise. Kellen thought he was so clever, moving his cattle about under cover of darkness, when all along one of Robert's own men helped guard the weedy beasts.

He liked feeling as if he moved players about a chess board, determining outcomes. The thought raised his mood. The heathen was moving into exactly the position Robert wanted him. Robert was in charge. He would hurt Marshall, make him sorry, and eventually make him die.

"You sent for me," MacGregor bowed his head mockingly. "And here I am."

"It took you long enough. I sent word that I had information two days ago and I have not seen my man since."

MacGregor shrugged. "I had to make some inquires. I like knowing who it is I do business with."

"And my man?"

MacGregor shrugged again then whistled loud and shrill. A yell and a smacking noise was heard inside the darkness of the trees and moments later a horse bolted out. The horse galloped past, a man bound, gagged, and wearing only underclothing tied across its back.

As Robert turned to gape at MacGregor, the barbarian simply shrugged again. "I did no' care for his attitude. I hope I like yours better."

Robert's mouth snapped shut as he stared at MacGregor. How dare this savage threaten him? "Do you want the information I have or not?"

"You seem to want me to have it, so what is it you know?"

"Lord Marshall's cattle are hidden on the north side of his property." As MacGregor stared at him, Robert had to fight the urge to move in the saddle.

"Tell me, English. Have you no problem betraying your kinsman?"

"Lord Marshall is no kinsman of mine."

"Your countryman then?"

"Why do you care?"

"Care? I do no'. I simply want my curiosity appeased, for I have often wondered, does your type have any loyalties at all?"

Robert shrugged off the insult, determined to get this meeting over with as quickly as possible. "I have relations aplenty and they are no concern of yours. Do you want the information or not?"

"Why no'? But I warn you. I do no' like my time wasted."

Again, Robert sensed a threat. The laird was a big man. Huge, in truth. Perhaps as big and powerful as Kellen, himself. And wild, too. Powerful and wild enough to bring Kellen down if it came to it?

One could hope.

The thought of the two powerful men coming together, clashing, perhaps dying, made Robert shudder. But beyond the physical threat of the man before him, Robert knew what would hurt Kellen the most. Kellen had stood guard over Lady Corbett like a dog with a stolen hunk of meat.

Robert hated the girl now. He had given her a chance and she had barely paid him any attention. She had seemed incapable of appreciating his finer qualities and practically ignored him as she gazed at and fawned over Marshall.

Unlike her sister, she actually seemed to prefer that uncivilized, unkempt barbarian. Mayhap she would like the Scot, too. In fact, perhaps Robert would do her a favor. "Then mayhap I should make sure your time is well spent with additional information. Lord Marshall has a new bride he guards like a precious treasure."

"And this affects me how?"

The man really was stupid. "She would bring a bountiful ransom."

"You would have me take his woman?" His tone was amused.

Robert thought for a moment, then sighed. "As if you could get to her," Robert said sourly, realizing just how hopeless that would actually be. A savage taking an English castle? Impossible. "So just dismiss it from your mind." But Robert hoped he wouldn't dismiss it. That he would take it as a challenge. The Scot was known to be relentless when roused. Perhaps the temptation would be too much for him to resist.

MacGregor studied him for a long moment. "It seems this grand gesture may be more about petty jealousy than any other motive, with me the knife you hope to stab in Marshall's back."

Robert's fists bunched. "I am not jealous of him! I have my reasons and they are none of your concern. I've not asked you to kill Marshall, but merely humble him. Are you going to do it or not?"

That infernal shrug once more. "Oh, I will do it. For reasons of my own. I do not plan to overlook such a gift as this. My thanks." He bowed his head.

Did the savage mock him? Robert wasn't sure, but suddenly felt as if he were lacking somehow. But what did he care what a filthy, heathen savage thought of him? The brute likely was not capable of thinking overmuch, anyway.

"One more thing," MacGregor said. "Just so we understand each other. I hope your information is correct, because I would truly hate to be disappointed. It might make me feel I was played for a fool, and that could make me verra, verra angry."

Robert swallowed, and realized he was sweating. Could he be causing future problems for himself by turning this wild dog against Marshall? But mayhap Marshall would go after MacGregor and they would kill each other? That would be a perfect solution to his problem.

"'Tis all true. I heard it straight from his own mouth." He didn't have to admit Marshall had lied. "At his own dinner table, not two nights ago."

"He fed you? And this is your repayment? Ah, a clever man, indeed."

Sarcastic brute. If somehow the savage *could* get to Lady

Corbett, so much the better. She did not like him? He would throw her to the dirty savages to be torn apart. She deserved it.

Signaling to his men, ignoring the chill it gave him to turn his back on the Scot, Robert dug his spurs hard into his mount and rode away, trying not to feel as if he ran. As if he had just tangled with the devil himself.

Robert glanced back once, but MacGregor and his men had faded away into the darkness.

Blasted creepy Scots.

CHAPTER 15

"*I* can't believe how many people showed up for this."

Gillian helped Beatrice unwrap a platter of cheese to set out by the bread as Amelia sat on the edge of the blanket playing with an ugly doll made of clay.

With resignation, Gillian looked at the knights, servants, children, craftsmen, laborers, cooks, squires, and others laying out blankets and food or playing by the river, conversing, laughing, and generally having a good time.

Tristan shrugged. "'Tis to be expected. Everyone wants to be invited to a field day."

"It turned into a bigger event than I'd anticipated."

Tristan nodded. "So it did. The more the merrier, eh?"

"I guess so." Gillian looked over to where Kellen was standing on the bank of the river. She'd wanted the picnic to be more intimate, had wanted to get Kellen alone. He'd been too busy lately, and had stayed out late the last few nights. Something about preventing raids on cattle, protecting the village, and setting traps. Medieval man waging war. Gillian sighed. While it was an attractive look for him, it put the romance she'd hoped for on the back burner.

Sir Owen walked over and knelt to help himself to a couple of slices of cheese. "You look charming this day, Lady Corbett."

"She does at that," Tristan agreed.

Gillian smiled and glanced down at the new yellow gown Beatrice and a few of the other girls had sewn for her, minus the feathers Beatrice had tried to sew into the sleeves. It was easy to look good when you dressed like a princess. "Flatterers."

Tristan laughed. "'Tis not flatter if we speak true."

Gillian felt her cheeks warm. "Well, thank you." She turned away to watch Kellen and the boys fish then glanced back to Tristan and Owen. "Can you believe I've been here for an entire week already?"

"And only four more until your wedding," Tristan said.

At the reminder, Gillian's heart sank. Four more weeks until the real fiancé showed. *That Cow Edith* as she'd taken to calling her in her thoughts. "It's gone so fast."

"Mayhap because you have enjoyed yourself," Tristan said. "If you find your enjoyment waning or the time slowing, it could be a sign you tire of your betrothed. If that be the case, perhaps you should choose to marry me rather than Kellen?"

Owen laughed. "No chance there. Have you not seen the way she looks at him?"

Gillian's cheeks heated all over again, but she smiled just the same. She *was* having fun. But it might be time to start thinking about getting back to her own time. Before Edith showed up and ruined everything.

Gillian looked at Kellen and acknowledged that she wasn't quite ready to go home yet, but at least knowing how would be a good idea. She'd thought living the life of a fairytale princess might get old, what with the garderobes, and the lack of malls in the area, but no, she was still having the time of her life. Granted, still no kiss. Apparently, Kellen had been too busy trying to foil would-be rustlers to spare time for any more late night visits. But a girl could hope. One thing was for sure. She was getting that kiss before she left. Maybe even tonight. "I'll see you guys later."

They protested, but Gillian stood anyway and Amelia followed to walk over to where Kellen fished with Francis. The boys stuck worms onto hooks and looked to be relishing the task. Another boy stood nearby, and Gillian recognized him and swerved in his direction. "Valeric. Hi."

The boy looked startled and almost dropped his pole. "My lady."

"Caught anything yet?"

"No, my lady."

She put a hand on his bony shoulder before moving on. "Well, good luck." She moved on to see Peter and Ulrick plucking worms out of a bowl. "Yuck. Make sure you wash your hands before you eat anything. Worms have germs."

After a quick glance the boys laughed and then ignored her.

Kellen, holding a fishing pole and jerking it rhythmically backward, sighed. "Gillian, you are babying again. 'Tis unacceptable and you will confuse their training if you continue to coddle them. I will thank you to stick to womanly matters."

"Fine. I can tell when I'm not wanted." She took Amelia by the hand. "Come on, Amelia. I'm going to tell you everything I know about men. It won't take long, because there isn't much to tell. Men are very simple creatures."

Kellen scoffed. "I did not ask you to leave. I wish you to stay. Perhaps I will want to hear such tales myself."

Gillian smiled at him. "No. You really don't," she teased as she glanced back and saw Kellen was watching her with appreciation in his gaze.

She glowed and didn't leave. Just stood there like a goof smiling at him smiling at her. She finally turned away, embarrassed. Talk about wearing her heart on her sleeve. No wonder Sir Owen had been confident of Gillian's affection toward Kellen.

She glanced around at the people starting to eat. There was a lot of laughter and joking, and she soaked up the whole family atmosphere. Her house had been so quiet after her family died. The noise, the togetherness, the acceptance, was an absolute joy. This was what she'd been looking for when she'd gotten conned into a relationship with her ex-fiancé.

Tristan pointed to the distance. "Someone comes. Kellen, see you the colors?"

"I'm not blind."

On the other side of the village heading down a hill was an entourage of some sort with at least twenty riders, some carrying flags. One man broke away from the group and rode forward and Kellen walked to the end of the path and waited to meet him.

As Gillian noticed women in the group, her heart started to pound and she stood rooted to the spot. When the man finally arrived, she slowly followed Kellen to where he chatted with the rider. The Corbett's hadn't come early, had they? Was Gillian about to be exposed?

Kellen turned. "'Tis my stepmother."

Relief left Gillian feeling weak as she watched the group of riders move closer, veer to the picnic and, finally, come to a stop.

One of them, a beautiful lady with covered hair, jet black brows, white skin, and red lips stopped before Kellen. Snow White in person.

Kellen helped her dismount and the woman straightened, smoothed her dress, and folded her hands together. "Your father sends his greetings. He is pleased with the betrothal. He thinks you a fine son in need of a son of your own."

She looked beyond him to Gillian and Kellen took a step back and beckoned her forward. "This is Lady Corbett." He gestured to the lady. "My stepmother, Lady Hardbrook."

Her lips barely smiled. "You must call me Marissa."

Gillian was unsure whether she should curtsey or not. "Please, call me Gillian. It's so nice to meet you."

Marissa looked at the child. "And is this Amelia? You've grown so much, my dear."

Amelia held up the doll but Marissa didn't take it and simply looked around before turning to Gillian once more. "Where are your parents? Your ladies? How progress the wedding plans, servants, meals, weaving, and such?"

Gillian looked to Kellen then back at Marissa. "Uh. My parents aren't here yet. It's just me. I haven't really started planning anything yet."

Marissa's firm mouth slackened in seeming shock. She looked back to the ladies still seated on horseback then again at Gillian. "I do not understand. Why not?"

"Well, I'm still getting to know Kellen and all, so . . ."

Marissa's mouth was still open and it snapped shut at the same moment she turned to Kellen. "'Tis good you sent for me. I will take everything in hand, including your betrothed."

That didn't sound good. "What do you mean? I don't want to be taken in hand. I'm enjoying my free time with Kellen."

Marissa drew her head back and looked at Gillian like she was some sort of oddity. "Free time? There is not such for the lady of a castle. Proper cultivation of discipline and decorum seem to be in order, do they not?"

Gillian looked to Kellen hoping for a rescue, but Kellen didn't say a word. He simply clasped his hands behind his back and looked at the ground.

Marissa turned away. "I will go to the keep and organize my possessions in your bedchamber. I'll be waiting."

"Waiting?"

Marissa's gaze swept over the gathering. "For this spectacle to end."

Feeling helpless, Gillian watched Kellen help Marissa mount again, and then the entire entourage left for the castle. Apparently Snow White hadn't arrived but the wicked witch instead. So much for Gillian's vacation.

Kellen turned to look at Gillian, who gazed at him as if he had betrayed her. But all he could think on was the fact that when he'd sent for Marissa it had not occurred to him that she would sleep with Gillian.

He couldn't help the disappointment he felt. Kellen couldn't seem to get Gillian out of his thoughts. She was attractive, amusing, charming, and she seemed to like him. All good qualities, to his way of thinking.

He straightened his spine. Still, Kellen had to admit he was relieved his stepmother was there. He would be married to Gillian soon enough, and while the wedding was being planned, he would simply have to concentrate on *knightly* endeavors rather than *nightly* endeavors.

Gillian looked worried, which he did not care for, but did understand. She had not taken over her duties and established herself as lady of the castle. She seemed uninterested in cooking, servants, or anything else that would fall in her domain. This had concerned him. He had not forgotten her comment about her stay being but temporary. She still had not given him the ring.

He had told himself not to worry. She was simply getting to know her place here and taking her time. But he had to admit he was glad Marissa had arrived to force the issue. The sooner Gillian settled, the better.

Except now there would be no more going to see Gillian in the middle of the night.

Devil take it. So much for seducing her.

CHAPTER 16

*T*he bed curtains were drawn back. "'Tis time to wake," urged Marissa. "You must bestir yourself, Lady Corbett."

Gillian rolled over and moaned. She cracked an eye to look at the window. The wooden shutters were still in place, but the slits around the edges showed it was still dark. Maybe there was a sliver of light but that might just be her imagination. She rolled over again, pulled the blankets up around her chin, and snuggled into her pillow.

"Come, Lady Corbett. The morning is a fine one." Marissa's voice was more insistent this time. "You have had your time of rest."

Gillian moaned. "Please. I just want to sleep in." The night before hadn't been a restful one, what with having to share her bed with Kellen's stiff-sleeping step-mom. The woman had continually shoved Gillian back to her own side of the bed, waking her several times, and Marissa had snored softly when she slept on her back. Couldn't she just leave Gillian alone for a while longer?

"The lady of the castle does not sleep in. She sets the example." Now the voice was disapproving.

Gillian cracked an eye open. Kellen's stepmom was completely dressed and ready for the day. "How? By having the bleariest eyes? That'll show them."

Marissa gestured to Beatrice, who hurried forward to lay a gown at the end of the bed. "The lady of the castle must hold herself to a higher measure."

Gillian groaned, rolled onto her back, and threw an arm over her eyes to block everything out. This wasn't sounding good for her.

"Beatrice, dress your lady so she might instruct the household and plan her wedding. Things that should already have been done. Apparently, your mistress is sorely in need of a few lessons."

Gillian heard the edge to Marissa's voice and Beatrice jumped to do her bidding. "My lady?"

Gillian sighed. "It's not even light outside." She tried to pull the covers over her head, but they were yanked away by a disapproving, tight-lipped Marissa. Gillian wasn't too happy herself. "I don't need any lessons. I'm on vacation."

Marissa turned and spoke to others, and for the first time Gillian realized there were three other ladies in the room. Marissa walked them to the door. "I will meet you downstairs directly."

She waited as they left, shut the door, and turned back to Gillian, her face calm. "When you embarrass yourself, you disrespect your husband. I expect you to stop whining and make the correct choice to work hard this day."

Whining? The heat rising in Gillian's face made her mad. She wasn't a lazy whiner so she had nothing to be embarrassed about. The loony woman was dragging her out of bed before dawn. She was trying to force her to plan a wedding for a girl who probably didn't deserve Kellen. Gillian wasn't doing it and she wasn't going to feel bad about it, either. "I already have plans for today. I'm busy."

"Busy with what?" Suspicion was thick in Marissa's voice.

Drooling over Kellen? Holding his hand? Getting a few kisses? Enjoying her time in medieval England? Finding a way home? "Well, I . . . I just have things to do, okay?"

Marissa straightened. "Yes, you do. I know you will want to live up to the expectations of your parents and make them proud of you. You will want to have Kellen happy to take you to wife. You will want to be an exemplary wife so as to blot the stain your sister's actions left upon this family's honor."

Enough with the guilt! Gillian tried to stifle a groan but was unsuccessful.

Marissa ignored her. "I want to know exactly what has been done to prepare for the wedding in four weeks' time."

Gillian looked away. "There's still plenty of time, right?"

There was a long silence before Marissa took a breath. "I am shocked by your lack of industry, but we will remedy that together. As to the running of the keep, you will need to take over every aspect as soon as possible to ensure the respect of your people. I will help with that also. Is there a reason your mother did not come to assist you during this period of adjustment?"

Gillian shrugged and resisted saying, *'maybe she's a lazy whiner like her daughter.'*

"Illness?" She prompted.

"Sure."

"Ah." Marissa nodded. "Then it was wise of her to send you early." She started to pace. "This morn we will begin with the kitchens, then instruct the servants, and perhaps afterward we will contend with the sewing and weaving. That should take up the morning, and in the afternoon, we will begin the wedding plans."

Whoopee. It sounded dull and boring and Gillian had no intention of complying. No way was she planning Kellen's wedding to another girl.

She glanced at Marissa, feeling uneasy about disappointing

her, which immediately ticked Gillian off. She didn't even know the woman! And she wanted to please her? Enough! She wasn't going to let Marissa make her feel guilty. She didn't have the time. She needed to find out how to get back home and, from the looks of things, she might need to leave sooner than she'd intended.

Marissa was studying her again. "I am also prepared to teach you all I know about gardening and herbs. 'Tis a skill that has proven a worthy one and is beneficial to all in my care. A skill your husband will be proud you possess. We will spend time each evening doing this. Also . . ."

Marissa continued to organize every hour of Gillian's day, week, and month as Gillian listened with growing horror.

"What about fun?"

Marissa turned dark eyes on her. "What of it?"

Gillian was starting to feel desperate. The woman obviously wouldn't be swayed from her course and Gillian wondered how easy it would be to sneak away to spend time with Kellen. "I need to get to know my fiancé better, we need bonding time, and then I'll start planning the wedding, okay?"

Marissa glanced away, seeming embarrassed. "You will have years in which to ah, *bond,* and get to know one another better."

"But . . ."

Marissa glowered. "Up!"

Gillian resentfully stood and Beatrice helped her into her dress, and then Gillian put on her shoes.

Marissa sighed. "I do not understand your attitude. Sluggardly behavior in anyone is unacceptable. In the lady of the castle, 'tis reprehensible."

Gillian glared at her shoelaces. Now she was a sluggard? What did that even mean? Stung, feeling desperate, Gillian finished tying her shoes and headed toward the door. "Excuse me, but I need to use the facilities."

She hurried down the hall, made quick use of the privy, and decided on a plan of action. She'd simply sneak away. She'd find

Kellen and explain to him that his stepmother was a slave driver, and let him take care of the situation. He could deal with the woman. Didn't he say he'd slay her dragons? Did his stepmother count?

Decision made, she went out into the hall to find Marissa waiting outside the door. Gillian's sense of desperation increased. She could outrun the woman. She was sure she could. Her athletic shoes would be far superior to the slippers Marissa wore, and she doubted Marissa would suffer the indignity of running after her, anyway. But she might send the servants.

Gillian was still on vacation. She still needed to find a way back home. She didn't need training to run a castle, and she certainly didn't need to be planning Kellen's wedding to someone else.

Besides, Gillian would either (a) be there for a very short time or (b) be dead, because when the saintly, already-knows-how-to-run-a-castle Edith showed up, Gillian would be hung as a spy. So, she really needed to spend her time (a) finding a way back home and (b) kissing Kellen while she had the chance.

The last part made her smile. She might want to know how to get back to her own time eventually, but Gillian wasn't quite ready to leave Kellen yet. Gardening and planning weddings? Menus and directing servants? No, thanks. Anyway, *That Cow Edith* would have her wedding already planned when she got there and all Marissa's work would be wasted.

Marissa snapped her fingers at a servant and started down the stairs, motioning for Gillian to follow. Gillian sighed. It wouldn't kill her to keep the woman happy for the next few hours. Probably. In the meantime, she'd have to think of better ways to avoid training with Marissa in the future.

She yawned.

Once she was actually awake, she was sure to think of something.

STANDING OUTSIDE THE STABLES, Kellen caught two of his foster boys by the backs of their tunics as they tried to run by him.

Tristan caught the third.

"Where do you think you are going?" asked Kellen.

They desperately tried to get away, squirming and fighting as they looked back toward the keep. "Let us go!" yelled Peter. "Lady Marissa will see us!"

Tristan looked to the open doorway of the keep, then back at the boys. "Why is that troublesome?"

Ulrick grimaced "She's trying to turn us into . . . into . . . into . . ."

Francis opened his eyes wide and finished the words Ulrick couldn't spit out. ". . . into *gentlemen!*"

All three faces flushed with outrage.

Kellen pressed his lips together to keep them in a straight line.

Owen rubbed his nose.

Tristan laughed aloud. "The indignity."

They released them and the boys quickly ran off.

Kellen glanced up at the keep. "That reminds me." He cleared his throat. "I need to check on something. I had best run up to the hall for a moment."

Tristan and Owen exchanged a knowing glance, and Kellen stared them down. Tristan leaned back against the stable wall and crossed one leg over the other. "Sir Owen, why do you suppose he needs to go up there?"

Owen's eyes widened. "I don't know, Sir Tristan. Mayhap to get a bite to eat?"

Tristan rubbed his chin. "I do not understand. Did we not eat our noonday meal of bread and cheese while moving the cattle? Did he not get his share? He cannot possibly be hungry. For what other reason would he go inside on such a fine day?"

Kellen glared at them both as he moved away but refrained from commenting on the fact that they were idiots.

"Don't come back a gentleman!" Sir Owen yelled after him.

Their laughter followed as he walked away, but he ignored them. He had missed seeing Gillian at both the morning and noon meals. Indeed, he had not seen her this day, and she was all he could think of. He wanted to spend time with her and cared not who knew it.

Kellen went inside to find Gillian surrounded by Marissa and her ladies, her head downbent, applying herself to a task. Seeing her thus reminded him of his first wife, Catherine, and the cold reception he'd received from her and her circle of ladies whenever he'd ventured near.

His chest tightened and he thought to leave again, but Marissa and her ladies looked up at him, trapping him with their gazes. His tunic seemed to tighten around his chest, cutting off his air supply, as he bowed and backed away. "My pardon, ladies."

Gillian's head shot up. *"Kellen!"* She stood and ran to him, a panicked expression on her face. At the last moment, Kellen opened his arms and caught her as she threw herself at him, clinging, her cheek pressed to his shirt.

His arms tightened about her as his chest seemed to burn from the inside. He could not help the smile that spread across his face, could not have imagined this reception. "Gillian?"

She looked over her shoulder before turning back to look earnestly into his eyes. "Please, save me!" she whispered.

He glanced between the ladies and Gillian. "What is amiss?"

"Kellen," Marissa's voice cut across the hall. "We are otherwise occupied and you are disrupting us and need to be about your business."

"Certainly." Kellen, feeling chastised, tried to disengage himself, but Gillian refused to release her hold on him. He bent his head to smile against her hair. "Gillian?"

"I want to go with you," she whispered again.

Kellen looked to Marissa and the others, all sternly watching them. "I have been gone all morning and am only now off to train in the lists. And it looks as if you are busy, also."

"Couldn't I just watch you?"

He'd like nothing better.

"Lady Corbett?" Marissa called. "We are waiting."

Her gaze beseeched him.

Marissa sighed heavily, put aside her sewing, stood and crossed to join them.

Gillian's eyes closed and her shoulders slumped. Kellen wanted to help. "Gillian?"

She finally opened her eyes and her expression turned mutinous as she released her grip and turned to face Marissa, clutching his arms to keep them tightly about her. "As much as I'd like to stay and help, as an engaged couple, we need to spend time together."

Kellen's arms clenched convulsively around her.

"I disagree," Marissa said. "There is too much to do. Please move away from him. He is filthy and smells of horse and you are dirtying your gown by brushing against him. 'Tis unseemly besides. You need to come away, and you most certainly need to practice decorum."

Kellen felt his face heat, and loosened his grip, but Gillian pushed tight into his embrace. She didn't seem to care about the dirt or the smell as she clutched his arms.

Marissa gave him a pointed stare and Kellen hesitated. He didn't want to distress his stepmother.

But he did not care to turn Gillian away. He liked that she clung to him and would not wish her to feel rejected.

But, of course, he was the one who'd invited Marissa in the first place. He'd asked for her help and knew he should bow to her dictates.

But the way Gillian pressed herself against him like a second skin was heady and exciting. He wanted to be with her.

Marissa sighed. "You will see each other at supper in a few hours."

Kellen bent his head to Gillian. "I am happy you are learning the running of the keep. Marissa is a good teacher. There is none better to ease your way."

Gillian looked as if he'd betrayed her. 'Twas like a dirk in his chest. He straightened and faced Marissa. "But Gillian can't be expected to learn everything at once."

Gillian expression relaxed and she gazed at Kellen as if he were her champion. He liked it.

"I disagree," Marissa said. "There is not much time and she has much to learn."

"I . . ." Ruefully he accepted that he cared more about what Gillian thought than Marissa. "I understand, but no more today. Ready yourself, Gillian. I will return for you shortly. I came in to tell you that I am riding into Thropworth this day." He knew he was contradicting what he'd said earlier about training this day, and that everyone would know he was lying, but he didn't care. He turned to a tight-lipped Marissa. "Gillian should watch as I mete out judgement. As my lady, 'tis important for all to see her."

He was finding he would do about anything for her.

"Can I ride with you on your horse again?"

Marissa let out a harsh breath.

Kellen cupped Gillian's cheek as he looked down at her. He couldn't believe she was his. He didn't want to part with her for as long as it would take to get everything ready. "Of course."

The thought of facing his men . . . well . . . they would think him crazed when he changed course for the day. At his command his men were already gathering in the north field. Besides rounding them up, he'd also have to send word ahead to announce his intent of arriving in the village this day. The teasing would be merciless.

'Twas worth it to be with her.

CHAPTER 17

"How fare you with Marissa?"

Snuggled in Kellen's arms, Gillian enjoyed the warmth seeping from his chest into her back, the possessive way his arms surrounded her, and the rocking motion of the horse. She was exactly where she wanted to be. "Fine."

"Truly?"

"No." Gillian bit her lip as Kellen laughed. She didn't want to come off as a complainer but didn't want to lie, either.

"She means well."

Gillian snorted and craned her neck to look up at him. "I think she means to drive me crazy. Do you suppose she'll make things worse because I went off with you today?"

Kellen shrugged. "She is not vindictive. Do not concern yourself."

"Easy for you to say." Amused by his lordly proclamation, Gillian huffed out a breath before relaxing against Kellen once more. "You're not the one who has to sleep with her tonight."

Kellen laughed. "If you are truly concerned, I'll speak on your behalf. Or better yet, you can sleep in my bed. I promise not to snore or steal the bedcovers. And I vow to keep you warm."

Gillian smiled. "I suspect staying warm would be the least of my concerns."

Kellen leaned down, his mouth near her ear. "I can hardly wait until we are wed." His whispered words, low and full of meaning, had Gillian shivering. She glanced around quickly to see if any of his men had heard. They hadn't, but Gillian ducked her head and searched for a change of subject, positive her flaming face would give her thoughts away if anyone cared to glance in their direction.

Her gaze fell to her ring and she gave it a tug. It didn't budge. "Um. I think I've gained weight since I've been here. You're feeding me too much."

Kellen chuckled, ran a hand down her arm, then back up to cup her shoulder. He squeezed. "I admire every single curve and cannot wait—"

"Kellen, hush!"

His laughter had Gillian blushing all over again as she searched frantically for another subject. "Where are we going, anyway?"

Kellen chuckled. "Perhaps we are simply enjoying the seeing of the sights. Would that not please you?"

She smiled up at him. "Actually, it would."

They soon rounded a hill and Gillian saw a village nestled below filled with cottages, huts, and assorted buildings; but it was the big church with an imposing steeple and light-colored stone that immediately caught her eye. She straightened. "Hey. I know this place." Surely this was Marshall, the town she'd been staying in before heading out to draw the castle.

"You have been here? When?"

"Uh . . ." Oops. She couldn't tell him she'd stayed here in the twenty-first century, that she'd bought chocolate in a shop that wouldn't exist for hundreds of years, and gotten directions to the ruin of Marshall Keep from the plump woman behind the counter. Directions to Kellen's castle.

Kellen suddenly stiffened. "Is this where you were robbed of your possessions?"

Gillian breath caught. "Um . . ." She was going to have to plead the fifth on that one. "I have no memory of that event."

Kellen's arms tightened, pulling her back against his chest. "If someone has made you fearful, have no worries on that score, my lady. I will find the miscreants and they will be duly punished."

Gillian thought it unlikely, but nodded as if she believed him. Said miscreants were safely in another century and most likely continuing their reign of terror against unwary travelers.

When she didn't say anything, Kellen sighed, then pointed. "I own all this land and the manor house yonder and have placed in its charge one of my most trusted knights. I believe you will like his wife. She is friendly and would make you a good companion."

"Oh yeah?"

It didn't take them long to get to the outskirts. As they rode through the town, everyone stared at Gillian. Well, almost everyone. A pretty young woman waved then placed a hand on her hip, her smile beckoning as if she silently offered her services to Kellen.

Gillian glared at the woman and laid a hand on Kellen's shoulder, staking her claim, before turning her glare on Kellen. "A friend of yours?"

Kellen's lips curved. "Not at all." He didn't even bother trying to hide his grin. "Is this your way of letting me know you wish me to be faithful?"

Gillian smiled sweetly. "Only if you wish to keep all your bodily parts intact."

Kellen laughed, causing his men and nearby villagers to stare. "Do not concern yourself, Gillian. I will ever be true and will want no other."

Gillian turned to look at him, and the heated, possessive way he gazed at her made her want to melt into a puddle. She reached up to cup his jaw and he captured her hand and pressed a heated kiss to the center. She gasped, held his gaze for a moment longer, and then looked around self-consciously. People were definitely staring. "I'll hold you to that."

After they'd dismounted, Gillian watched curiously as Kellen and another man formally greeted one another. The knight bowed. "Do you desire to pass judgement this day?"

"I do."

"We are honored and look forward to your discernment." The knight gestured and chairs were brought forward as Kellen introduced Gillian to the knight, Sir John Teasdale, and his wife Lady Teasdale, who looked to be about Gillian's age. Lady Teasdale curtsied and quickly introduced her four young children, three girls and a boy, all blonde like their mother, and all probably under eight years old.

Gillian tried out a curtsy and didn't think she did too badly. "It's so nice to meet you all."

Lady Teasdale beamed. "The pleasure is ours. I'd not thought to meet you until your wedding day, so this is most pleasing."

"Thank you. I'm glad to be here."

As Kellen led Gillian to her seat, he leaned down. "I do not normally deal with such small matters," he said in a low voice. "My man does this. I am only called in to deal with murder, arson, robbery, and assault, but make an exception this day."

"To spend time with me?"

Kellen's mouth quirked up on one side. "Verily you are a lot of trouble."

"I know."

Gillian was joined by Lady Teasdale and Kellen took his seat at the front, beside Sir Teasdale.

"You look nothing like your sister," Lady Teasdale said.

"No?"

Lady Teasdale studied her. "The same coloring, 'tis true, but your features are much finer." She hesitated. "None here believe he killed Lady Marshall."

"Is that what some people think?"

Lady Teasdale looked suddenly worried. "Some say so."

"Kellen would never hurt a woman in a million years. There's just no way."

Lady Teasdale studied her. "You defend him so vehemently. 'Tis nice to hear."

"Of course, I do. Anyone can see he's innocent."

Lady Teasdale nodded. "You are not who I was expecting."

Yes, well, that was pretty much a given. Gillian lifted a shoulder, glanced at Kellen, and made sure her voice stayed low. "I don't mean to sound so defensive, but not only does he have to deal with being almost murdered, but then he's the one who gets the bad reputation out of it? It's not fair."

"You do have the truth of it." Lady Teasdale agreed then turned her head as the noise escalated in the gathering crowd.

Gillian glanced from Kellen to the crowd, wondering what was happening. One of Kellen's men stepped forward. "Lord Marshall will now hear any grievances brought before him."

Gillian leaned closer to Lady Teasdale. "So, he's like a judge or something?"

Lady Teasdale nodded, but there wasn't time for a longer response as an indignant man pushed his way toward the front, pointed at another man, and loudly proclaimed, "I would accuse Gilbert the Baker of stealing the affections of my wife."

An audible gasp went up from the crowd as everyone turned to look at a man who gaped unbecomingly, yellowed teeth on full display. He glanced around for a quick exit, but his peers relentlessly pushed him forward.

Kellen motioned with one hand. "Both men advance and give me the details."

The first man moved toward the front, bowed quickly and pointed at the other man, who closed his mouth and straightened skinny shoulders. "He has been gazing upon my wife, praising her, and he touched her hand. My wife smiled at him and I caught her eating a pastry that I had not given her."

Kellen motioned to the other man. "What say you?"

The man flushed an unbecoming shade of red but stood his ground. "'Tis all innocence, my lord. Naught has occurred. I swear to it."

Kellen turned toward the first man. "He says naught has happened between them and has sworn it. If he agrees not to talk to your wife further, will you forgive this man?"

"Aye." The man straightened. "For a chicken."

"What?" Incredulity colored the other man's tone. "A whole chicken?" Mouth slack he looked to Kellen. "'Tis unthinkable."

Kellen glanced between both men, then leaned forward. "Perhaps half a chicken?"

A laugh escaped Gillian before she even knew it was bubbling up. She quickly turned it into a cough as everyone, including Kellen, turned to stare at her.

A moment later the argument continued, capturing the crowd's attention once again; and Gillian couldn't resist, she got out her sketchpad and started to draw.

After a few more minutes of haggling, the half chicken was finally accepted.

Stifling another giggle, Gillian drew faster as Kellen nodded toward the husband. "By forgiving this man you show great strength of character and are to be commended."

He turned his gaze upon the other man. "And you, sir, need to find a woman of your own and stop trying to lure the wives of other men. 'Tis unacceptable."

Gillian's sketch started to take shape. Two men tugged on a pretty chicken, each pulling a wing as the long-lashed hen struggled between them, panicked. Drawing all those caricatures at fairs during college stood her in good stead as she over exaggerated the determined features of the men, making them sinister yet silly at the same time.

Lady Teasdale glanced over and muffled a laugh. Kellen turned, his brows raised, and Gillian pulled her pad against her chest, smiling innocently.

Another man caught Kellen's attention as, soft-spoken but upset, he claimed some of his grain had been stolen but didn't have any proof against the accused other than he'd witnessed the man leaving his hut and had less grain upon checking.

Kellen considered the situation as the accused shifted in place, looking down. "Did you take the grain?"

The man took a breath, but before he could respond, Kellen held up a hand. "Keep in mind," he said sternly, "that you not only answer to me but must stand before God and His judgement for what you say this day."

The man visibly wilted, his shoulders and head dropping. "I did take the grain, my lord."

"Is it gone?"

"Aye, my lord, 'tis gone."

"Then you must pay your debt by helping this man work for seven days' time, doing whatever he needs of you."

"Yes, my lord." Both moved away, seeming satisfied by Kellen's judgement.

Another man came forward, bowed, and pulled on his forelock. "My lord, the blacksmith," he pointed into the crowd, "'e killed me goat."

A burly man, thick with muscle, pushed his way to the front. "You lie!"

Kellen looked between the two men. "Let me hear the details."

The accuser crossed his arms over his puffed-out, bony chest. "'E gave me goat the evil eye one morning as 'e walked past. The goat died the next day."

The blacksmith, jaw clenching, shook his head in disgust. "I never did such a thing."

"Have you any witnesses?" Kellen asked the accuser.

At first no one came forward, but the claimant smacked an

adolescent boy on the back of the head and, cap in hand, the kid moved forward. "I witnessed it, my lord." The boy didn't look up from the ground or sound very convincing.

"And you are?"

The blacksmith shook his head in disgust. "'E's his son."

Gillian stifled another giggle as Kellen sighed. "Any other witnesses?"

No one came forward. "As there is no real proof that the blacksmith did indeed harm your animal, I will have to deny your claim."

"But, my lord—"

"The matter is closed."

Good call, in her opinion. Gillian glanced around at the crowd to see that more people had gathered. It looked as if the entire town had turned out. The scandal sheets apparently had nothing on medieval England.

A tall, well-dressed man came forward next. Stern-faced and confident, he dragged a shorter man by the arm who pulled and tugged and tried to escape.

Lady Teasdale leaned forward. "'Tis the reeve bringing a man to justice. He supervises work on Lord Marshall's property and reports to my husband."

"Ah." That might account for the air of self-righteous indignation. He was doing his job. The reeve dropped the man's arm and the guy danced away, then glanced around and finally settled in front of Kellen, bowing his head and wringing his hands.

The reeve gestured. "This man poached a fish from my lord's stream."

Murmurs flowed through the crowd as the accused looked at Kellen beseechingly. "My lord, if I might defend myself?"

The reeve's lips curled and Kellen nodded. "Continue."

The man's eyes darted about constantly as if seeking escape. "I was merely cooling my hands in the water, my lord, and the fish swam right into my curled fingers, it did, or I would have thrown it back."

The reeve snorted. "He used a hook."

The accused ignored the reeve and glanced around at the crowd. "In truth," he said, raising his voice and straightening, "I did throw the fish back for it was so very big and was obviously meant for his lordship's table." He gestured toward Kellen.

"But then another fish, an exceedingly puny and worthless one, swam right into my hands; and my wife, being very ill and with a great desire for fish, she came to mind."

"Did she now?" asked Kellen, irony lacing his tone.

"Aye, my lord."

Gillian couldn't help a smile as she started to draw again.

It wasn't hard to see where this story was going.

"I could not help myself. I did take the puny, feeble, insignificant fish home with me. Barely a mouthful it was. For my wife, that is to say."

Everyone laughed, clearly not believing he didn't get his share of the fish; and Gillian, a broad smile on her face, stood. "Kellen? May I make a comment?"

Kellen glanced back, surprise flickering across his face as he motioned her forward. "As you will."

Stepping beside Kellen's chair, her sketchpad pressed to her chest, she smiled down at the man, then turned to Kellen. "I hesitate to interfere in something I don't understand, but aren't fish washed downstream and into the ocean? That being the case, couldn't they be considered free fish?"

"No." Kellen shook his head. "All fish belong to the landowner. If they are taken without permission, shortly there would be none to speak of."

"Ah." Since she had no idea if the fish population would decline if everyone suddenly took up fishing, or if the river would replenish itself with new fish coming downstream, she didn't comment.

She lowered the sketchpad and glanced down, then back at the defendant. "Well then, sir, may I ask you a question?" At his hopeful expression and nod, she continued. "Exactly how big was the fish that got away?" She managed the words with a straight face.

"It was this big, yer ladyship." He held both hands quite far apart and Gillian bit her lip. Hard. "That big, huh?" At his nod, Gillian lifted her pen and added another detail to her drawing. "Well, that was certainly generous of you to let that one go. And what illness does your wife suffer from?"

"A babe on the way is wearisome. It vexes her so."

She glanced down at Kellen. "I ask you, what is a man to do in such a situation? Perhaps you could be lenient this once concerning the fish?"

"I cannot. Then all would expect leniency and the fields would be neglected in favor of the river banks."

"Well then, might I suggest that this man's payment could be in amusing us all so well?"

Kellen's amber gaze, sparkling amusement and approval, captured her own. "Are you amused, Lady Corbett?"

Gillian turned her sketchpad around and handed Kellen the finished artwork, an exaggerated caricature of a man, eyes gleaming lustfully, a huge fish escaping his grasping fingers.

Kellen laughed aloud and she couldn't help her own smile. "Why, yes," she said. "I do believe I am."

Leaning over his shoulder, she studied the picture and lowered her voice so no one else could hear. "Taking into account the fact that the one that got away is always the biggest fish ever caught, I believe you should give the man a break for being so generous in giving up such a catch; and also for being willing to tell such a good . . . ah . . . tale, don't you think?"

Kellen's mouth still quirked at one corner as he studied the picture. "Aye." He didn't bother lowering his own voice. "He did tell the story well, did he not? And as he amused her ladyship, I

will excuse him this one time with his tale being sufficient repayment. But were such to happen again, I would be most displeased."
His gaze bored into the man. "Most. Displeased."

Gillian, feeling unaccountably triumphant, straightened and
bowed her head toward the man. In turn, he bowed repeatedly to
her. "You are wise and beautiful, my lady." Bow, bow. "Generous
and a true noble." Bow.

Well, as to that, she couldn't say, but she might have made a
fine defense attorney if she hadn't become an artist. As Kellen
grasped her hand, Gillian jumped. His look of approval had her
brows raising, especially since she hadn't been sure he'd welcome
her interference.

She squeezed his own in return, took the proffered sketchpad
and turned toward her seat. Kellen was gratifyingly reluctant to
let go of her, only releasing his grip when their hands had
stretched too far apart. He waited until she was seated before he
called the next case.

Luckily there weren't many more complaints and, since
Gillian didn't interfere again, they were soon free to walk around.
Kellen was quick to reclaim her hand and she tried to control
her grin.

"Everyone is staring, my lady," Kellen said. "I cannot fault them
as your beauty seems to glow as does the sun at noontime. You
radiate happiness."

"Thank you." Gillian could feel herself blush. She didn't look at
him but kept her gaze firmly on the wares being sold by the
townspeople. Vases, cookware, cloth, her eyes skimmed them all
as her attention was taken up by the man at her side.

He leaned closer. "I was truly proud of you this day." His
breath stirred her hair and caused goose bumps to break out at
the base of her neck and along her arms. "These are our people.
They are as important to us as we are to them. Thy prompt aid,
and my acceptance of your judgement, showed us as unified. I am
well pleased with you."

Gillian looked up at him, her heart beating hard, leaving her lightheaded and breathless. "These compliments have to stop."

He grinned.

"And so does the way you're looking at me."

His warm gaze, his forbiddingly beautiful face, the attraction flaming between them, it all had to stop.

"I would spoil you. I wish to fill the pack you value so with all the treasures it can hold. I want to be gentle with you. And more." His voice deepened on the last two words as he gazed at her mouth. She shivered.

"Stop already."

"I merely want to please you and make you smile."

Gillian ducked her head and his chuckle sent another shiver up her spine.

Kellen tugged her to a nearby stand and bought a bundle of colored ribbons. Laying them across his palms, he presented them to her with a slight bow. "For your hair, fair Gillian."

Her cheeks were heating again as the shopkeeper smiled and listened in. Gillian lifted the bundle, studying the different colors as they walked away. "I haven't worn ribbon in my hair since I was in grade school, and now I'm wearing them all the time. They're beautiful, thank you."

She searched desperately for another subject before he could say anything else to make her blush. "What is the name of the village?"

"Thropworth."

"Really? Well, someday, it will be named Marshall. For you."

Kellen laughed. "Think you I would name this village after myself? You talk nonsense."

Gillian glanced up at him and smiled. "I think Marshall is a good name. Strong and masculine."

He stared down at her, eyes intense, then cleared his throat. "Let us hope 'tis not too masculine a name as it will soon be yours to share."

"I suppose it will." She looked down. "And if we were married, then you would belong to me as well, wouldn't you?" A girl could wish for a moment, couldn't she?

"Let me assure you, my lady, that I am yours, even now."

His words, spoken in that gravelly tone, had Gillian's breath catching and her knees weakening. She slowly raised her head to see the possessive way he looked at her, like she was dessert and he had a sweet tooth that hadn't been slaked in a very long while. The way his gaze dropped to her mouth, his slowly drawn-in breath, his firm and inviting lips.

Bundling the ribbons in one hand, she reached up and touched his warm, stubble-roughened cheek with the other. "Right at this moment you do belong to me, don't you?" She slid her hand behind his neck, her fingers tangling in the thick, silky hair at his nape and slowly she pulled him down and stood on tiptoes.

When their lips met in the lightest of kisses, Kellen groaned, and the sound, the vibrations, the surprising softness of his mouth pressed gently against hers, caused Gillian to shiver.

Applause snapped her out of the enticing daze and she let him go. He slowly released her, stroking her hair once as she glanced around to look at their smiling audience. Gillian, cheeks heating, did the only thing she could think to do. She smiled and waved at everyone.

Kellen chuckled. "'Tis glad I am to see you blush, my lady. I would hate to be the only one. And can I say that your timing could not be more disappointing. I finally get to taste you and cannot pull you into my arms as I long to."

Gillian laughed, her heart pounding, her face heating. "Sorry about that."

"Never fear. When next I get you alone, 'tis a problem I will rectify."

That's what she was afraid of. Their relationship had gotten too serious, too fast. Her emotions were engaged. His might be, as well. She certainly hadn't meant for that to happen. Maybe it was time to pull back.

She met his gaze once more, saw the heat, longing, and satisfaction burning there and felt herself weaken once more.

Maybe it was already too late.

CHAPTER 18

With Gillian sitting in front of him, wrapped in his arms, Kellen was in no hurry to return home. She seemed contemplative as she rocked with the motion of the horse and took in the scenery, and Kellen wondered what she was thinking. "You are very quiet."

Gillian glanced over her shoulder then back to a copse of trees. "I'm just thinking about our kiss and questioning your courage."

Kellen's eyes widened of their own accord and every muscle in his body tightened in outrage. "What?"

"Well," she lifted a shoulder. "I did kiss you first. It left me wondering if you are simply shy or a bit of a scaredy-cat."

Jaw clenching, Kellen bit off a sound of disgust. "I am no scared cat. I had desired to kiss you sooner but worried you might be skittish and had vowed to woo you first. I had not realized I had such a bold lass on my hands, else I would have acted sooner."

"Bold? Whatever!" Gillian turned and hit him in the shoulder, pretending to be upset, but he could now see the laughter in her eyes and the curve of her lips and realized he was being teased. His muscles relaxed and he couldn't help a slow grin.

A couple of his knights tried to stifle their laughter and Kellen slowed his horse. When his knights did the same, he jerked his head. "Ride on."

Reluctantly his men obeyed, and when they were out of hearing, he adjusted Gillian in his arms and cupped her cheek. "Now what say you?"

Gillian looked at his mouth, then into his eyes. "I'm not sure this is such a good idea." Her voice, weak and whispery, made him feel strong, powerful.

"I disagree. 'Tis the best idea I have had of late." He lowered his head and kissed her gently, his mouth moving over hers, his hands sweeping into her hair as he held her in place. His heart pounded and he couldn't believe the incredible softness of her mouth, the way her lips parted to let him taste her. Her arms slid around his neck as if to hold him to her and he moaned, unable to stop the sound. She was exquisite.

When he broke off the kiss and lifted his head, his voice was rough and his arms tight about her as he claimed, "Mark me, Gillian. This is our first kiss. The other, a weak, paltry attempt on your part, does not signify."

Gillian, chest rising with quick breaths, laughed as she released him. "If that's the case then we will never be able to point to a spot as our first kiss. It will be an ever-changing location."

He lowered his forehead to hers. "I assure you, lady, that whenever I ride my mount I will remember this kiss. And since I ride daily, I will never forget."

Gillian lifted her hand to his neck and the tender gesture, her cool fingers against his skin, had his arms tightening about her. "You're very sweet," she said.

"Sweet?" he chuckled. "Enough with these insults. I insist you stop—"

The pounding of hooves had Kellen's head jerking up and he saw his men riding toward them, fast. Kellen adjusted Gillian, clutched her tight, then urged his mount forward.

The knights pulled up and he did the same, their horses

heaving and prancing as the men tried to control them. His other men backtracked to join them.

"My lord," Sir Reginald de Lacey bowed his head. "Some of the cattle are stolen and the guards missing."

Kellen's mouth tightened. "Scots?"

Sir Reginald shook his head. "I know not."

"Whoever has dared such will soon feel my wrath. Where?"

"The east side."

"When?"

"Perhaps as early as this morning. It could have happened soon after the guards were changed."

Digging his heels into his mount, Kellen set a fast pace for home, his men following, Gillian clinging. Once inside the court-yard, he yelled orders as he stopped in front of the steps to the keep.

As his men ran for their arms calling for squires and more horses, he dismounted then lowered Gillian off his horse to stand with the women gathered on the steps, watching the scene unfold. Kellen touched her cheek, then turned to Marissa. "See to her safety."

Marissa rolled her eyes. "Lady Corbett will be well protected within the walls of the keep."

With one last look at Gillian's confused face, Kellen remounted his horse and called to his men. They would get his guards and his cattle back, and make whoever took them very sorry they did.

GILLIAN, heartbeat speeding, leaned against the stone wall behind her since there wasn't anywhere to sit. Kellen looked like a warrior, his body thick with muscle, covered in armor and chain, helmet gleaming in the sun, his shield emblazoned with the black bird of prey that made her shiver. Wow. Just *wow*. Could she help it if her knees went weak?

His men were impressive. Fast at following orders and incredibly well organized, they rode well-trained horses behind Kellen's out of the keep. She wouldn't want to meet any of them in a dark alley. These guys were intimidating.

The women stood still watching the men ride away without moving. Almost as if this were expected of them? After the last man disappeared under the gate, Marissa finally turned and walked into the hall. Gillian followed. "Will they be okay?"

Marissa looked surprised. "Of course. None can defeat Lord Marshall."

"Will there be a fight, then?"

Marissa shrugged as she moved away. "Doubtful. The miscreants will likely run and hide. Why were you away for so long this day?" She asked over her shoulder. "What were you about?"

"Oh. Um, well . . . what with the traveling there and back, and the judging, and we may have stopped to look at a few things in the village and—"

Marissa waved a hand. "I find I've no stomach for excuses. We will simply have to make up for lost time now that you have finally arrived."

Gillian's own stomach sank as she followed Marissa inside, the two ladies following directly behind her, hemming her in. She glanced back to see the blue-eyed woman, a big cat embroidered on her skirt, give her a malicious smile. Just as Gillian had suspected, she was to be punished for going off with Kellen.

The second lady, her eyes dark brown and malevolent, offered a patently insincere smile. "'Tis certain you are much like your sister Catherine, are you not? She, also, was ever one to shirk her duty."

While Gillian had expected the attack, her mouth still fell open. "Hey! I wasn't shirking. I was just spending time with my fiancé. That's important, too."

"I agree," said the cat lady to her companion, ignoring Gillian completely and certainly not agreeing with her. "She is much like her sister, is she not? If not in looks then certainly in character."

Stung, Gillian took a breath. "Look, I'm nothing like Catherine. And I'd appreciate it if you didn't try and paint me with the same brush. It's not very fair."

"What has fairness to do with it? You are her sister. What more is to be said?"

"I agree." Blue eyes flashed limpidly once more. "There can be no more to say of the matter."

What a couple of hags. Even if Catherine *were* her sister, which she was not, it wouldn't be fair to judge them the same. She knew plenty of sisters who were nothing alike. How would they like it if she blamed them for something someone else did?

Sort of like she was doing with Edith?

Gillian's heart sank. Wasn't she romancing Kellen and justifying it by telling herself that Edith didn't deserve him? Because of the way Catherine had tried to murder him?

Dismayed, Gillian looked at the ground. Kellen wasn't hers. Ultimately, he belonged to Edith who might just be a perfectly nice person and well suited to him.

Gillian didn't like it when Marissa and her friends blamed her for Catherine's failings. But wasn't she doing exactly the same thing to Edith? Catherine was bad, therefore so was Edith? Therefore, Gillian could do what she liked?

Gillian felt sick. She'd taken this whole thing too far. She needed to find a way back home before she ruined Kellen's chance of a good marriage.

She needed to get out of there.

MARISSA APPRAISED the forlorn expression on Gillian's face and barely refrained from rolling her eyes. Enough of this mooning about. "Come then," she said, clapping her hands. "We'll not dawdle in the hall all day waiting for the men to return. There is work to be done."

Turning, she led the way, and her ladies followed. A glance over a shoulder assured that Gillian was slowly climbing the stairs. The girl looked upset. Was it because Kellen had left? Or because of the biting comments made by Yvonne and Vera?

Marissa shook her head. If the latter were the case, the girl needed to grow a backbone if she thought to take her rightful place as lady of the castle. Otherwise, Gillian's own ladies—when they arrived—would soon disdain to follow her lead.

Marissa climbed the stairs to the solar, and when Gillian finally entered the chamber, Marissa stood patiently beside the head chair and waited to see if Gillian would offer the seat or take it for herself.

Politeness dictated Gillian give up the place-of-honor as Marissa was Kellen's stepmother, but the girl said nothing at all and simply sat across the way, leaving not only the head chair available, but also the one she should have rightfully claimed next to Marissa. Lady Vera promptly sat therein with a smirk toward Lady Yvonne.

Marissa sank down with a sigh. The girl had much to learn. And learn she would. If Gillian's mother was such a sad case as to allow her daughter out in the world with so little training, then for Kellen's sake it was Marissa's duty to teach the girl.

"Lady Corbett, let us start with castle fare. Know you how to plan a menu?"

Gillian sighed. "Look, Lady Hardbrook, I understand you're trying to help me, and I appreciate it, I do. But I really have somewhere I need to go. And the sooner the better." She stood. "So, it's been really nice to meet you, but—"

"Sit down."

"Um—"

"*Now!*"

Gillian sat.

Marissa schooled her expression. She didn't enjoy raising her voice and didn't like that this girl had managed to goad her into doing so. "'Tis obvious you've been allowed your way too often." Marissa was proud of her patient-yet-stern tone. "That will change. You have much to learn. I will not have this family disgraced by your laziness."

A flush rose in Gillian's cheeks and she crossed her arms.

"I've never been called lazy in my entire life."

"Then 'tis obvious someone thought to spare your feelings."

The ladies giggled and Gillian's mouth fell open. Marissa raised a hand. "No more. There is work to be done."

"But if you'd just let me explain—"

"I'm not interested in excuses." Marissa cut in. "We will now begin. Let us start with castle fare. Lady Corbett, know you how to plan a menu?"

Leaning back in the chair, arms and legs crossed like a sloven, Gillian shrugged. "Not really. Mostly I've just done take out."

Marissa stared. "You have never planned a menu for an entire keep?"

Gillian shook her head. "I'm afraid not."

This was worse than Marissa had realized. "How many servants had you the responsibility of directing?"

"None. If I wanted something done, I just did it myself. My mom was a big believer in self-sufficiency. We never had a maid or anything. We all just pitched in."

Marissa stared, appalled. "You've not been trained in the instruction of servants?"

"No."

Marissa's chest tightened. This was not to be believed. "Do you sew?"

"No."

"Nay?"

"Well, I sewed an apron once in school, but I sewed the ties on backwards and they wouldn't reach around my waist. I made a mess of the material trying to unpick the whole thing. My teacher still gave me a C for effort, which I appreciated."

Marissa knew when she was being mocked and her voice sharpened as she asked. "Do you embroider?"

"No. But I've always wanted to learn. I did knit a hot pad once. It was actually supposed to be a scarf, but when I lost interest, my mom used it to protect the table until the yarn unraveled."

Marissa didn't even try to hide her disgust. Gillian's mother should be ashamed of herself and certainly of her daughter. "Can you do nothing womanly?"

Gillian raised a brow.

Lady Yvonne snickered. "It almost seems as if your mother thought to train you for the life of a peasant."

Lady Vera laughed. "The lowliest of peasants. With your lack of skill, 'tis no wonder you had to wait for your sister to die before you could find yourself a husband."

That was over-harsh, and Marissa thought to rebuke her ladies, but at Gillian's unconcerned expression, decided to allow the rudeness. Perhaps their words would shame the girl into a desire to learn.

Lady Yvonne smirked. "Do you possess any skill at all, Lady Corbett?"

"I can draw."

"You can sketch?" Marissa wasn't sure she believed her.

"Yes. Very well."

At the display of confidence, Marissa felt slightly relieved. At last, a womanly accomplishment. But she was skeptical, too. Gillian's standards might be low and her skill merely adequate.

"Would you like to see?"

Marissa's mouth half-opened to respond in the affirmative, but the half-smile, the excitement in Gillian's expression stopped her. Because what Marissa saw was that Gillian truly wanted to sketch.

"Sewing first." Marissa grabbed up a garment from the top of the pile. "Kellen has torn this sleeve to such an extent as to render the garment useless. You will sew it back together. Later you can demonstrate your skill at sketching."

After getting Gillian set up with needle and thread, Marissa ignored her for the next ten minutes and listened to the chatter of her ladies. When she finally could stand no more, she checked Gillian's progress and her heart sank. "This is very poor work, Lady Corbett."

Looking crushed, Gillian held up the garment. "What do you mean?"

"The stitches are too far apart and uneven. You need to apply yourself." Marissa took the garment and demonstrated.

Gillian watched carefully, then sighed. "How long is this going to last? When will Kellen be back?"

Marissa tried to check her exasperation. "Do you want your lord to be poorly clothed or to have his garments fallen to shreds? Are you not ashamed at your lack of skill?"

Gillian shrugged.

"I warn you, 'twill be unpleasant if your people think you slothful. The servants won't respect a lady that refuses to set an example."

Gillian's lips tightened.

Marissa sighed. "Lady Corbett, I don't understand your belligerent attitude. I am trying to aid you."

Gillian's face slowly relaxed and she nodded. Finally, the girl straightened in her chair. "I see that. I'm sorry. I'll try harder."

Marissa resumed her seat and relaxed a little as Gillian seemed to concentrate on her stitching. When Kellen's daughter wandered in with a maidservant, Gillian beckoned to her. "Come sit by me, Amelia. I'm learning to sew."

Marissa watched as Gillian situated the child and the two of them took up stitching. Marissa shushed Lady Vera when she loudly whispered that Amelia's skill might outshine Gillian's.

Gillian seemed determined to make the task fun as they played a game of who could make their stitches the tiniest.

A few minutes later Marissa checked on Gillian's progress again. "Better. But try to make your stitches more even, each one the same. And watch that you don't take too much material into the stitch. It still has to fit his arm when you're done else you'll have to take the stitches out and start again."

Marissa demonstrated once more before resuming her seat. At least the girl improved with direction, so she wasn't totally hopeless, but Marissa was truly concerned about Gillian's lack of skill. After Marissa went back home, Gillian would be in charge, but her attention seemed on flighty matters. Mostly she seemed to want to spend time with Kellen. And, Marissa had to admit, Kellen seemed to feel the same about her.

How could one so lacking in skill attract a man? She was pretty, certainly, but beauty didn't get the work done.

Lady Yvonne smiled sweetly at Gillian. "Lady Corbett, 'tis admirable how well you work with the child. Perhaps 'tis because you seem such a child yourself. Might I ask thy age?"

"I'm twenty-four."

Lady Vera rolled her eyes. "Thy true age, Lady Corbett. Though you act no more than four."

"I am twenty-four," Gillian said, her tone firm.

Lady Vera's brow crinkled as she lowered sewing to her lap. "Truly?"

"Truly."

Marissa slowly lowered her own sewing, shocked to realize Gillian told the truth. She was older than Marissa had realized. How awful. "I had thought you younger than thy sister. You've never married? You have no children?"

"Nope. Never been married. No children."

"At thy age?"

Gillian sighed and glanced up. "At twenty-four I'm hardly in my grave yet. My biological clock isn't even ticking."

Pity for her burned in Marissa's chest.

Lady Vera finally took a breath. "You must forgive our shock, but you are so old."

Lady Yvonne jumped in. "You must feel gratified that Kellen is willing to take you in. Is he aware of thy true age?"

Gillian laughed. "Kellen is five years older than I am. I don't see the problem. Would you want to marry him off to a child?"

Marissa tried to hold onto her pity, but it was hard to feel sorrow for one who did not regret their own sad plight. Besides, her throat had tightened uncomfortably. Her own husband was twenty-three years older than she. Did he see her as a child? Was that what bred his lack of interest?

Gillian glanced up from her work. "So, what age did you ladies marry?"

Lady Yvonne straightened proudly. "I was but fifteen when I wed. Were my husband still alive, we'd be celebrating our eighteenth year of marriage."

"Oh. I'm sorry for your loss. Thirty-three is so young to be a widow."

Marissa's eyes widened at Gillian's quick calculation, but she only said, "Lady Vera wed at fourteen, and I married at the age of eighteen, but only because my betrothed had died. It was needful for the king to grant permission for a new match, else I'd have married sooner."

"So young," Gillian said.

At least they hadn't been so old. "By the time I was your age I'd borne two children."

"You are Kellen's stepmother, right?"

Stung, Marissa nodded once and resisted lifting a hand to her face to check for wrinkles. "I am barely older than Kellen."

"So, you must be a lot younger than your husband?"

"Yes."

Gillian shrugged. "Well, May-December romances work out all the time, right?"

Romances? Again, Marissa felt the sting and grasped for something to say. "There is not much time for romance in a marriage. I take joy in running the household, in doing my duty, and in my two young sons."

Gillian lowered her stitching, a look of incredulity spreading across her face. "No time for romance in marriage? That's a sad thing to say. It sounds like the two of you need some time away together. Something certainly needs to change."

The pity on Gillian's face offended Marissa and she swallowed past the tightness in her throat. "People do not change."

"People change all the time. They just have to want to." Gillian looked around. "Did you say you have two sons? I've only seen the one."

Marissa glanced to where her young son sat on a blanket, playing with a wooden sword, and her heart filled with love and grief. "Quinn, my child of eight, has recently been fostered to Lord Waldegrave."

Gillian looked shocked. "Fostered? What is it with you people and farming your kids out? Eight is too young for a child to be separated from his parents. Don't you miss him?"

Miss him? Marissa's eyes burned as she bent over her sewing. She ached for him, worried for him, and prayed hourly he was being treated with kindness. She could only hope Lady Waldegrave cared for him with the love of a mother.

"I'd never allow anyone to separate me from my children."

At that, Marissa lifted her head. "You'll not have a choice."

"We'll just see about that, won't we?"

The challenging words and stubborn tilt of Gillian's chin had Marissa's brow drawing together. She wondered if perhaps Gillian would get her way in this. Marissa had no doubt the first thing Kellen would do when he returned was search for Gillian. If he continued his infatuation within their marriage, mayhap he'd indulge her.

How did she do it? Putting vanity aside, Marissa knew she was pretty, yet she couldn't seem to hold her husband's attention more than a moment. And this . . . this . . . unskilled . . . well she could hardly be called a girl . . . this woman, so effortlessly received what Marissa would give her eyeteeth to have. Her husband's caring, his attention, and . . . affection.

Lady Vera lifted her chin and glared at Gillian. "Your education certainly seems to be lacking. You don't appear to know anything about the way of things."

"Yes," Lady Yvonne concurred. "'Tis quite sad, actually."

Marissa was aware her ladies were responding to her distress over her son, and that she should intervene. But she could not make herself.

Her chest burned, and bitterness crept like acid up her throat. Why should this girl have it all? How did one such as she receive everything, while Marissa, who worked herself to the bone, was barely noticed?

Marissa bore and taught her children, planned food stores, menus, she kept her husband's home comfortable and well run. She sewed, embroidered beautiful tapestries, and kept herself attractive.

This girl planned outings, field days, and the like. Frivolous activities. She wanted to swim, to see sights, and Marissa had no doubt Kellen would accommodate her. The girl brimmed with an unfounded confidence. Yet, how could she? She did not know the first thing about running a keep. And her speech was strange. A trait Kellen simply seemed to find charming.

And if she had sons, would she have them wrenched from her if she did not desire it? Or would her husband abide her wishes out of his love for her?

Marissa couldn't sit with Gillian another second. She stood, and startled, her ladies followed suit.

"Are we done?" asked Gillian.

Marissa started toward the door. "You are not. You will sit

there until the work is done correctly. Even if that takes the whole night through."

As she exited the room, she could still see Gillian's confused face and was dismayed at her own shrewishness and for taking her inadequacies out on the girl. But all the same, she could not stay another moment. She had to get away before she did something stupid and out of character. Like burst into tears.

CHAPTER 19

*H*ours later Gillian finished darning a sock, tugged at
the stitches to see if they'd hold and, satisfied they
would, set it down in the finished pile. She looked at the sewing
still to be done and closed her eyes.

She felt like Cinderella but was trying hard not to have a pity
party. She didn't have the time. There was still at least half the
clothing to be mended. Beatrice had come in and offered to help,
but Gillian hadn't let her. The last thing she wanted was Marissa
believing Gillian hadn't done the work.

Kellen's stepmom was a certified witch, but regardless, Gillian
was determined to prove to the woman that she did *not* have a
lazy bone in her body. This went beyond her reluctance to do
Edith's work. Gillian's reputation was on the line. She'd finish
every bit of the mending and would do an excellent job.

She quickly sewed a small tear on a pair of boys' hose and held
them up to check for more rips. She thought she was getting
better and faster, too.

Anyway, it hadn't been all bad. For the first time since she'd
been there, she'd actually had time alone to think and had come to
a decision.

She was taking Kellen and Amelia with her.

Yes, she'd only known him a short time, but Edith didn't know him at all, so Gillian refused to feel guilty for stealing him. She had strong feelings for him and was convinced he did for her, too. She'd be a wonderful mother to his child. They could have a great life together.

So, rather than miss him like crazy, she'd just take him with her. The twenty-first century had a lot to offer.

They could live in the house her parents had left her. It was nothing like his castle, but it was a good-sized home. Once he'd tried the food, the entertainment, the *bathroom*, he'd be hooked. He could find a job—probably some type of outdoor physical labor—and they'd be happy together. Make more babies. Raise a family.

She tried to picture him living and working in Seattle. Perhaps he could work a job in construction? Or as a police officer or maybe a fireman? A gardener? She sighed when nothing seemed to click.

Here, he was already in his element. A knight-in-shining-armor, running his castle, training his men. She was having a hard time picturing him anywhere else.

Still, technology had a lot to offer. *She* had a lot to offer. Maybe she could tempt him?

"Gillian?"

Kellen's voice broke into her thoughts and she glanced up to see him poking his head into the room. When he spotted her, she smiled. "I was just thinking about you."

He looked pleased and a little shy, his gaze falling as he entered the room. "Missing me, I hope? I searched everywhere and none seemed to know of your whereabouts."

He'd bathed. His masculine face was clean-shaven and his hair damp on his shoulders. The long shirt and belt he wore didn't hide the well-developed muscles of his chest and arms. Maybe he could learn to play football? He might like that. She couldn't help the sappy grin she was positive adorned her face. She really didn't want to lose him.

"Do you wish to join me in the kitchens to find some supper?"

Forcing herself to stop ogling, she glanced instead at the sewing pile. She was hungry, but determined to finish. "Not yet. I still have a lot of mending to do."

"I could help."

"Really? I thought this was considered women's work. Since when do big, strong, handsome," she drew the last word out and grinned at him, "knights sew?"

"Ah, flattery." Kellen grinned and closed the door. "Now you'll not be able to rid yourself of me. Leastways, two will finish more quickly and we can be on our way."

"True." Suspicion had Gillian's brows drawing together. "But do you even know how to sew?"

Kellen crossed the room and retrieved another candle, bringing it back to hold the wick against the flame beside her. "Not many women grace the battlefield, yet there is still torn clothing aplenty. I was a squire once, and had to sew my lord's clothing as well as my own."

He shrugged. "Of course, that was years ago and expected. I must issue a warning. If you happen to mention that I helped you this day, I will, of course, have to slay you."

"That sounds ominous." Gillian smiled as she retrieved another needle and threaded it for him. "How exactly will you do me in?"

Kellen hesitated, and Gillian glanced up. Suddenly serious, his smile gone, he said, "There are many and varied ways I am capable of doing the deed, though I will say I do not count poison among my skills. I tend to be more forthright."

He was talking about Catherine. Well, Gillian was sick and tired of Catherine and the damage she'd done this man. He'd been playful only moments before and she wanted that back.

"I never thought you did. But what about drowning? I bet you could make it look like an accident if you tried. You could tell everyone we were going swimming and when you return alone you could fake tears and that would be that."

Kellen laughed. "Too much effort, especially the weeping part. Besides my dagger is sharp and handy."

Gillian grinned. "But think of the mess. What if you arranged a horse riding accident? Everyone knows I can't ride. Or better yet, what if you threw me off a cliff, or placed a snake in my bed?"

Kellen smiled, then chuckled, almost as if he couldn't help himself. "Again, 'tis all too much effort. Adders are especially difficult to find. I suppose I must needs keep you and suffer the ribbing my men are sure to give."

"You're assuming I'll talk. I won't, you know. All your secrets are safe with me."

Kellen glanced up, a quick upswing of his head as he studied her face, before he snatched up a piece of clothing and searched it for damage. Long enough for her to see the vulnerable, seeking expression. She breathed out slowly. Catherine had a lot to answer for.

"Tell me about the stolen cattle. Did you get them back? I hope no one was hurt?"

Kellen shrugged. "We found our men tied up and, other than a few scuffle marks, unharmed. We found most of the cattle and have two men in the dungeon." His sudden smile was edged with satisfaction.

"Will you try and retrieve the missing cattle?"

"'Tis pointless." When he finally looked up again, his expression was unreadable, the earlier traces of vulnerability gone. "They are long away by now and the further into Scotland they go, the more likely we are to face ambush and loss of life."

He really was a good leader. He cared more about his men than his pride. As Gillian watched the play of candlelight on one of Kellen's high cheekbones, she realized the sappy expression was probably back on her face.

Kellen finished the shirt and held it up for her inspection. "Well? What think you?"

He'd done a better job than she could have. "Not too shabby."

"Do I receive payment?"

"What kind of payment?"

"You are sure you have no more of the chocolate?"

She chuckled. "I wish. It really is all gone."

"I suppose." His look was sly. "I will have to settle for a kiss then, as payment."

Gillian glanced at Kellen's mouth and, suddenly breathless, barely refrained from licking her lips. "Settle, huh? I don't think so. Anyway, that's hardly fair since you're the one who tore it in the first place."

Kellen crossed his arms and narrowed his gaze. "You would deny me payment?"

"Are you going to pout if I do?"

Kellen glanced away, his brows drawing together. "Nay."

"You are!" She laughed. "Well, perhaps I'll kiss you when the work is all done."

"I always think it best to deliver payment as work is completed."

Gillian laughed. "For each piece? An installment plan?"

"Yes, I wish for an installment."

"All right." Still smiling, unable to resist, she leaned forward. "One kiss."

Kellen quickly took advantage of her capitulation and leaned in and fitted his mouth to hers, kissing her gently. He coaxed her mouth open and tasted her, making her boneless, making her moan.

She lifted an arm and slipped it around his neck and Kellen dragged her across his body. Her other arm rose of its own accord to circle his neck. She was getting dangerously addicted to him. To his taste and—

The door creaked slightly as it swung open. *"Saints protect us!"*

Gillian scrambled back as Kellen let her go.

Marissa's shocked expression was quickly replaced by a glare directed at Gillian. "I leave you to work and this you do instead? Have you not the pride to fulfill your duties?"

Heat fired Gillian's cheeks. "Uh . . . I was actually sewing," Gillian pointed to her pile. "And got quite a bit done. This was the first time I'd stopped working since you left."

"Do you take me for a fool?" Marissa turned and pulled the door closed behind her.

Gillian sighed and looked at Kellen who didn't seem upset in the least. She glared at him. "Well?"

"Yes?"

Gillian gestured frantically toward the closed door. "So much for impressing the woman. Now I'm not only a sluggard, but a slut."

"A slut?"

"A wanton."

Kellen laughed. "I could but wish."

Gillian sank back with a laugh of her own. She looked over at the pile of clothing still to be done. "Well, no point in continuing now." She turned to an unrepentant Kellen and his smile irked her. "But for the record, you're a jerk."

He laughed. "Shall we go down to supper now? Or we could stay here and finish. I find I'm not as hungry for food as I had believed."

His eagerness made her laugh. "If we stay here, I'm sewing. I'm not risking her coming back and finding us making out."

"Making out?"

"Kissing, necking, smooching, snogging, sucking face. Whatever you call it."

Kellen laughed and leaned in, obviously intent on kissing her again.

"That's it." Gillian stood. "I'm out of here."

Kellen scrambled to his feet. "No, wait. I must needs discuss this sucking of face with you."

"Not another word." Gillian was out the door before he reached her.

~

AFTER THE MORNING fast had been broken, Kellen knew he should leave. He had much to do but lingered anyway.

Marissa and her ladies moved to sit by the fire and, after a flatteringly long look in his direction, Gillian followed. Kellen, unable to help himself, followed too, stopping nearby to lean against a whitewashed wall.

After they'd *raided the kitchen* the night before, as Gillian had named their foraging, they'd sat in the great room before the fire until complaints from those trying to sleep had sent them abed.

Kellen smiled at the memory of Gillian's dread of bedding down with Marissa. He'd offered to let her sleep with him; but she'd rolled her eyes at the suggestion, so he'd walked her to her chamber instead. The lack of privacy had allowed for but a few kisses, leaving Kellen yearning for more throughout the night. He couldn't wait until she was his the whole night through.

Marissa sat with her ladies and sorted through the mending, checking the clothes and Gillian's work. "Lady Corbett, I'm pleased with what you've accomplished." She held up a shirt. "Look here. If you but decide, you are quite capable of doing an adequate job."

Recognizing the shirt as the one *he'd* sewn, Kellen pushed himself off the wall. "Adequate?" He asked, offended.

"Yes, adequate. The stitches are not precisely even," Marissa said. "But 'tis a start. She is doing well enough."

Kellen leaned back and crossed his arms while Gillian, her face turned toward him, struggled not to laugh.

"As you did so well last night," Marissa continued, "you may now demonstrate your skill at sketching."

Gillian squealed, ran over, grasped Kellen's hand, and tugged him toward a chair. He offered little resistance.

"Sit here." Gillian was gleeful as she pushed him down, then pulled up another chair and sat across from him.

"Gillian, I cannot stay. I have much to do. My men are no doubt waiting for me to show myself."

"Oh, come on. Please?" She wasn't even looking at him, but digging in her pack, sure he'd give in. He sighed. For her, he would. "To please you," he said. "But I will demand payment."

She chuckled and jumped up to give him a quick kiss on the cheek. "Payment."

He shook his head at her but couldn't help smiling at her contagious joy. She gave him a slow grin that had his heart speeding as she arranged him to sit as she desired, his legs outstretched, hands enfolded on his lap.

He was gratified at how easily she touched him, something his first wife avoided even after four years of marriage. Gillian smoothed a hand down one of his legs and patted his knee.

"Aye, touch me wherever you like," he said quietly. Gillian winked at him and his grin broadened.

"Now sit still and don't fidget." Gathering her paper and sticks, Gillian seated herself and studied his face a moment before beginning her sketch. She looked carefree, her blue eyes shining, a half-smile on her full lips. He was pleased she was settling in. She was fast becoming Kellen's weakness and he wanted her happy.

He quickly reminded himself that he possessed no weaknesses and anyone who said otherwise would not live to tell the tale.

"Don't scowl. Just give me a slight smile."

Amelia entered and wandered over to see what Gillian was doing. "Amelia!" exclaimed Gillian. "I have an idea. Come and stand beside your father. Now Kellen, I want you to put your left arm around her."

Again, Gillian arranged them to her satisfaction, moving their bodies into position. "There. Perfect. Now don't move."

Kellen was rigid, the tiny body next to his own, no less so. He didn't like being this close to the girl. He didn't want to look at her for fear he would see she was not his, that he was raising another man's child. One of his men's? He was determined not to think on it. To wonder if one of his own had betrayed him.

"Relax, both of you."

The child, stiff and unbending, stood for only a few minutes before jerking free and running away.

"Amelia, come back!" Gillian tried to coax the child into returning but to no avail. The girl ran out of the room and, looking confused, Gillian asked, "What was that about?"

Kellen shook his head. "I did nothing."

"Well, I wasn't accusing you of pinching her. I just wondered why she left." Gillian shrugged and picked up her sketch. "I'll put her in later. In the meantime, keep your arm up as if she's still there."

"Lady Corbett," Marissa called out. "You do not have the day through. You must finish soon. There is work to be done."

Gillian mouthed "there is work to be done" along with Marissa and rolled her eyes, making Kellen stifle a laugh. Then he wondered if she was being made unhappy, if perhaps he should send Marissa away?

He glanced over at the ladies, working industriously. No. Marissa was teaching Gillian well. He wanted her settled and wanted her to take her rightful place. Marissa would make sure she was comfortable in her role, and after the marriage Gillian would have none to gainsay or arrange her time.

"Kellen," Owen came into the room. "There you are, lazing about as always, I see. The men are training and wondering what you are about."

Gillian waved a hand. "I'm keeping him. Go away."

Her words produced a warm glow in Kellen's chest, and

embarrassed that his feelings might show on his face, he lifted a fist to his mouth and cleared his throat.

Tristan came inside. "What are you doing? Sketching?" He moved forward to look over Gillian's shoulder. "No, no. You are making him too handsome."

Gillian withered him with a stare. "Go away, Tristan."

"Wouldn't you rather use your talent to sketch a well-favored face?"

Gillian snorted. "Yours, I suppose?"

"If you insist, I could be persuaded to—"

"Leave!" Kellen said.

Tristan sent him a disdainful glare. "Come, Owen. As ever, it looks as if we will have to train the men ourselves."

Kellen snorted and watched them go.

After she'd been busy a few minutes more, Gillian spoke. "I need to ask you something."

"Aye?"

"I was thinking we could take a walk today. Out to the cemetery. You, me, and Amelia. Just the three of us. What do you think?"

Kellen's brows drew together. Again, with the cemetery? "Nay."

Gillian stopped sketching and looked up. "Why not?"

Kellen rubbed the back of his neck. "'Tis not safe."

"It's just outside the village. We'd be with you. What's not safe about that?"

Kellen tried to think how to deny her. "What captivates you thus? Cemeteries are nasty, gloomy places, fit only for the ghosts that haunt them."

"I just want to go."

"Another time?"

"Soon?"

"Of course. When we both have a free moment, we will get my men together and—"

"No. Just the three of us."

He was suspicious again, but could not fathom what she could be about. Was there someone waiting? A man she hoped to see? A lover she wanted to leave with? And if so, did she think Kellen would be easily overpowered? The idea was ludicrous. "For what purpose?"

"It'll be fun."

Kellen didn't want to take her to the cemetery. Not with the thieving Scots about, and not when the hair rose on the back of his neck in warning every time she mentioned the blasted place. It wasn't likely she could have a romantic tryst in mind. Not with the child there. And by the saints, it was a graveyard!

"Okay?"

What was she hiding? She was tying him in knots. Her sister Catherine had ever been secretive. She'd met with a man somehow, and been so tightlipped about it, Kellen had not been able to find the culprit.

Gillian's face was open, without guile. But she had such a different way about her that she was still difficult to read. Where women were concerned, he didn't trust his instincts anymore.

Kellen was relieved when Owen came back in the room. "Kellen? A word with you?"

"I must leave."

"No!" Gillian said. "Just a little while longer."

Marissa lifted her head. "'Tis best he goes. He has much to do, as do you."

Kellen looked into her distressed face and desired to give her whatever she wanted. Within reason.

Tristan came up behind Owen. "Is he coming?"

Kellen gave Gillian one last searching look and realized Catherine was making him doubt Gillian. He knew it wasn't fair to her, but didn't know how to feel differently.

Marissa glanced over. "Gillian?"

Owen gestured from the door. "Kellen?"

Before Gillian could protest, before Kellen could even be tempted to stay, to accuse or apologize for suspecting her of foul deeds and worse, he vaulted out of his seat and hastened after his men.

CHAPTER 20

A week later, in the middle of the night, Gillian yawned widely, not bothering to cover her mouth or look away from the sketch she worked on. No one else was around anyway.

To say they'd been keeping her busy was an understatement. Marissa and her ladies were slave drivers, granting very little free time, and zero access to Kellen. Not that he'd seemed to mind.

To add insult to injury, after keeping her busy every day, Marissa had tried to stop Gillian from drawing at night, scolding her for staying up late, for wasting candles, and for keeping Marissa awake with the scratching noises.

Gillian smirked at the memory of *that* particular accusation. The feather-light sound of her pencil was completely drowned out by Marissa's soft snoring. It was nice to see the paragon wasn't perfect.

Gillian bit her lip to try and hold back a smile as she sketched, knowing she shouldn't be mean. Marissa might not be warming to her, but all the same, she was teaching Gillian all she knew and, if she were actually staying, it would be very useful information.

She used a finger to smudge the curve of Kellen's jaw on the page, creating a shadow and softening the line. She was just about finished with the portrait and was happy with how it was turning out. She stared at Kellen's masculine face, the full lips, high cheekbones, neck and shoulders thick with muscle. Yummy. The man was gorgeous, no doubt about it.

Amelia's petite form nestled within Kellen's arm, her pixie little face, so lifelike it almost looked like a photo. Dealing with Amelia's wiggling and squirming had turned out to be well worth it. The likeness was good. This might be the best family portrait she'd ever done. It would make a fantastic gift for Kellen. She just hoped it wasn't a goodbye present.

Gillian turned to look at the snoring woman on the bed and wondered if Marissa would wake if Gillian snuck out to see him. He'd been avoiding her the entire week and Gillian was starting to feel desperate. She needed to get him and Amelia out to the cemetery, and for some reason he was against taking them. Perhaps if she sneaked to his room and had a little chat with him she could lure him with her feminine wiles.

Gillian grinned at the thought and glanced at the door. Should she chance it? She deserved a little free time, right? She'd certainly done her part lately. She knew how to plan a menu, discuss said menu with Cook, keep kitchen accounts, instruct servants, mend, instruct spinners and weavers, plan a wedding feast, and check wheat for mold.

While the work itself wasn't bad, and was even quite interesting at times, she really needed to kidnap Kellen and Amelia; and no one was making it easy for her. She was busy. Kellen was busy. Everyone was busy. But she had to get them out there if she wanted to take them home.

She'd been thinking about it and had come to the conclusion that there had to be a reason she'd been sent to Kellen. A reason for the attraction and connection they'd felt from the beginning. That being the case, there had to be a way for the three of them to get back, so they could be together as a family. She was starting to feel very possessive. Edith could find a new guy. Kellen belonged to Gillian now.

She was pretty sure Amelia would be fine. Kids adapted quickly. But she wondered how Kellen would react to the twenty-first century. If he could go. If he *would* go. If he'd be happy if he did. Gillian was starting to wish there was some way she could stay. Medieval England was definitely missing some basic necessities, but overall, she was sort of getting used to it. If Kellen couldn't or wouldn't go with her, she wasn't sure she'd have the will power to leave him.

She sighed. It wasn't as if she'd have a choice. How would Kellen react when Edith showed up? He'd be shocked, hurt, angry. Would he put Gillian in the dungeon? Arrange a hanging? Keep her as his mistress and marry Edith? Gillian wasn't going to chance any of it.

In the morning, they were supposed to meet with the priest. The banns were to be posted, whatever that meant. Maybe afterward she could talk him into going.

Still tempted to see him immediately, Gillian carefully inserted her sketchpad into her pack, put away her art supplies, blew out the candle, and sat in the moonlight, shadow, and glow of coals from the fireplace. As Marissa snorted, Gillian smiled and looked at the door. She just might risk it. So what if she got caught? It wasn't as if Marissa held a very high opinion of her as it was and anyway—

As she watched, the door slowly, silently opened and someone eased into the room. Kellen? Gillian smiled. Great minds thought alike. She looked to where Marissa snored softly. If she caught Kellen there, she would raise an unholy racket, but the risk was worth it.

Glancing back, she suddenly realized the wraithlike figure was too small to be Kellen. She watched the shadow start toward the bed and whispered, "Hello?"

So quick she almost didn't see the motion in the murky darkness, the guy lifted his arm and threw something just as Gillian stood and took a step to the side. At the sharp thwacking noise, Gillian looked behind her. The moonlight revealed a dagger protruding from her high wooden chair.

If Gillian hadn't stood, she would have been skewered in the neck.

Shocked, heartbeat speeding, Gillian put a hand to her throat and turned her head; but it was all she was capable of doing. The man moved a few more steps toward her; and finally, after a choked gasp and a quick scramble backward, Gillian was able to scream.

Marissa sat upright, instantly screeching, adding her voice to Gillian's. The shadowy figure took one more step forward, hesitated, then melted into the darkness and out the door.

Gillian stopped screaming to stare after him, her heart pounding hard and her breath coming in gasps. She looked at the chair then at the door again. If it weren't for the knife, she could almost believe it hadn't happened.

Marissa stopped mid-scream. "Gillian?" She sounded breathless, scared. "What has happened?"

Kellen ran into the room and this time there was no mistaking his large form for anyone else and Gillian, shaking and relieved, started to cry as she stumbled toward him.

Kellen rushed forward and pulled her into his arms. "What is it? Are you well? Did you have bad dreams?"

"Someone . . . someone . . ."

After skimming his hands up and down her body, he lit a candle and Gillian pointed to the chair and the knife. His face disbelieving, he asked, "Are you hurt? Where did you get this blade?"

"No. I'm not hurt. A man was in here." She shuddered. "I was sitting in the chair and he threw the knife at me as I stood."

Kellen ran his hands over her body a second time, then lifted her into his arms and crossed to the bed. He stuffed her under the covers next to Marissa and; looking dangerous, he grabbed the knife, studied it, then thoroughly searched the room before posting a man outside the door. He turned back, giving Gillian a stern look. "Stay here. Bar the door."

Fine with her. She wasn't going anywhere. Someone had just tried to kill her.

Kellen left, yelling for his men as he went.

"FIND HIM!"

As his men rushed to the roof and down to the great hall Kellen searched above-stairs, looking behind curtains, under furniture, and out windows to see if a villain hung, or climbed a rope to the roof. Whoever tried to kill Gillian needed to be captured. So Kellen could personally kill him.

He glanced back toward Gillian's door. He did not dare move too far from her bedchamber, though he knew the women had it barred. Why would anyone want Gillian dead?

Owen came out of the ladies' solar and shook his head. "I found naught."

Tristan ushered Marissa's ladies out of their room. They were visibly upset and Lady Vera repeatedly hit Tristan who had an arm raised to defend himself. "None hid in the ladies' bedchamber. I searched everywhere."

Lady Vera's eyes burned fire as she continued to slap Tristan. "And used the opportunity to touch my underclothing!"

Kellen raised a brow.

"Not apurpose!" said Tristan. "I was searching for a villain!"

Lady Vera hit him again.

"Enough!" Kellen turned away to search the corridor. "Take them to Lady Marissa." He noticed the boys standing against one wall, wide-eyed and frightened. "Did any intrude upon your room?"

Peter shook his head. "No one, my lord."

Kellen turned to Owen. "Take the boys, also. Make sure Lady Marissa bars the door."

Kellen checked the boys' chamber himself but found it empty. As he exited, three of his men came down from the roof. "Well?"

"Nothing, my lord."

Kellen's teeth clenched as his frustration grew. Three more of his men came upstairs. "Did you find anything?"

They all shook their heads. "Nothing suspicious, my lord. We questioned all below stairs, but none report anything amiss."

Kellen felt blood rushing to his face as he tried to hold his temper. "How can a murderer slip in and out of my keep? Threaten my lady?" His voice rose with each word. *"Find him!"*

Kellen checked Gillian's door, found it barred, waited to see if they would open it and, when they did not, told the guard to stay put and headed down the hall and descended the stairs. When he reached the great hall, he looked around. His people were visibly frightened and Kellen didn't see any who did not belong.

Another guard came into the room. "The outer gates are all secure, my lord. None passed that way."

Kellen nodded once. "Detain any who look in the least suspicious, even if they are known to you." His frustration levels mounted as he looked around. It could be anyone, any of his men, his guards, his knights, his servants.

He again wondered about Catherine. Who had been her mysterious lover? One of his own men, perhaps? Was this revenge for her death? Had she even spoken true? Had there ever been a lover? Or was the attack related specifically to Gillian? Or to himself?

He studied the knife he'd confiscated, but it yielded no clues. It was ordinary, one any knight could own or any peasant steal. Its sharpness reminded him of its former location in the chair, directly at throat level.

Gillian could have died.

He felt himself sweating and wiped his brow as two more of his men came in. "There is naught to report from the village. All has been quiet. None saw any pass who did not belong."

Kellen seethed. "We've missed something. Search again. Question everyone."

Nodding, they left.

Kellen studied his people gathered in the hall, their expressions nervous, fearful. Some stood, some sat on sleeping pallets, but none slept. He studied each face. They were all familiar to him. He moved forward and ripped the hood off an adolescent. The boy screamed, defensively raised his hands and, recognizing the lad, Kellen let him go.

He didn't want to believe it could be one of his own people. Perhaps it was the Scots? Had men come in to rescue their own and plotted revenge? If so, how did they get in? How was it they weren't seen?

He would question the Scots sitting in his dungeon. But first, he would question Gillian again and see if she'd remembered aught. See if she was still safe.

CHAPTER 21

*W*hen Lord Marshall grabbed Valeric by the shoulder and ripped the hood from his head, Valeric screamed, defensively raising both hands to protect himself, awaiting a blow. Lord Marshall only searched his face a moment, then let him go and, without a word, moved away.

Valeric stared after Lord Marshall's retreating back in disbelief. He'd thought himself caught. He'd thought himself *dead*.

Breathing hard, Valeric watched Lord Marshall walk away, heart pounding so hard he wondered if he might die this night, regardless. Perhaps his treacherous heart would stop of its own accord and save Lord Marshall the trouble of slaying him.

On boneless legs, he backed the few feet to the wall and slid down to sit among the rushes, pulling his knees close and wrapping his cloak tight about him. He listened to Lord Marshall shout orders, and the hunger that had been with him for years surfaced once more. Why could not Lord Marshall have been his sire rather than Sir Royce? Would Lord Marshall have acknowledged him? Would he have trained him up to become a knight?

Shame had his eyes closing. That dream was now impossible. He'd tried to harm a lady. He'd tried to *kill* a lady. He leaned his head against the wall and fought against the tears burning his eyes. A lady who had been nothing but kind to him. Now he could never be a knight.

And what of Lord Royce? When he found Valeric had failed, what might he do? To him? To his mother? He considered staying at Marshall Keep and never returning to Royce Castle. In any case, he could not set forth. They had men everywhere, searching, watching. But he could not leave his mother unprotected.

All here knew and accepted him as one of their own. Lady Catherine had seen to that when she'd needed a message boy in place for her trysting with Sir Royce.

Might he not help his mother escape somehow? Find her a place, either here or in the village?

He opened his eyes to watch Lord Marshall until he moved out of sight, still shouting. He wished he could trust him enough to ask for aid, to beg protection for his mother at the very least; but did not doubt Lord Marshall would kill him if he realized he were the culprit. And then what would happen to his mother?

He took a shuddering breath and lowered his head to his knees. He hadn't actually hurt Lady Corbett, he reminded himself. He hadn't *wanted* to hurt her. He'd been relieved when she was unharmed. Perhaps he had missed apurpose?

He rubbed his face against his hose, wetting the material with the tears he could not seem to subdue. He remembered the accuracy of the blade and knew nothing could excuse his behavior.

After he'd thrown the knife he'd been more shocked than Lady Corbett and walked a few steps into the bedchamber to assure himself she was unharmed. When she'd screamed, he'd realized she thought he was coming to finish the task.

He lowered himself to the ground, curled into a ball of shame and tears, and realized that he was, indeed, his father's son.

~

THE TENSION in the room was unbearable and, when someone pounded on the door, Gillian jumped, Vera gasped, and Yvonne placed a hand to her chest. Only Marissa slid off the bed where they were ensconced in furs and blankets and hurried to the door. "Who is there?"

When Kellen identified himself, Gillian let out a breath as Marissa unbarred the door. When he came into the room, he was tight-lipped and stern; but Gillian was relieved to see him and scrambled off the bed and hurried over with Yvonne and Vera, asking questions with the others.

Kellen put both hands in the air. "Enough!"

When everyone fell quiet, Gillian put a hand on one of his arms. "Did you find the man? The one who threw the knife?"

Kellen gave a curt shake of his head. "Not yet. Come." He took her arm and ushered her first toward the chair, then changed directions and, when they reached the bed, grasped her waist and effortlessly set her on the high mattress. He put pillows behind her, propping her up, and pulled a blanket across her legs. When he'd arranged her to his satisfaction, one of his hands gripped the nearest bedpost, and he looked down at her. "I need to hear every detail, no matter how trivial. All you remember."

Feeling slightly overwhelmed by the way he was looming and still shaken by the attempt on her life, Gillian nodded, drew her knees to her chest, and hugged them. She still couldn't believe someone wanted her dead, that someone had snuck into her room in the middle of the night to accomplish the deed.

As a woman who lived alone, she'd always checked and rechecked the doors and windows and set the alarm before going to bed. Here, inside a fortress, with a big, burly, overprotective man down the hall, she hadn't given it a thought.

She took a breath. "When the guy came into the room, I'd just barely blown out the candle and was sitting in the dark." She gestured toward the small table. "I was actually looking at the door when he slipped in the room or I might not have seen him because he was so quiet. At first I thought it was you."

Gillian felt her face heat a bit as she remembered planning to sneak to Kellen's room. "But then I realized he was too small; and I whispered to him, and the next thing I knew there was a knife in the chair. If I hadn't stood when I did . . ." Gillian placed a hand at her throat and swallowed.

"How much smaller than me?" Kellen barked out the words. "Who is of similar size?"

Gillian's brows drew together as she remembered how the guy had strode toward her, how they'd been about the same height. "Actually, I don't think he was much bigger than I am."

"Could it have been a female?"

Gillian looked at the three ladies standing at the foot of the bed. Vera and Yvonne looked affronted, Marissa calm. Gillian shook her head. "The way he moved, it seemed like a man."

Kellen's face tightened with frustration, and Gillian wished she had more information to give.

"Mayhap it was a youth?"

Again, Gillian shook her head, trying not to be irritated by his snapping. "I don't think so. The knife hit hard, and I'm assuming it landed where he'd intended it to. Wouldn't that take a lot of skill?"

Kellen walked a few feet away, his hand lifting to rub his neck before he turned back. "You did not see any feature that set him apart? Hair color? Clothing?"

Gillian shook her head. "No. It was dark and he was dressed in dark colors." She watched Kellen continue to pace back and forth. "I wish I knew more."

"Surely there must be some tiny detail you have left off?" His tone was sharp, again.

Gillian's mouth tightened for a moment before she took a breath. "Well, sure I do. But I'm purposely hiding what I know." She threw out a hand. "Bring out the thumbscrews or you'll get nothing out of me."

Kellen gave her a narrow-eyed glare then jerked his head toward the door. "Why was the door not barred?" He was getting louder. "*It must be barred every night!*"

Gillian's chin lifted as she leaned forward. "I didn't realize I needed security in my own bedroom." She threw out a hand. "Maybe you should post a guard outside the door or get me a big dog since I'm obviously the target of a madman and I'm *completely without protection!*"

Both of them were breathing hard as they glared at each other. Only the opening door had Gillian glancing away to see several of Kellen's men come into the room. She raised a hand to gesture, palm up, toward the door. "*You* didn't bar the door."

Kellen gave her a fulminating glare then turned to his men. "Well?"

Sir Owen stepped forward. "'Tis bedlam outside, my lord. Word of the assassin has spread and many are panicked, seeing shadows, ghosts, and murderers."

Gillian didn't blame them. She didn't feel safe, either.

Kellen started across the room and Gillian lifted a hand. "Wait! I want to ask you something." When the men turned back, she continued. "Is there any way this could be related to Catherine's death?"

Kellen turned back toward her. "I cannot deny there might be a connection." He stared at a spot above her head. "If I had found the man responsible for turning Catherine from her duty, it may have prevented this attack."

"But I don't understand why you haven't already figured that out?"

Kellen's teeth clenched as he bit out, "I tried."

Gillian didn't know what to say. She hadn't meant to offend him. She just saw him as super-competent and was genuinely surprised he hadn't found his wife's cohort and dealt with him accordingly.

With a growl, he turned away. "You will stay in your bedchamber on the morrow."

"What?" She got to her knees. "No! Why should I? You told me you'd keep me safe!"

Kellen kept walking. *"I will!"*

"But I want to go home!"

At the door, Kellen stopped, then turned back, his gaze icy. It was the first time he'd looked at her like that, almost as if he hated her. "You are home." The words were cold, hard, final. He turned and left, jerking the door closed behind him.

Gillian, stunned by his harshness, by everything that had happened, burst into tears.

As Yvonne rushed to bar the door, Marissa walked around the bed and pulled Gillian into her arms and stroked her hair. "He did not mean to be so heavy-handed. As a male, being told he is inadequate is the worst of insults."

Gillian managed to sob out, "But I never said that!"

"Whether you said the actual words or did not, he believes you think it," Marissa said.

Vera cut in. "Never tell a man he cannot protect you. 'Tis devastating to their ego."

Yvonne stroked Gillian's back. "Very true. Either they will rush off to prove you wrong and get hurt, else they will cease caring and go into a depression of the spirits. Either way, 'tis not a good idea."

Gillian's chest ached as she continued to cry. "Kellen hates me. I could see it in his face."

"Shh," Marissa stroked Gillian's cheek.

"And . . . and . . . someone is trying to kill me! I mean, I knew I could die of the plague or the pox or something, but a knife in the throat? What is that about?"

Yvonne continued to rub her back. "Hush now. You will make yourself ill. 'Twill all be sorted in the morning."

Gillian remembered the way Kellen had looked at her and cried harder.

Marissa tried to calm her. "Shh. Sit up now. Dry your tears. This is no way for the lady of the house to carry on."

They pushed her into a sitting position and Gillian wiped her face with the cloth Marissa provided and tried to stop crying.

Vera handed her a cup. "Here. Drink this."

After a few hiccoughing sobs, Gillian drank a bit. "Ugh," she made a face. "It's nasty."

"Drink it down," Marissa insisted. "'Twill make you feel better."

As soon as she'd finished, they tucked her in and Gillian wondered if perhaps she'd been wrong about the culprit being a woman and if she'd just been poisoned, but couldn't work up the energy to care.

Eyes closing, she buried one side of her face in the pillow, and her breath continued to hitch as she struggled to suppress more tears. "I'm not supposed to be here. You know that, right? In the morning, I'm finding a way to go home."

"Shh," Marissa tucked the blanket around her shoulders. "Of course you will, dear."

Gillian finally slept.

LATE THE NEXT AFTERNOON, there was *finally* a knock and Gillian's level of anger flashed to boiling point as she leapt off the bed and hurried to the heavy door. "Who is it?"

"'Tis Kellen. Unbar the door."

Mouth tight, Gillian shook her head. What a piece of work. Without so much as a word he'd left her to twiddle her thumbs the entire day, then showed up giving commands. She had no intention of making this easy for him. "How do I know you aren't a murderer? One can never be too careful about these things."

"Nay, my lady," an earnest voice responded. "'Tis truly Lord

Marshall." Her guard, anxious to please after trapping her inside the entire day, was no doubt relieved to offer the good news. She crossed her arms and glared at the door, torn between throwing it open to let Kellen have it, and forcing him to stew in the hall.

Easy decision. After the day she'd had he could cool his heels. "But how do I *know* it's him? It could be anyone. It could be a murderer who's also a voice impersonator. I saw this guy in Las Vegas who—"

"Gillian! Open this door! Now!"

She hesitated, considering. She didn't want him to disappear in a huff before she finally had the chance to give him a piece of her mind; so she lifted the bar, swung the door wide, and glared at Kellen.

He stared back, face impassive, his amber gaze raking up and down her gown-clad body before he moved forward, forcing her to step back. He crossed the room, pulled in the sheet she'd dangled out the window, lifted it up and looked at the painted words. Throwing it across the bed he asked, "What is written here?"

"Trapped in the tower. Call 911. But maybe it should have said 999. It might have brought better results here in England."

His brows furrowed. "What does it signify?"

Gillian stepped forward to admire her handiwork. "It means rescue me. I *thought* with all those knight-in-shining-armor types running around I'd get a few takers, but *apparently,* you're all a bunch of poseurs." She glared at the guard hovering in the doorway, and Kellen, following her gaze, quickly dismissed him.

He sighed. "Gillian, you are well aware keeping you thus is for thy protection."

Gillian's fists clenched. "The other ladies weren't confined to quarters. Only me." Her eyes started to burn and she looked down, unwilling to cry and suffer swollen and gritty eyes again.

She took a calming breath. "I hated being grounded as a child and I find it even less appealing as an adult."

"Gillian." He reached out, held her arms, and tried to draw her forward, but when she jerked away he sighed again. "I understand your anger with me. 'Tis my fault you were not kept safe. 'Tis a mistake I won't repeat."

"What are you saying?" Her calm deserted her as she threw a hand in the air. "I get to be confined to my bedroom for the rest of my life so you don't make any mistakes?"

He gritted his teeth. "'Tis only until I find the culprit."

"Did you find him? Or is it visiting hours in the prison?"

He stood a bit straighter. "I've not yet discovered the villain, but I swear I'll not rest until I do." He held out his hand. "Come. Make peace with me. The priest has returned and summoned us both."

Gillian thought of refusing, but wasn't about to miss the chance to leave her cell. Instead she crossed her arms and lifted her chin. "After you."

Kellen's hand dropped; he turned and led the way, and Gillian was left with the impression she'd hurt his feelings. She hesitated, a pang of guilt making her wish she'd simply taken his hand; but then she remembered the long stay in her bedroom, hardened her heart, and followed.

When they reached the great hall, servants were setting out tables and benches and getting ready for supper, but there was no sign of Marissa and her ladies.

Beatrice rushed forward. "My lady? Is there anything I can get you?"

Gillian shook her head. "I'm fine, thank you."

Beatrice glanced uneasily at Kellen, then bent forward to whisper. "I managed to procure some pheasant feathers. If you would like I can sew some onto the hem of your blue gown?"

Gillian glanced at Kellen who waited impatiently. "Uh. Feathers. Yeah, I don't think so. Maybe later we can think of something else to do with them."

Beatrice looked so crushed that Gillian almost changed her

mind, but she didn't want to be kicking feathers around every time she wore the dress.

Once outside, Gillian looked toward the castle gate just as Kellen stopped to wait for her; and he intercepted her glance. "I would catch you well before you reached the gatehouse. And were I not here, I have ordered the guards to deny you passage. You'll not escape me, Gillian. This *is* your home now."

"Do you have to be so irritating? Maybe you'll be the one who doesn't escape me; did you ever think of that? And maybe once I have you where I want you, I'll lock you in my bedroom all day and see how you like it."

A laugh escaped him, quickly stifled. "As you will, my lady." His carefully neutral tone and the realization that it would take him about two seconds to break down her Seattle bedroom door, earned him a heated glare. She said nothing more as they crossed the bailey yard, side by side, in silence.

When they reached the open chapel entrance, Kellen offered his arm; but any soft feelings she'd felt earlier were well and truly squelched. She ignored him and walked the few steps into the chapel.

The priest, a plump, middle-aged man wearing a black robe, a brown bonnet that did nothing to hide his thick salt-and-pepper hair, and a cross at chest level, must have been waiting. He immediately came forward. "Welcome, welcome, Lady Corbett!"

Gillian politely stuck out her hand and the priest took it in both of his, a delighted smile on his kindly face. "I am so happy to know you. I am Father Elliot."

"It's nice to meet you, Father."

"I am so pleased Lord Marshall is to wed again and to such a beautiful maid. 'Tis not right for one such as he to be alone."

Gillian wiggled her hand loose. "Why not? He doesn't mind it when I'm all alone."

The priest looked surprised and glanced between the two of them.

"You must forgive her," Kellen said. "Lady Corbett is not herself this day."

The priest nodded. "Of course, of course!" He turned to Gillian. "You are not to worry, my dear. Lord Marshall will make a fine husband. You are lucky to be wedding such a one as he."

"*I* am the fortunate one," Kellen said.

Father Elliot's mouth fell open and he looked a bit shocked. "Of course, of course! I meant no offense." He turned to Gillian.

"All are excited for the wedding, my dear. The clothing, the romance, the dancing, the drink, the food." He placed both palms on his stomach and smiled at Gillian. "Most especially the food. Wedding feasts are beyond compare. Do you not agree?"

Gillian managed to keep her eyes on the man's face and not on his protruding belly, but couldn't hide the smile, which he quickly noticed.

"Ah," he chuckled. "So you do. Good, good. I'm pleased with Kellen's choice of bride. You come from an esteemed household. Your father, Lord Corbett, is an outstanding example of courage and nobility, and his wife the image of grace and beauty. A fine family."

Gillian noticed he didn't mention Catherine. She wasn't about to bring her up, either.

Father Elliot turned to Kellen. "Did you catch the culprit who dared to infringe upon Lady Corbett's bedchamber?"

"We are still searching. I gather you arrived last nightfall?"

"Aye, I did."

Kellen silently regarded the man.

Father Elliot's eyes widened. "But surely you do not believe *I* had aught to do with the attack on Lady Corbett?"

Kellen hesitated, then said, "The man who attempted this crime is of similar size to my lady."

Father Elliot, looking relieved, laughed and patted his belly. "None will mistake me for a delicate female."

"No. But the tutor under your direction is quite slender, is he not?"

The priest's mouth fell open again and he took a quick breath. "I can assure you we had naught to do with any deviltry."

Kellen simply stared, saying nothing. The priest seemed to be trapped by Kellen's gaze, prey to his predator; and Gillian, feeling sorry for him, finally interrupted. "So, what are we here for?"

The priest was visibly relieved by the change of subject. "Come, come." Waving his hands around, inviting them further inside the stone chapel, he rounded the altar and said, "Now I am returned, 'tis time to post the marriage notice on the chapel doors."

"What for?" asked Gillian

He looked surprised. "'Tis required, my lady. I will write thy names on the notice, and if any come forward with valid reasons why either of you cannot wed, the marriage will be prohibited."

Gillian shifted from one foot to the other. Would the fact that she wasn't actually Edith Corbett be a valid consideration? "What sort of reasons?"

Kellen stiffened beside her and when she glanced up, his jaw tightened.

Father Elliot glanced between the two of them and cleared his throat. "Ah, if either are married, or have taken vows of celibacy, or are perhaps too closely related. None such applies to you?"

Gillian shook her head. "Not to me." That, at least, wasn't a lie.

Kellen relaxed. "Nor me."

The priest flattened out the paper, dipped his quill, and looked at Gillian expectantly. "Tell me thy full name, my dear."

Gillian bit her lip, and looked from one man to the other. "Shouldn't we wait until my parents get here to do this?"

"No, indeed. We would do this even had you not arrived."

Gillian thought a moment. She had no idea what Edith's full name was and couldn't begin to guess. Taking a breath, she wondered if she was about to give herself away. "Edith Gillian Rose Corbett," she said, giving Edith's and her own name.

She watched them closely, but neither man seemed to think anything was wrong. Kellen was simply watching the priest, almost with satisfaction, as he wrote slowly and carefully then sat back to admire his handiwork before beginning again.

"And Lord Kellen William Spencer Marshall." Father Elliot wrote as he spoke each name.

Gillian, relieved that the jig wasn't up, smiled at Kellen.

"It's nice to meet you."

He smiled back, a bit hopefully. "Aye, my lady, 'tis a pleasure."

Gillian remembered she was mad at him and looked away. "Father, maybe you should fill out my death certificate, as well. You know, just in case. That way I won't put Kellen to any more trouble than I have to."

The priest's mouth fell open once more.

Kellen took a deep breath and put up a hand to rub the back of his neck. "Gillian." He growled her name. "I would simply keep you safe. And, whatever you believe, you are no trouble to me. I am most anxious to please you."

Gillian turned to him hopefully. "Do you mean that?"

He lowered his hand and nodded. "Aye," he said fervently. "With everything in me."

She held out both hands and he quickly grasped them in his own. As the warmth from his skin and eyes engulfed her, she swallowed. "Then take me to the cemetery. Come with me." *Come home with me.* She couldn't say it out loud but tried to convey how much this meant with her gaze.

Kellen looked conflicted and she held her breath as she waited for his response. Then his face hardened and she let out her breath, knowing she'd lost.

"Nay. Your safety is all that matters."

She jerked her hands out of his grasp. "You're never going to take me, are you?"

"I will when it is safe. I swear it."

When it was too late, she thought, but didn't dare say the words out loud.

"The cemetery beyond the village?" Father Elliot sounded confused. "They say that it, as well as this chapel, was blessed by Saint Cuthbert himself, a known miracle worker who . . ."

As Gillian looked at the stone floor and listened to the priest prattle on, desperation overwhelmed her. Someone was trying to kill her. Edith and the wedding party would show up who knew when, and when they did, Gillian was in so much trouble. If she hadn't already been murdered, she'd be locked in the dungeon or worse.

For her own piece of mind, she had to at least see if she could get back. Once she was actually in the cemetery, she had no idea what would happen. Would she simply go back to her own time or find she had some control over the situation? Maybe she'd be able to stay a while longer to try and persuade Kellen to go with her. But either way, she had to know. Even if it meant she'd never see him again.

Unexpected pain rippled through her and tears filled her eyes as she turned her head to look at him. She really did like the big goof. She might even love him.

Whatever anger she'd been harboring melted away at his pained expression, and she held out her hands to him once again. He quickly grasped her fingers, kissing the knuckles of first one hand, then the other, gazing into her eyes as he did so. Maybe it would be okay. Maybe she'd find she could come back for him.

But tonight she'd give him the drawing, just in case it really was goodbye.

Tears spilled over and she dipped her head.

"Ah, good, good," said Father Elliot. "A love match. 'Tis just as it should be."

CHAPTER 22

*K*ellen paced while he waited at the base of the stairs and noticed Owen try, and fail, to hide his smirk. "You are sure to wear a path in the stone if you continue thus, my lord."

Tristan didn't bother to hide his grin. "True, but perhaps we can find a use for such a rut. We could fill it with water for the dogs to drink, or store fish in the winter months. 'Tis a brilliant notion, my lord. Continue on."

Kellen shook his head and glanced to where Royce stood flirting with the ladies at the head table; leaning over them, his oily charm a success if the smiles and laughter he earned were any indication.

No. Better to ignore his men and intercept Gillian before Royce tried to attract her attention. Kellen wanted to ensure the lout didn't so much as speak to, look at, or touch Gillian. And if Kellen had to suffer the ribbing of his men to achieve that end, he would do so gladly.

She finally appeared, her guard trailing behind. She'd changed into a green gown, and her blonde hair caught the torch light for a moment, shining brightly as she descended. The slight smile on her face indicated she wasn't upset or angry and Kellen exhaled. He did not wish to fight with her.

As she halted a few feet above him, he finally noted the flat package she carried under one arm, wrapped in linen, a blue ribbon tied at its center. "Who is the gift for?"

"You'll have to find out along with everyone else, won't you?" She stepped down and entwined her free arm with his. As they walked into the great hall, Kellen was not surprised to see Royce saunter over to intercept them. No doubt he'd been watching for Gillian.

"Lady Corbett! I have heard of the attack on thy person and have come to offer my support."

"Thank you, Sir Royce. That's very kind of you."

With one hand occupied with the gift and the other clutching his arm, Kellen was pleased Royce had no excuse to touch her. As Gillian chatted with Royce, Kellen signaled to his men; as arranged, they hurried to sit on the benches surrounding the ladies, taking every available space.

When he led Gillian to the head table, he was gratified by Royce's frustrated expression as the dolt realized there was nowhere for him to sit. As Royce was about to protest, Kellen called out, "Music!" and the musicians in the corner immediately started to play, their timing perfect, as Kellen helped Gillian into her seat.

He had not cared to let the performers inside but wanted to please his lady more, and so he had instructed his men to watch them closely.

Royce, stiff, looked around as Kellen took his own place, well satisfied with the arrangement. Royce turned to join his men at the next table, when Marissa called out, "Wait! Sir Royce, you must come sit between myself and Lady Corbett. Everyone slide down to make room."

His men looked at him helplessly. "Go on," said Lady Marissa and, reluctantly, they did as she asked.

Royce, all smiles now, took his seat and Kellen fumed, pulling Gillian close to his side as the meal was brought around.

Gillian clapped as the musicians ended their first song. "Where did the band come from?"

"Can I not spoil my lady if I so choose?"

"You're just hoping the present is for you." She indicated the gift, now propped a few feet away against a wall.

Kellen laughed. "Is it?"

Gillian lifted a shoulder, smiled, and turned her attention toward the musicians once more.

Kellen leaned closer. "Do you like the performance?"

Gillian nodded. "I love it. I hadn't realized how much I missed music. I used to listen to it all the time when I was drawing."

"Who played for you?" asked Kellen.

Gillian shrugged. "I like all sorts of music. One of my favorite English musicians is Elton John, or I guess I should say, Sir Elton John."

Jealousy swamped Kellen at the thought of Sir John playing for her as she sketched. He wondered that her mother had allowed such as Gillian obviously thought on the man with affection. Perhaps he was a eunuch.

As they ate, he brooded as Royce flirted with Gillian, thankful Marissa kept pulling his attention away.

"Lord Marshall," Royce said, addressing Kellen for the first time. "I understand you hold several Scotsmen in your dungeon."

"Aye."

"Have you questioned them?"

"Of course. They claim to know nothing of Lady Corbett's attack."

"Ah. Do you believe them?"

"No. I've sent a message to their laird. I'll trade his men in exchange for any information that might be of use to me."

"Ah. Of course."

As everyone finished eating the first course, Gillian stood. "I have a gift." She paused as everyone looked up. "For Lord Marshall."

Everyone clapped as she retrieved the gift and handed it to Kellen.

"What is this for?"

"Your birthday?"

"'Tis four months' past."

"Consider this a belated birthday gift. But you have to guess what it is before you can open it."

Kellen, his chest tight, held the flat package in both hands. "Is it a new sword?"

Gillian smiled. "No."

"Armor?"

She laughed and so he tried to think of something more foolish and absurd. "A horse?"

Everyone laughed now. "You are horrible at this," Gillian said. "Open it."

He untied the bow and pulled off the linen to reveal a portrait of a man sitting in a chair, a girl leaning against his side. He turned to look at her. "This is me?"

She nodded. "And Amelia. The blacksmith was able to make the frame for me. He didn't think it was fancy enough, but I'm really happy with the rustic way it turned out. I just wish I had a piece of glass to protect . . ."

Gillian's words washed over him as he stared at the portrait. Her skill was unbelievable. Their faces were so lifelike. Of course, he'd seen his reflection in still water before, and in the smoothness of his shield. Catherine had owned both a polished mirror and a water bowl, but surely Gillian had made him more handsome than he truly was?

"I wanted you to have it."

At her saddened tone, he glanced up. Was she trying to tell him something? Did she want peace between them as he did? A true marriage?

The ladies surrounded them. "Your skill is amazing," Marissa breathed. "You've captured their faces exactly. Look how much Amelia looks like my son, Quinn."

Gillian's brows rose. "The one I haven't met?"

"Aye." Marissa traced the shape of Amelia's nose, mouth and eyes, not quite touching the paper. "See here? All Marshall features."

"Aye," agreed Lady Vera. "Though, of course, Quinn's eyes have Marissa's blue color, while Amelia's are amber like Kellen's."

Kellen looked at Amelia's likeness, then at his own face in the portrait. Everyone knew of his wife's infidelity, but there was no denying the resemblance. Kellen was astounded to realize the ladies were correct.

Which meant Catherine had lied. Amelia *was* his child.

His chest tightened and his throat constricted as he looked at Amelia's little face. She *was* his daughter. Ever since Catherine's death he had not allowed himself to believe. He had done his duty by the girl but had not so much as looked at the child if he could help it.

"Well? Do you like it or not?" asked Gillian.

He didn't dare lift his gaze until his emotions were under control.

"Kellen?" she pressed again.

He cleared his throat and was finally able to answer. "Your talent has overwhelmed me." The words came out hoarse, but audible.

Marissa nodded. "'Tis amazing. I see why thy mother never made you learn castle work. They no doubt kept you busy with thy incredible talent. I would ask you to do a sketch of my two boys. Mayhap at Christmas you might travel to Hardbrook Hall? I could call Quinn home for the event?"

Gillian hesitated, but finally nodded. "If possible, I will be glad to."

Kellen's chest filled with pride. "I will place this in my bedchamber in the place of honor."

Gillian grinned. "You'd remove the wolf skin from off the wall for me?"

At her teasing, Kellen smiled. "Surely you ask too much. Mayhap I can spare a dark corner of the chamber."

Everyone groaned as Gillian struck him in the shoulder.

Kellen laughed and glanced toward the stairs. "I wish to see Amelia. Perhaps someone should go and fetch her?"

"The child is no doubt asleep," Marissa chided him. "She can see it in the morning."

Kellen wasn't sure *he* could wait until morning to see *her.* Again, he fought tears back.

Gillian had no idea what she had given him this night.

She had given him back his daughter.

HAND SHAKING, Robert set his spoon down and tried to make his face blank as the rage bubbled inside him.

The portrait showed the truth. He could not deny the girl looked like Marshall. That she was, in fact, Marshall's daughter. Robert had always loved the thought that Amelia was *his* baseborn child. That Kellen was forced to accept and raise a child of *Robert's* seed. It would only have been fair as Catherine had loved *him!* Had lain with *him* at every opportunity. By all accounts the child should have been his, as well as Marshall Keep and everything in it.

How did everything always turn to Marshall's advantage?

Robert glanced at Gillian. While her sister's eyes had only been for him, Gillian barely deigned to look in his direction. Once again, Marshall had everything. Why did the goddess Fortuna *always* smile upon him? Did he wear a lucky toad around his neck? Cast runes? Control the very fates?

And why *did* Gillian feel naught for Robert? Had Catherine truly been the love of his life? Did Gillian sense his heart was already taken and so settled for Marshall? He calmed at the thought. That must be it. Otherwise, Gillian would fall under his spell as Catherine had, as all the ladies did. Ultimately, it was Catherine with her soft looks and touches who should be at his side and not her inferior sister. This was unbearable.

Marshall and his harlot needed to feel the pain that Robert felt. With luck, they would both die before dinner was finished. Only then would Robert's misery finally come to an end.

Robert nodded at his servant who, as instructed, had ingratiated himself with the staff and helped serve the dinner as Robert and his men had caused extra work. The man dipped his head once, an almost imperceptible movement, then moved away. After he did his work, he'd melt away to help elsewhere, a shadow no one quite remembered.

Everything in place, Robert turned to smile at Gillian; but once again her back was to him as she spoke with Kellen. It was an insult, of course, indicating that she found Robert tiresome.

He forced himself to smile and chat with the other ladies who more than welcomed his attention. This was not to be borne and would not be for much longer.

His man returned with a platter, but another intercepted and took it, lifting a spoon and taking a few random bites. A food taster! The man took one last bite then set the platter between Gillian and Marshall.

Robert could not move his gaze from the morsel of meat Gillian picked up and lifted to her mouth. Happiness overwhelmed him and he tried to hide his expression by taking a drink of wine. Yes. Take a bite. Just one should do it.

The food taster knocked over a platter and a jug of water when he went down, but still, Gillian's food was almost to her mouth. Just one little bite . . .

GILLIAN WAS STARTLED when Kellen knocked the food from her hand then grabbed her mouth, squeezed her cheeks together and looked inside. She smacked his shoulder and jerked away. "What are you doing?"

Kellen grabbed her chin again and forced her to meet his gaze. "Did you take a bite?"

Shocked by his behavior, his savage demeanor, she didn't answer; he stuck his finger in her mouth, running it around. Gagging, she pushed him away. "Kellen, please, what are you—"

"Did you eat anything?" His voice was louder this time.

She looked down at her platter. "N . . . no," she stammered.

"Did you drink?"

Her breath caught in her throat; she looked at her goblet and nodded as Kellen grabbed her drink and sniffed it then gave his own drink the same treatment.

She heard the whispers. *Poison.*

Fear gripped her and she slowly stood. "What's going on?"

The crowd parted and to her left she could see a man on the floor and watched as others helped him to sit up. Moaning and clutching his stomach, he vomited into a bowl that an old woman held to his mouth.

Gillian searched the crowd to see worried and fearful faces, people crossing themselves, and leaning to whisper to neighbors. She lifted her gaze to Kellen. "Someone poisoned that man? I don't understand. Why?" she asked, and pressed a hand to her pounding heart.

Kellen didn't answer but ordered someone to help the healer and make the man comfortable as they carried him out. He instructed Marissa to take the ladies up to their chamber and to stay inside with the door bolted. They were not to eat or drink anything. Kellen scanned the crowd.

Marissa tugged Gillian away.

"Someone was . . . was . . . poisoned?" Gillian asked again. "But why?"

"It was your platter that was tainted," Marissa said. "Your food taster."

Gillian stopped walking. "A food taster? What do you mean?"

Marissa gave her a push to get her going again. "Lord Marshall is a cautious man. Things are not as they seem here."

"Someone really wants me dead?"

"You and Lord Marshall, it would seem."

"But why?"

Marissa shrugged. "'Tis what Lord Marshall will discover."

Gillian paused to look back at Kellen. He was shouting commands to lock the doors. No one was to leave. He turned to meet her gaze and his was as hard as granite. She shivered and let Marissa drag her away.

A HALF HOUR later Kellen's fists clenched and unclenched. First someone tried to stab Gillian then poison her? Who? Why? It made no sense.

He could fool himself no longer. When Catherine had tried to kill him, she'd had help; someone had turned her against him, and that someone was now a threat to Gillian. The fact that he'd never found Catherine's accomplice made this his fault.

Tristan and some of the guardsmen excused a group of servants and approached. "Any witnesses?" asked Kellen.

Tristan shook his head. "None remember who brought the platter; and other than a girl positive she saw demons flickering in the fire, none saw anything suspicious."

Owen came into the hall and everyone stopped talking to watch his approach. He halted before Kellen and took a deep breath. "Frederick is dead. He could not give a name."

Tristan swore.

Kellen's mouth tightened and he looked at the ground. When he'd assigned Frederick as food taster, the man had been pleased to have the important task. No one, least of all Kellen, had truly believed the position a dangerous one. "Question the guards at the gates. Someone must have noticed something."

The men turned and left.

Who were his enemies? Men he'd bested in battle? Or angered by having the King's favor? And they'd sent assassins across the whole of England to kill his betrothed? Ridiculous.

He glanced to where Royce stood questioning servants in the middle of the hall. Granted, there was no love lost between them, but Kellen still considered him an ally. Besides, Royce had nothing to gain by Gillian's death and had not been around when she'd been attacked with the dagger. Kellen headed to join him. "You were seated at Gillian's side. Did you notice aught amiss?"

Royce gave an angry shake of his head. "Nothing. Would that I could name the blackguard who desires Lady Corbett's death. I have questioned each of my men and many of the servants and they saw nothing awry. I suspect treachery from the north."

The Scottish? Kellen doubted it. He scanned Royce's men, but again, suspicion failed to take hold. Royce would not benefit by Gillian's death.

"What can I do?" asked Royce. "I would help in your investigation of the matter."

Kellen shook his head. "We will manage the search."

Royce's mouth tightened, but he nodded. "I understand. The less people milling about the better. But do not hesitate to call upon me if I might be of assistance."

Kellen followed Royce and his men outside, watched as they mounted up, and wondered at Royce's earlier assertion. Could it be the Scots? Two of their men resided in his dungeon. But the Scots generally dealt in physical attacks: rescues, ransoms, thievery, and the like. Not poison. And what would Gillian's death profit them? If they murdered a lady, their men would be executed, there would be war, and they could gain nothing by antagonizing England. If they wanted their men back, they had only to return the cattle. Killing Gillian would accomplish naught.

Owen and Tristan returned. "No strangers were seen lurking about, and no one suspicious passed through the gate," said Tristan.

A growl issued from Kellen's throat as he went back inside, his men following. He could not fight who he did not see.

Group by group, the stragglers were questioned then sent on their way. The dwindling crowd was a relief after the earlier madness. Kellen headed for the kitchens and, upon entering, found Cook crying. She looked up at his entrance. "Is Frederick truly dead?"

Kellen hesitated, then lips tight, nodded. "Aye. 'Tis true."

Cook turned away and started cleaning, banging pots and pans, instructing servants to throw out food she had doubtless worked the day through to prepare.

"I am truly sorry about Frederick. I know he was a friend to you. We will find his murderer." He paused. "Did any come in here who should not have?"

Cook shook her head. "No one came in but Lady Gillian herself. No food left this kitchen poisoned, I can tell you that. I do not let just anyone dally about." Cook grabbed a piece of cooked meat, lifted it for Kellen to see, and stuffed it in her mouth. As she chewed with difficulty, tears ran down her face.

Kellen put a hand on her shoulder. "I assure you that I do not distrust your loyalty in the least. I have known you my entire life and none could be so entirely above reproach as yourself."

Cook swallowed, nodded, and wiped her eyes; but the tears continued to flow as she turned away.

Owen and Tristan appeared in the kitchen doorway. Tristan elbowed Owen, and sighing, he pulled Kellen aside. "In considering the matter," said Owen, "I note that on most occasions, poison is a woman's weapon."

He shifted on his feet, his cheeks reddening, but his gaze remained steady. No doubt he thought on Catherine, but Kellen couldn't care less about her at the moment and only nodded.

"Marissa, her ladies, and Gillian are the newest members of the keep," said Owen, his tone careful.

Brows rising as he caught Owen's meaning, Kellen shook his head. "Nay. Marissa and her ladies could have no motive for killing Gillian."

Tristan and Owen exchanged a glance. "If you were to die, Marissa's elder son would be heir to your father rather than yourself; but regardless, I agree. I do not suspect Marissa, nor her ladies."

He hesitated, looked at Tristan who nodded again, then continued. "But Gillian's sister tried to kill you. Perhaps this day you were the target again, and not the Lady Corbett. The platter was to have fed you both. Perhaps she'd not meant to dine?"

Kellen shook his head again. "I knocked meat from her hand as she was about to eat."

"But she did not actually partake, did she?" asked Tristan.

"Someone attacked her with a dagger also, remember?" Kellen said. "She is the target."

Owen took a breath. "We have only her word there was an assassin. A common knife was found and she the only witness."

Kellen remembered Cook's claim that Gillian had gone to the kitchen before the meal started. Perhaps to arrange something? Immediately he shook his head. If it was Gillian, she was the best player he'd seen in his life. He'd known Catherine had despised him, but Gillian's feelings seemed quite the opposite.

But she did continue to try and leave the keep. To visit the rocks and the cemetery. To meet someone? To acquire poison left by another? Did she blame him for her sister's death? Or for her broken betrothment? Would she have Kellen dead rather than wed herself to him?

His chest tightened and, turning away from his men, he waved a hand. "Go talk with the men. See if they have learned aught."

They left, but he could not erase the suspicion forming in his mind and burning deep in his stomach. Perhaps Gillian was simply more clever than her sister? Did she think to gain his confidence, draw mistrust from herself, then kill him?

He had never asked about her broken betrothal but thought on it now. If Kellen were dead, would she return to a former love? Or was her father the enemy? Had her father ordered both his daughters to kill him? Did Lord Corbett desire his death?

Closing his eyes tight, he lifted a hand to rub his forehead before turning and heading up the stairs. He needed to speak to Gillian. If she knew anything, he would get it from her.

CHAPTER 23

"*W*hy would anyone want me dead?" Gillian paced across the floor to the fireplace, tremors occasionally running through her body. She turned her back to the flames, hoping to capture some warmth. "I mean, poisoning? Seriously? The whole thing is . . . it's just . . . *crazy.*"

The three ladies, busy with embroidery, looked at each other; and Marissa set her sewing in her lap. "Perhaps it has naught to do with you? Perhaps Kellen has an enemy and you were simply in the way?"

"In the wrong place at the wrong time?"

Lady Yvonne nodded. "Aye, just so."

Gillian couldn't help a laugh and wasn't surprised when the ladies exchanged another glance. Even she could hear the touch of hysteria. "Then I guess I'd better get back to the right place at the right time. *Aye?*"

All three sets of brows furrowed and Marissa lowered her sewing once more and motioned toward the maid. "Beatrice, help your lady to lie down."

Beatrice jumped up, but Gillian hugged herself and snorted. "Yeah, because I'd be able to sleep."

As Beatrice subsided to her chair once more, Vera shook her head but, needle flashing, didn't look up. "Sarcasm is never becoming. If you refuse to lie down then why not sit and—"

There was a knock on the door, and Gillian hurried forward; but Marissa, who jumped up faster than Gillian would have thought possible, beat her to the door. She leaned her head close to the wood. "Who is there?"

At Kellen's harsh but recognizable command, Gillian scrambled to help Marissa lift the bar and open the door.

Once inside, Kellen's sharp-eyed gaze scanned the room, lighting on each woman. When his attention moved to her, Gillian crossed the space between them, threw her arms around his waist, and pressed her head to his chest. He tensed and, when he didn't reciprocate or react in any way, Gillian slowly sank away, looking up to meet his harsh gaze.

"What's the matter?" she asked.

"Frederick is dead."

Gillian's hand flew to her throat and she took a step back.

"The food-taster?"

Kellen nodded once.

"It was poison?"

Kellen nodded again and continued to study her, his gaze penetrating.

Feeling vulnerable, she turned away. The room, Kellen, the ladies, everyone and everything suddenly seemed so foreign, unfriendly, and frightening. She pressed a hand to the ache in her stomach and shook her head. "This isn't right. This just isn't right. Did he have a family? A wife? Children?" She glanced back to see Kellen shake his head.

"He was unmarried. None will carry his name, though he did have many friends and will be sorely missed."

Tears filled her eyes. Kellen watched a moment longer before turning to answer the questions Marissa peppered him with.

Gillian pivoted away. The room spun and she grabbed the

back of a tall chair to steady herself. People didn't die of poison. In her whole life, she'd never known one person who'd died of poison. But here . . . Catherine had died, and now a man was poisoned with food meant for them?

She wiped a hand down the front of her gown and stumbled as she walked to the window and looked out, seeing nothing. She had to get out of there. All along it had been a given that she needed to leave before Edith and her family arrived, but now she needed to go before someone actually killed her.

She lifted a hand to her throat, remembering the dagger. Whether this was about Kellen or not, it felt very personal. Like someone wanted *her personally* dead. Because she was Kellen's fiancé? She had to get out of there.

She turned to look at Kellen. The thought of leaving him tore her apart. What if he missed her as much as she was sure to miss him? What if he would go with her if she only had the courage to tell him everything? What if she would be saving his life too?

Kellen was still talking to Marissa but glanced up, as if feeling Gillian's gaze. "I must needs question Gillian. Alone."

Marissa hurried forward to put an arm around her. "Now is not the time. Note how pale she is. The girl has been through too much this night. On the morrow is soon enough."

Gillian shook her head. "No, it's okay. Really. I want to talk to Kellen."

"Nay." Marissa's tone was firm.

After one brief frustrated glance, Kellen turned to the other ladies. "Come. I offer escort to thy chamber. You need not fear, I am well aware of whom the murderer targets." He looked at Gillian.

Gillian put a hand to her throat. "Do you know something you haven't told me? Do you know who the poisoner is?"

Kellen stared for a long moment before shaking his head. "Not yet."

After they left, taking Beatrice with them, Marissa barred the door; and they started to undress, neither speaking as they went about getting ready for bed. Gillian pulled a nightgown over her head. Why had Kellen been so indifferent toward her? He'd been icy cold, his expression grim.

She huffed out a half-sob, half-laugh. How should he act? His friend had just died instead of the two of them. She was freaking out, why shouldn't he? If only she'd had a chance to talk to him about it, to comfort him over his friend's death, to be comforted.

"Do you feel unwell?"

Gillian climbed into bed. "I feel sad."

"That is to be expected. But worry not, Kellen *will* find the murderer and he *will* be punished."

It still wouldn't change the fact that Frederick was dead, and it didn't change the fact that Gillian couldn't do this anymore. She couldn't make any more half-hearted plans to go home. She had to go. But that didn't mean she had to be happy about her decision.

Marissa's breathing grew heavy, and Gillian turned onto her side, tears filling her eyes and dampening her pillow at the realization that this was likely her last night here.

She was going to miss Kellen so much. She wished she could stay. She wished things were different. That she really was Kellen's fiancé. That they loved each other and could raise a family together. That no one was trying to kill her.

She'd give up a lot to have him: modern medicine, her career, indoor plumbing, and chocolate. But she wasn't willing to give up her life. Especially since he probably wouldn't want her anyway once Edith arrived with her bags of gold, her land, and her family connections.

Or would he?

That was the thought eating at her. What if he would choose *Gillian* if given the chance?

She remembered how he'd looked when he'd left the room. Cold, indifferent, frustrated.

What if that was the last time she ever saw him? What if he were busy in the morning or gone when she got up? What if she never got the chance to ask him to go with her or to say goodbye?

Some time later Gillian slid out of bed to the sound of Marissa's soft snores. If this was her last chance to see Kellen, if only to say goodbye, she was taking it.

KELLEN HAD ALMOST TALKED himself out of his suspicions and was considering his warm bed, when he heard the scraping of a bar being lifted. Immediately tense, he straightened from the wall, moved back into the shadows, and waited.

The door opened and a small figure slipped into the darkness of the hall, her motions furtive and stealthy, the blonde hair that flashed in a slice of moonlight unmistakable.

Trying to rein in his doubt, to excuse her somehow, to squelch the dark suspicions rising within him, he watched and followed silently as Gillian made her way down the hall.

Perhaps she simply wanted to make use of the garderobe? Or mayhap she was hungry? After all, she'd had little supper this eve. None of them had.

But no, she went directly to his chamber and slowly pushed the door open. His jaw clenched, and a slow burn started in his chest as his mouth tightened into a straight line.

He should have known.

He should have known she had no true feelings for him. He should have sensed that beneath the lighthearted and cheerful facade she was a betrayer like her sister.

Did she think to kill him, as well? To finish what she'd tried to accomplish earlier when Frederick had been struck down? Perhaps she thought to stab him in his sleep? Smother him?

When she slipped inside, he was directly behind her, watching by the light of the small fire burning in the hearth, blood starting to throb painfully in his head, fists clenching. Kellen had truly believed in her, in her feelings for him, in their future together.

And it had all been a lie.

Darkness spread inside him, dangerous and vicious, as he watched her approach the bed. She hesitated and he waited for her to act. Was it to be poison dripped into his mouth? A knife? At this point he'd not be surprised if she drew a sword.

She stopped short of the bed, hesitated, then took a step back, seeming almost on the verge of leaving. Had she changed her mind? Did she harbor a small bit of the feeling she'd feigned for him? Had a portion of it been real?

She straightened her shoulders. "Kellen?" she whispered his name, and took a step forward. "Kellen? Are you there?" She closed the distance and reached out to feel the blankets, then sighed as if disappointed when she realized he wasn't there.

What was she doing? He hadn't expected her to wake him. He shut the door behind him with a solid thud and threw the bolt.

Gillian whirled and put a hand to her heart. "Kellen? My goodness, you scared me."

She ran at him and he tensed, ready for anything. She threw herself at him and he grabbed her wrists, felt for a weapon, but found nothing.

"Kellen? It's me. Gillian."

Kellen slowly let her go and instantly his arms were full of soft, fragrant female. He allowed the embrace, but didn't relax his guard. Just because she didn't have a weapon at the ready, didn't mean she wasn't carrying one.

He closed his arms around her and resumed his search, hands skimming over her back, her hips, up the arms she'd lifted around his neck, kneading and tightening every few inches, sure there was a trick somewhere, a hidden danger.

She giggled and pressed closer and he realized the danger too late as his anger drained away. His breath caught and he broke into a sweat and escalated his search, bunching the sides of her nightgown in his fists, fighting his body's reaction to hers.

If he could find a weapon and prove she intended to kill him, he could protect himself, harden his heart. He truly needed to despise her right now. Before it was too late.

WHEN KELLEN'S hand touched her thigh, Gillian jerked away, startled. She tried to read his expression, but his back was to the fire and she couldn't see his face in the shadows. He reached for her again and continued his octopus impression, his hands wandering above her waist again.

Sheesh. Whatever happened to romance? She'd never tried to seduce anyone before, but was pretty sure it was supposed to start slower. His hands moved up her sides, cupping her shoulders, then around and under her chest.

Gillian gasped, jerked again, then giggled. It was sort of endearing that he hadn't had much practice with seduction and was so clumsy at it. Not that she was an expert, but rubbing his hands all over her seemed a bit abrupt. Maybe she should do the same to him and see how he liked it?

She smiled. He probably would. "Kellen, slow down. We have all night. What if we start with a kiss?"

His hands stilled. "A kiss?"

He sounded so confused she worried she'd offended him by questioning his lovemaking skills. She knew she had to be careful. She'd heard men had fragile egos where stuff like that was concerned.

She petted his chest and the muscles bunched, making her shiver in response. She looked up and tried an alluring smile. It was probably wasted as it was so dark, the fire mostly burning embers, but it made her feel enticing anyway.

"Yes. A kiss," she practically purred the words. Then thinking about the way his hands had just roamed her body she thought she might want to be specific. "On the lips."

He was still for a long moment before clearing his throat. "You left the protection of your room for a kiss?"

She nodded.

"You could have been hurt. Injured."

She smiled and moved closer. "I knew you were just down the hall. I knew you'd protect me."

The flattery didn't work. He stayed stiff and stilted, so she reached for him, placing a hand on his arm. They were in the dark, just the two of them, and *her* heart was certainly pounding. If his roaming hands were any indication, he seemed to like her well enough, too. This might be her first attempt at seduction, and off to a slow start, but she wasn't giving up.

"So," she tried to sound like a temptress. "Is that what you were doing? Checking me for injuries? Did you find anything interesting?"

As if reminded, his big hands started to move again, up and down her arms, clenching every few inches. It was almost as if he were searching her. He checked her fingers one at a time, pausing to feel her ring, then his hand went up to her hair, feeling every inch of her scalp, then trailing down its long length. She laughed again. "Kellen! What are you?—"

Was he searching her?

Surely not. She was almost embarrassed to ask. "Are you . . . are you frisking me?"

"Frisking?"

"Checking me for weapons?"

Kellen stepped back, and his hands fell away. He sighed. "None but you saw the dagger-throwing villain. And this night you could have easily poisoned our trencher when you entered the kitchen. I but thought to wonder if your father sent you to murder me, and if perhaps Catherine was trained to the task, as well."

Gillian's breath caught and her mouth went slack as she gaped at him, unable to speak.

"Gillian?"

She sucked in air and jerked away. "How . . . *how dare you!* You think I'm a suspect in my own murder attempts? You think I'm responsible for the attacks? For a man's *death!*" Her voice rose on the last word.

Moisture filled her eyes and, disbelieving, she lifted a hand to wipe away tears. Why was she crying? She'd never been so angry in her life and she was crying? She couldn't breathe, couldn't get enough air.

"So much—" she gulped in oxygen. "So much for the big seduction. I wouldn't seduce you now if you were the last man on earth. The last man in this century!" Face crumpling, she turned away. *"You can stay here and rot!"*

More tears flooded her eyes as she ran for the door. She never wanted to see him again. *She hated him!* She unbolted the door and at the last moment remembered what she'd come to say. She didn't bother to turn. "Goodbye, Kellen. Goodbye *forever!*"

She fled toward her room. She would never forgive him for this. *Never!*

~

GILLIAN HAD NOT SOUGHT to kill him but had desired to seduce him instead? Confusion held Kellen rooted to the spot. Why would she want such? Did she. . .did she bear true feelings for him?

He shook his head and the movement somehow loosened his feet, and he started after her. Who was he to think to fathom the workings of a female mind? All he knew in truth was he'd mismanaged the entire event and was the veriest of louts.

Within moments he spotted her white nightclothes floating ahead in the darkness. "Gillian, wait! I beg you, hold up!"

Moving fast, he caught up just before she reached her chamber. "Please! I beg you," he said. "Take pity on my vile and wretched self." He gently gripped her shoulders but she spun away.

"Don't touch me!"

He tried again, but she was slippery as a trout. He couldn't get a good hold without handling her roughly and, unwilling to risk hurting her, moved to block access to her room, his arms spread. "Please hear me. I am truly the worst of bunglers. I have spoiled much with my unfounded suspicions. 'Tis obvious you are no murderer. My wits had gone begging."

As she tried to slide around him, he managed to catch her wrists and hold her. She tugged, trying to free herself, making a sound of frustration when she couldn't. "You are *such* a jerk!"

She tugged again but he held fast. "Do you know that?" she said. "You're a big, fat, stupid *jerk. Let go of me!*"

"Agreed on all points. I am also a half-wit and a fool. Come back to my chamber. We must needs discuss this further."

She reared up, taut as a bow, to study his face in the darkness. "I'm not interested in talking to you." Her voice was low, yet fierce, and the underlying hurt tugged at his heart. "Or in going to your room. Or in doing *anything* with you, *ever* again!"

Turning her face, she sobbed, just once; and concerned that he injured her, he released her. She quickly ran around him into her room and shut the door. The bar dropped into place.

He grimaced, thumped the door with the side of his fist, then turned and paced down the hall before returning to knock. There was no response. He leaned his forehead against the wood. He truly was an idiot. He'd gotten it all wrong. Of course, she was no murderer. The idea was ludicrous. Where had his wits been? He must make it up to her somehow.

He paced again as he considered items in his treasury, which might bribe his way back into her good graces, when a torch appeared and two of his men climbed the stairs. 'Twas unfortunate they were not the miscreants who'd cast suspicion on Gillian's honor, thereby turning his thoughts to mush. Those two probably had more sense than to show their faces.

"My lord? All is well?" asked the knight holding the torch.

Embarrassed to be caught skulking in the hall, Kellen threw out a hand. "All is well. Go. You are not needed here."

The man lifted the torch high and waved it back and forth, apparently trying to penetrate the shadows, then with a nod, went back the way he'd come, his friend following.

Kellen knocked again and this time the door opened, only slightly, and Kellen was disappointed to see Marissa. "I must see Gillian."

When he moved forward, Marissa held up a hand. "You may see her in the morning."

Kellen could hear Gillian crying and tried to look into the room. "But I must needs speak—"

"In the morning."

"I'm never talking to him again!" Gillian half-yelled, half-sobbed.

Kellen started forward and tried to push the door open, but Marissa held her position, her body blocking the door, and perhaps her bare foot also. Kellen stopped, unwilling to risk harming her.

"In the morning," she said again.

With a growl of frustration, Kellen pivoted and stormed away. What difference would sunlight make to the situation? He doubted he would sleep a trice until he had put things to rights with Gillian. Marissa was a meddlesome busybody. Why, he wondered, had he invited her to stay?

Tomorrow could not arrive soon enough.

GILLIAN LAY on her side with the covers tucked around her and sucked in a shuddering breath as she tried to stop crying. "He is such a . . . a *jerk*."

Marissa appeared around the side of the bed and handed her an embroidered handkerchief, and Gillian blotted her eyes. "I had to work up my courage to approach him, you know?" Gillian said. "I almost chickened out, and then suddenly everything seemed to be going so well."

Gillian remembered the dark, just the two of them, his hands roaming her body. It had been a bit awkward at first, but exciting nonetheless. She snorted and rolled her eyes. "He'd *seemed* willing enough."

She took a deep breath and leaned up on one elbow. "And then he accuses me!" She patted her chest. "He thinks *I'm* the poisoner!" Another pat. "That *I* faked the knife that was thrown at *me*. I *hate him!*"

Marissa moved to stand at the end of the bed, arms crossed and lips pinched. "Then why do you cry so?"

"Because I'm mad at the big creep, *that's why!*" She sobbed out the last two words. "He's ruined *everything!*" Another sob and her face crumpled. And afterward, he hadn't made much of an effort to get her to listen, had he? *"Jerk!"*

Marissa continued to stand at the foot of the bed, arms crossed, a disapproving expression plastered to her face.

"What?" Gillian snapped. "You think I'm the murderer, too?"

Marissa waved a hand. "Not at all. I am simply concerned with thy lack of morals. This sneaking about in the middle of the night like the basest of serving girls is unacceptable. What would thy mother say? Apparently, I must needs sleep with one eye open so as to keep abreast of the goings on after dark."

Gillian snorted. "Don't bother. I certainly won't be sneaking off to meet Kellen anymore." Gillian's fist tightened around the handkerchief. "To think I was going to seduce him! That I was going to try and find a way to take him home with me. And all the time he thinks I'm some sort of murderer? Like his horrid first wife! What a suspicious *man!*" Tears pooled in her eyes again. "I'll die a virgin before I ever go near him again."

Marissa bent her head and put a hand to her mouth.

Gillian sat up in bed and sank her face into her hands. "Do you know what the problem is? Our relationship happened way too fast. Our feelings probably aren't even real." She shook her head. "His obviously weren't."

"True," Marissa agreed. "Else he'd have trusted you."

Gillian's head reared up and she threw out a hand. "But why *should* he have trusted me? He doesn't really even know me. And neither does anyone else around here. So, who is trying to kill me? And why?"

Suddenly she worried Kellen would be harmed when she left, but tried to suppress her concern. He didn't deserve it. Anyway, he was on his guard now. He'd be okay.

Gillian glowered. "If I *had* died, he'd probably forget all about me and marry Miss Perfect and Polished who no doubt already knows how to run a castle and how to live happily ever after in it."

More tears flooded her eyes. "What if tonight really was our last goodbye? What if I never see him again?" She started to cry once more and held a hand, palm up, to Marissa. "Look at what this place is doing to me? I'm a mess. I need to get out of here. That should make you happy, right? Won't you be relieved to get rid of me?"

Marissa didn't respond, and her lips were pressed tightly together.

Gillian hung her head. "The fact that I'll never see Kellen again is for the best. I'm *glad* he's not coming with me. In the future men only want to cheat on you. They don't accuse you of trying to kill them. He's welcome to his flawless, faultless wife who—"

Trilling laughter rolled out of Marissa, a deep belly-laugh, and she gripped her stomach and doubled over before finally taking a breath so she could do it all over again. It surprised Gillian enough that she stopped mid-rant. Marissa never unbent enough to smile, let alone laugh until she had tears in her eyes.

About a minute later, still smiling, wiping her eyes, Marissa finally got hold of herself. "I must say you are most amusing, Gillian."

Arms now crossed, Gillian glared at her.

"I suddenly feel grateful my relationship with my own husband is much more subdued," Marissa sighed. "I almost feel sorry for Kellen." She studied Gillian's face for a moment, then looked down and placed both hands on the bedspread, and sighed. "What you must needs remember is that, before all else, Kellen is but a man, and males are often wrongheaded." She glanced up. "For all that, he is intelligent, and will soon see the error of his ways."

Gillian glowered. "Too little, too late."

Marissa threw her hands up, laughed again, and rounded the bed. She blew out the candle on the table and climbed under the covers. "All will look better in the morning."

Hearing the smile in her voice, Gillian lay down and rolled onto the side facing away from Marissa, hunching her shoulder. "Yes, way better. Because I'm going home in the morning."

Gillian heard what sounded suspiciously like a muffled giggle.

She sighed. Tomorrow couldn't come soon enough.

CHAPTER 24

*A*nger carried Gillian away from the keep, and Beatrice's pilfered dress swished around her legs. She glanced back at the imposing castle in the semi-dark, early morning air. It had been easier to get through the gates than she'd thought. While the guards were thoroughly checking the villagers entering, she'd barely gotten a second glance. Cloaked and dressed as a maid and carrying the blanket-covered basket, she'd left the castle.

And she wasn't going to feel guilty, either. After the way Kellen had accused her, he deserved to wake up and find her gone. She knew he'd be upset, but only until his real bride showed up. Then he'd forget all about her.

At that thought, tears unexpectedly filled her eyes. She willed them back and concentrated on making her way through the bustling village, dodging animals and people alike. When the buildings began to thin, she ditched the blanket and basket at the side of a hut, put on her backpack, and headed up the hill toward the cemetery.

How long would Kellen search? Edith wouldn't arrive for several weeks; and while Gillian was mad at Kellen, she didn't necessarily want him to suffer. She'd considered leaving a note but doubted anyone could read her modern handwriting. She'd also briefly thought about giving Beatrice a watered-down version of her travel plans but knew she'd have run straight to Kellen and tattled.

Gillian's brow furrowed. If he'd just cooperated, she could have taken him and his daughter with her. They could have been a family. Her steps slowed. Was she leaving too soon? With her gone, what would Kellen think when Edith arrived? After he found out Gillian was an imposter, would he believe she'd really been the one trying to murder him? If he did, would he let his guard down and give the murderer a free shot at killing him?

The last of her anger evaporated, and she admitted to herself that the further away she got, the more miserable she was. Maybe she'd just go to the cemetery and see if she could get back to the twenty-first century. She could see if a time travel portal opened or something; and once she'd assured herself that she *could* go, then she'd turn around and stay with Kellen for a bit longer. Surely, she could find a way to talk him into going with her?

When she heard hooves thundering behind her, relief flooded her, and she let out a breath. Kellen. Sure, he'd be angry, but he'd get over it. She'd just tell him she was upset and had gone for a walk. He'd take her up on his horse and feel so bad he'd take her the rest of the way to the cemetery. She'd somehow prove she was from the future and give him the chance to choose between her and Edith. He'd forgive the deception, marry her, and love her the rest of her life, right?

Gillian suddenly remembered the hard look on Kellen's face the night before. He could be incredibly ruthless when he chose to be. What if she ended up in the dungeon? What if he chose Edith instead?

The horse came closer and she finally turned to face him. A man she'd never seen in her life grinned at her as he swung off his horse quicker than she could process. Her mouth fell open and the man, muscular and wild, gave her a flourishing bow.

"Greetings, Lady Corbett. I be Quinn MacGregor. 'Tis verra nice to make yer acquaintance." From his accent, the guy was Scottish and from the looks of him a barbarian, all animal skins, wool, and long, tangled hair. "Laird MacGregor will be wanting his men back, so I'll just be takin' you as a bit o' insurance. How does that suit ye?"

Her mouth snapped shut and she glared at the guy, unaccountably angry that he wasn't Kellen and that one more guy was trying to tell her what to do. "Are you freaking kidding me? I'll tell you what I think. I think this is really not happening today. I have some important things to get done, and I want you to step away from me and perhaps go find somewhere to bathe. Get lost."

At his grin, she shook her head, clutched the shoulder harnesses of her pack, turned, and walked away.

Laughing, the man easily wrenched the pack from her back and threw it in the long grass, snatched her up, and mounted his horse in seconds.

"Let. Me. Go!" Gillian kicked and squirmed, but her effort proved fruitless; she was thrown over strong legs and smacked on her bottom. Hard. She took a breath to scream and got smacked again.

"I'll bash ye on the head next time if ye doona settle," he said cheerfully. "Ye ken?"

Fuming, she settled. As they rode for the trees, she looked back at the castle in the distance. The sun was barely lighting the tips of the parapets, and she doubted anyone had seen a thing. She'd really messed up this time.

When they hit the tree line, three more men joined them, one taking the lead, and two bringing up the rear. Her anger quickly dissipated as fear had her heart beating hard in her chest. Her captor rearranged her, easily swinging her around so she was seated behind him. "Hold on. If ye fall, ye'll just get hurt and 'twill make no difference ta us. We willna leave ye behind."

After a quick glance at the distant ground, she gripped the washboard abs in front of her as all four men urged their mounts to run.

"What does Laird MacGregor want with me?" she yelled.

Quinn turned his head and she saw he was still grinning, clearly enjoying the situation. "He'll be sure ta use ye as ransom. Think you Lord Marshall values ye enough to pay the price?" He ran a hand down her leg and laughed.

She pinched him on his stomach, hard, and he laughed again but did release her leg. "Ye made it easy," he said over his shoulder. "We saw ye leavin' the village, had heard tale of yer wee bright pack and couldna believe our luck when ye slung it on. It fair glowed in the darkness."

"But why go to all this bother?"

"The MacGregor wants the men that Lord Marshall keeps in his dungeon. And he'll no' be gettin' ye back 'til he returns them."

"Why not simply give back the cattle you stole?"

"Give it back? Are you addled?"

"It would be the right thing to do."

He snorted. "'Tis the principal of the thing. Besides, we doona have to as we have ye now."

Gillian closed her eyes. Kellen was going to kill her for giving the Scots this advantage. Of course, she might be headed directly toward the guy who wanted her dead, so Kellen might never get the chance. This just wasn't her day.

KELLEN WALKED to where Owen and Tristan trained with the men, unsheathed his sword, and started hacking at them both, forcing them to defend themselves.

"Uh," Tristan gasped after a bone-jarring strike. "You seem in a foul mood this day."

"Think you?" responded Kellen, not letting up and using all his strength to drive both men backward, alternating his strokes between them.

Owen, face aghast, defended himself when the sword slashed his way. "My lord? Has aught occurred we should know about?"

Kellen struck out at him. "Let." *Another strike.* "Me." *Another.* "Consider." Their swords clashed and held, and Kellen was happy to see the strain shaking Owen's arm and the nervousness on his face. "What could have happened betwixt the last time I saw you both and this moment?" Kellen used his strength to throw Owen back a few paces. "Ah, yes. The lady Gillian did not show to break her fast this morn."

Tristan defended himself when Kellen turned on him. He skipped back a few paces, trying his best to anticipate Kellen's slashing movements. "Nay? Was she not hungry then?"

Kellen disarmed Tristan and he went scrambling after his sword. Kellen slashed the air twice and turned his attention back toward Owen. "Mayhap she was not. Of course," Kellen's sword clashed with Owen's. "The two of you could not know she was absent as you did not show yourselves either, else you might have noted the way I mooned about, also not eating, as I waited for the fair Gillian to arrive." He slashed again. "Which, as I've stated, she did not."

"She did not then?" Owen deflected, but Kellen threw him back so hard he stumbled, coming down on one knee before jumping back to his feet again.

"She did not."

Owen and Tristan shared a look and Tristan hastily raised his sword as Kellen attacked him again. "Is there any reason the fair Gillian did not break her fast this morn?"

"Hmm." Kellen cut with a sweeping stroke, forcing Tristan to jump back. "Let me consider. Oh, that is right. It was because, after being influenced by two of the most feebleminded men in the kingdom, I accused her of being a poisoner last eve. Of murdering Frederick. Oh, and also of staging the entire event whereby a villain attempted to stab her in the throat." He slashed hard, driving Tristan to his knees; and then as Tristan scrambled back and tried to regain his feet and his balance, Kellen turned his sword on Owen.

"Did I mention that my attack on my fair lady occurred when she did come to my chamber intent upon seduction? Of course, after getting such wise counsel from my two most trusted men, I did not chance to grasp what she was about. Oh, no. I believed she tried to murder me and searched her for a weapon before accusing her thus."

Owen sidestepped, but Kellen kicked out and knocked him to the ground. Owen scooted backward as Kellen held the sword to his throat. He swallowed audibly. "Dear, me. What did she do?"

Kellen stepped back, then went after Tristan again and knocked him to the ground next to Owen. Kellen, breathing hard, stabbed his sword into the dirt in disgust. His men looked at the waving sword, obviously aghast that Kellen would treat his weapon thus.

"What think you she did? With wounded feelings, and a newfound disgust of me, she ran to her room and barred the door."

Owen lifted a hand to his forehead. "Kellen, I do most humbly apologize."

Tristan backhanded Owen's shoulder. "*We* most humbly apologize."

Owen lowered his hand. "It had seemed—"

Kellen raised a palm, and shook his head in disgust. "Would that I could blame you. You are both idiots, 'tis true, but I am the biggest of all. When Catherine tried to poison me, 'twas no great surprise. But the thought of Gillian doing so? It shocked me to my bones. And why? Because she is no murderer. I knew this in here." He pounded his chest. "You can imagine her dismay when I accused her thus."

They were all silent a moment, then Owen shook his head. "We are truly imbeciles."

Tristan blew out a breath. "It seemed most reasonable last eve with Frederick dead on the floor and no enemy in sight; but in the light of day, the charge does seem exceedingly foolish."

Tristan and Owen regained their feet as Kellen sheathed his sword. They looked around to see the men watching them and Owen shouted for them to get back to their training. But for themselves, they continued to stand about saying nothing. Finally, Tristan whistled. "You did not comprehend her attempt to seduce you?"

Owen pushed Tristan's shoulder and Tristan barely maintained his balance. "Mayhap if you were to offer a bauble or two?"

Kellen pulled out a pouch of gems tucked in his belt and shook it. "She has to actually see me ere I can gift them to her."

"Ah," Tristan grinned. "You have already considered such. Mayhap you could send them with a love poem?"

Owen nodded. "Or we could deliver them for you and admit our part in turning thy thoughts."

"What if—" Tristan paused then pointed and Kellen turned to see Marissa running toward them, her skirts lifted.

Marissa never ran.

The men surged forward to meet her.

She put a hand to her heaving chest. "Lady Gillian is nowhere to be found. She is gone, as is her pack."

Kellen seized Marissa's upper arm. "What do you mean, gone? She must be about somewhere."

Marissa shook her head. "When I awoke, I thought her elsewhere. We've looked everywhere, my lord. She is not to be found."

Marissa hesitated. "Gillian had claimed she was going home this morn. She was upset. I had not thought to take her serious."

"Keep looking," Kellen said. "Get everyone to search." Kellen headed toward the gatehouse, as Owen and Tristan shouted orders to the men.

BREAD CRUMBS WOULD BE *nice right about now,* thought Gillian. *A nice long trail of them leading back to Marshall Keep.* Because hours later, she had no idea where she was or how to get back. Panic nipped at her again, rising and falling with her thought process, leaving her exhausted.

The horses moved at a steady pace, walking single file through the forest. There wasn't even a real path and certainly no trail to follow home.

She could hear the two horses behind her and one leading the way, but with her arms locked loosely around Quinn's waist and her head ducked behind his back to avoid the occasional branch, she felt pretty isolated. Luckily, she'd gotten used to Quinn's smell, because it didn't bother her anymore, which was a blessing.

She should have fought harder. Why hadn't she fought harder?

Once their ride through the forest had begun, it hadn't taken long to realize how much trouble she was in. No one knew she'd been kidnapped, and no one knew where she was.

Kellen was not going to come charging to her rescue. He wouldn't even know where to look until a ransom demand was made; and by that time, he'd think Gillian had gone home to her father. He'd look for her at Corbett Castle and find Edith there instead. He'd have his new bride in hand by the time he got back home to find a ransom note for Gillian. He'd probably just throw it in the fire with a hearty good riddance, glad to forget all about her once he realized she was a liar.

There would be no help for her, no ransom paid, no way back to the cemetery, and no way home.

So, now what did she do?

AN HOUR LATER, Kellen was convinced the woman was a half-wit. And so was he for not putting a guard on her door after she'd gone to bed the night before.

She'd snuck out at dawn without protection, which meant she'd been gone for hours at this point. One of the guards remembered a maid carrying a basket, and it had been found at the edge of the village.

Guilt tightened his chest as he crossed the bailey, dodging people scurrying hither and yon. The entire keep and village were still in an uproar looking for her, but Kellen was convinced she wasn't about. He never should have accused her. This was his fault for making her unhappy.

She'd told Marissa she was going home, which made no sense. The horses were all accounted for and she could not walk the entire way. She'd be accosted or murdered if she tried. She had never struck him as stupid, but obviously, he'd have to rethink his judgment.

Some of his men were already on the way to her father's keep with instructions to retrieve her even if she'd made it all the way home, which he deemed doubtful. If she had gone that direction, she would not have gotten far. Kellen would follow the minute he was convinced he'd done all he could here.

One of his men brought a young village boy forward. "This child claims to have witnessed a man on horseback early this morn."

The thin boy's frightened eyes were visible under his cap of messy blond hair, and Kellen knelt before him and tried to tamp down feelings of dread. "You saw a man on horseback?" he asked softly.

"Aye, my lord."

"Did you know him?"

"Nay, my lord. I tried to see but 'twas too dark and too far away to see much of anythin'. But I saw him riding up toward the graveyard. I thought maybe it 'twere a headless ghostie comin' for the dead." The boy suddenly grinned, showing he'd recently lost a few baby teeth. "Me brother would have near died of envy had I seen such!"

With a nod, Kellen sent two of his men to the cemetery. They mounted horses and were gone within moments.

"Did you see or hear aught else?"

"I waited, and then he went back the way he come and 'twas the slightest bit brighter; and I saw hair flying about his head, so I knew he weren't headless." The boy's disappointment was palpable.

"Did he have anyone with him?"

The boy shrugged, then looked up, hope gleaming in his eyes. "Think you he carried a spirit or two?"

"Mayhap. Where did he go?"

The boy pointed toward the northern tree line and Kellen's teeth clenched. Scots? Would they dare? "Did you see my lady?"

"Nay, my lord."

After dismissing the boy and telling him to find a treat in the kitchen, Kellen paced as he waited for his men to return. Minutes later, one rode fast through the gate house, only pulling up short when he approached Kellen. "My lord!" He lifted Gillian's pack. "We did a quick search, but did not find her."

Kellen's jaw tightened as he grimly accepted the brightly colored bundle. She was very attached to her treasures and would never have willingly left her possessions behind. Could she have been taken so close to the village? Perhaps by the man who'd tried to murder her?

His guts clenching, Kellen mounted up and he and his men headed toward the tree line. After only a short search they found evidence of three or four horses. And tied to a tree branch was a piece of Scottish cloth.

A message? Or a trap? Either way, Kellen was immensely relieved they'd not found Gillian's dead body. "Gather the men," Kellen yelled. "And bring the Scottish prisoners."

If Gillian had been harmed, he'd gut the men while their people watched. Then he'd slaughter the lot of them.

CHAPTER 25

*G*illian heard people before she saw them.

Her captors, fists raised in the air, shouted in triumph as they rode out of the trees and into a camp where a band of wild-looking, filthy men gathered. Some stopped their training, others came out of tents, and more stood from where they lounged near a campfire. But one and all they moved forward, at least forty men, some shouting responses to her captors, and every one of them staring at her.

Gillian's throat tightened and, mouth dry, she gripped Quinn and watched as a huge guy made his way toward them. Men moved out of his way and, the closer he came, the more Gillian tensed. The man's thick dark hair and beard was randomly braided and messy, though it at least appeared clean. His shoulders and arms bulged with muscle. Tall, strong, and in command, he was obviously their leader. When he reached them, Quinn half-turned, a wide grin on his face.

"Laird MacGregor, meet Lady Corbett, recently of Marshall Keep."

The laird bowed mockingly. "My lady, welcome." His voice was deep and loud. "I am most pleased to make thy acquaintance."

The men around them laughed.

Before she could respond, he spoke to the men on horseback in a language she couldn't understand and, when Quinn laughed and responded in kind, the laird grinned. Without any warning, he grabbed hold of her arm and dragged her off the horse, catching her before she plummeted to the ground. She screamed, slapping, scratching, and pushing for freedom, her feet touching the ground as the men around her laughed. She could barely walk after hours on the horse, but tried to run anyway.

The behemoth easily caught and held her with her back against his front, his arms around her, her wrists crossed and captured in his large hands. He laughed. "Little cat, sheathe thy claws."

Gillian bucked, trying to get away, but all she did was amuse the crowd, if their hoots and hollers were any indication. *"Let go of me!"* Breathing hard, she twisted and turned but remained trapped.

The man's warmth seeped into her chilled body, his wild, campfire smell settling over her with every gasped breath. The guy simply held on and let her wear herself out.

She finally stilled. Was he planning to assault her? Kill her? It was too much: leaving Kellen, being captured, the travel, the men surrounding her, and her helplessness. She started to cry. "Leave me alone." She bucked one more time. "Just leave me alone."

"Calm thyself." His chest rumbled against her back. "You willna be harmed, lass."

"Then why am I here?" She kicked at his shins with a running shoe. He grunted but remained unbending. "What do you want?" When he didn't respond, she tried to think of a way to keep herself unharmed. "Do you want to marry me? Is that it? For my family's wealth?"

He turned her around to look at her, keeping one hand tight on her wrist, speculation in his expression as he looked up and down her body. He grinned, his gaze settling on her chest. "Ye come well dowered, do ye?"

As the men around them guffawed and snickered, Gillian ignored his lewd implication and decided Kellen was the best weapon to threaten him with. "Yes, my family settled a large amount on me. Lord Marshall already has it."

The laird chuckled. "Clever man. But it doesna matter. We simply mean to use you as ransom to get our men back. Mayhap he'll part with a bit of your portion, eh?"

"But Kellen . . . Lord Marshall, doesn't know where I am."

"He does by now."

Gillian stared at him for a moment and then tension drained from her, leaving her weak and unsteady. "You left a note?"

He nodded once. "Aye. My men left a message."

Kellen would be coming for her? Gillian bowed her head as relief surged through her. With his hand still clamped around her wrist, Laird MacGregor hauled her, unresisting, to a tent; and she stumbled behind him. He pushed her inside and pointed to a blanket. "Sit there. I'll return directly."

Gillian considered running but realizing how pointless it was, sank to the blanket, and pulled her knees to her chest.

A moment later Laird MacGregor returned with meat and dark bread. He passed her a portion and sat across from her. "Eat."

Gillian hadn't eaten since noon the day before and didn't have to be told twice. She bit into the meat, some kind of fowl. The wonderful campfire taste hit her tongue, and she moaned then glanced up to find him watching her. Self-conscious, she stopped chewing. "What?"

"Ye just surprised me, lass. Ye didna cross yourself against me, nor," he pointed to a stick nearby, "wave the elder branch over thy food, nor even pray over the fare. I hazard I am used to the superstitious lot out there." He jerked a thumb toward the tent's entry.

Gillian swallowed then broke off a small piece of the dry bread and popped it into her mouth. "How are they superstitious?"

The laird shrugged. "In all the ways a man can be. My men think me a warlock if I forget to stir my oats in the proper direction to ward bad spirits." He pointed to the stick again. "I humor them in favor of peace."

When she snorted, his brows rose. "Have I shocked you? Do you fear me the worse now?"

She chuckled and relaxed a bit more. "No. I don't believe in warlocks."

He smiled slightly. "Don't you then?"

She shook her head. "I believe in evil men and women doing evil deeds but not in witches and warlocks."

He studied her for a moment. "Now ye've shocked me, lass. I've not met a female who doesna cast wards against evil, cross herself ten times in a day, throw salt over her shoulder, and plant mugwort, foxglove, and the like. Do ye none of those things?"

She chuckled again and shook her head. "I've been known to salt my food on occasion, but only for the taste."

"Hmm." He finally applied himself to his food, and she had the chance to study him while they ate. He truly was scary to look at, savage. His brown tunic, stained at chest and hem, hit his knees when standing but now, rucked up, exposed most of his strong, bare legs. Fortunately, he looked to be wearing shorts of some kind. He also wore an animal skin vest and had brown wool draped over one shoulder, fastened somehow. There wasn't a kilt in sight, which she had to admit surprised her.

He met her gaze and she asked, "Have you been planning to kidnap me for long?"

It was his turn to snort. "We had no thought to take you at all. We thought you too well protected. You fell into my men's hands like a plump partridge."

Well, of all the rotten luck. Brows drawn together, she bent her head to hide her chagrin. "Why were your men there then?"

"Hoping for the chance to rescue their kinsman."

"You sent them?"

"Aye."

She finally lifted her head. "You're very loyal to your men."

He laughed in a humorless way. "I could but wish my men were as loyal to me."

"What do you mean?"

He didn't explain and resumed eating.

"What do you mean?" she asked again.

He shrugged.

Gillian sighed. "So . . . Scotland is nice. It's really pretty. I've always wanted to come here."

He shot her an incredulous look.

"So . . . who are you, anyway? What's your name, rank, and serial number?"

He ate some bread.

"So . . . why are you camping in the forest? Are you related to Robin Hood?"

He gnawed the meat off a bone.

She took a breath and he threw up a hand. "Stop nattering on!"

"Then tell me why you think your men aren't loyal!" she whispered fiercely.

He sighed. Shrugged. "'Tis no great secret. My mother is English and I did much of my training in England. When my father died, I was expected to come back and lead, which I did. But loyalty has to be earned through time and action." He threw a handful of bones through the tent opening.

Gillian resumed eating and studied the man. While he looked and acted tough, he'd actually seen to her comfort, fed her, and put her at ease. Maybe she could do something to help him. "I once read a book called *How to Win Friends and Influence People* by Dale Carnegie. It said that you need to smile, be friendly, treat people kindly, and find out their interests and try to share them." She nodded. "You need to make people feel important and appreciated and always try and remember their names. Maybe you could try that with your men?"

He stared at her, brows raised, mouth agape, and then laughed. When she glared, he laughed harder, openmouthed, until he fell over backward.

Gillian straightened her spine and pursed her lips. When he finally sat up, his laughter subsiding to chuckles, she said, "Don't knock it until you try it. When I was in junior high, I didn't have any friends and my mom read the book to me. It's good advice."

He chuckled a few more times then shook his head and wiped at his eyes. "You're an agreeable lass to talk to. You must keep Lord Marshall well entertained." He studied her, and she refused to look away. "You're also verra easy to look upon."

She grinned. "Flatterer. You're kind of cute too, in a barbarian-at-the-gates sort of way. A girl could feel very protected with you around."

He actually looked down and blushed above his facial hair, and it was Gillian's turn to laugh at him.

He glared. "Watch yourself ere I lose my patience."

She managed not to roll her eyes. The guy was turning out to be a pussycat. "Obviously, you don't live here in the forest. Why aren't you home? What *are* you doing out here in the middle of nowhere?"

He shrugged. "The usual. Trapped between two kings who use us as puppets for their own amusement." Gillian heard bitterness in his tone.

She studied him for a moment. "You don't seem very happy in your chosen occupation. Couldn't you just give it up? Stop being Laird and go back to England?"

He shrugged. "I am the MacGregor. There's no altering that. Ye cannot change what is."

"You'd be surprised."

When she finished her meal, he cut an apple with his knife, gave her a piece and then grinned when she made a face at its tartness. He then cut and ate a slice himself before giving her another.

"Are you married?" she asked.

"Are ye offerin' for me, lass?"

She looked at him. Under all the hair, he was young, probably mid-to-late twenties and might even be good-looking. He was as tall and broad through the chest as Kellen and had shown he could be kind. All in all, he sort of reminded her of Kellen. A decent man hardened by the time he lived in. "Let me ask you something. Would you take a wife without a dowry?"

"O' course. Chances are I will. Heiresses are not thick about the ground for men such as me."

"What about Lord Marshall? Do you think he'd take a bride without a dowry?"

"Why do ye ask? I've said I'll return ye to him, and I will. If you're worried on that score, put your fears to rest."

"Just answer the question."

He shrugged. "By all accounts the man is wealthy, but you ne'er ken. Some men are ne'er satisfied but with more. You know him. What is your take on the man's character?"

Gillian shrugged and looked down. That was the problem. She did know him. She knew how much his land and people meant to him. How responsible and practical he was. She loved him, but didn't have the courage to tell him the truth about herself and hope he'd choose her over Edith and her money.

"What's it to be, then? Did you not fancy Lord Marshall? Is he a cruel man? Disfigured? Would you prefer to take your chances on me? Lord Marshall would never give up your dowry, but I'd never rebuke ye for the lack."

Startled by what sounded to be a genuine proposal, she glanced up, warmth flooding her. Would Kellen feel the same? She smiled at Laird MacGregor and gently said, "I'm afraid my heart has already been given to another. But thank you. I'm honored."

He lifted a shoulder. "Ye've crushed me, lass."

She laughed. "Like I said. Flatterer."

He grinned, and when she'd finished the apple, he gave her

some water from some sort of bag. He stood and held out a hand. "Come, I'll let you have privacy behind a tree, ere we get ye settled for the day."

Embarrassed, but grateful, she was once more dragged through camp and allowed a few minutes to herself. She was thankful for the thick foliage and, after briefly considering escape, discarded the idea as foolish and impossible and returned. Wouldn't this group of crazy men just love to chase her through the trees? The laird took her by the wrist again and led her back to the tent. She noticed the men breaking camp.

"Why are you packing up?"

He didn't answer but simply stopped in front of his tent and shoved her inside. "You're to stay here and keep quiet, ere my men decide you be a witch with your strange way of speaking." He followed her in, pulled out some long cloths, took hold of her wrists, pushed her to the blanket, and knelt beside her.

She glanced up, startled. "What are you doing?"

He quickly bound her wrists together.

She tugged against his hold. *"Stop it!"*

He paused and gave her a fierce look. "Doona fight me. 'Tis for your own protection."

With one hand holding her, he reached for another cloth and Gillian tugged again. *"Don't!"* She fought him with all her strength, got free, and bashed him in the face with her bound wrists before he recaptured them.

Holding his nose, he laughed and swore. "Blast it, lass. Ye'd make me a fine wife. If you reconsider, the offer stands."

"Let." She continued to struggle. "Me." She pulled as hard as she could. *"Go!"*

He released her and she fell backward onto the blanket and he held up a strip of cloth. "Is it to be the gag then?"

At the thought of that filthy material in her mouth, all the fight flowed out of her. "No. I'll be quiet."

"There's a good girl." He quickly tied her ankles together, taking time to study her athletic shoes, twisting them one way, then the other. "I've never seen the like. Doona let my men see them." He finished, covered her feet with her skirt; and when he was done, looked to see her glaring at him. He grinned, reached out, put a hand on her cheek, and rubbed his thumb over her tight lips. "I truly am tempted to keep ye but my clan would likely not accept an Englishwoman, especially one who talks and acts so strange. You'd as like be burned as a witch."

"Thanks a lot." He turned to leave and Gillian struggled to sit up. "Wait." He turned back to look at her. "What will happen if Lord Marshall doesn't come for me?"

He stared at her for a long moment then chuckled. "Oh, he'll come for ye. Of that I have no doubt." And with a quick grin and a wink, he was gone.

TEETH CLENCHED AND MOUTH TIGHT, Kellen rode with his men deeper into Scotland. He tried not to think of what could befall Gillian in this foul place, tried to convince himself the savages wouldn't harm a woman. If they acted on even one of the things riddling his thoughts, if they . . . well, he would kill them all.

Again, he couldn't help but question her motives. *What had she been doing? Why had she left the protection of the keep? What had she been thinking?* None of it mattered at the moment, of course. All that mattered was getting her back safely. When he had her in his possession, then he could strangle the answers out of her at his leisure.

A new thought worried at him. What if, once they had spoken to her, looked upon her, they decided to keep her rather than ransom her? She could be headstrong and capricious but also charming and fascinating, and she was far too beautiful for her own good.

Or what if that were the true purpose for which she'd been taken? Not as a prisoner to ransom or exchange, but as a bride. The Scottish savages were known for kidnapping brides. It was no doubt the only way they could get them. Had Gillian been kidnapped by a man looking for a wife? Kellen's hands clenched and unclenched on the reins. Had she been brought before a priest? Handfasted? What if—

"My lord, look ahead," Tristan yelled and pointed to a man in dirty wool coming out of a grove of trees. His hair, braided, uncombed, and wild, looked a good place for nesting creatures.

Kellen pulled up and the man rode forward, his teeth flashing straight and white.

"Out for a ride in our fine woods?"

"Where is she?"

"Where be our men?"

Kellen stilled and the tension in his body lowered a notch. Was this simply to be a trade then? Were they to willingly give her back? "We have them with us. Who are you?"

"You may call me Sir Angus." The man smiled at the claim of gentry. "I'm to take you to The MacGregor.

"I will call you Sir Horse's Arse. Lead the way."

The man's eyes narrowed. "We thought you wasna comin'. 'Tis been hours since the lass was snatched."

Kellen had no intention of telling the oaf he'd not known his own bride was missing while he'd mooned over ways to win her favor.

"We thought perhaps you'd changed your mind about your English bride. That mayhap you didna want the lassie after all." He raised a brow. "She is a handful."

Had that given them reason to believe they could hurt her?

Kellen's muscles clenched and his horse moved under him skittishly until he tightened the reins. Kellen could feel heat rising in his body. Through clenched teeth, he grated, "If she has been hurt, you will all pay with your lives."

"They would not dare to harm her, my lord," said Owen. "They know if they do they die."

Angus snorted. "She was aright when last I saw her."

If he lost her, if she was gone from him . . . he pushed the thought aside. If they failed to give her up, he'd kill them. If he could not find her, he would call in every ally he possessed if needs be, and he would find the culprits and kill them. If they hurt her—

He swallowed. She was delicate, but fearless. Always wandering about without protection. What if they accidentally killed her?

He found himself sweating as they followed Angus MacGregor.

"What if the English don't come for her?"

Gillian hugged her knees to her chest and listened to the group of men. It wasn't as if she had a choice. For all their attempts at whispering, they either weren't very good at it, or the clear Scottish afternoon air easily carried sound through the tent. The fact that they spoke English made her wonder if they wanted her to overhear.

Anyway, she shared their concern. What if Kellen didn't come? What if she had to spend the night there? She shivered at the thought of being surrounded by these men overnight but didn't so much as move otherwise. She didn't want to draw their attention.

"Perhaps the wool tied to a tree wasna enough of a message?"

"Everyone knows the English are slow-witted. Mayhap we should deliver a note?"

"But then another of our men might be captured."

"Perhaps they rode in the wrong direction and never met up with Angus?"

"Nay, we left a trail a half-wit could follow."

"Mayhap they killed Hamish and Donald? Mayhap they have naught left to bargain with."

"They are not dead!" A man bellowed. Gillian heard footsteps stomp to the tent and a corner was pulled back to reveal a bushy, red-bearded face. "Girl!" Gillian jumped. "Be our men murdered by your lord?"

Gillian swallowed. "Nope. Last I heard they were doing just fine."

"See. They are well." The tent flap fell again and Gillian breathed a sigh of relief. She knew a mob mentality when she heard one and didn't want them reminded she was there.

It was quiet for a while. "'Tis said he killed his first wife. Perhaps he willna be fashed should this one disappear, as well?"

"She's comely enough and has plenty enough atop to please a man. Her hips seem shapely, as well."

"And she's young."

"Still, mayhap she could be infertile?"

"Nay, not with those hips. Perhaps he hopes to find a wealthier bride?"

"If he doesna want her, I'll take her."

Gillian took a breath and decided that keeping quiet might not be such a good strategy after all. "I can hear you." She called out through the tent. "I'm right here."

The men were silent a moment, then she heard more whispering before another man approached the tent. "Does your lord care for you, lass?"

"He likes me just fine."

"His first wife died and you were left to wander. Mayhap he seeks to rid himself of encumbrances? Think you he will come for you?"

"Yes." She tried to infuse confidence in her voice. "He will come for me. In fact, you'd better treat me well or I'll tell him that you didn't."

She could hear more whispering as the man went back to the group.

"I've heard he can cleave a man's head off without breaking a sweat."

One man scoffed. "No, he canna."

"'Tis true. 'Tis said he has the eyes of a warlock and he can freeze a man so as to split his head without hindrance. 'Tis said he's not lost a fight. If he comes after nightfall, we will all be killed!"

"Mayhap his bride is a witch, as well!"

This was getting out of hand. "I'm *not* a witch."

"Witches are paid in gold. Her ring looks to be worth a fortune. Mayhap we should take it ere we trade her for our men."

"It doesna come off! I tried to pull it from her finger and 'tis stuck as if by magic!"

Gillian heard a gasp or two and rolled her eyes.

"If someone cut off her finger—"

She took a breath, determined to show no sign of weakness. "Yeah. I dare you to. My betrothed, *Lord Marshall,* surely won't notice my finger missing or me bleeding all over the place. I'm sure Mr. MacGregor will be pleased, as well."

It was silent again for a moment, and she hoped they were cowed by the threat of Kellen's name but she cursed MacGregor for leaving her unprotected with this bloodthirsty lot.

"Look at my arm! 'Tis covered in gooseflesh. She must be a witch!"

"Mine, as well!"

"Witch . . ."

"Witch . . ."

"Witch!"

"She's no witch," said a deep, authoritative voice. "Just a scared lass surrounded by a pack of slathering idiots. Now mount up men, and bring the girl. The English come!"

Gillian couldn't help it. She actually sagged with relief. As much as she wanted to bash the guy, she was thrilled MacGregor had returned. She wondered if Kellen were actually there or if the barbarian was simply trying to control his men. Either way, she'd be glad to get out of the tent.

CHAPTER 26

*K*ellen arrived at a big meadow and stopped. The men behind him followed suit as their guide hurried forward to greet his kinsmen.

Kellen's gaze took in the line of men seated on horseback. The Scottish Laird, reputed to be a large man, was no doubt the hulking giant in the middle. Other fighters were thick upon the ground, weapons at the ready; however, Gillian was nowhere in sight.

Kellen looked to the trees, trying to determine how many men they might have to fight. As far as he could tell, his forces outnumbered the Scots both in men and training; but he wouldn't underestimate them. He knew them to be sly and vicious fighters.

As the two forces faced each other, the biggest of their men urged his horse forward, confirming Kellen's suspicions as to his identity. "Wait here," Kellen said to Owen and Tristan. "Be ready."

"Aye, my lord," said Tristan, man and horse spoiling for battle.

"Aye. Be on guard against trickery," said Owen.

Kellen nudged his mount forward until he faced the other man and was surprised to find he recognized Laird MacGregor. "What do you here? We have met on the jousting field."

"I remember. You won my horse and armor. The armor was shite, but I hope you treated the horse well."

"I did. 'Twas a fine animal. Again, I ask, what do you here? Are you not English?"

A shrug. "Half."

Kellen's brows rose. "And your men accept a leader with English blood?"

"I am The MacGregor," he said simply.

Kellen lost interest and got to the point. "Was she harmed?"

"Nay. You have my word that she's no' been harmed. I canna say the same for my nose. She's a feisty thing, is she not?"

Kellen sucked in a breath at the thought of Gillian having to defend herself against this towering savage and suddenly wanted to kill the man.

From the smirk on the other's face, Kellen could see his feelings were obvious.

"A man in my keep was poisoned. You're doing?"

"Nay. Nor that of my men. Do not think to blame us for thy failure to clean house." MacGregor motioned with his hand and Gillian was pulled through the crowd of Scots and given a shove.

She started walking toward them and Kellen was so relieved to see her it was all he could do to wait while she crossed the distance. Kellen motioned to his own men to release the two prisoners and then waited while the three crossed the field.

"She has a strange way of speech, does she not?"

"'Tis charming," growled Kellen.

"Ah, you care for the girl then? She wondered, you know, if you would want her if she came undowered. A question a girl asks if she's feelings for a man. I offered to marry her without payment, but she turned me down."

Feeling murderous, Kellen snapped, "She's mine."

"Aye, well, as to that, I let her know the offer stood were she to change her mind."

Kellen tried to tamp down his rage. "Was she touched?"

"She was not."

Gillian finally arrived.

"Are you hurt?" demanded Kellen.

Eyes wide, she looked at them both for a long moment, her gaze moving between the two and, the longer she didn't respond, the more tense Kellen became.

The MacGregor, losing his mocking grin, tensed as well, his horse moving skittishly beneath him.

Someone was going to die if Gillian uttered so much as a word of complaint.

"Gillian?" Kellen waited for her reply and gripped his sword. If she was so much as breathed on, he was going to kill them all, starting with the giant before him.

"No. No, I'm fine."

Both men relaxed and both exhaled.

Good. That was good. She was aright and still his alone. Kellen held out his hand.

After a hesitant glance at his horse, she reached for him and he hauled her atop his lap, turned his mount, and moved away.

Behind him MacGregor called out, "Watch thy back about thy kinsman, English."

Kellen turned his horse around. "What is your meaning? Is that a threat?"

The laird laughed. "Not at all. A warning. One of yours told me of the, ah, delicious cattle to be found were I to cross the border." He smiled at Kellen, then gave Gillian a less mocking smile. "Doona forget my offer, lass." His tone gentled. "'Twas genuine." He laughed at Kellen's thunderous expression and turned his own mount away.

"Someday I will get the chance to pay you in kind," Kellen said. "Count on it."

The MacGregor saluted him. "I look forward to it, English."

AT FIRST, Gillian was so happy to see Kellen, to get away from the Scots, and be on her way back to England, that she didn't realize how angry Kellen was. It didn't take long for the excitement over her rescue to fade or for the questions to start.

"Why did you leave the protection of the keep?"

Kellen's clipped, angry tone had Gillian's arms crossing and her lips thinning. She didn't answer.

"Did someone lure you out?" he asked, his voice hard and forbidding. "Or mayhap you simply had a fit of temper and placed yourself and others in harm's way?"

Tristan and Owen, riding on each side of them, tried to intervene. "'Tis simply that his lordship was considerably worried on thy behalf, my lady," said Tristan. "Such things can upset a man, and the fright has overset our lord greatly."

"Aye, my lady," said Owen. "Pay him no heed. He'll soon be back in high spirits and will be more civilized company."

"Both of you fall back," snapped Kellen.

After a few minutes, and with the men behind them, Kellen spoke again. "Well?" his voice was slightly calmer, but still frosty. "Have you naught to say?"

Goaded, Gillian said in a pleasant tone, "The weather is nice today. Not too hot, not too cold. The breeze feels good. Also, I think the trees are pretty."

They both sat stiffly and after a moment, the strain became too much and she cleared her throat. "If it's all the same to you, I'd rather ride with Tristan or Owen."

Kellen's arms tightened around her. "We *will* discuss this," he said, ignoring her request. "You *will* tell me why you left."

Gillian sighed and threw up one hand. "I wanted to visit the cemetery, okay?" Her tone was belligerent but she didn't care. "I told you I wanted to, remember? I asked you to take me there and you wouldn't."

"Why did you want to go?" he snapped. "I see no point."

"I lost something there and I want it back."

"What?"

Seven centuries she wanted to say, but since she couldn't; and since he was waiting for an answer, she crossed her fingers under her rough work skirt and lied. "Um . . . a bracelet?" Not necessarily a bad lie. Maybe having a reason to go search would get Kellen to take her there.

Kellen snorted impatiently. "I would give you a hundred bracelets if I but knew you desired such. There is no need to place yourself in danger for a trinket. You will *never* go there again, do you understand?"

She let out a breath. *Or maybe he'd dig in his heels instead.*

"I want that bracelet. It has special meaning to me."

"Why? Did a male give it to you? A sweetheart? Perhaps Sir Elton John?"

"What?" She craned her neck to look at him. "What are you talking about?"

His eyes narrowed to slits. "Think you I forgot thy affection when speaking of the musician? 'Tis a wonder your mother allowed such a man in your company."

She let out a breath, faced forward again, and shook her head. *Incredible. Fighting over a fake bracelet and a faker boyfriend? Like she didn't have real problems to solve?* "Just so you know, my father gave me the bracelet, and Sir Elton John prefers men to women."

After a long moment, Kellen cleared his throat. "Ah, well then. Just so."

She rolled her eyes. "Back to the subject at hand. The cemetery? My bracelet? I need to go there. I need to look for it."

"If you insist on its return, I'll send others."

"No. I want to go myself. I told you I like to go sightseeing."

"Sightseeing? As you did this day?" his voice roughened again.

"Well . . . yes." A quick glance showed that, yes, indeed, he was clenching his teeth. "Granted, today I saw more than I'd intended, but Scotland is pretty."

She felt him stiffen again and sighed. "Kellen, I'm not an idiot. I know today was bad and that people could have died." Some of the tension eased out of her. "You know you're my hero for saving me, right?" She turned and put her hand on his cheek and finally looked at him so he could see she meant it. "Thank you for coming to get me. I was so scared. I didn't know if you knew where to find me, and I didn't know if you'd come."

His jaw slowly relaxed as he searched her eyes. "Gillian," his tone was less harsh, but still frustrated. "Perhaps the real reason you fled was because you are angry with me for accusing you of treachery. Truly do I beg thy pardon."

Gillian turned away again and bent her head so he couldn't see her face and couldn't see that she was still hurt by the accusation.

"Why *did* you accuse me?" She rubbed at a stain on her brown skirt. "Because of your first wife? Because we have the same blood you think I'm tainted by association?"

His grip tightened on her. "Nay. I truly do not believe such. My wits had gone begging in the heat of the moment. I know you to be steadfast and unlike your sister. In truth, I have no excuse and ask your forgiveness."

After a long pause, she finally let out a breath. "Okay, but I'm only going to say this once. I may not be perfect, but I'm no knife thrower, or poisoner, and I'm certainly not a murderer. I'm going to forgive you this *one time,* but I have no intention of paying for Catherine's sins ever again. I have enough of my own to worry about."

He hugged her to him. "Nay, you are *perfect.* Thank you, Gillian. I do not deserve you."

"You've got that right." She considered how he'd react when he discovered she wasn't Edith, but a liar and a fraud. "I'm not perfect, you know."

He sighed. "'Tis true. I only said such to cool thy temper. You are overly stubborn, obsessive about the oddest concerns, and quick to cause inconvenience."

She elbowed him lightly in the gut and he laughed. "Thy father will no doubt arrive soon, as I sent men to Corbett Castle to find you. Shall I take him to task for all thy faults to spare you more chidings?"

"What?" Gillian actually felt blood drain from her face, leaving her dizzy. She slowly straightened in Kellen's arms and stared unseeing at the landscape. "My father is coming?"

"Aye. Marissa said you had thought to go home. When I couldn't find you, I immediately sent men toward your father's keep. No doubt he will be worried to hear you've gone missing and come to help the search."

Gillian's body stiffened further. No doubt the man would be surprised to find someone was impersonating his daughter and come to find out what was going on!

Gillian's heart pounded furiously in her chest. She no longer had the luxury of waiting to go home. *She had to go now.*

"What ails you? Why do you tremble?"

Gillian tried to force herself to relax. "When do you expect my father?"

"'Tis about eight days' fast travel there and back."

Eight days.

"Are you fearful?" Kellen gave her a slight tug. "Lie back again and do not worry so. I'll not allow thy father to scold you." When she remained stiff, he sighed. "Peace?"

She finally remembered to breathe. "Uh, yeah, sure." She was a dead woman. She was so, so dead. Slowly she sank back against Kellen, glad for his warmth since she suddenly felt chilled. "Peace."

She had eight days before she had to be out of Medieval England. She slid her hand down Kellen's arm until she found his hand at her waist and held it tight.

He gripped hers in return and kissed the top of her head.

She had eight days to get to that cemetery. Eight days to convince Kellen to go with her. Eight days until she was exposed as an imposter.

Hours later as they passed the cemetery in the distance and stayed on a straight path to the castle, Gillian considered asking Kellen to turn. She might be able to talk him into taking her there if she insisted enough; after all, they'd have the protection of his men.

Only two things stopped her. First, if something strange or unusual occurred, which it might, and she didn't or couldn't get back to her own time, the last thing she needed was a bunch of witnesses branding her a witch. *Again.* And second, if she could swing it, she was taking Kellen and his daughter back with her, which would require some extra thought and planning.

Before long, they arrived at the castle and Kellen dismounted in the bailey, handed the reins to a waiting squire, then reached up and easily lifted Gillian off the horse. When she would have turned away, he cupped her cheek. "You've been quiet this day. Are you sad, then? Worried?"

"Truthfully?" She looked around and feeling tired and vulnerable, told him the truth. "I just want to go home."

"You are home. I am your home."

Gillian bit her lip and couldn't help it, she moved forward, wrapped her arms around his waist, and lay her head on his chest. She hoped he still felt that way when she took him back with her. "You have no idea how much I want that to be true," she whispered.

"Shh. Shh. You are not to worry. I *will* keep you safe." His arms engulfed her for a long moment then he leaned back to regard her, expression serious.

"Think you I know not where your true concerns lie? Come." Kellen took her hand and tugged her to the middle of the bailey so she could see into the gate. "Look you there. See the extra men guarding the gate?" He pointed up. "The towers? I know you are concerned that whoever murdered Frederick will try for thy life once more. You need fear no longer. None will be allowed in or out without my express permission."

Her mouth parted as dread built in her chest. In or *out?*

"There is more. Let me show you." He tugged her toward the entrance of the keep and dragged her through to the kitchens, where Cook and her helpers prepared food.

"Thy lady fears more poison. Can you not set her mind at ease?"

Cook's ample chest puffed up and she shook her head. "You've naught to fear, my lady. Any food you eat will have no chance at poison. None but myself will serve you, I can assure you of that."

"You see? I learn from my mistakes. A guard will be set at your door each night. My enemies will never again threaten what I prize most." He cupped her face and looked as if he were making a vow.

Gillian's knees weakened. "Kellen—"

In an abrupt move, he once more grasped her hand and pulled her after him, rounded a corner, and pressed her into an alcove. "I want you to feel safe and happy here. I have decided I will court you, and then you will desire to stay with me always."

"Really," she said weakly. "That's not necessary."

"I assure you, what I want is you, relaxed and happy, looking forward to our wedding day." He dipped his mouth toward her ear. "And night." His lowered voice caused her to shiver, which made her mad. She didn't have time for this right now. She gave him a shove and he backed up a step, his eyes questioning. "Gillian?"

He just didn't get it. He wanted her relaxed and happy? He wanted to court her? With Edith's father, no doubt riding toward the castle to expose her as an imposter, with Kellen making sure she couldn't slip out to the cemetery again, and with her uncertain of whether she could even return to the future, she was stressed to the max! And now he wanted to court her?

She felt like smacking the seductive look right off his face.

What she wanted was his assurance that when Edith showed up he wouldn't like her better. A silly thing to worry about in light of everything else, but there it was.

What she wanted was the assurance that he'd choose her, Gillian, over Edith if given the chance, even without a dowry, even without Lord Corbett as her father. What had he said the day she'd arrived? That he'd stick her in the dungeon or hang her as a spy if she didn't turn out to be Edith?

Gillian gave a slight laugh and a shake of her head. She had other things to worry about right now besides being courted.

"Fine. Whatever. Give it your best shot, big guy."

In the meantime, she had some planning to do.

As GILLIAN APPROACHED the long table the next morning, Kellen rubbed his sweaty palms against his tunic then fingered the pouch at his waist. It felt heavy but that was no doubt his imagination as the gold bracelet, set with pearls and sapphires, did not weigh much at all.

He had retrieved it from the blacksmith early that morn. The man had worked the night through to craft the piece and, though not an artisan, he had done a credible job. The sapphires, shining brightly between the pearls, reminded Kellen of Gillian's eyes. He also had gems he could gift her to decorate her gowns, or they could be made into jewelry if it so pleased her.

He tried to decide whether to give them all to her at once or to keep some back so as to have more to offer later. The decision was easy. He'd spread them out and thus have more opportunities for gratitude coming his way.

He stood as she neared, as did Tristan and Owen; but while the other men easily exchanged greetings with her, Kellen swallowed a few times and could feel sweat slicking his back. *He could do this. He could court Gillian without mucking it up.*

Gillian stopped in front of him. "You've assigned guards to follow me?" He finally noted the scowl on her face as she threw both hands in the air. "Really, Kellen?"

He took a breath. "'Tis for your safety. A good morn to you, my lady."

Gillian took a seat on the bench. "Good morning. All I'm saying is I just don't think it's necessary."

Kellen resumed his seat. "Regardless, you will humor me."

Cook brought food and, bushy brows drawn together over a red face, mumbled to herself, *"I should like to see them try it again. Poisoning my food and killing my friends? Threatening my lord and lady thus? I will deliver it my own self and see if they dare such trickery again."* She left the food and a somber mood as she marched back to the kitchen.

"I will try it first." Kellen picked up a piece of bread and took a large bite.

Gillian reached for a different slice. "Don't think I don't know why you're so willing to put your life on the line. You just took the best piece."

When she winked at him, Kellen laughed and finally relaxed a bit. "You know me well, my lady." He considered how to gift her the bracelet, how to charm her. He would chat with her, put her at ease, have more of her smiles, then give her the gift. "I trust you slept well?"

Gillian didn't answer, didn't seem to hear, only stared across the table and over Tristan's shoulder at the stone wall behind him.

"Gillian?"

Her head jerked and she looked down at the piece of bread in her hand as if surprised to see it. "Hmm?"

"Did you sleep well?"

"What? Oh, yes. Thank you."

"You look beautiful this day."

Her attention was caught by Marissa and her ladies joining them and he wasn't sure if Gillian heard his compliment over their chatter. What he really needed was to get her alone and have all her attention to himself. "I would be most grateful if you could find the time to walk—"

"Lady Gillian, you must tell us about Laird MacGregor," Lady Yvonne interrupted. "Is he as fierce as they say?"

Lady Vera seated herself and leaned forward. "Was he handsome?"

Gillian shrugged. "He had hair all over his face, and he's pretty wild looking; so it's hard to say if he was handsome or not. He's big and strong like Kellen, and I thought he was nice enough. We had a pleasant conversation in his tent, and he was a perfect gentleman the whole time I was there."

The two ladies exchanged a look and giggled.

Kellen's fists clenched and he snorted. "Would that I had killed him when I had the chance."

Gillian turned to see his expression, laughed, and touched his arm. "Are you jealous? That's so sweet."

He shook his head and rolled his eyes. She found him sweet when he *was not* trying.

"His men seemed a bit superstitious," Gillian said. "They actually thought I was a witch."

"A witch?" Kellen thumped his fist on the table. "Would that I had killed them *all* when I had the chance." As he'd hoped, Gillian laughed again and he reached for his pouch. With her laughing, cheerful, and looking at him thus, now would be the perfect opportunity to gift her the bracelet.

"We buried Frederick yesterday," Marissa said. "In a place of honor."

Kellen's hand dropped away. Or not.

Gillian's brows furrowed. "In the cemetery up the hill?"

Marissa nodded. "Aye."

"I'd like to go and pay my respects today," Gillian said.

Marissa waved a hand. "There is no need. My ladies and I stood for our family."

Gillian placed her hand on Kellen's arm. "I insist. He died protecting us."

Kellen placed a hand over hers. "That he did. Do you really want to disrespect him by placing yourself in danger? When I have discovered the villain who is throwing knives and poison about, you shall have more freedom. You may pay your respects then."

"But—"

"Frederick would be the first to agree."

Gillian searched his face, scowled, then shot a glare at Tristan and Owen, who murmured their agreement from across the table. She looked down at the trencher in front of her.

"Come, Gillian. Let us have no hard feelings between us this day."

"You keep forgetting that *I'm* the one who owns *you*, not the other way around."

Amused by her crossness, by the reminder of the day they had met, Kellen smiled. "I wholeheartedly agree. I am yours."

Gillian looked at him, her eyelids fluttered, and she glanced away. "Then take me to the cemetery."

Kellen sighed. She was like a dog with a bone. "I will send villagers to look for the missing bracelet. If it is there, they will find it."

He'd thought to please her, but she continued to frown. He reached for his pouch, sure he had something to put a smile on her face.

Tristan slapped the table. "I have no doubt 'tis the mangy, puking, Scots scum who are responsible for Frederick's death."

"What think you, my lord?" asked Owen. "You spoke to their laird. Did you sense the Scots are behind the attacks?"

All eyes turned to Kellen and, with a sigh, he dropped the bracelet back into the pouch. Why could they not discuss such matters when Gillian was not about?

"I cannot see them trying to slay Gillian. Kidnap her? Aye.

Ransom her? Most assuredly. But poison? Murder? Nay. There is no point to it. But it would be easier were it the case, because the thought of one of my own doing the deed sits ill."

Everyone went silent, and Gillian placed her hand on Kellen's arm and rubbed it for a moment. At her softening, he thought to get her alone, to give her the gift in private, and perhaps earn a kiss or two. "Would you care to take a turn about the orchard?"

Sir Owen cleared his throat. "Do you forget we hunt this day?"

Gillian looked to Sir Owen, then back. "You're going hunting?"

"Aye," said Sir Tristan. "'Twill be great sport."

Kellen shot a glare in his direction. "We go because we need the meat, and to train the men. 'Tis of necessity, not for the sport of it."

Gillian's brows drew together. "If you're leaving anyway, why can't you just drop me off at—"

"*You*, however, are to stay here."

"So, you get to go out, but I don't? That is so unfair! You were targeted for poison too, you know."

Kellen sighed. So much for any kisses coming his way. He shot Tristan a glare that promised retribution as he cast about for another subject. "No doubt you have much planning still to do for the wedding?"

When her eyes narrowed, he stood. Forget trying for charm, at this point he would go for appeasement. With fumbling hands, he pulled out the bracelet and set it in front of Gillian on the table. "A betrothal gift for you."

It suddenly occurred to him he didn't want her thinking it had been Catherine's. "It did not belong to my first wife. I commissioned the blacksmith to create it especially for you. I chose the sapphires as they are the color of your eyes."

The ladies leaned forward for a better look, but Gillian just stared at it, her face expressionless. Kellen could feel himself start to sweat again. "Do you not like it?"

She bit her lip then slowly looked up. "You have to marry me, right? Because you need more land, more money, and an heir. Would any of my . . . um . . . sisters . . . have been just as good?"

Kellen's mouth parted. *"Nay!"* The last thing he wanted was Gillian believing such. He truly wanted none but her.

Wishing they were alone, Kellen spared a quick glance at their audience, but there was no hope for it. He could not leave Gillian believing such nonsense. "More land means more opportunity for my knights, my dependents, and someday, for our children. So, aye, the dowry you bring will be of much benefit to all. Those are the reasons I have to marry you."

Gillian nodded and looked down at her hands as Tristan and Owen frantically motioned him to cease talking.

Kellen sank to the bench and took her hand. "But now let me tell you the reasons I want to marry you." He gently squeezed her fingers. "Your sweetness, intelligence, and playfulness. The way I cannot help but smile when you are about. Your willingness to argue with me which tells me that, despite my size, you know I would never harm you, which I would not. Your kindness and humor." He cleared his throat as it started to close. "The way you returned my daughter to me."

She finally looked up, her gaze questioning.

He shook his head. *"You* are the reason I want to marry you. You alone."

One of the ladies sighed and Gillian looked hopeful. "Do you mean that? Even if I came to you with nothing but the clothes on my back, with no dowry, would you still mean that?"

"Aye. I mean it with everything in me."

Tears in her eyes, Gillian clutched his hand, then released him, picked up the bracelet, slipped it on her wrist, and admired it. Finally, she smiled. "Thank you. It's beautiful."

He cleared his throat again. "But not half so beautiful as you."

Another sigh from the ladies and a smile from Gillian.

Kellen, deciding it was time to leave, stood and bowed. "My

lady." He strode away, unable to stop his chest from swelling with pride.

The bracelet had been an excellent idea. And although he'd thoroughly embarrassed himself in front of his men and the ladies, he decided Gillian's was the only opinion that mattered.

His men followed and Kellen stopped at the entry and looked back to see Gillian still watching him. He raised a hand and she nodded at him, smiled slightly, but still looked a bit worried.

When she looked at him like that he wanted to go back, take her in his arms, remove all her concerns, and slay all her dragons. He was glad he'd have the rest of his life to do just that.

CHAPTER 27

*G*illian held the stick over the pot with both hands while Marissa coated the wool string, hanging down the middle, with beeswax. "My husband will be one of the guests, of course."

The tiny bit of breathlessness in Marissa's voice had Gillian smiling as she jiggled the stick to shake off the excess drips into the warming pot, splattering the table in the process. "Missed him, have you?" Gillian wiggled her brows and was rewarded by Marissa's blush. "If he shows up early, does that mean I get to sleep in Kellen's bed?"

"Gillian! The things you say." Marissa turned away to busy herself at another table the servants had placed beside the rose-bushes. "Now pay attention. These candles are for your wedding procession and if you are not more careful, the beeswax will harden before you get the desired shape."

As if she cared about Edith's stupid candles. Gillian grimaced at the dripping string, the melting pot, and the small mess she'd made on the table. She had more important things to worry about. "I was thinking we might plan another picnic soon, you know, right outside the village. What do you think?"

"I think you need to keep your mind on the wedding. After the candles are finished and bleaching in the sun, I would like you to help Vera and Yvonne with the altar cloth." She gestured to where the two ladies sat on chairs on the lawn. "I know you will want to have a hand in the embroidery so you can remember it with fondness in the years to come. Then we must needs finish planning the feast and alert the musicians as to the . . .

Gillian felt a tug on her apron. "I want to go on a picnic."

Gillian glanced down at Amelia's cute little face and smiled. "Of course you do, darling. And you're the first one I'll take with me. I promise."

As the little angel grinned, Gillian wanted to grab her up, give her a hug, and spirit her away. Along with her father, of course.

"Gillian, are you listening? 'Tis time to spoon more wax on. Keep your mind on task. The wedding will arrive before you know it."

"Yeah, yeah." Gillian dutifully spooned more wax on the string. "So, about that picnic—"

"You do not fool anyone as to your purpose, Gillian. There will be no picnic and no visit to the cemetery, of that I can assure you. What there will be is attention to seating arrangements and flowers. You will turn your attention thereafter to the embroidery."

Yep, that's what she wanted to think about. Kellen seated next to Edith while Gillian languished in the dungeon. "As if I give two hoots about seating arrangements."

Marissa clapped her hands. "Enough! You will cease being difficult and will act with grace and decorum."

Gillian carefully set the stick along the top of the pot, untied her apron and threw it on the ground. She shot Marissa a glare. "You think I'm being difficult? I haven't even begun yet." She turned and walked away.

"Where are you going?" More clapping. *"Gillian!"*

Gillian headed for the front gate, marched under the long stone arch and, when she finally reached the exit, completely out of breath, held her head high and attempted to pass by the two guards stationed there.

They scrambled to block her path. "You will halt, Lady Corbett."

Gillian tried to get around them, dodging their flailing arms this way and that, but it was no use. She finally took a step back and sighed. She looked at the taller of the two guards and her eyes narrowed at seeing his overlarge nose. "Hey, I remember you." She looked at his brown-eyed companion. "And you, too. You guys tried to stop me from going up to the battlements when I first arrived."

The brown-eyed man's brow creased. "Aye, my lady," he said apologetically.

Big Nose snorted. "Aye, you were difficult then and look to be difficult now; always going where you should not."

"Do you know who I am?"

"Aye, my lady," said Brown Eyes.

"That's right. I am your lady. Basically, that makes me your boss, so stand aside."

The big nose lifted into the air. "Never."

"I'm sorry, my lady. We have our orders."

"Who gave you these orders?"

Big Nose threw back his shoulders. "Lord Marshall, himself."

Gillian crossed her arms. "Lord Marshall has gone hunting. With him away, who do you suppose is in charge?"

They looked at each other then back at her. "Lady Marissa?" asked Big Nose.

"No, not Lady Marissa. *I* am the lady of the castle."

"Er . . . not yet," said Brown Eyes apologetically.

She sighed. "Look. I just want to go to the village. What would be the harm in that?"

"Only that our lives would be forfeit if we disobey our lord."

Gillian tried to get past them again and ended up in an undignified wrestling match before she was thrown back, barely retaining her balance. They both tried unsuccessfully to hide smirks and laughter.

Gillian felt heat rising in her cheeks, looked down, and brushed at her skirt. "Fine." She looked back up and narrowed her eyes. "But you know what? Maybe there's a secret exit you don't know about."

They looked at each other then back at her. Brown Eyes looked worried again.

"That's right. I *will* find a way out; you just see if I don't. And when Lord Kellen comes back and I'm out in the village, I'll tell him you guys let me through."

"My lady, I beg of you," Brown Eyes held out a hand. "Please do not do this thing."

Who was smirking now? There might even *be* a hidden passageway but, if so, she had no idea where it was. At least they looked worried. It would have to do.

Footsteps crunched on the path behind her, and Gillian glanced over her shoulder to see Marissa approaching. She turned her back and rolled her eyes but managed to hold in a scream.

"Gillian, come here."

Gillian held up her hands to the guards in a pleading gesture. "Please let me through and I won't tell Lord Marshall," she whispered.

Big Nose and Brown Eyes drew their swords and it took Gillian a moment to realize they weren't threatening her as they turned as one to confront three riders traveling up the path on the other side of the gate.

Marissa arrived in time to watch as wedding presents were delivered. Wedding presents for Kellen and Edith. She smiled. "Ah, yes. We've already received cattle and other goods. Is that not wonderful?" When Gillian didn't react, Marissa nudged her shoulder with her own. "So generous. Do you not agree?"

Tense and overwhelmed, Gillian's throat tightened in sudden fear, and she couldn't respond. She couldn't even look at the wedding gifts. They made it seem so real, so scary. The wedding would be here before she knew it. *Lord Corbett* would be here before she knew it! What would happen to her then? Kellen said he'd want her, only her, but when the truth came out, what would happen?

"Gillian, is it not generous? Are you not pleased?"

Gillian shook her head and Marissa sighed. "'Tis very generous. We must make sure we are ready when the guests arrive. That the menus are planned and entertainments provided. Come, Gillian, all must be in order."

Gillian wanted to scream but restrained herself. She really, really, needed to go and find the place where she was attacked. That had to be the place she could travel back to her own time. It had to be. She sucked in a shuddering breath and followed Marissa. "What I desire is to forget it; to forget the whole thing. I'm going to take Kellen and Amelia and elope."

Marissa laughed.

But Gillian was dead serious. The three of them were out of there at the very first opportunity. She didn't have a choice.

"FATHER ELLIOT, CAN YOU REMAIN?" With dinner cleared away and everyone gathering in the great hall, Marissa played the part of the good hostess, talking to guests, instructing servants to set out games for the men, and readying a sewing area for the women. It was not as if *Gillian* stepped forward to do the task. "The men are to play games and would greatly enjoy thy company. Please stay."

"Gladly, my lady." His fingers tapped his overlarge belly, and he smiled as he looked about the hall. "I thank you for the invitation."

Marissa found a seat among her ladies, enjoying the antics and yells of the men as they started playing games of chance and skill. "Come ladies, what plans have we tomorrow to prepare for the wedding? Think you we should . . ."

Marissa realized she was talking to herself. Vera and Yvonne watched Kellen watch Gillian flirt with Sir Royce. Kellen's face started to flush with anger. Foolish girl.

Marissa hated to admit it, because she enjoyed Sir Royce's company so much, but she should not have insisted their neighbor gain entrance when he came calling this eve. Kellen had turned all Sir Royce's men away, but let Sir Royce in to please Marissa. She wished now she'd not interfered.

Gillian curled a piece of blonde hair around one finger as she smiled up at Sir Royce. "The thing is, I lost my bracelet and . . ."

Gillian was yammering away about the bracelet again?

Kellen moved forward to join the pair. "As I told you, I have instructed the villagers to search, but none have found it as yet."

A sharp pang of jealousy bit Marissa and she tugged too tightly on the embroidery string, puckering the material. If her husband felt half so possessive of her as Kellen did of Gillian, she'd be a happy woman.

When Kellen continued to glare at Royce, the man finally turned away to flirt with Vera and Yvonne. Moments later, when Kellen's attention was distracted by Father Elliot, Royce turned his attention back to Gillian. 'Twas like watching a live game of chess, acted by very poor players.

Gillian did not help matters by laughing and flirting with the man. Kellen's attention was soon back upon her; and he was so obviously incensed, Marissa wanted to feel sorry for him. Instead, all she could do was wonder how Gillian did it? How did she make a man such as Kellen feel so possessive?

Yes, the girl was pretty, but she did so many things wrong. She was not proficient at running a household, her sewing was barely passable, she spoke sharply, and could be demanding. She never left Kellen in any doubt about what her needs were, and yet he seemed willing to do anything to keep her happy.

It no doubt helped that she was also kind, caring, and merry. But still, the girl seemed to instinctively know how to get what she wanted from the man in her life. And Kellen seemed so different around her, no morose or dour moods. It gave Marissa hope and made her wonder if perhaps she might change, as well.

Mayhap she could smile and simper her way into her husband's heart? Mayhap she could even make him forget his perfect first wife and fall in love with her instead?

Marissa dropped the sewing to her lap and sighed. She was tired of suppressing her emotions, tired of trying to convince herself love wasn't necessary, and tired of being last in her husband's affections.

Royce moved forward and bowed to Marissa. "My Lady, you look stunning this eve, but then you always do." Marissa couldn't help but smile. It was gratifying and it soothed her ego that he made the effort to speak with her.

"I thank you, Sir Royce, I—"

"Sir Royce!" Gillian called out, then glanced flirtatiously at Kellen once more. Marissa could almost see the girl thinking to cause mischief as she purposefully gave Royce a big smile. Royce certainly seemed happy enough with the attention as he hurried once more in her direction.

Marissa sighed again. Men were such simple creatures. Could Royce not see Gillian was using him to make Kellen jealous? Could Kellen not see? Marissa wondered if she should interfere but decided against it, curious to see what Kellen would do.

Gillian played with fire, whether she realized it or not. She smiled at Kellen's frowns, seeming pleased, and then flirted with Royce all the more. "Sir Royce, I feel so safe with you. If you were to take me for a ride tomorrow, I know I'd feel protected. I've been completely cooped up here with nowhere to go."

Royce's chest expanded and he smiled, obviously flattered by the attention. Marissa rolled her eyes. Flattered? Truly? And Kellen was jealous? Truly? Could not they both see she was using them to achieve her own ends? Verily, men were simpletons!

"If you could take me to the cemetery, I know a big strong man such as yourself wouldn't fear anything." Gillian reached up and placed a hand on Royce's arm; and Kellen growled, surged forward, grabbed Gillian's wrist, and dragged her away.

Marissa half rose from her chair, thinking to intervene, but the foolish girl didn't even look upset. If anything, she looked triumphant!

Marissa sank down again. It would serve her right if Kellen took her off to beat her for her unseemly behavior.

Everyone in the room quieted as they listened to Kellen yelling at Gillian and then . . . laughter? Kellen and Gillian were laughing?

Marissa's mouth parted. How? How did that girl do it? How did she wrap Kellen around her finger the way she did?

Perhaps Marissa should be asking herself how *she* could do the same with her own husband? She wondered what he would do if he caught her flirting with Sir Royce. Would he drag her off to laugh with her?

Perhaps Marissa should be more demanding and . . . and . . . *flirtatious* with her husband? Her heart started to beat hard in her chest at the thought.

"My lady? Are you well?" asked Sir Royce.

"I am well," she answered, her voice breathless.

Perhaps instead of trying so hard to teach Gillian lessons she had no desire to learn, Marissa should pay more attention to the girl and learn from her.

Learn to flirt with her own husband. Learn to seduce her own husband. The thought made Marissa feel faint. She would not dare to talk to her husband the way Gillian spoke to Kellen. Would she? *Could* she act like Gillian?

She remembered catching Gillian kissing Kellen in the solar like a common maid. And what was her reward for such base behavior? Only that Kellen looked upon her as if the moon and sun rose from her as he lavished gifts upon her.

"Lady Marissa? Are you well?" asked Lady Yvonne.

Marissa waved a hand. "I am fine." She smiled. She was more

than fine. She stared at the exit where Kellen had dragged Gillian and considered how she would feel if her own husband did the same to her. Perhaps she would wear a look of triumph on her face as well.

She sucked in a ragged breath, caught the look Vera and Yvonne shared, forced herself to smile at everyone, and picked up her sewing as if nothing was wrong. As if nothing had changed.

But it had.

Lady Marissa Hardbrook was going to start paying attention and figure out how to seduce her husband. As a man, and therefore a simple creature, he did not stand a chance.

GRIPPING GILLIAN'S WRIST, Kellen pulled her out of the great hall and around the corner from the kitchens. He needed privacy to discuss the fact that *he* was Gillian's betrothed, and *she* needed reminding.

When he reached the relative privacy of the alcove, he whirled her about, only to catch her smiling at him. His brows pulled together and he frowned. "You flirt with another man in my presence and think it amusing?"

"Yes. Yes, I do. You're easy to tweak and I got exactly the reaction I'd hoped for."

He gaped for a moment, at a loss for words, then finally inhaled. "You made me feel this," he hit his chest for emphasis, "apurpose?"

"Yes."

He shook his head, trying to clear his wits. "So, you do not have feelings for Sir Royce?"

Gillian laughed. "Hardly. He's like a little boy next to you. I was only trying to make you jealous." She reached up to pet his arm and, when his muscles bunched involuntarily, she practically purred. "Mm. I have to say, it was pretty easy to do."

He could not think clearly with her touching him, muddling his thoughts, but was so relieved she touched *him*, that she *did not* want Sir Royce, he could not help laughing. He intentionally tightened his arm, and his mood lightened as she tested his strength with her fingers, a pleased expression upon her face. "To be more precise," he said, "Royce is like *a little girl* next to me."

She laughed and slapped his arm. "Don't be mean," she said, but continued to giggle. Triumphant, he laughed again, finally able to relax completely, the rage and confusion gone.

"I am surprised you would admit to a desire to make me jealous."

Gillian tilted her head. "Why wouldn't I? It worked, didn't it?"

His brows drew together. "Aye. It worked all too well. I wonder that you would do this thing? To what purpose? Mayhap to capture my attention?" Strangely enough he could not help feeling flattered; no one had ever cared to try and make him jealous before.

She chuckled. "You like that, huh? Well, don't get too excited. It turns out you're a pushover and an easy target."

"Well, then? Why would you do such a thing?"

"I'm glad you asked. I *am*," she poked him in the chest, "going out to that cemetery. If you don't take me, I'll keep trying until I find a way there; even if I have to find someone else to help me."

Kellen looked down at her stubborn expression and raised chin. He had a difficult time believing a lost bracelet meant so much. "What of the bracelet I gave to you? Do you not care for it?"

She bent her head and touched the metal, running her fingers over the stones. "I like this one too; if I ever lose it, I'll certainly go looking for it."

He'd noted before she was an acquisitive little thing, carrying her pack about at the oddest moments. Mayhap she would get it into her head to acquire *him* and be as unbending and possessive? He would not mind if she did.

Kellen lifted his head, listened, and realized the hall was silent, everyone no doubt trying to hear their conversation. He exhaled a pent-up breath, grabbed Gillian's wrist again, and dragged her away.

"Now where are you taking me?"

"Wait and see." Accompanied by Gillian's occasional giggle, he dragged her across the bailey, started up the stairs, and headed for the top of the wall. He easily held her upright when she tripped and, when she giggled again, he had a difficult time biting back his own smile. No doubt he was a fool for Gillian, but there was no need to bare the fact to the guards manning their posts.

When they reached the top, he gestured to his men and they melted into the darkness. Gillian moved forward to lean into the short, stone wall and lifted her face to the slight summer breeze. She glanced at the torchlight, then out over the ramparts, and into the darkness. "It's so romantic up here at night."

"Think you?"

She looked over her shoulder and grinned at him. "You're not planning to throw me off, are you?"

"'Tis tempting, to be sure." Placing hands on the stones on either side of her, he trapped her within his arms, bending his head to hers so he could press his cheek against her own. "It would be no more than you deserve for upsetting me so."

"Mm." Gillian moved her face against his, and he couldn't help a tremor of pleasure. He'd thought to take her to task again, either for her stubbornness or for succeeding in driving him mad; but when she leaned back into him, his breath caught and, instead, he wrapped his arms around her and nuzzled her cheek.

"We are to be married soon," his voice deepened at the thought. "I can hardly wait for our wedding night."

Gillian shivered and he smiled, well pleased with her response.

After a few moments, Gillian stirred in his arms. "Kellen, about that picnic—"

"Nay. Mayhap later in the summer."

"Fine. No picnic. Just take me out there for a short while and let me look around."

"Nay."

After a long pause, Gillian shrugged. "Maybe you're worried you can't protect me. That you aren't strong enough, after all, to fight off any threats."

Kellen tensed and thought to pull away, but she held fast to his arms wrapped around her waist and he settled. He was not an idiot. He could see she tried to manage him again. He could also see she would not give up the idea. She was relentless.

He hoped it bade well for their future. If she were to fall in love with him, would she be as unmoving in her feelings? He could only hope. He inhaled her intoxicating scent, like the sun after a storm, and gave in. "All right."

Gillian squealed and turned in his arms. "Really?"

Kellen straightened, stepped back, crossed his arms, and sighed long and loud so she would know he was put upon. "I will take you. I will have the men search the trees, the rocks, any hiding places beforehand. You may look about the place to your heart's content, but that is all. No picnic, and there is to be a price."

"Tomorrow? You promise?"

"Aye. *For a price.*"

"What price?"

"A kiss."

Gillian laughed and he tensed, which only seemed to make her giggle all the more. "That's not a price. I've been wanting to kiss you again anyway. But I accept your terms." She pushed at his stiff arms until he opened them, pressed against him, wrapped her arms around his neck, and tugged.

After a moment, he allowed his head to drop, and she pressed her mouth to his. He could not help the moan that escaped when her lips moved against his own in the lightest of kisses.

His arms encircled her, tightened, and pulled her closer,

higher, his mouth tasting hers, one hand rising to slip into her hair, to hold her close, as he gave himself up to the moment, to the feel of her lips against his own.

Minutes later, heart pounding in his chest, he broke away from the kiss and was glad to note he was not the only one breathing hard.

"More," she whispered and, gratified, he bent his head and kissed her again, holding her to him, and loving the way she clung. He finally ended the kiss with one last gentle brush of his lips across hers.

Trembling, she pressed her face into his chest as she tried to catch her breath and he laughed softly. "Gillian," he whispered as he held her tight. "What am I to do with you?"

"Keep me forever?"

He chuckled, bent and kissed her soft neck, and was gratified when she shivered. "I will have to, will I not? For I have not the strength to let you go."

"Then don't. Don't ever let me go. I feel safe and protected in your arms, weak against your strength."

He could not help it. He leaned back and kissed her once more; one quick kiss to her soft lips, then taking a deep breath, he forced himself to release her, to step back while he still could.

She clung and he could not help but feel pleased by her reluctance to let him go. She might be bossy, opinionated, and difficult; and she did not stay where she was told; but by the saints, she pleased him.

"Come." He took her soft hand in his rough one and descended the stairs. He did not regret letting her goad him into going to the cemetery on the morrow. It was becoming over important to her.

He just needed to let her visit the place, get it over with, then allow her to focus all her obsessions onto him. A fine plan, if ever there was one.

CHAPTER 28

"Kellen, I'm taking her."

"Nay, Gillian, you are not. You already have your pack and there is no place for the child."

Gillian raised her chin and shifted Amelia on her hip. "Then we can walk. I'll carry her."

Kellen threw his arms up in the air, turned away, and then back again. Muttering under his breath, he took Amelia, set her on the ground, lifted Gillian onto his horse, handed Amelia up, then mounted.

He sat unmoving for a moment. "Must you take your pack?" he asked with exaggerated patience.

She risked a glance at his gorgeous face, at his lips, compressed in a tight line, and tried to shift so the pack on her back wasn't against his chest. "Yes, I must," she said in a small voice.

He sighed, giving up any pretense of patience. "I will yield. But only as I want this finished. I do not wish to give you an excuse to insist we go once more. I want your word that after this day you will not mention the blasted place again. Not once until I am an old man and 'tis time to place my weary, browbeaten bones into the ground. Only then may you remember the location."

Gillian laughed at his vehemence. "You have my word." When they finally moved forward, she couldn't help glancing back, missing the place already. To the best of her ability, she'd said her goodbyes to Marissa and her ladies, to Sir Owen and Sir Tristan, to Beatrice, Cook and the others. She hoped they'd remember her fondly and felt bad for the confusion they were sure to feel when the three of them didn't return.

She tried to ignore the heavy weight of guilt squeezing her chest. She couldn't imagine this place without Kellen. But Sir Owen and Sir Tristan would keep things running smoothly until something could be figured out. She loved Kellen and, selfish or not, was taking him with her.

Anyway, who was to say it had to be forever? She didn't know how the whole time travel thing worked. They might be able to come back again. Right? After his ring was on her finger and Edith could no longer lay claim to him.

Kellen took them outside the gates and looked around. "My men have searched the area."

"No!" She tightened her arms around Amelia. "I just want it to be the three of us."

Another exhalation, then he spoke again. "My men are further afield, 'tis simply a safeguard. They have been told to keep their distance unless needed. We will be alone."

"Oh. Okay." She hesitated. "Thanks."

They rode slowly through the village, and Gillian tried to soak it all in. She waved at two young women who waved back energetically, watched a group of children tease a kitten with pieces of long grass, and noticed the respectful way the men greeted Kellen as he rode past. She was well aware this could be the last time they saw this place and these people who depended so much on him.

Guilt pinched her conscience. She wished she could let him know this might be his last chance to say goodbye to everyone but, of course, she couldn't.

For some reason, it seemed to take forever; but they finally arrived at the cemetery, and Gillian's heart pounded with fear and excitement. She wondered what Kellen would think of the future and couldn't wait to show him everything, couldn't wait to see his amazement.

After he helped them off the horse and they stood on solid ground, Gillian held hands with Kellen and his daughter, took one last look at the castle, and jerked her head toward it. "Look how beautiful it is." She wanted him to remember it as it was, not the crumbling ruin he'd soon see in the future.

Kellen, not particularly interested in the view, searched the ground.

"Kellen, look at the castle."

He finally glanced up, smiled, and his chest lifted with pride. "Aye. 'Tis impressive, is it not?"

"Yes. Very much so." And so was he. Large and strong, with chiseled features, his dark hair lifting in the wind, a lord surveying all he owned, in his element. She hoped he wasn't too angry with her for stealing all this from him; for taking him from his time, his people, and from Edith. Surely, she could make him understand?

She studied the two of them, Kellen back to kicking the dirt, and Amelia squatting down to pick tiny yellow flowers with chubby fingers. Why did Gillian feel she was about to kidnap them both?

She remembered how confused she'd been and knew they'd feel the same. But she'd be there to guide them through it. Maybe they could even come back again sometime. She did like it here. She just had no desire to find herself in the dungeon awaiting execution when her deception was discovered.

Anyway, the future had a lot to offer them. She was sure both Kellen and Amelia would thrive there. She'd love them so much they wouldn't have regrets.

Tugging them both forward, the hair rising on the nape of her neck, she took a deep breath, and walked onto the grounds.

Nothing happened.

She didn't know what else to do; so she kept walking, moving forward, trying to feel something. Kellen tried to release her hand as he searched the ground, but she held tight.

He started kicking at tufts of dirt and grumbled again. "'Tis doubtful we will find the bracelet as the villagers went over every tuft of grass and clod of dirt. But for your sake, I will search."

Gillian could feel tremors start to run up her arms, causing her to shake a bit. She glanced back to see the castle still there. It wasn't working. She tried to remember the day she'd arrived.

She'd shoved the ring on her finger and, the next thing she knew, the castle was before her. She reluctantly released Amelia and Kellen and tried to tug the ring off so she could put it back on, but it held fast. Regardless, she'd worn it that day and wore it now; so if the ring had anything to do with it, it should be okay.

She'd also been running. Grasping their hands once more, she dragged Kellen and Amelia to the far side of the cemetery. "Okay, I'm going to try and recreate where I went that first day." She tried running with them but it was slow going with Amelia. The little girl laughed, thinking they were playing a game.

"What are you doing?" asked Kellen. She could see he thought her crazy but thankfully, went along with it, his large strides easily keeping up with the slow pace.

When they finally exited the cemetery on the other side, nothing happened. The castle was still there, sturdy and strong, the village in front of it. When they finally stopped, Kellen was staring at her, his brows raised.

"What? I'm simply trying to remember what happened the day I arrived."

"You were running?"

"Yes, I was being chased."

His eyes narrowed. "Who chased you?"

She could see he was getting angry and tried to let go of his hand, but he held tight. "Just some young men."

"No doubt they stole your bracelet after you dropped it. Describe the knaves and I assure you they will be caught and punished."

Gillian barely heard him. The boys chasing her hadn't come with her. Did that mean she might have to go alone? That she might not be able to take Kellen and Amelia with her?

"Gillian? You will answer my questions."

She tugged her hand free. "I'll tell you all about it later. Right now, I need you to stand right here." Reluctantly, she had them stand at the edge of the cemetery. "Stay here. I need to try something."

Her heart pounded as she tried not to cry. She knelt and gave Amelia a kiss on her soft cheek and hugged her. "You are such a good girl." A wisp of Amelia's blonde hair lifted in the breeze, and Gillian's chest ached when the little girl smiled and offered her a tiny yellow flower. Gillian took it, sniffed the flower, and tucked it in her hair by her ear, making Amelia smile. "Thank you, sweetie." She so badly wanted to be Amelia's mother.

Gillian straightened and turned to Kellen. She took his big, warm hands in hers and looked up at him. "Kellen . . ." She found she didn't know what to say. She wanted to tell him she loved him. That the thought of living without him made her heart ache in her chest and that she needed him.

But she knew it wouldn't be fair to tell him and then leave, so instead she let go of his hands and wrapped her arms around his neck. At his look of surprise, she smiled, tugged him closer, and he willingly bent his head and kissed her, his arms closing around her.

She kissed him back, her lips clinging, relishing the feel of him, yet unable to help the tears springing to her eyes at the thought that this might be the last time she saw him, touched him, kissed him.

He broke off the kiss, lifted his hand, and gently wiped a tear off her cheek with his thumb. "Gillian?"

"Stay here." Wiping her eyes, she pulled out of his arms, turned, and walked away; shaky, nervous, and so sad she felt her heart was breaking. She walked to the other end, tightened her pack, then started to run toward them, fast like the day the boys chased her.

Kellen's brows were drawn together and Amelia grinned and jumped up and down as she held tight to her father's hand. Gillian's heart ached in her chest as ran, as she waited for them to disappear. She finally ran out of room and overshot the cemetery boundaries.

It hadn't worked. She could feel the blood drain out of her face; and breathing hard, feeling strangely lightheaded, and relieved, she glanced wildly about.

The castle, the village, Kellen, Amelia, nothing had changed. Why hadn't it worked? Suddenly dizzy, Gillian placed her hands on her knees and bent over, trying to catch her breath.

It could be anything. Was it because she was wearing medieval clothes? The time of year? The day? The month? The temperature? The season? The weather? The spot she'd exited? The boys who had been chasing her? She really couldn't rule anything out. There were too many variables. Even if Kellen would allow it, she could do this all day long and still be unsuccessful. Whatever the case, she was stuck.

"Gillian?"

While her breathing evened out, she walked back toward Kellen, whose incredulous gaze never wavered from hers.

She threw herself at him and burst into tears, so glad to be with him still, yet so scared to be with him still.

He held her tight. "Gillian, have you lost your wits, then?" He gently rubbed her back. "Never have I seen lost articles searched for in such an unlikely manner."

She cried harder.

"I am trying my best to understand why the loss of some

trinket matters so much to you. You must tell me that I might make it right. What is the matter?"

Gillian gripped his tunic and wanted to blurt out that she wasn't Edith, that's what was the matter!

He tried to pull away, but she clung. "Listen to me. I will make you a new bracelet. A better one. There is no need to upset thyself this way. I did this to please you. If you but describe its likeness, I will have an exact copy made. Better yet, you could use your skill to sketch a likeness and I will send it to London to the best of artisans. 'Twill be better than the original and surely of more value."

He continued to rub her back. "Come, Gillian. Cease. I do not care for your tears."

She pressed her cheek to his tunic, sucked in a shuddering breath, and made an effort to stop crying. She didn't know what to do. She's been so sure this would work that she hadn't planned any further. So now what? Should she run away? Wait and see what Kellen did to imposters? Explain everything to him and hope he chose her? If he threw her out, what would she do to survive? She didn't know. The tears started up again, and she sobbed.

Kellen growled, grabbed her by the waist, and set her on his horse. His face pulled into tight lines; he grabbed Amelia and handed her up then mounted behind them. "I brought you here to make you content. To give you what you desired. Not to upset you."

Maybe she should just tell him and get it over with. Let the chips fall where they may. What was she waiting for? Edith to witness the spectacle? She took a deep breath and looked forward, over the horse's ears. "Kellen . . . I . . . I don't belong here."

"This is your home now." His voice hardened.

"I . . . I . . . came from the future."

"You came from the south. We are not so backward here as you would make us out to be."

She shook her head. "No. No, you don't understand. I'm from another time."

"Gillian, I will not take you to task if you desire to do things differently here. As lady of the castle, 'tis your right to make changes. If your preference is the way of your father's keep, I'll not interfere."

"I'm not Edith." Fear tightened her throat as she strangled the words out, making it hard to breathe, but she'd said it. She'd finally said it.

"I will always call you Gillian. 'Tis my preference, as well."

Her shoulders slumped as she ran out of courage and his arms tightened, drawing her back against him. She had to face facts. She might never go home. She might live here forever or die here quite soon.

Fine tremors shook her stomach and, when Amelia started to cry, Gillian realized she was scaring the little girl. She hugged her tight and kissed the top of her head. "It's okay, sweetie." She sniffed. "It's going to be okay."

"By the saints! Two crying females are more than I can bear! I will fix this if you will only give me a task! I will take you directly to my treasury and let you have whatever you like; whatever catches your eye. I promise you I have treasures worth much more than your wretched bracelet, but you must be silent!"

Gillian nodded, sucked in a shuddering breath, and tried to control herself. Anyway, she needed to be clearheaded so she could decide what to do next. Unfortunately, she didn't have the slightest clue.

THE NEXT MORNING, one hand hidden behind his back, Kellen waited behind some shrubbery as Gillian approached. He was determined to court his lady. If he did it aright, perhaps Gillian would settle and cease pining for her old life. Mayhap if he did it correctly, she would even cede her heart and reward him with a kiss or two.

When she rounded the corner, his heart beat harder as he quickly moved forward to walk with her. "My lady?"

Gillian started and stared up at him, her eyes blank as if lost in thought, her face pensive, her usual vitality missing. "Oh. Hello."

"Good morrow. Where are you off to, then?"

"What?"

"Where go you?"

As if looking for an answer, Gillian glanced around the bailey at knights, servants washing laundry, and at the wagon rumbling through the gate. She seemed a bit distracted, which to Kellen's mind, was not necessarily a bad thing. Taking her arm, he pulled her to a stop at the other end of the shrubbery, blocking her view of the goings-on around them.

"I have something for you," he said. "A gift." Taking his hand from behind his back, Kellen dangled a string necklace on two fingers, the pearls and gold beads gleaming in the sunlight.

Gillian's eyebrows rose and her mouth parted. "Oh, wow." She placed a hand to her heart. "It's gorgeous."

Kellen smiled at her reaction. She had not been interested in recreating her bracelet or in choosing something from his treasury, but he hoped the shiny piece would please her and in some way, make up for the missing trinket. Perhaps it would even cause her to *forget* the cursed piece.

"I thought you might wear it on our wedding day." Kellen spread the necklace apart with both hands and lifted it toward her head. "May I?"

Gillian bent slightly and Kellen slipped it over her hair and smiled when she arranged it against her bosom where it looked very lovely indeed. She glanced up and smiled weakly. "It's beautiful. Thank you."

"Ah . . ." Kellen rubbed the back of his neck. "I have something more for you." He glanced around, glared at one of his men who happened to walk too close until he hurried away, and then reached inside his tunic and pulled out a piece of parchment. "I've written a poem for you."

Gillian tilted her head to the side. "A poem? Really?"

Kellen cleared his throat. The troubadour had declared his efforts feeble. Mayhap the man had even dared to laugh until Kellen had half-strangled the pansy-faced she-goat. But afterward he'd been in the proper frame of mind and tried to help Kellen finish the missive. Kellen had not allowed it; however, at that point he'd realized he'd wanted it to be from himself and no other.

Another quick glance assured him they were alone, and he took a breath and began to read. "My lady's smiles do suffer my heart to wake. Take pity on the pain, for 'tis drunk on thy beauty and laughs for the future; for when I die, I will know I have lived well. For passion is a pleasing thing and bonds as strong as horse or hound or blade."

Kellen swallowed, held his breath, and looked to see if Gillian understood what he was trying to say.

Laughter erupted from directly behind the shrub. Kellen recognized the high-pitched squeals of his foster sons as, still shrieking, Peter, Ulrick, and Francis ran along the length of the greenery and out the other side.

Face heating, Kellen was about to go and thump the spying miscreants when Gillian grasped his arm, and he allowed her to pull him in the other direction. Mayhap he should have let the troubadour help him after all.

Gillian stopped and faced him. "Did you write it yourself?" she asked softly.

Kellen swallowed. Glanced at the retreating figures of the boys, who had best run faster if they wanted to escape unscathed, then reluctantly turned his attention but did not lift his gaze.

"Did you care for it?"

"Yes. Very much."

Kellen let out a breath and nodded. "Aye. I did. I wrote it myself, with no aid."

Gillian held out a hand. "May I?"

Kellen gave over the small bit of parchment and Gillian took it, looked at it for a moment, then gazed up at him. She pressed it to her heart. "Thank you. I'll treasure it always."

He sucked in a breath, nodded, willed the heat to leave his face, and finally met her gaze. She still did not seem herself, her usual liveliness absent. "Is aught amiss, my lady?"

Gillian shrugged then smiled wistfully. "Will you make it better if it is?"

"Aye. Think you I cannot carry your burdens?"

Her blue eyes looked troubled, but finally she nodded. "You probably could."

He longed to erase the look. "Then let me. What were you thinking of? Earlier, when I stopped you."

She tucked the poem inside the bodice of her gown and held out her hand. "Come with me."

After a lingering glance at her bosom and a fleeting press of envy for his poem, he grasped her small, soft hand and walked with her toward the gardens.

"I never told you about . . . well . . . about the couple who raised me." Gillian took a breath. "Their names were Alan and Christina, and they were wonderful people; I loved them so much. They had a son named Nicholas and he was . . . like a brother to me."

Kellen squeezed her fingers, willing her to continue.

"They all died in an accident and, well, I wanted to die, too. I felt very alone. I've been thinking about them today and wondering what they'd want for me."

Kellen squeezed her fingers again. "'Tis hard to lose loved ones." He led Gillian toward a bench and, after a quick glance around, sat and pulled her onto his lap, feeling pleased when she did not protest.

Kellen opened his mouth to speak, closed it, then tried again. "I did not truly know Catherine. She went about her life, as did I. When she died, I felt cheated and angry; my chance at an heir gone with her. While I did not love her, I wanted to. I tried to be a good husband and was happy about the coming babe." He lifted a hand and tucked a length of blonde hair behind her ear so he could better see her profile.

"Life can be difficult at times, Gillian, but you will never be alone again; I swear it. You have me now. It sounds as if your foster family treated you with love. I believe they would want you happy. Can you be happy with me?"

Gillian turned and placed her arms around his neck, pressed her face against his skin, and hugged him.

Kellen, pleased by her reaction, wrapped his arms around her, held her tight, and realized he was the one in danger of falling in love. He only hoped it was requited.

After Catherine, he'd not thought to trust a woman again; but Gillian easily breached his defenses with warmth, sincerity, and candor.

He admitted to himself that Gillian had captured his heart completely.

He felt hope again, anticipation, and desire. His arms tightened further, but she did not protest, relaxing against him, her arms about his neck, her breath warm against him.

"Can I ask you something?"

Kellen relished the feel of her in his arms. "Aye. Anything."

"What are you planning to do with the dowry my father paid you?"

"It will go to help our people. I also want to improve our position here on the border. The more men we have, the better trained and outfitted they are, the better our situation and strength."

"Oh."

"Do not worry on that. I will always keep you safe." Kellen considered what more he might do to further his suit and remembered her curiosity about his marriage proposal. She had wondered at the romance of it.

For her, he could be romantic. He could propose and it would be everything she might wish for. He *would* capture her heart as she had his. She could depend upon it.

HOURS LATER, Gillian lay in bed, wondering once more what she was going to do. The Corbett's impending arrival and the imminent threat of exposure had left her exhausted, feeling like a sword was hanging over her head. Maybe she deserved it for blatantly stealing Kellen's affections from Edith, but she couldn't dredge up even a smidgen of regret. Kellen was hers now and Edith could get lost.

Gillian turned over, unable to get comfortable. She was going to have to tell Kellen everything before the Corbett family arrived. Either that or run away.

She snorted. She could leave a note, *don't look for me, it might be plague;* because, yeah, for sure she'd be able to survive in medieval England on her own.

Anyway, even if it were an option, she wasn't sure she could get herself to leave Kellen at this point. She loved him. Really, really loved him. And she was starting to suspect that he just might love her back.

Earlier, she'd practically melted into a puddle at his feet when he'd asked if she could be happy with him. If she just told him everything, threw herself on his mercy, surely he'd choose her and forget about the fortune Edith brought?

Gillian turned over again. "Marissa, are you awake?"

Marissa sighed. "Must you move about? Are you not tired?"

"When you got married, did you bring a big dowry to your husband?"

"Of course."

Gillian hesitated. "Kellen wrote me a poem today. It was so incredibly sweet. *He* was so sweet. Do you think he'd take me without a dowry?"

Marissa jerked the covers up. "The land and money are for the good of his people. Your people now. Never underestimate what you bring to this marriage. Lord Marshall has many to care for."

"But my sister already brought him a dowry. Why does he need another one?"

"It will make his position even stronger. It will help more of his knights secure a place. It means more property and crops to feed his people. It will earn gratitude and respect for you, as well. You must cease trying to turn everything into a romantic gesture."

"Right. Of course, you're right." Gillian sighed. "But you should have seen his face today when he read me that poem. He was so earnest and wonderful and . . . and . . . just so cute." She knew she was gushing but couldn't seem to help herself. "Is your husband romantic?"

Marissa turned onto her side, her back to Gillian. "He has no flowery words but is dependable and offers loyalty and protection."

"Oh. Right."

"Go to sleep, Gillian," Marissa said wearily.

Gillian turned over. She wished she could sleep and forget about her troubles, if only for a little while. She knew she'd soon have to tell Kellen everything and throw herself on his mercy. She probably ought to do it tomorrow.

She remembered the way he'd looked at her earlier, his expression tender and possessive. Would that change? She had to admit, despite the poem and the way he'd held her so close, she was concerned. Her ex-fiancé had been romantic, too, but in the end, he'd only wanted her for what she could give him. Would Kellen be any different?

As worried as she was about being put in the dungeon or hanged, she was actually more troubled about her heart. When her fiancé had revealed his true colors, it had definitely hurt, but she'd gotten over it. If it turned out Kellen only wanted her for the money she was supposedly bringing, if his expression changed from tender to contemptuous, she just wasn't sure she'd recover from the pain.

CHAPTER 29

*M*arissa would *not* lose her temper. She would not allow Gillian to affect her mood. Lord Corbett was expected soon and perhaps his family as well, so they needed to finish the final touches for the wedding. But it was not easy to concentrate with Gillian pacing about the solar.

"Gillian," Marissa forced a genial tone. "Will you please settle? We need to finish stitching these gifts for your mother and sisters."

Gillian walked to the window, yet again, and looked out. "I can't. I need to talk to Kellen."

Marissa forced her jaw to relax. She would be patient. She would not let Gillian drive her to madness. "Later. At the moment, you need to work. Perhaps you can help Beatrice sort her . . . feathers." Marissa stopped herself from rolling her eyes. Was no real work to be done this day?

"No, now. I sent the boys to go and find him."

Marissa's mouth opened and shut as she tried to decide how to chide Gillian without losing her temper. Finally, she gave up. "Honestly, Gillian, you will cease moping and pacing about. 'Tis affecting us all and getting on my nerves."

She set her stitching aside. "Kellen is mooning about and trying to find ways to please you and must I remind you, *yet again,* that as lady of the castle, 'tis your responsibility to set the tone for your home. If you have your husband running about after you, trying to win your smiles, then he has no time for his duties. You must needs—"

"*Lady Hardbrook! Lady Hardbrook!*"

The three boys, Peter, Ulrick, and Francis came running into the solar.

"Gentlemen." Marissa shot them a stern look as they slid to a halt. "You forget your manners."

Ulrick bowed quickly and the other two boys copied him. "Apologies, my lady, but Lord Hardbrook is at the gates!"

"He is riding a huge stallion!" said Peter. "Come on!"

As the boys ran out Gillian stopped, turned to look at her, and Marissa found she was struck dumb.

Gillian's head tilted to the side and she looked concerned. "Are you okay? What's the matter?"

Marissa's fingers started to shake and in that moment, she hated Gillian more than she'd ever hated anyone in her entire life.

If Gillian's husband were to turn up unexpectedly, she would toss her dignity to the wind, run down the stairs, and throw herself at him; regardless of the fact that she'd only embarrass them both.

Of course, Kellen never seemed embarrassed. He seemed to admire Gillian more than any husband Marissa knew of.

Marissa was suddenly at a loss about what to do. She was fearful to meet her own husband or at least fearful to meet him in the manner she'd been intending.

Gillian's brows furrowed. "Marissa, are you all right?"

The longer Marissa stared at Gillian the more she thought about her decision to follow Gillian's silly and immature lead in this. What if she *were* to act like Gillian? What if she *were* to go downstairs, right this moment, and throw herself at her husband? What if she were to flirt with him? Kiss him?

Her stomach tightened so much it ached and, when dizziness assailed her, she remembered to breathe. Would he set her aside in disgust? Would he shove her away in embarrassment for them both? He might. But what if he hugged her back? What if he greeted her in kind?

Before she could turn coward, she stood. "Come with me, ladies. I need your assistance."

Vera and Yvonne jumped up at the urgency in Marissa's voice; and they followed, as did Gillian.

"Not you, Gillian. You, you just . . ." She waved her hand. "Just . . . do something."

Her ladies hurried with her to her bedchamber. She needed to change into her most beautiful gown, uncover and brush out her hair, one of her best features, pinch her cheeks and bite color into her lips.

"Wait!" called Gillian from behind them. "What's happening? Where are you going?"

Marissa found she could not answer. She was scared spitless.

DETERMINED to talk to Kellen and tell him everything, Gillian waited until Marissa was out of sight before leaving the solar. She'd explain who she was, or rather, wasn't. She'd tell him where she was from, how she felt about him, and her hopes for their future together. Everything.

At the thought, her heart rate increased and her hands felt cold and clammy; but she really couldn't stand the suspense a moment longer. With shaking fingers, she slipped on her pink pack for the proof it contained to back her claims, smoothed her yellow dress, and headed out to find Kellen.

When she reached the top of the stairs, she immediately saw

Kellen talking with a well-dressed older gentleman below who, from the looks of him, could be none other than Kellen's father.

Kellen looked up, smiled, and beckoned to her. "Gillian," he circled his hand a few more times. "Come and meet my father."

Taking a shaky breath and feeling a bit deflated by the fact that she'd have to put off her talk, she went downstairs and joined them, slipping her hand around Kellen's arm, linking them.

He patted her hand possessively then held his own over it. "Gillian, this is my father, Lord Edward Hardbrook. Father, this is Lady Edith Corbett, my betrothed. I call her Gillian."

Gillian smiled at the pride in Kellen's voice and held out a hand, which Lord Hardbrook took in one of his, and bowed over in a graceful gesture before kissing the back. "I am very pleased to meet you, my dear."

Gillian arched a brow at the smooth move. "Thank you. It's nice to meet you, too. I can certainly see where Kellen gets his good looks and charm from."

Kellen grinned and Lord Hardbrook laughed in surprise. "Thank you, my dear." She could see he was flattered, but she'd meant it. His father was just an older version of Kellen, and it was nice to know Kellen would still be yummy to look at in a quarter-century. The thought made Gillian's hand clench on his arm. Would it be her at Kellen's side or some other wife?

"My son seems well pleased with his choice of bride, as am I," said Lord Hardbrook. "I welcome you to our family."

"Thank you."

Lord Hardbrook's eyes widened as he looked beyond Gillian and up the stairs. Gillian turned to see Marissa descending, dark hair floating about her shoulders, looking pale but beautiful in a royal blue gown, her fine features slightly strained.

When she reached the bottom, she took a deep breath then ran at her husband, throwing herself at him, her arms wrapping around his neck. Lord Hardbrook's mouth dropped and he gaped for a moment but quickly encircled his wife and chuckled as she clung to him. "Hello, wife, I have—"

Before he could say more, Marissa grasped his head, pulled him toward her, and kissed him thoroughly. The man seemed frozen in place for a moment, but quickly relaxed and got into the spirit of the kiss, his arms tightening about his wife.

Gillian wiggled her brows at Kellen who brought a fist to his mouth to clear his throat and hide a smile. As the kiss continued, they both looked everywhere but at the couple in front of them.

Finally, Kellen took a step back, pulling Gillian along with him. "Well, yes, then. We will see you at supper," he said, as he turned around, caught Gillian's hand, and pulled her away.

They both walked fast until finally they were almost running out the front doors. They barely made it outside before they burst out laughing.

WHEN HER HUSBAND finally broke off the kiss to gaze down at her, surprise, pleasure, and interest in his expression, Marissa was pleased to see his breathing was as unsteady as her own. His gaze fell to her lips, his color heightened, and he clasped her in his arms as tightly as she could have ever wished for.

Her hands lowered to his chest and she could not help but smile up at him as she gasped for breath. "I have missed you, husband."

A smile curved his lips as he gazed down at her. "I can see you have. I have missed my own sweet wife, as well."

At his words, tears filled her eyes and the last of her misgivings melted away. She leaned up on her toes to whisper, "My ladies have moved Gillian's things to their chambers. I thought perhaps you would wish me to show you our bedchamber and help you get settled?"

Edward glanced about quickly, nodded, released her, and practically shoved her toward the stairs, his hands firm on her waist. "I would like nothing better."

Disbelief, relief, and happiness bloomed inside Marissa as she hurried up the staircase with her husband directly behind her, urging her onward.

She conceded that she had definitely been too harsh with Gillian. It turned out the girl knew a thing or two about managing a household, after all.

∼

KELLEN HEADED with Gillian across the bailey, toward the training field, and smiled when she giggled. "You are amused?"

"I couldn't believe that was Marissa. I never would have guessed she had such a passionate marriage. Never."

Kellen laughed. "Nor I. I have not seen the two of them act in such a way as that before, but I am happy for my father." Marissa had seemed cold in the past, and he knew what it was to be married to a passionless wife.

Looking down at Gillian, he let go of her hand and put his arm about her shoulders, pulling her close, enjoying the sunshine, the walk with his lady, the way she so easily slid her arm into place about his waist, and the way his heartbeat sped at her touch. "My father is here, and soon yours will be, also. I cannot wait for you to be mine."

He could not help but notice the way Gillian tensed at his words, her expression bordering on fear.

"You need not distress yourself. I will be gentle with you; I swear it."

Gillian nodded and squeezed his waist. "I know you will."

"Are you worried over the wedding?"

She shrugged but remained silent.

"I cannot wait until is it over, as well. Life will be more

peaceful afterward. I swear I will do all in my power to help you settle into your new role. I want you to be happy, Gillian."

Gillian pulled him to a stop and looked up at him. She opened her mouth to speak, closed it, and then sighed.

"What is it?"

She took his hand. "I have something I need to tell you. It's important."

Gillian looked about as if searching for privacy, and Kellen realized this could be the perfect opportunity to carry out his plan. "And I have something to say to you, as well. Come."

Grabbing her hand, he pulled her toward the training fields, past his men and the orchard, and to the private garden beyond. He was relieved to see it was unoccupied as he dragged her toward a pretty little bench and settled her upon it.

She slipped off her backpack. "Kellen?"

"Aye. Give me a moment." He could feel the pulse beat in his own throat, and could feel himself start to sweat as he paced back and forth. Finally, he stopped, took a breath, and rubbed the back of his neck. "Gillian, you are . . ."

He studied her beautiful face, the soft blue eyes, thickly lashed, the full and inviting lips, the high cheekbones framed by her disheveled blonde hair, and tried to remember the words so painstakingly memorized. Finding the distance between them intolerable, he knelt on one knee, his face almost even with her own, and grasped her hands in his.

His mind blanked, all the memorized words going straight out of his head. He swallowed and looked into her eyes. "Gillian, I have not the pretty words that some men do, but I . . . I have loved you from almost the moment we met."

Tears filled her pretty eyes and, when she tried to speak, he put a finger to her soft lips, silencing her. He had to finish this or he'd kiss her and be done with it.

"The first day I met you, when I took you from Royce, I knew you were mine. But do you remember at the rocks? When you took my hand as we walked back to the keep?"

She nodded.

"When you took my hand, I was certain I was yours."

He lifted her hand to his mouth and kissed the back, turned it over and kissed her palm, and then holding her trembling hand to his cheek, gazed into her tear-filled eyes. "You are everything. My life, my love, my all. Will you marry me, Gillian?"

~

"OH, KELLEN . . ."

Gillian felt her face crumple as he blurred before her. She'd been concentrating so hard on what she was going to say to him that when he'd sunk down on one knee, when she'd realized he was proposing, she'd been taken completely by surprise.

She blinked against tears as she looked into his earnest face, felt his warm, raspy skin against her fingers, and all the problems between them fell away.

She loved him, and he loved her. She could see it in his face; *feel* it as he looked at her. She wanted him to choose her *so much,* and here he was, this strong, capable, gorgeous man, barely breathing as he waited for her answer. He had such a tender expression on his face, it was all she could do to not simply melt into a puddle at his feet. He'd choose her when given the choice between her and Edith. She really believed he would.

His brow creased in sudden worry and he swallowed audibly. More tears rushed to her eyes. "Kellen, I love you so much."

He let out a breath, grasped her hand on his cheek, and turned his head to kiss her palm again. "You had me worried for a moment, dearest."

Her heart fluttered at the heartfelt endearment, and she watched as he dug in the pouch at his waist and pulled out an intricately braided silver ring. Tears blurred her vision. "It's beautiful."

"You have not answered my question. I know 'tis all arranged, but I would have you want me for your own self, as I want you, and not out of a sense of obligation." He swallowed again as he studied her face, his vulnerable expression clearly revealing how much her answer mattered to him. "I would call it off if you did not truly want me."

Gillian's heart pounded. She loved him so much at that moment her heart ached. "Yes. If you could ever want me, just for me, then yes, I'd marry you in a heartbeat. It's what I want with everything I have in me. I want to marry you, and be your wife, and have your babies, and love you until the day I die."

He released a breath, lifted one of her hands, and kissed the knuckles hard. "Good, that is good." He lifted his gaze and grinned at her. "Particularly as I am not sure I was being honest and could let you go if you said otherwise."

She laughed. "Oh Kellen. I do love you. So much."

He took a deep shuddering breath, slipped the ring on her finger, stood, and swept her into his arms. He kissed her roughly on the mouth, holding her almost too tight, before gentling.

A moment later he pulled back to study her expression and whatever he saw there made him smile. "You have made me very happy. I will make you happy, as well. I swear it."

He leaned in to kiss her once more and as she clung to him; she hoped his words were still true when he learned the truth. And she'd tell him. Just as soon as he stopped kissing her.

A LONG WHILE LATER, Kellen's head lifted and he glanced around. It took her a moment, but Gillian realized she heard voices and started to pull away, to move out of Kellen's arms, but he wouldn't let her go. He quickly stole another long kiss, and another, smoothed back her hair, then reluctantly released her, and stepped back.

Peter's voice called out. "Lord Marshall! Lady Corbett! Are you there?"

Excited chatter from the foster boys gave Gillian the strength to finger comb her hair, press her fingers to her swollen lips, and ease back a few more paces before the boys rounded the corner.

They let out a cheer when they spotted them. "There you are!" said Ulrick.

Peter glanced between the two of them, one brow arching.

Francis hooted at the sight of them. "We've searched everywhere for you! What have you been doing?"

Kellen cleared his throat, and Gillian bit her bottom lip to keep from smiling as Kellen, still catching his breath, stumbled out a hearty greeting. "Just showing Lady Corbett the flowers in the garden."

Three faces crumpled in disgust. *"Flowers!"* said Francis.

Kellen shot Gillian a wide-eyed look that said *help me out;* but she only smiled and glanced down, glad she wasn't the only one flustered.

It was good the boys had shown up. Kellen's kisses were mind-scrambling, and they needed to talk. She needed to admit she was from the future, that she wasn't Edith Corbett, and hope he still chose her. After his heartfelt proposal, she was starting to believe he just might.

"Flowers are foolish!" said Peter. "We've been looking everywhere for you! Lady Marissa has sent everyone out searching, and we found you first!"

"Ah, yes, very good, boys. You are clever indeed to have found us."

"Lady Marissa promised an extra tart after dinner if we did!" exclaimed Ulrick, but his brows suddenly furrowed. "Do you think she means us to share one, or to have one to ourselves?"

Kellen's expression was grave. "I'll talk to her and make sure you each get one." He winked at Gillian.

Gillian, her heartbeat finally slowing, asked, "What does Lady Marissa want?"

Peter grinned. "Oh, we did not tell you! Your family, come from Corbett Castle, have finally arrived! Lady Marissa and Lord Hardbrook had to wake from a mid-day nap to greet them without you, and she is quite put out at your absence. You must come quickly!"

Francis nodded vigorously. "Before she changes her mind about the tart!"

"My family is here?" Gillian's voice trembled.

Kellen turned to smile at her. "We are one step closer to being wed."

Fright had Gillian pressing a hand to her chest and she could actually feel her heart speeding, thumping. "But . . . but . . . you said it would take them three more days to get here."

He shrugged. "Mayhap they had already left. No matter, let us greet them." He reached forward to rub Francis's hair. "I am sure young Francis is glad to see his parents again, as well."

The boy smiled at him, but when the other boys took off running—yelling how they must tell Lady Marissa they'd found them first—he was quick to follow.

Kellen helped Gillian put on her backpack, tucked her into his side, and they started walking. Cold inside and out, she didn't resist, didn't know what to do. Her heart beat rapidly, thudding in her chest as they left the gardens and headed toward the orchard. Her instincts told her to run and hide, but she was well aware it was too late for that.

There was nowhere to go, and the moment she'd been dreading was upon her. She looked up at Kellen, who gazed down at her, a pleased and loving expression on his face and, again, though her throat had closed and her mouth was dry with fear, she felt a spark of hope.

Maybe Kellen really would choose her?

She swallowed and pulled to a stop. "Kellen, wait a moment. I .
. . I . . . have something to tell you."

"And I am anxious to hear. I want to learn each detail of how
you came to love me. I want you to assure my poor heart that I am
not alone in this feeling." He suddenly pulled her into his arms
and gave her another long, mind-blowing kiss.

When he finally broke it off, he pressed his forehead to hers
for a moment, then smiled, grabbed her hand, and tugged her
along. "We will talk later, without fear of interruption." His smile
widened. "Mayhap tonight?"

"But . . ." She let out a shaky breath. It was too late. She'd left it
far too late and didn't know what to say, anyway. She'd just have
to face the music and see if Kellen chose her. The thought made
her shiver.

She stumbled and he caught her easily, smiling down at her,
his expression excited, eager. "Careful, we do not wish your father
to think you ill-used."

She sucked in a shuddering breath, nodded, and tried to return
the smile. She'd never been so afraid in her entire life.

CHAPTER 30

*W*hen Kellen and Gillian entered the great hall, Tristan and Owen surged forward and tried to stop him, to tell him something; but he pushed past them, anxious to see Lord Corbett, and to assure the man he was a good choice for his daughter. To assure Lord Corbett that Kellen was well pleased with the match.

All eyes turned toward them—Marissa and his father, Lord and Lady Corbett, their daughters, even Kellen's knights and servants—and the silence was unnerving.

Regardless, Kellen moved forward to warmly welcome Gillian's family. He had no doubt Lord Corbett had taken great care to give Kellen his best daughter this time, so 'twas important to Kellen to show there were no hard feelings from the nastiness with Catherine. Now that Gillian was his, he could afford to be high-minded and forgiving. "Welcome, Lord Corbett. Lady Corbett. I see you have brought some of your lovely daughters, as well. You are all most welcome here."

Pandemonium ensued as everyone started speaking at once, or rather, *yelling* at once.

Lord Corbett, his voice rising above the others, pointed at Gillian and demanded, "Who is this girl?"

Kellen turned to look at Gillian who, rather than greeting her family stood stiffly next to him, clutching his hand, her face a mask of fear.

Kellen quickly placed a comforting arm around her to protect her from her crazed family. First her sister Catherine had proved to be unsound, and now her father did not know his own daughter? Were she and her brother the only sane ones among them? Little wonder she'd arrived early. She had no doubt run away from home.

Lady Corbett now yelled at Kellen's father, who bellowed in return as he pointed repeatedly with his finger at one of the Corbett daughters. Another of the girls, a younger one, cried and carried on in the most irritating way.

Kellen finally lost his temper. "Quiet! What is happening here?"

Silence reigned for a few moments, then Lord Corbett, spittle dotting his lips and beard, pointed his finger at Gillian. "That is not my daughter, the Lady Edith Corbett." He turned and pointed at one of the girls in the gaggle behind him. "That is."

Kellen followed the new direction of Lord Corbett's finger to see a girl who closely resembled his dead wife. Instantly repulsed, he scowled. "I think not." Did the man think to renege on the betrothal and foist off an inferior daughter? Did he think to give Gillian to another? His arm tightened around her shoulders. He'd not give her up.

Lord Corbett's jaw thrust forward. "What is happening here? You think to go back on our agreement? You *insisted* you have another of my daughters. I had to break her betrothal to make it so. Now you do not want the girl and have replaced her with another? Do you seek revenge, after all?"

Kellen looked at Gillian, then at Corbett's daughter, at Lord Corbett, and then back to Gillian's fearful expression. Lord

Corbett may have gone insane, but he swore to himself he would never hold Gillian's parentage against her. He lifted her chin and forced her to meet his gaze, anxious to reassure her. "Tell me they are lying and I will send them all away."

Gillian looked up at him, her gaze wide-eyed and afraid. She slowly shook her head.

"Gillian?"

GILLIAN'S RACING heart felt as if it might explode. "K-Kellen," she stuttered, barely able to say his name. Face hot, she glanced around the room and could practically feel the weight of the hostile gazes drilling into her. Finally, she took a deep breath and tilted her head to meet Kellen's worried gaze.

"I-I'm not Edith Corbett." Her voice, barely a whisper, broke on the last word. "My name is Gillian Corbett and I traveled through time. I-I'm from the future." She swallowed hard. "I'm Lord Corbett's granddaughter, seven hundred years from now. At least, I think I am." She lifted a pleading hand to Kellen. "I wanted to tell you. I tried. I didn't know how."

Kellen's mouth parted and he looked at her and then at the others around him. "Is this entire family gone mad?"

Gillian didn't move, didn't say another word, just stood frozen within Kellen's arms.

Kellen glared down at her. "You truly believe *that girl*," he jabbed his finger in the air twice for emphasis, "is Edith Corbett?" Kellen gestured toward the beautiful girl Lord Corbett had pointed out. The girl straightened her shoulders as several of her sisters laughed and her mother's expression turned especially snide and haughty.

Gillian nodded, her heart pounding so hard in her chest it hurt. "Yes." She took a gasping breath. "But if you'd rather ch-choose me, I-I'm okay with that."

Kellen didn't respond for a moment, his expression colder and angrier as the seconds ticked by. He suddenly let go of her, took a step back, and thrust his fingers through his hair. "You deceived me? You are not the Lady Edith Corbett? You *lied?*"

Gillian swayed on her feet. He wasn't going to choose her. She could see it in his face. Despair sank deep within her. He'd just told her he loved her, and now was looking at her as if he hated her. Did people really only want her for what she could give them? Couldn't he just love her because he did? "I am not Lady Edith Corbett," she said again, trying to rein back tears.

Marissa stepped forward and instructed her husband to remove Gillian to the chapel. "We will come to you when this discussion is decided."

Kellen's father moved forward and gently took her arm. Gillian left with him, stumbling a few times as they headed out the doorway. Angry voices broke out once more behind them. She no longer cared what happened. All she could see was Kellen's cold, angry, bitter face.

She glanced back once, but tears blurred her vision. Apparently, she'd been right to be afraid for her heart. If she didn't come with money, he didn't want her.

KELLEN WATCHED Gillian walk away and saw the betrayed look she cast him. It was as a knife in his gut. He was not the betrayer here, she was. Deceiving him, leading him on, lying to him. Just as Catherine had done.

No, she was worse than his wife. At least Catherine had not attempted to sway his affections before trying to kill him. He felt as if his guts were being ripped out. His heart. And then to spout nonsense besides? He was simply at a loss, hollow, and empty as he watched her go.

Lord Corbett started to yell again, demanding and grating, his voice curiously insubstantial as numbness spread throughout Kellen's body. When Kellen ignored him, unable to think or care enough to form a reply, Marissa stepped forward to appease the man; and Kellen glanced at Edith, the real Edith, who looked so much like Catherine he had to turn away.

He accepted that Gillian was not Lady Edith Corbett but was having a hard time believing Gillian was not still his, that she was not the girl he'd been given to marry. The girl he'd fallen in love with.

Now he had to decide what to do. She'd lied to him, betrayed his trust, used him, and all he wanted to do was run after her and force her to admit she truly did love him.

Again, he compelled himself to look at Edith, who stared impassively back, her chin rising. She arched a brow in a disdainful fashion he well recognized and, again, he felt revulsion. His decision was made.

He would not marry a woman he did not love. He would marry Gillian. Even if she was a lying, deceitful, double-tongued pretender. She had convinced him of her feelings, made him feel impassioned and alive, and she could bloody well continue to do so. She would keep her promises to him. He would insist upon it.

Kellen looked at the door and wanted to follow Gillian and have this out with her. Whatever her purpose in coming here, he could not give up on the idea that she *did* love him. He could not believe their entire courtship had been a ruse. When she had told him earlier she loved him, he'd believed her, and the relief had fair weakened his knees.

Regardless of her deception, he loved her still. But what of her true feelings? Her true motivations in coming here? He thought of her strange way of speech, so unlike anything he'd heard before. The pack she carried about so frequently. Was she a spy? A girl who sought to improve her station in life through marriage? A thief? He wanted to see her face as he asked these questions. He needed to know.

His jaw ached as he clenched his teeth. Regardless of her answers, he would do whatever was necessary, including paying a fine to the king if he had to, but would marry none but her. If she did not love him, she could learn to do so. He would insist upon it. She was his.

He looked at Edith's stiff expression again and acknowledged he had been arrogant. He had thought one wife as good as the next so long as she gave him an heir.

Not so. Gillian was the only woman for him. He could not be happy without her and would not give her up. Not only for his own sake but for Edith's, as well. He was sorry for the humiliation she would suffer, but she also deserved better than a loveless match. He'd been on the other end of one of those before and it hurt.

As Lord Corbett continued his rant, his finger now pointing repeatedly in Kellen's direction, Sir Tristan and Sir Owen moved to stand beside Kellen, ramrod straight, in a show of support.

Kellen eyed Edith one last time and shook his head. He looked at Lord Corbett, held up a hand and, when the other man stopped talking, Kellen informed him, "The wedding is off."

Lord Corbett gaped like a landed fish, his face blooming redder than before. *"How dare you?"*

Kellen, uninterested in any discussion that did not involve Gillian, turned and headed for the doors; but Lord Corbett ran after him and grabbed his arm, fingernails digging into skin. Kellen reluctantly stopped and exhaled a pent-up breath.

Lord Corbett, practically frothing at the mouth, shook Kellen's arm. "You will marry my daughter! I had to break a betrothal with Lord Phillip's son so you could have her." Spittle flew. "It cost me much."

Kellen's eyes narrowed and he bit out, "Only fitting as your eldest daughter cost me a son."

Corbett gaped and drew his hand to his chest. "But . . . but . . .

you do not understand! He will not take her back. Only my alliance with you keeps Lord Phillip from attacking."

Marissa stepped forward, composed and serene. "Sir Tristan is in need of a bride, my lord. Might he not be persuaded to take her?"

Edith's mother burst into tears.

"*My lord!*" Lord Corbett sputtered. "Take her? Take her indeed! He should be so fortunate!"

Kellen remembered Tristan mentioning how lucky Kellen was to marry an heiress and arched a brow at his friend. "Well, then?"

Tristan looked at Edith, who eyed him back.

Her coldly blank expression reminded Kellen of Catherine once more, so he stipulated, "Only if you are willing. I'll not force the issue."

Tristan smiled. "Aye, if she'll have me, I'll take her and be glad of it."

Lord Corbett's wife wailed and Lord Corbett sputtered, but Marissa raised her voice to be heard. "A marriage between Lady Corbett and Sir Tristan would be beneficial for all concerned." She turned to Kellen. "Except, of course, there will be no dowry for you. It will go to Sir Tristan."

Kellen started forward again. "I care not."

Lord Corbett made a wild grab for Kellen's sleeve. "I care! He has not your standing! He can offer me no protection against Lord Phillip."

Kellen shrugged him off. "You need not worry on that score. I will stand behind Sir Tristan."

Feeling the matter concluded, Kellen slapped Tristan on the back and headed out the door toward the chapel. He needed to find out just who it was *he* was marrying.

As confused and angry as he was about Gillian's identity, he did not wish to doubt her. There must be some explanation for her behavior. He thought of her strange speech again and wondered at her origins. In all his travels, he had never come across such.

No matter. He would solve this mystery and marry the lady. She was no doubt fearful and confused, and he meant to go to her with assurances that all would be well. He'd find out how she came to be here, who she was and, most important, if she really did love him.

He hurried, having the strangest feeling that if he did not, she would disappear from his life as quickly as she'd appeared.

Lord Corbett followed, yapping at his heels. "This is unacceptable. I will not be treated this way. What of our alliance? What of your daughter, Amelia? Does she not have Corbett blood running in her veins? Do you wish to diminish her position by marrying this girl?"

Kellen stopped and glared at the man. "Were it not for Gillian convincing me otherwise, I would not have a daughter. Catherine thought to steal her from me, along with my heir. As she lay dying, she claimed Amelia was not my child, but her lover's."

Lord Corbett's mouth dropped. "She would never!"

"Aye, she did."

"'Twas the poison polluting her mind!"

"You were not there. She was most convincing." Kellen strode away.

After a long moment, Lord Corbett ran to catch up. "You must attend me!"

When they finally reached the chapel, Kellen stood in the doorway and watched Father Elliot trying to comfort Gillian, who was crying, the two of them seated on a bench, her pack beside them.

Kellen sighed, tension draining out of him, his feeling of dread subsiding. He caught his father's gaze upon him and his own brows rose in question, but his father simply shrugged.

Lord Corbett pushed past Kellen to point at Gillian. "She is a fraud, a liar, and insane!"

Kellen dragged the man back, yanking him around to face him. "You will not speak of her in such a manner!"

Lord Corbett attempted to shake him off. "Why should I not? She could be anyone. A temptress, a swindler, a villain sent by your enemies to defeat you from within. Or even my enemies, to prevent this advantageous match."

"You will cease such slander or I will be forced to make you. I will—"

"There will be no such talk in this chapel!" Father Elliot raised both hands. "Saint Cuthbert himself blessed this sacred place, and there will be no fighting within these walls. Until you can comport yourselves in a manner fitting Lords and Knights, you will stay outside."

Kellen met Gillian's reddened gaze and, seeing she was safe enough, he dragged Lord Corbett outside. He did not want the man slandering Gillian in her hearing and needed to convince the old fool to accept Tristan and be on his way.

Lord Corbett grabbed at Kellen's tunic. "What of Edith's dowry? We will double it!"

Kellen took a breath, determined to be patient.

"Think what you could do with the coin Edith brings! This girl? Who is she? Who is her family? She has nothing. She is nothing."

With a growl, Kellen grabbed the man by the throat.

SHE HAS NOTHING. *She is nothing.* Gillian's stomach clenched at the words Lord Corbett yelled so convincingly. It almost sounded as if the man was trying to bribe Kellen to take Edith over Gillian. She almost felt . . . hope. Was Kellen going to choose her? Regardless of everything? Could he?

She knew Kellen would lose out financially by marrying her. She knew he had plans for the money: To help more of his knights secure a place, to expand his property and his crops, to improve his influence and his military along the border.

All along she'd consoled herself with the thought that he'd received Catherine's dowry. If his wife hadn't died, Kellen wouldn't have more. But now Lord Corbett was offering double the amount if he married Edith.

Gillian's hands clenched open and closed on her skirt. She desperately wanted Kellen to choose her. She'd been risking her heart and counting on it, risking *his* heart. Only now was she considering, at what cost to others?

On the other hand, if he didn't choose her, what would happen to her? She had no way back home. She was basically at his mercy. Hysteria bubbled in her chest. Did she take Laird MacGregor up on his offer of marriage?

A few minutes later Kellen came back inside; and Lord Corbett followed, rubbing at his throat. Both men looked grim as they moved toward her and, at the last moment, Lord Corbett grabbed Kellen's arm, pulling him to a stop. "She could be an assassin, sent by your enemies to slay you."

Kellen jerked away. "If I feared murder, I need only marry one of your daughters."

Lord Corbett gasped, then shook his head. "What of the king? Think you he will not exact a high price when I tell him of your refusal to wed Edith? After your demands to produce her? 'Tis yet another way this girl will cost you."

"Think you *your* reputation will survive the revelation of the manner of Catherine's death?" Kellen's voice was low and fierce. "Perhaps I shall run to the king with tales of my own if you interfere in my affairs."

Kellen's father stepped forward. "I, for one, would be pleased to have my son's name vindicated."

Gillian made an inarticulate sound as tears flooded her eyes. It did sound as though Kellen wanted to choose her. But again, at what cost to himself? To others?

Father Elliot patted Gillian's hand and stood once more. "My lords. I believe I have been quite clear on the subject of fighting within the chapel. You must remove yourselves if you wish to continue in this vein."

Kellen ignored the man and moved forward to stand in front of Gillian. "Who are you?" His tone was gentle. "Where do you come from?"

Gillian wiped her eyes and reluctantly lifted her gaze as all four men stood in front of her. "I told you. M-my . . . name is Gillian Corbett. I was born in the future, seven hundred years from now. I was running through the cemetery and," she shrugged. "I just a-appeared here." She gazed into Kellen's eyes, willing him to believe her. "I think that I may be a descendant of Lord Corbett."

The man made a scoffing noise.

"Look." She lifted her hand and revealed her ring.

Lord Corbett grasped her fingers. "Where did you get that? You stole this from my rooms at Corbett Castle!"

She snatched back her hand. "No, I didn't! It belonged to my father."

Lord Corbett held out his hand. "Give it to me."

Gillian tried to take off the ring but, as always, it stuck fast.

Lord Corbett shook his hand, palm up. "Now, girl!"

She yanked again, sobbing with effort, and pulling so hard she cut her finger; and blood welled up, bright red against the white of her skin.

Kellen slammed the back of one hand into Lord Corbett's chest, knocking the man back a few paces. "Now look what you've caused with your shouting and abuse!"

Gillian looked at the blood coating her finger and ring. Her hand seemed to waver a bit, like a mirage; and the ring seemed to loosen. She sucked in a breath.

The blood.

She'd been bleeding when she'd arrived. She'd cut her finger when she'd shoved the ring into place, and then right after, she'd traveled through time. She looked around and the men seemed to fade, the chapel to crumble, and another thought occurred to her. The chapel had been blessed by Saint Cuthbert, the same as the cemetery. She didn't know if that meant anything or not, but Father Elliot sure seemed to think highly of the man. Or rather, the *saint*.

Goose bumps erupted all over Gillian's body as the men came back into sharp focus, the chapel new again. She was on the verge of time travel.

She suddenly had a choice.

Would she stay and fight Edith for Kellen and possibly endanger his future?

Or did she let him go?

It wasn't a hard choice, only difficult to make herself comply. She loved Kellen so much and wanted him to have everything he needed. She wanted him to have the money. If she stayed, if she fought for him and won, he could lose everything. Kellen needed that dowry. She didn't want the king angry at Kellen, fining him, and jeopardizing everything he had. He'd end up hating her in the end.

He couldn't choose her. Too much was at stake. Too many other lives depended on him. She knew he was having a hard time with all this. She'd deliberately stolen his affection thinking they could have a life together. That being the case, she should be the one who made things easy on him. Even if it devastated her.

She stood, slid on her backpack, and tightened the straps. Her heart started beating too fast, a staccato rhythm thumping in her chest and ears.

She looked at Kellen and tried to memorize his face, his chiseled features, the thick, tousled, black hair, the dark stubble covering his bold, masculine jaw and strong chin. The amber eyes, and even the scars on his cheek and forehead. The memories would have to be enough.

Her lip trembled. "Kellen."

He continued to argue with Lord Corbett.

"Kellen."

He glanced up.

"Goodbye, my darling." Tears welled in her eyes. "I-I will always love you. I swear it."

All four men turned to look at her, but she only had eyes for Kellen. She tried to burn his image into her mind one last time as she slipped off the ring.

CHAPTER 31

*T*he hair on the back of Kellen's neck rose and he surged forward when Gillian started to waver, fade, and then disappear. He was too late. She was gone. There was nothing but empty air where she'd been standing. His mouth open, his heart beginning to thunder, every muscle stretched taut; he turned wide eyes on his father, Lord Corbett, and the priest. "Did you see her?"

Father Elliot's mouth was open as he loudly sucked in deep breaths. *"'Tis the second miracle of Saint Cuthbert!"*

Kellen searched the chapel, but there wasn't much to explore; only the altar, and a few benches, including the one Gillian had been sitting on. He even looked up at the beams in the ceiling.

He felt the air where he'd last seen his bride, but she was truly gone. He threw back his head. *"Gillian! Where are you? Come back to me!"*

White-faced, Lord Corbett sank onto a bench. "Perhaps the girl was speaking the truth?" His voice was hoarse. "Perhaps she truly was my granddaughter? That or a witch."

Father Elliot snorted. "No witch could ever cross this particular threshold, or take communion herein. 'Tis a *miracle*."

Kellen's clenched his fists, battling the desire to destroy the room, to smash walls, tear off window shutters, and lay waste to everything. He looked around wildly. *"Gillian! Come back!"* Kellen stared at the empty space where last he'd seen her and swallowed. If Gillian had been telling the truth about where she was from, then mayhap she'd told the truth about loving him as well.

So why would she leave him? Why would she *abandon him?* He had every intention of asking her just that when he found a way to get his hands on her. She had to come back. He could not live without her.

GILLIAN'S EYES BURNED, dizziness overwhelmed her, and she fell, landed on one knee, and hit a rock. Pain, sharp and intense, bit hard around her kneecap and her vision blacked for a moment. She couldn't breathe.

Finally, sliding off her pack, and clutching her knee, she groaned, reached out, and touched rough stone. Her shaking fingers grasped for a handhold, found one, and she pulled herself up.

As she blinked away tears and glanced around at the graffiti-decorated stone and crumbling walls, she realized she was definitely in the ruins of the chapel. She could see what was left of the keep beyond and knew she was back. Back in her own year? She hoped so. She was counting on the fact that she didn't leave Kellen only to show up in some other time not her own.

At the thought of Kellen, her face crumpled and the tears started to flow. She sank against the crumbling stone wall as it really hit her. She was never going to see him again. He'd marry Edith and *she* would be the one to give him children. *She* would be the one who made him smile. It would be *Edith* who held Kellen close, teased him out of his somber moods, and saw the vulnerable man beneath the strength.

Gillian started to cry in earnest. *Edith would* never *love him as much as* she *did. Never! Edith couldn't possibly, and it wasn't fair!*

A long while later, Gillian swiped at her tears and took deep, shuddering breaths. She looked at the drying, congealing blood on the finger of her left hand. She was pretty sure the blood had somehow loosened the ring and triggered the time travel.

The ring had become so much a part of her; she'd been convinced she'd wear it the rest of her life. Her eyes filled with tears once more. She'd also been convinced that somehow, she'd have Kellen for the rest of her life, and look how that had turned out.

She opened her right hand to see the gold circle still within her cupped palm and picked it up to study the engravings on the inside. Again, she wondered at the words before closing her fingers around it once more.

According to the priest, she'd been on holy ground both in the cemetery and in the chapel. If the combination of blood and holy ground had somehow sent her back, that meant she could have returned at any time.

If she had, she'd have never met Kellen, never have fallen in love with him, or had his love in return.

Gillian leaned back against the crumbling wall, completely worn out, eyes swollen, and tried to hold back a fresh onslaught of tears.

What did she do now? Did she go home and somehow put her life, and her shattered heart, back together? Or did she do what her heart was telling her to do and put the ring back on?

The memories she'd made just didn't seem enough. She sat in the rubble of the chapel for a long time, remembering, crying, and feeling sorry for herself.

Finally, completely chilled and shivering, she got up. Yes, she was tempted to put the ring on her finger and try and go back, but she wouldn't. She was in her own time now, and he was in his. It was for the best.

She needed to step aside so Kellen could have everything he needed. So he could have everything Edith's property would bring. Kellen wouldn't have to pay a fine to the king, and he wouldn't have to try and explain her presence to anyone. By marrying Edith, he'd be ahead money rather than behind and, like Marissa had said, he had many to take care of.

So, Gillian would go home, get over Kellen, and get on with her life. It hurt. But it was still the right thing to do.

HER RENTAL CAR was long gone from where she'd parked it. Still swiping the occasional tear, Gillian walked all the way into town, glad of the exercise in the cool mid-afternoon air and the time to think. When she finally arrived, the first thing she did was head to the hotel. When she explained who she was, the manager's eyes widened and his mouth fell open.

"Miss Corbett! Where have you been? Your car was found and the police searched the area looking for you!" The manager, tall and thin, with a shock of thick, black hair and dark brown eyes, looked worriedly at her clothes. "Why are you dressed like that?"

Relieved that he knew her, that she'd made it back to where she was supposed to be, Gillian ran a hand down the skirt of her yellow medieval gown. "Uh . . ." She wasn't sure what to say.

"You look like you've been crying? Have you been harmed, Miss Corbett?"

"No. I'm fine. I went off with my boyfriend for a while, and we recently broke up."

"A local boy?"

Gillian nodded.

The manager's brows pulled together. "You went off with some bloke for over a month and didn't think to tell a soul?" His lip curled in disgust. "If that isn't just like an American girl."

Gillian, feeling numb, simply shrugged. "Do you still have my luggage?"

"Yes." His tone had cooled considerably. "We still have it."

"Can you rent me a room?"

The manager turned to his computer. "I shouldn't after the way you took off. So inconsiderate. But the police will want to see you, and I'll have to call the car rental place and let them know you've turned up. They brought your cellular phone in. It's with your luggage. They were very worried about you. Everyone was." He shook his head and tapped his fingers on the keyboard. "So inconsiderate."

Gillian opened her backpack, pulled out her Visa card and ID and, after what seemed like forever, she was finally checked in and given a key.

The manager's expression was icy. "Your things will be sent on to your room. Of course, there will be an additional fee for storing your possessions while you were away."

Gillian lifted one shoulder. "Thank you. That will be fine."

The man nodded and, apparently somewhat appeased by her response, softened a bit. "All right, then."

Gillian headed to her room and, after her luggage arrived, she cried in the shower as hot water streamed over her. She already missed Kellen so much.

Was he already married to Edith? After she'd left had they just got on with it? She realized he'd actually have married, lived his entire life, and had a family with Edith. He'd be long dead by now.

That made her cry even harder.

After the water cooled, she got into her pajamas and lay on the bed, only to be awakened some time later by a knock on the door. She quickly slipped into her robe.

The two burly gentlemen at the door, a redhead and a thinning brunet, identified themselves as the police. "Miss Corbett? Can we come in?"

She stepped back and let them enter.

"Are you alone, miss?"

"Yes."

They looked around; the brunet, a hard-jawed man with a strong cleft chin, searched the bathroom, apparently unwilling to take her word for it. When they'd all been seated, her on the bed and them in the two available chairs, they started the questions.

Had she been injured? *No.* Was she held against her will? *No.* Was she robbed? *No.* The name of her boyfriend? *Kellen Marshall.* His address? *They'd just traveled around a lot.* Was there anything she wanted to tell them? Anything she'd left out? *No.* Was she afraid to report a crime, because they could assure her they had the ability to protect her. *She was fine.*

Standing, looking exasperated and no doubt thinking the whole process a waste of time, they headed for the door; and the redhead turned back. "It was inconsiderate of you to worry everyone so. There was a search after your car was discovered, you know?"

Gillian hung her head. "I heard. I'm sorry."

The man nodded once, they both left and, exhausted, she crawled back into bed and immediately fell asleep.

THE NEXT MORNING, Gillian went outside into the chilly spring air, bought a local newspaper, and sat on a bench. She looked at the date in the corner, May 24. Sure enough, it was springtime again, and over a month had passed since she'd been there last.

She thought about all that had happened, and stupid tears welled in her eyes again. She knew she needed to get control of herself. She was a mess. But all she could think about was, did he miss her? Think about her? Would he be happy? Did she want him happy with *That Cow Edith?*

"Miss, are you okay?" Gillian looked up to see a pretty, middle-aged woman looking at her with concern.

Gillian sniffed, wiped at her eyes, and chuckled. "Sorry, I'm fine, just thinking about something . . . sad."

"Is there anything I can to do to help?"

Gillian shook her head. "No, I'm fine. Thank you, though."

The woman nodded. "Okay, if you're sure." She smiled and started to walk away.

"Wait. Do you know if there's a car rental in town?"

The woman nodded. "Sure. There's one just outside the Gillian town square."

Gillian stared at the woman. "Excuse me. Did you say the *Gillian* town square?"

"Yes. I can give you a lift if you'd like."

Gillian looked at the newspaper in her hand. *The Gillian Gazette* was printed at the top of the front page in big, bold letters. How had she missed that? "I thought this town was named Marshall?"

The woman shook her head. "No, you're thinking about the ruin outside of town. It's called Marshall Keep. The town is named after some obscure lord's true love." She waved a hand. "I don't remember all the details, but there's a guidebook over at the local bookshop." She pointed across the street to a charming cluster of honey-stoned cottages. "It tells the whole story."

Gillian stared at the hanging bookstore sign as chills raced up her body. "Thank you."

"Are you sure you don't need a lift?"

Gillian shook her head. "No, I'm good. But thanks for your help."

She walked across the cobblestone street to the bookstore, asked for and purchased the guidebook, and was soon back outside and sitting on a pretty wooden bench. She flipped to information about the castle.

Lord Marshall, later Lord Hardbrook after his father's death, had named the town after his true love. *Curse it!* The tears started up again and she tilted her head back and willed the moisture away. After a moment, under control again, she continued reading.

Historians weren't sure what the whole story was there. Lord Marshall's first wife had died, and it had been rumored he'd killed her. For this mystery girl? No one knew, which was why Lord Marshall had become such a figure of speculation and mystery over the years.

Some historians ventured that Gillian had actually been Catherine, perhaps a nickname? Apparently, her death had left him disconsolate as he'd never remarried. Another theory stated that perhaps Gillian was a lover who had died too? Or had married another?

What was clear was that, after his wife's death, Lord Marshall had contracted to marry his wife's younger sister, but she'd married one of Lord Marshall's men instead.

Tears flooded her eyes again. It was *her* that he'd wanted? Not riches or wealth or a connection to Lord Corbett? Just her? Had Kellen believed her story after she'd disappeared? Was he leaving her a message with the name of the town? He'd never married Edith because he loved Gillian? And then he'd been alone his entire life?

She swallowed convulsively. *That wretch Tristan!* If she could get her hands on him right now, she'd hurt him! She might not have wanted Kellen to marry Edith, but she hadn't wanted him lonely, either!

She wiped away more tears as she tried to sort through what this meant. Kellen had found out that she'd lied about being Edith. He knew Gillian wasn't an heiress. And he'd still wanted her? He'd given up wealth and property and even a chance at the heir he'd wanted when Gillian had nothing to give but herself? He'd meant what he'd said?

She pressed her hands to her face and cried harder. She'd felt he couldn't love her unless she had something to offer, specifically money, but that wasn't the case. *That wasn't the case!* If he couldn't have her, he hadn't married anyone?

Gillian started to laugh and pressing the guidebook to her heart, she jumped up and started toward the hotel. She'd grab her things and run back to him. She had to see him, to tell him. She stopped, realized a passerby was staring at her, probably seeing a crazy, giddy woman, and put her head down and walked at a more sedate pace to the hotel.

She wanted to see him immediately, this day. She wanted to hold him, be held by him, tell him how she felt, and listen to his assurances; but there were some things she needed to do first.

A FEW HOURS later Gillian was sitting on the hotel bed, her newly charged cell phone in hand, and the notes she'd made to herself spread out before her. Taking a breath, she dialed a number in her contact list.

"Hello?" A deep voice answered the phone.

Gillian clutched the receiver. "Mr. Frost? Uh, Walter?"

"Yes, who is calling, please?"

"It's Gillian. Gillian Corbett."

"Gillian! My dear. It's wonderful to hear from you. How are you?"

"I'm doing well." She smiled, seeing the easy-going older gentleman in her mind, always perfectly groomed, and most comfortable in slacks and a sweater. Ten years older than her dad, they'd been good friends in the years before his death. "Better than ever, actually."

"I'm so happy to hear that. We've been worried about you, you know. How was England?"

"Well, I'm actually still here. I've met someone and I'm getting married." Saying the words out loud sent a thrill through her.

"Married?" He cleared his throat. "To that young gentleman

you told me about? I thought—" he hesitated. "Did the two of you make up, after all?"

"No. This isn't Ryan. This is someone I met in England."

Walter paused. "Oh, but my dear, that was awfully fast." He hesitated again. "Gillian, as a good friend of your father's, I feel I have to caution you against jumping into marriage too soon. And so quickly after you ended a previous relationship. You've been in a vulnerable place ever since, well, your family . . . uh . . . left you alone. He's English?"

"Yes. And I understand your concern. I do. But please don't worry. My fiancé is rock solid. He's a really great guy."

"Hmm. Tell me about him. What does he do for a living?"

"He's a farmer. He has a lot of people working for him and depending on him."

"How do you know he's not some sort of con artist?"

Gillian laughed, thinking of Kellen's reaction to such an accusation. No doubt a sword would be involved. "I've been living with him and his family for a while now. I think I'd know if anything shady was going on."

"Well then, how do you know this gentleman doesn't just want you for your money? I hesitate to say hurtful things to you, my dear, but you've been taken in before. Didn't you tell me Ryan turned out to be less than honest in his feelings for you?"

She looked at the guide book and thought about the fact that Kellen didn't marry Edith for her money, that he'd named the town Gillian, and she couldn't help but smile. "I promise you I'm not even the smallest bit concerned about that. He doesn't even know I have any money. He's actually been supporting me for the last month or so."

There was another hesitation then, "Gillian, you've been through a lot in the last few years. Are you sure?"

"Positive. Listen, I know Ryan and I didn't work out, but this is different. In terms of character, Kellen reminds me of my father and of you, for that matter. He's honorable, dependable, and always does the right thing. I know he loves me. He's a wonderful guy and I'm so glad to be marrying him. You have no idea how happy I am about this."

Walter sighed. "Well, I can see you're not going to change your mind. And I appreciate you calling to tell me. Are you coming home before the wedding?"

"That's why I'm calling you. I'm not coming home at all."

"What do you mean?"

"I'm hoping you can sell my parents' house for me. Quickly."

"Well, Gillian, of course I can. I still do a little real estate from time to time, and I'm glad you've come to me; but why the rush? What if the marriage doesn't work out? I can list your house, but why not wait for the market to recover?"

"No. I want it sold."

He paused. "Look, I know your parents left you some money, and I'm aware your art career is going well. Surely there isn't any hurry? After all the work your parents did to the place, it's a gem. If you sell it, you may never get it back if you change your mind later."

"I promise I'm not coming back. This is happily ever after for me. I'm all right and I'm happy. Please don't worry about me. Here's what I want . . ."

After a lot more talking back and forth, she finally convinced him to sell the house for the lowered price she'd decided on so it would sell fast.

"Everything? What about keepsakes? Furniture?"

"All I want is for you to overnight my family genealogy album and the big red photo album. The one with all my family photos."

"This just seems so fast. So permanent. Can't I talk you into waiting?"

"No. My mind is made up."

He sighed again. "All right. If you don't care, I'll buy your house myself if you're determined to sell it for that price. Then I'll wait out the market and make the profit you should have had."

Gillian smiled. "That would be wonderful. Thank you so much. That's generous of you to offer."

Walter blew out a breath. "I'm the one getting the good deal. I feel like I'm cheating you."

"And yet, I feel like you're doing me a huge favor. Please get the paperwork started immediately." She gave him the hotel and fax number, the name of the city, and her bank account info. He already had a spare key.

After everything was taken care of, he sighed loudly. "Just so you know, I'll be paying all the closing costs. It's the least I can do. And I'll be calling the local police so I can make sure none of this is being done under coercion."

"That's fine. I have their number here if you want it. I took off with my boyfriend for a while, and when I came back they paid me a visit."

"Hmm. Actually, I prefer to look up the number myself. You realize it's looking even more suspicious to me now, right?"

Gillian laughed. "Please don't worry. I promise I'm fine. But call the police if it will put your mind at ease."

When she got off the phone, she added a visit to the police station to her to-do list. No doubt they'd think she was a flake and an idiot for making up with her boyfriend and marrying so quickly, but that didn't matter. They just needed to believe she was all right so they could convince Walter.

She picked up the phone again. A call to her money manager, then another to the leading gold and gems expert in England got the ball rolling, and when she'd finished making the calls she picked up her purse and headed for the door. It was time to go shopping.

CHAPTER 32

Two weeks later, Gillian drove to the ruins of the castle exhausted but happy. She looked down at her yellow medieval gown, dry-cleaned, pressed, and bunched around her knees so she could drive. She couldn't help but smile.

She knew she was looking her best, with subtle make-up, her hair freshly washed, trimmed and curled, and she wore a fortune in gold jewelry.

She was, however, feeling a bit paranoid because she had so much of value with her. She glanced at the one of the large duffle bags, taking up the entire passenger seat and floor, and gave it a pat before glancing in her rear-view mirror to assure herself no one was following.

She drove along the road near Marshall Keep, saw no one, doubled back, and parked as close to the castle as she could get, in the spot she'd instructed the car rental place to pick up the vehicle in a few hours. She didn't want it getting back to the police, and then to Walter, that she'd gone missing again.

She glanced at the castle ruin, then carefully studied the entire area, but there were no cars, no people, just the deserted rubble in the morning sunlight, the softly rolling hills, and the cemetery in the distance.

Her body humming with excitement, she got out, double-checked the pepper spray and knife in her pocket, then slipped on her backpack, tightened it, and dragged out the two padlocked duffle bags full of gold coins, gems, spices, and essentials.

She catalogued the essentials in her mind: Her genealogy book, with added family pictures from her photo album, chocolate, antibiotics, and a fully stocked first aid kit. A few books on natural healing, and seeds for some of the healing plants. Ibuprofen, a hand mirror, menstrual cups, a manicure set and nail polish, toothbrushes, and some make-up and underwear. Also, a little something for Kellen on their wedding night. There was so much more she could have brought, but she didn't want to push her luck. Anyway, there was only so much she could carry.

She'd closed her social media accounts, said her goodbyes to work contacts, college friends, Walter and his wife, and hoped they'd all be so busy with their own lives that it would be a long time before they realized she hadn't been in contact. Hopefully, they'd just assume she'd moved on with her life as had already happened with a few of her friends.

As an added precaution, she'd let it slip to the police that she was ready to completely break ties with her old life, start a new one, and probably wouldn't be in touch with her friends again. No doubt she'd come off sounding irresponsible, selfish and cold, but the last thing she wanted was for Walter to worry about her or feel responsible for instigating a search and rescue if he tried and failed to get in touch.

She still had to laugh about the last time she'd spoken to him. He'd found her ex-fiancé, Ryan, living in her parents' house, claiming he wanted to get back together with Gillian. Walter had had him arrested for trespassing. It couldn't have happened to a nicer guy.

Placing the car key under the mat, she shut the door, glanced around, hoisted a pack onto each shoulder, and groaned at the weight. She staggered toward the ruin and couldn't help glancing around the entire time, feeling paranoid that the young men who'd attacked her, or someone else entirely, would show up. Thankfully, she was completely alone.

She hauled everything to the ruin and, after much heavy breathing, a few rest stops, and quite a bit of sweat, through to the chapel.

She went to the spot she'd landed the last time and dropped the duffle bags, straightened, rubbed her lower back, and tried to catch her breath. She looked at the bounty at her feet and couldn't help but feel pleased with all she'd accomplished in such a short amount of time. Darned if Kellen was ever going to feel he'd lost out by marrying her.

Not that she'd tell him about her dowry before he declared himself willing to take her without it. She had her pride, after all, and wanted to actually hear the words. She wanted to hear that he loved her for who she was and not what she brought to the marriage. Apparently, she was still feeling a little insecure.

He would still want her, wouldn't he? Now that he'd had a chance to think about it? Gillian looked around the ruins of the castle and admitted she was stalling because she was scared. Scared the time travel wasn't going to work, scared he'd already moved on, scared that the history books had it all wrong.

She took one of the gold chains off her neck, looked at the ring dangling at the bottom, then at the writing engraved on the inside. When her family's genealogy book had arrived, she'd found a receipt from the man her dad had hired to decipher the markings. The ancient words meant *Life flows for all time.* Gillian, thinking of Kellen, certainly hoped so.

She clenched the ring in one fist. It had to work; because if it didn't, she didn't know what she'd do. She finally took a deep breath, squatted down, hefted one strap onto her left shoulder, another onto her right, and straightened. The heavy packs dangled against each side, and she opened the chain and removed the ring.

She grimaced as she cut her finger with the small knife she'd bought for just that purpose. She folded the blade, put it back in her pocket and, taking a deep breath, slid the ring onto her bleeding finger.

Within seconds, the chapel was whole again. Father Elliot let out a startled yelp. "By sweet Saint Cuthbert! Lady Corbett!"

Gillian fell to her knees, the duffle bags clanging noisily to the ground beside her. She was so relieved it had worked, that she was back, that she'd made it, that she'd reached Kellen. Stupidly, she started to cry. "Father Elliot," she said between sobs. "It's so good to see you again."

The rotund man rushed forward. "And you, as well. Welcome home."

Gillian wiped at her eyes and laughed, glad to see he didn't look as if he were ready to gather firewood for a witch burning. "Thank you. How long have I been gone?"

"A fortnight at least, my dear."

"Kellen didn't marry Edith, did he?"

He smiled at that. "Nay, my dear. He awaits your return."

"Oh." Another sob burst from her and more tears burned her eyes, but she still couldn't help smiling. "Good. That's so good." Relieved and elated, Gillian shrugged off her backpack, stood on unsteady legs, and headed for the door. She stopped and turned around. "Do you think you could have my things sent up to my room?"

Father Elliot nodded. "Certainly."

And then she was outside, running toward Marshall Keep to find her man, marry him, and live happily ever after.

MARISSA WALKED out the front doors to greet Sir Royce and his three men as they handed off their horses to the boys. As she lifted her hand in greeting, Gillian ran up behind them. "Hi. Where's Kellen?"

Marissa gaped at her. *"Gillian!"* She looked beautiful, her blonde hair gleaming in the sun, her brilliant blue eyes striking and vivid, her lips a soft color. "You . . . you are back! I . . . I . . ." Marissa threw up her hands. "Where have you been?"

Gillian grinned at her. "We'll talk later, I promise. But right now, I need to see Kellen. Gillian started to move around Marissa. "Is he inside?"

"He is not here."

Gillian stopped short. "What? Where is he?"

"He is at the river. But Gillian—"

"I have to go see him. We'll talk later, I promise!" Gillian took off running toward the gatehouse.

"You cannot mean to go alone!" Marissa yelled after her. *"Gillian!"*

Sir Royce, bowing slightly at the waist, straightened and smiled. "Fret not. I will take her safely to him."

"Will you?" Marissa placed a hand to her heart. "Oh, thank you, sir. You are most kind."

Sir Royce and his three men hurried after Gillian on foot, Sir Royce raising a hand and calling after her. "Lady Corbett! Wait! *Lady Corbett!"*

Gillian sprinted past the gatehouse and Marissa rolled her eyes as more voices joined in as the guards yelled after the girl. She shook her head. "Decorum, my girl. Decorum."

Still, Marissa couldn't help smiling as she headed inside to find her husband. First, she would share the news, then go and meet with Cook. No doubt they would be feasting this night.

KELLEN STOOD at the side of the slow-moving river, glad of the privacy the trees provided and of the time alone. He needed to think and was tired of his men watching him, giving advice, and pitying him. He was especially weary of Tristan alternately offering to give Edith back or trying to hide his happiness over his upcoming marriage.

As if Kellen wanted Edith back. He wished Tristan to marry the girl as soon as the banns were declared fulfilled, hopefully in the next week, so he could take her and her blasted family away.

He was sick to death of Lord Corbett trying to prove unfounded impediments to the marriage, tired of Owen's hovering concern, and fed up with his father attempting to convince him to see reason and reclaim Edith or find another bride.

None but he believed Gillian would return. But fate would not be so callous as to gift her to him then snatch her away forever. The belief that she would return was all that steadied him.

With all his might, he threw a small stone out into the river and, as it splashed, swore he could almost hear Gillian calling his name, that fate was letting him know—

He heard it once more, louder this time, and whirled. He caught a glimpse of a yellow gown moving through the trees and lost his breath as he awaited another.

"*Kellen!*" Gillian broke from the tree line and ran toward him, smiling, happy, and breathless.

Disbelieving, he started toward her, slowly at first then faster when she did not vanish. His heart hammered, and his head spun with the thought that simply thinking of her had made her appear.

It was not until she threw herself at him and he clasped her within his arms and lifted her tight against his chest that he actually believed she was back. Eyes clenching as he buried his face in her neck, he breathed her in. "Gillian," he whispered, his voice low and ragged.

After a moment, she laughed and squirmed. "You're holding me too tight!"

Kellen forced himself to loosen his grip but did not release her. He could not. "What I should do is wring your neck for leaving me." His voice shook and tremors shivered throughout his body.

"So, you missed me?"

Kellen lowered her to the ground, clasped her shoulders, and touched his forehead to hers. "Aye, sweet. I missed you. So much."

Her hands caressed his face, and her eyes moistened. "And you love me? Even though I'm not Lord Corbett's daughter and even though I don't have a dowry?"

Kellen finally lifted his head so he could give her a shake. "None of that matters. Aye. I love you. I love you with everything in me, and it has slowly gutted me to have you gone. You love me, as well? Say it. I need to hear the words."

Gillian laughed. "I do. I love you." She kissed him, her soft lips clinging for a long moment before she sank back. "I love you, so much, with everything in me."

"Why did you leave? Why did you stay away? Could you not return to me?"

"Well, I thought you were better off without me. I thought you needed Edith's money. Then I found you'd named the town after me."

Kellen's grip tightened as he whispered a prayer in thanks. "It was all I could think to do. I could think of no other way to send you a message. I also had the stone mason fashion a tribute. Did you see it?"

She shook her head. "No."

"I tried to think on how to let you know I needed you to return. Why did it take you so long? Were you prevented?"

"I needed to get some money. To bring a dowry. It took some time to sell my father's house and buy gems and gold."

Kellen stared at her in disbelief. "You stayed away for money?"

"I had nothing. I didn't want you to feel you'd lost out by marrying me."

His hands clenched and unclenched on her shoulders and he managed not to shake her. Barely. "What if you could not have returned? I have been in cursed misery for fifteen long days on account of riches?" His voice rose. *"Possessions?"*

Gillian looked worried, as well she might. "I was trying to do the right thing."

Kellen's mouth tightened as he tried not to lose his temper but the words were forced from him. "You left me, ripped my guts out *to get funds?"*

Gillian shook loose and took a step back. She placed her hands on her hips. "Do you know how hard I had to work to put this together? It's easy for you to act like it doesn't mean anything, but you know good and well your family, your men, and even your servants think you deserve the dowry your wife brings. I'm not coming to this marriage as a poor beggar."

"A poor beggar? *You are only the most precious of my possessions!"*

Gillian poked him in the chest. "That is exactly what I'm talking about! You don't own me. *I'm* the one bringing the dowry that *my* parents provided. *I'm* the one who owns *you!"*

He stared at her a long moment, then shook his head, and finally smiled. He tried to pull her back into his arms, but she stiffened and pushed against his chest, her expression mulish.

"Come now. Peace," he said softly. "You do own me. Heart and soul. I am yours for the taking."

She visibly softened and, after a moment, relaxed against him as he held her close. "And I am yours," she said softly.

"Aye. You are here. Nothing else matters. I will do whatever it takes to keep you."

She finally slid her arms around his neck and hugged him tight. He pulled her close, determined that nothing would ever separate them again.

CHAPTER 33

*S*ir Robert Royce smirked as he stepped from behind the trees. Watching the lovers reunite and knowing it would only last a short while filled him with an almost joyful rush of power.

He clapped approvingly as he walked forward. "How amusing; how very charming. 'Tis simply too precious for words."

He motioned and two of his men rushed forward and grabbed Kellen, who shoved Gillian behind him. While the three men scuffled, Kellen landing several blows and driving one guard to his knees, the third guard moved past them and grabbed Gillian. She wrenched away, ran, and the young guard barely caught her again, holding tight to her arm as she slapped him repeatedly with her free hand.

Robert rolled his eyes. "Get hold of her, boy!"

The boy finally overcame her by wrapping an arm around her waist and placing a knife to her throat. Wide-eyed, she finally settled, both of them breathing heavily.

Satisfied, Robert turned to see Kellen repeatedly punching a man in the stomach so hard he was lifted inches off his feet and, the second guard, his nose obviously broken, struggling to stand.

Robert sighed. Did he have to do everything himself? "Do I need to cut her?" His voice was loud, but pleasant. "I will, you know, and with pleasure."

Kellen glanced wildly around for Gillian, then, seeing the knife at her throat, stopped struggling. The two guards quickly grabbed and held him.

Robert laughed. "I thought so." He studied Kellen for a long moment, rather enjoying seeing him furious and helpless, caught by his own feelings for the girl. "I do hate to interrupt such a touching reunion." He glanced around. "And in such a deserted location, too."

Kellen glared at him. "What do you want, Royce?"

"What do I want?" His fists clenched. "Mayhap I wish to see you *put in a dress?*" Robert took a calming breath, then motioned to his men. "On his knees."

His men kicked the backs of Kellen's legs and, when he dropped, held him down. Robert smiled, enjoying the sight of the great Lord Kellen Marshall humbled and furious. He motioned to his men. "Not a mark to his face."

Needing no further instruction, they took turns slamming their fists into Kellen's back, chest, stomach, and arms. Robert smiled, enjoying every blow, grunt, and furious glare.

Gillian's enraged scream was cut off by the boy's hand over her mouth. "Please, my lady. Please be still."

Robert, irritated by the distraction, glanced around. "Yes, keep her quiet. We do not wish to be interrupted, do we?"

Gillian's hands fiddled with something and as Robert watched a blade opened in her hand. He moved forward swiftly and knocked it to the ground. He laughed as she rubbed her stinging fingers. "So very feisty." He snapped his teeth at her. "Save a bit for later, my dear."

Robert lifted a hand to his men. "That is enough." One jerked Kellen's arms behind his back in a cruel grip, and the other grabbed Kellen by the hair and yanked his head back, baring his face. Robert leaned down. "Do you know where the fair Gillian has been these last weeks? With me, at my castle, in my bed. When she ran away, that is where she went."

Gillian struggled against the hand at her mouth, unable to speak, and Robert laughed.

"*You* supplied the poison to Catherine," Kellen spat, bitter and fierce.

One of the guards slammed a fist into Kellen's face. Robert frowned. "Do *not* damage his face! How much more clearly can I state it?"

"Sorry, my lord."

Robert looked at the fresh cut on Kellen's cheek and chuckled. "Oh, well. What's another scar? Dear Catherine hated them, you know. It was her idea to use poison. A shame she drank it and killed not only herself, but your heir, as well."

Robert straightened and smirked. "Or would he have been yours? As much as she liked to crawl into my bed, there may have been some question as the child started to mature."

Suspicion marked Kellen's features. "You were in London most of that year. After her death, I checked your whereabouts."

Robert raised a brow. "You thought to suspect me?"

"I suspected everyone. Catherine herself told me with her dying breath she had a lover who was beautiful. You did come to mind."

Robert smiled. "Yes, well, I may have been in residence more often than I let on. Catherine preferred the secrecy. She loved to lie as a common maid in the forest. It was most uncomfortable and I ruined more than one tunic, but she wished for the risk and excitement. Who was I to deny the lady?"

Robert laughed at Kellen's murderous expression. "Of course, when it came time to kill you, I left. Catherine could be a fool at times, and there was always the chance she would get caught and betray me. I did not wish to be in the vicinity if she did."

Robert pressed his lips together. "She deserved to die. She was supposed to be mine. Her property and her child. The only thing she did aright was to give you a girl the first time. I thought perhaps the child was mine; and when I learned of your own doubts, it doubled my enjoyment."

Robert glanced at Gillian, enjoying her wide-eyed, tearful fear. "Then dear, sweet, Lady Gillian ruined it all with her sketching, making us all see to whom Amelia truly belonged." He shook his head. "Aye, Catherine betrayed me on many levels: having doubts, harping on her honor, bedding you. I'd wondered if she took the poison apurpose."

Robert shrugged. "It matters not. When you are gone, I plan to convince the king you killed your wife. I will say you admitted such to me after you killed Lady Gillian in a jealous rage upon seeing me escort her to you, and then remorseful, you killed yourself. I will say you could not live with double the guilt. Your father will share your shame and the king will give your land to me, his trusted and loyal servant. Everything you have will finally be mine."

Robert saw Kellen's gaze flicker to Gillian and smiled. "The problem is, you have no idea how to romance a girl. Catherine was easy. If I have the chance, perhaps the fair Marissa will join me in bed, as well. She is lovely and lonely. Tsk-tsk. Always a bad combination."

Robert moved forward and motioned to the boy to drop his hand so Robert could cup Gillian's cheek.

She jerked her head away and glared at him. "Don't touch me you filthy creep."

He grasped her chin tightly and forced her to look at him. "There was no turning your head, was there? Whatever did you see in that animal?" He jerked his head to indicate Kellen. "I think there must be something the matter with you to prefer such a scarred and overlarge man to me. I've often wondered if perhaps your vision is weak."

She tugged against his grasp again and, with a laugh, he let her go and turned back to Kellen. "You have had everything given to you while I have had nothing. I have been forced to scheme and betray to have what was easily yours. You, an uncouth and unrefined barbarian. But you will pay. Yes, now you will pay."

He smiled at Gillian. "I'm going to have your woman in front of you, then slit her throat, and then I will help you fall upon your sword in a fit of remorse. None will be surprised to learn you have killed a second woman, and the king will be most interested."

"Kellen, close your eyes," Gillian said. "Hold your breath."

Robert laughed as he looked between the two of them. "Do you believe if he does not see your death it will make it any less real?"

He turned to see Kellen actually closing his eyes and bending his head. Robert's brows rose in surprise. "I had not though you such a coward as to—"

The boy holding Gillian let her go and she stepped forward. Robert's mouth dropped. "Boy, grab her! Hold her!"

The boy shook his head and glared out of angry, tear-filled eyes. "My name is Valeric and I am your son. *Your son!* But I will have no part in this murder! I may never be a knight, but I will never be a cold-blooded killer, either!"

As Robert started forward, Gillian's hand lifted and sprayed red liquid at first one guard, then the other, coating their eyes and faces with red splatter. The men dropped to their knees screaming and clutching at their faces.

Confused, Robert stopped, then took a step away from Gillian, and then another. Her eyes, wild with rage, turned upon him, and Robert crossed himself against her. "What is happening? What did you do to my men?"

The guards writhed on the ground in obvious agony and Gillian ignored him to turn back to them. "I've sprayed acid into your eyes. You only have a few more moments before it starts to rot your vision away. If you don't wash them out with water for a very long while, you'll go blind and your face will melt like butter."

They scrambled to their knees and stumbled into the river behind them.

Kellen slowly stood, blinking rapidly, jaw thrusting as he started forward.

One look at Kellen's face and Robert turned and ran.

"VALERIC, take your lady to the keep!"

Kellen ran after the fleeing Royce and easily caught him, tackling the other man to the ground. He rolled him over and as they struggled, exchanging blows, they were soon covered in dirt and leaves. Kellen, finally getting the upper hand, punched Royce three times in the face in quick succession and was well pleased when the smaller man's nose crunched. Royce groaned in agony.

Kellen rolled off him, stood, and beckoned with the fingers of one hand. "Stand, coward."

Royce stood, his eyes filled with hate as he felt his broken nose and wiped at the blood flowing freely down his face to drip off his chin.

Kellen smiled. "That will mark you for the rest of your short-lived life, scum."

Royce pulled a knife from his boot, and Kellen jumped back when the smaller man slashed out with the blade. A dagger was thrown to the ground at Kellen's feet, and he wasted no time scooping it up.

"Traitor!" Royce roared at Valeric.

Kellen saw Valeric wince, agony in his expression, before the boy tried to tug Gillian away; and when she fought him, he turned and ran into the trees alone.

Kellen shook his head. "I have always considered you an idiot, but never realized the depths to which you were capable of sinking." Kellen balanced on his feet, waited for an opportunity, and when Royce slashed out once more, unbalancing himself, Kellen swung his own knife with considerable force; and the blade ripped into Royce's cheek, eliciting a scream.

Kellen laughed. "Oh dear, that will most certainly scar. If it has a chance to heal, that is."

White-faced, Royce jumped back and put a hand to his face, a look of horror spreading across his features as he felt the disfigurement then looked at the blood on his hand.

His face contorted in anger and with an incoherent yell, he ran at Kellen. Kellen grabbed his arm, wrenched it up, and drove his dagger into Royce's belly and upward. "For my wife and my son, you misbegotten cur."

Kellen looked into the other man's surprised face for a long moment before releasing him. Royce staggered backward, both his hands clasped around the dagger's hilt, then sank to one knee. He stared up at Kellen, a look of disbelief upon his bleeding face, then fell over dead.

FAINT AND DIZZY, feeling both sickened and relieved, Gillian put both hands to her face and covered her eyes. After a moment she swallowed, straightened, and hurried forward to wrap her arms around Kellen's waist. She carefully avoided looking at Sir Royce as she didn't have the luxury of losing it just then. Maybe later. "Are you hurt?"

Kellen glanced at his bloody arm, turning it so she could see. "No, love. 'Tis just a small cut."

Following his gaze, she winced at the gaping six-inch wound, fat tissue and muscle visible. It wasn't bleeding as much as she would have thought, but it would need to be stitched. She lifted his undamaged arm and put it around her shoulders, more for moral support than anything, and he winced.

"Oh, I'm sorry! Are you okay?"

Kellen pressed his arm against his side. "My ribs ache like the devil, but I'll live."

They staggered through the trees and back toward the castle; Kellen's injured ribs made him wince when they stumbled. When they moved into the clearing, it was to see Valeric leading Sir Tristan, Sir Owen, and several guards, all of them running fast. Gillian closed her eyes. "Oh, thank goodness."

When they reached Kellen, he motioned with his head. "You will find two men splashing about on the river bank. Put them in the dungeon. Also, retrieve Sir Royce."

Valeric stopped. "My father?"

Kellen shook his head. "I'm sorry, lad. It could not be helped. Come with us. I do not want you to see his body."

Eyes bright with tears, Valeric glanced toward the trees, swallowed. "Am I to go to the dungeons, as well?"

Kellen shook his head. "Nay. We will talk of this later."

They moved toward the castle, a subdued Valeric following behind and, upon their arrival, the healer was summoned as Gillian urged Kellen to go upstairs and lie in bed.

He rolled his eyes, headed for his chair in the hall, and demanded some ale. Marissa arranged for food and drink as he told everyone what had happened. His father and Marissa, her ladies, the entire Corbett family, and about ten of his knights listened incredulous and astonished.

Kellen finished with, "It was Sir Royce who planned my death and coerced Catherine into poisoning me. He also tried to stab Lady Gillian, poison her food, and murdered Frederick. Is that not so, Valeric?"

Valeric, his face a study in misery, threw himself to the ground at Kellen's feet. "My lord, I have a confession to make."

Kellen grabbed the boy by his shirt and forced him to stand. "Yes, yes. We already know Sir Royce was your sire."

"Aye, my lord, but the knife, the poison—

"'Twas Lord Royce's doing. It is at an end. Do you understand?"

The boy searched Kellen's face and swallowed, relief etched on his young features. "Aye, my lord. Thank you."

The healer finally arrived and tsked over Kellen's injuries. When the man went to stitch the cut on Kellen's arm, Gillian lunged forward and screeched. *"You didn't wash your hands!"*

Kellen sighed heavily. "Gillian, stand back. I do not wish you to hover."

"Just wait a minute, okay?" Gillian ran upstairs and was relieved to see her bags were in the room she'd shared with Marissa. She quickly found the key hanging on one of the gold chains around her neck, opened the padlock on one pack, and retrieved hand cleaner, antibiotic cream, alcohol swabs, and bandages from the first aid kit. She stuffed them in her pockets, snapped the lock into place, and hurried away.

When she returned to the hall, Kellen's wound was half stitched.

"You didn't wait!"

The healer snorted. "This isn't the first wound I've tended to, missy."

Gillian hovered, feeling helpless, on the verge of tears, and unsure about what to do.

Lord Hardbrook took her by the arm and led her toward a bench. "Lass, are you all right?"

She sank down and, feeling breathless and dizzy, raised a trembling hand to rub her forehead. "Fine. Fine. Just a little shaken up, you know?" When she realized she was the center of attention, she flapped a hand in embarrassment. "It's just not every day that you see . . . see . . ." She sucked in a breath. "I'm just not sure I can do this, after all."

The healer finished stitching, and Kellen quickly stood and moved around several of his knights to sit beside her on the bench. He firmly pulled her onto his lap. "You will be all right in a moment."

As tears pricked her eyes she realized the last thing she needed or wanted from the injured man was sympathy. It embarrassed her.

"Shh. Shh." His arms encircled her, pulling her to his chest. "You *can* do this. You will."

Gillian leaned her head onto his shoulder and sobbed. "What do you want from me?"

He chuckled and rubbed her back. "I want companionship, laughter, children, you. I want it all, love. I want you to marry me."

She noticed he didn't mention money and she appreciated it. She sniffed, wiped her eyes, and tried to get hold of herself. "Yes," she nodded, face flushing, feeling everyone watching. "I want those things, too."

"I also want to know your name."

That made her chuckle. "Gillian Rose Corbett."

"Of? Where are you from?"

She laughed. "Seattle, Washington."

Lord Corbett snorted and stepped forward. "Of Corbett Castle, daughter."

Gillian lifted her head, her brows knitting as she studied Lord Corbett's patrician features. The last time she'd seen the man he'd been denouncing her. Now he was claiming her? "I don't understand."

"There is nothing to understand." Lord Corbett looked around the room at all the wide-eyed family, friends, knights, and servants. "As much as you like to pretend otherwise, and I will say, you have been a most difficult and willful child, you are my daughter and we will have our alliance with Lord Marshall."

Lady Corbett, her beautiful face serene and confident, stepped forward to stand beside her husband. "Yes, child. No more of this dissembling. You will claim us as we do you. Gillian Rose Corbett of . . ." She looked pointedly at Gillian.

Gillian smiled at Kellen, chuckled, and then looked at Lord and Lady Corbett and bowed her head. "Of Corbett Castle."

AFTER SIR ROYCE'S body was sent to Royce Castle, Gillian tried to get Kellen to go upstairs to rest, but he wouldn't let her out of his sight. When she invited Lord and Lady Corbett to her room, he followed.

He wouldn't lie on the bed so she forced him to sit, gave him a quick kiss on the cheek for the intense, hungry way he watched her, and then dug her genealogy book out of one of the packs. She set it on the small table beside Kellen and opened it as the Corbetts gathered around.

"This is a genealogy book. I looked through it to see if I was truly related to the two of you." She glanced up shyly. "I am."

She opened the book to a page near the front and pointed. "See, here's my name, and here are my parents' names." She flipped through until she found Lord and Lady Corbett's information nearer to the end. "And here you are. See?"

"The paper is so fine." Lord Corbett leaned closer. "But the words are difficult to decipher."

"Not to me." She read aloud his entire name, his parents', and grandparents' names.

Lord Corbett pointed. "What is this?" he slid his finger across several black marks on the page.

Gillian sighed. Trust the man to hone in on the one thing she didn't want him noticing. "If you must know, they're death dates. I planned to show you this book at some point, so I crossed them out. Your childrens' and grandchildrens', as well. There are just some things a person shouldn't know."

His mouth parted and, after a brief hesitation, he nodded. "Just so."

She started turning the pages backward. "See this here? If you follow the names back to the front of the book, you'll see I'm directly descended from you." She flipped to the back and showed him the few treasured photos she'd chosen. "These are my parents. This is my brother. Here are some of our other relatives."

As Lord and Lady Corbett gaped at the photos, Gillian explained the time travel the best she could. "Father Elliot said the chapel and the cemetery were both blessed by Saint Cuthbert." She lifted her finger. "My ring has an inscription inside that says *Life flows for all time.* I don't know how it works, but somehow I'm able to use this ring to go back and forth between centuries if I'm in the right place."

Kellen sucked in a breath. "The day you were running through the cemetery? You were trying to take me and Amelia back with you?"

Gillian searched his face, but he didn't seem angry; he actually looked a bit smug. "Yes."

Kellen smiled. "I'd steal you away as well, sweet."

As they grinned at each other, Lord Corbett took up where Gillian left off and started turning pages again, his gaze fascinated. He picked up Gillian's hand and looked at the ring. "'Tis difficult to comprehend. But you are our daughter in truth?"

Lady Corbett turned to Kellen and she had tears in her eyes.

"Perhaps this fact might help to right the wrong done against you by our Catherine?"

Lord Corbett jumped in fast. "Yes. I would like to settle a dowry upon Gillian. Perhaps that would help to heal the past and start a bright new future. A strong alliance."

Kellen raised a hand. "That is not necessary."

Gillian agreed. "That's very generous of you, my lord, but my parents left me well provided for."

"Left you? Your parents are dead?" asked Lord Corbett.

"Yes, but they left me a . . . um . . . dowry. It's why I was gone for so long. I had to collect it."

Kellen straightened, then winced and rubbed one rib. "A

subject we have yet to discuss. I still cannot fathom that you left for money! What if you could not have returned? What then?"

"Kellen! Stop moving around. You're going to hurt yourself."

"You are not to leave me again, do you hear?"

Gillian sighed. "I had a good reason for staying away, you know. It's a rather large amount of money, thank you very much."

"I thought you'd gone forever. I believed I had lost you."

"But Marissa said you might be forced to pay a fine to the king—"

"I'd pay the fine ten times over rather than risk losing you. I am well able to provide for my wife and did not care for being abandoned! I did not need the money half so much as I needed you."

Gillian lifted her hands up in the air. "Where is the gratitude? Anyway, do you know how hard it was to leave? To think Edith would have you? If you hadn't changed the name of the city to Gillian, then I might have left you both to it and been miserable the rest of my life."

Kellen shot to his feet. "I knew it! You had no intention of returning, did you? You should never have left me! I could have lost you forever and for what? A blasted dowry I don't even need!"

Lord Corbett stepped in. "'Tis her father's right to provide such."

Gillian threw out a hand toward Lord Corbett, palm up. "Thank you! It was my father's ring that brought me here, and I can't help but feel that perhaps he even had a hand in all this! Did you think of that? I can't help but feel he would do everything in his power to see me happy."

"Ah. Just so," said Lord Corbett. "We will leave the two of you to sort it out. But remember, Gillian, we are your parents now. You are not alone and will never be so again. May I keep this for a while?" He indicated the genealogy book. "'Tis not easy to decipher, but it will bring me pleasure to try. And of course, the faces are fascinating to look upon."

Touched by Lord Corbett's earnest assurances, Gillian nodded. "Of course. But you probably should keep it to yourselves as everything about it will seem strange to others."

"Of course." Lord Corbett bowed, then quickly scooped up the book. "Thank you."

Within moments Gillian and Kellen were alone and she turned to see he was still angry.

She rolled her eyes. "What?"

Kellen glared for a moment longer, then sighed and sank back onto the chair. "Changing the name of the town was all I could think to do. I was lost without you. I remembered you telling me it would be named Marshall one day and I thought," he swallowed, "I thought you might live there."

The pain in his words had the tension leaving her body and tears filling her eyes. "So, you really do love me?"

"Aye. With all my heart."

Gillian went to him and he quickly pulled her onto his lap and held her tight. "I love you too," she said. "With everything in me."

"If I had not thought to change the name would I have lost you forever?"

"I doubt it. It spurred me to immediate action, but I'm sure I wouldn't have lasted a day before I was looking you up in any book I could find. If you hadn't married Edith, I'd have come back. Maybe I would have, anyway."

He looked upset again. He picked up her hand and tugged at the ring. He studied it, fear and loathing on his face. "I wish I could take this from you."

Gillian followed his gaze. "I wonder . . ." She twisted her finger, forcing the cut to reopen.

"Gillian!" He clutched her to him with both arms anchoring her tight.

The skin broke, just a bit, bleeding slightly and the ring slid right off.

After a shocked silence, Kellen snatched the ring from her and, fisting it inside one hand, stared at her with wide, incredulous eyes.

She stared back, equally stunned by what she'd just done. She could feel his heart pounding against her arm, her own matching its rhythm.

He cautiously relaxed his hold on her and when she stayed seated on his lap, let out a pent-up breath.

Gillian laughed a bit hysterically. "I guess I have to be on holy ground for it to work."

"You could not have known that!" He sucked in air and wiped at his brow with his closed fist. "I will be keeping this." He lifted the fist in front of her face. "You'll not be getting it back. Ever."

"Okay." Happiness engulfing her, she laughed again. "You look so upset." She slid a hand behind his neck. "Shall I cheer you up with a few kisses?"

Kellen wiped at his brow again, looked at her mouth, and chuckled. "Gillian. What am I to do with you?"

"Love me forever?"

"I intend to." He pulled her closer, captured her mouth with his, and neither one of them said another word for a very long time.

CHAPTER 34

*A*s the guests listened to the singer, Marissa sat at the head table and glanced around the great hall to make sure everything ran smoothly, that every table had been served the fifth course of roasted quail, and that the platters of cheeses, walnuts and tarts were plentiful. She could not help the slight smile that tugged at her lips, and she picked up her cup of spicy mulled wine to hide her satisfaction.

Her husband reached out and covered her hand with his much larger and warmer one. "Happy?"

She set her cup down, enjoyed the heat of his skin, the way his touch made her feel, and the fact that her husband knew her so well. Her smile widened as she looked around at the feasting, the tables set up around the hall, the guests laughing and teasing the newlywed couple, and their obvious happiness.

"Aye, husband. I am." Everything had gone beautifully. All the hours of planning and preparing had been worth it in the end; the bride and groom, as happy a couple as she'd ever seen.

Gillian was beautiful in green velvet with peacock feathers at ears, collar, and in her beautiful headpiece and bouquet. How Beatrice had thought of it, Marissa did not know, but the effect was stunning and would no doubt be much copied. Gillian's groom obviously thought her lovely. He could not seem to take his besotted gaze off her.

Marissa glanced at her husband, who met her gaze and smiled. "It is good to be married," she said.

He brought her hand to his mouth and kissed it. "Aye, wife, it is."

When the singer finished his song, Marissa motioned for the two jugglers to perform then glanced around, hoping the heat in her cheeks was not obvious to all.

Many had attended, it being midsummer and a goodly time for travel, but Marissa was sure Gillian would be glad when everyone finally left them in peace to enjoy married life.

Valeric, so obviously happy in his new role as squire in training, offered the happy couple more choice meats and cheeses for their platter, but she wondered that he bothered. She noted that neither the bride nor the groom ate much, but there was much touching, talking, and smiling between them.

Tristan and Edith were to be married in a sennight and, though the girl was still a bit distant with her future groom, he seemed to be keeping her well entertained as he tried to draw forth her smiles with his chatter.

She saw Lord Corbett questioning Gillian once more, as he seemed to do at every opportunity. When Gillian had turned to him before the wedding and kissed his cheek and promised to always be a good daughter to him, the man had nigh wept in front of the assembly.

Of course, she could not fault the man. When Kellen had placed the ring upon Gillian's finger and sworn an oath to be a good and true husband to her, and Gillian had made her own vows in return, the truth and love in their voices had left not a dry eye in the chapel. When he'd kissed her overlong and she had clung to him, everyone, including herself, had cheered.

She looked at her husband once more. He returned her gaze

with a heavy-lidded one of his own that had the heat rising in her cheeks and left her wishing for the feast to be done with.

Yes. Married life was good indeed.

"GILLIAN?"

"Just a minute. I'm looking for something."

Kellen shifted from one foot to the other and waited impatiently as Gillian went through one of her packs at the side of his bed. *Their* bed now. He smiled at the thought.

He glanced at the door he'd managed to bar against his men and considered that if he'd allowed them to strip them and place them naked in bed as was their plan, he would not now be wondering how to place his bride there himself. "Can this not wait?"

"Don't you want to see what I bought for our wedding night?"

Kellen glanced at the bed. At the moment, he really did not care what was in her pack, but could tell from Gillian's quick glances and the quaver in her voice that she was a bit nervous, so feigned interest. "You've already shamed any dowry ever brought to man. There is more?"

Gillian shrugged. "I didn't want you to feel you'd lost out by marrying me."

Kellen shook his head at the worry. "I have never in my life seen jewels or gold so fine. If your goal was to produce a dower greater than the king could have provided, you succeeded."

"I have other things, as well. Art supplies, sulfa drugs, band-aids, antibiotic ointment, a book on natural healing and—"

"Did you bring more chocolate?"

Gillian pulled the pack closed and glanced back at him. "No."

His mouth curved. "You lie!"

"Hey. I bought you. I own you. I'm the one in charge here, and don't you forget it."

He rubbed his chin. "Mayhap I am not for purchase."

"Oh really?" She pulled out a gold coin and to his amazement, peeled it like a piece of fruit.

"What is that?"

"A coin." She pulled what looked to be a thin sliver of chocolate from the middle and popped it into her mouth. "Mm, mm, mm."

"Chocolate?"

"Say it. Say, Gillian owns me." She pulled out another coin and peeled it.

Kellen looked at the coin, but in fact was simply relieved that Gillian seemed to be relaxing so continued to tease her. "You must wait while I consider the matter."

Gillian popped the chocolate into her mouth. "Mm. Yummy."

"Just give me but a moment to consider. But do not eat all the coins in the meanwhile."

She pulled out another coin and started to open it, and he lunged at her.

She screamed, then laughed as he took the thin sliver of chocolate between his teeth and ate it. He tossed the gold bits aside and picked her up in his arms and held her close.

Gillian lowered her gaze and, with her finger, traced a pattern on his shirt. "You didn't let me find what I was looking for." She parted the material enough to slide her hand onto his skin, making his heart speed. "I bought a nightgown for our wedding night. I think you might like me in it."

"I am most certain I will." His voice was low, gruff, and he could feel the shiver that moved through Gillian, engendering a matching response in himself. "Gillian what I was trying to say is that you cannot buy my love, because you already won my heart."

She cupped his cheek and smiled, and it was all the encouragement he needed. He kissed her and carried her toward the bed, protectiveness, satisfaction, and longing enveloping him as he lay her on the mattress and followed her down.

As he moved back far enough to gaze down at her, she clung, her arms around his neck, love and acceptance shining in her eyes as she looked at him.

She was everything he could want. She was everything.

And she was finally his.

She pushed back a strand of his hair with her fingers, tucking it behind his ear, making him shiver anew. "I love you," she said.

His heart squeezed tight. "And I you." He touched his mouth to hers and could not help but smile against her lips when her arms tightened ever more, as if afraid he would escape.

She *was* everything. She had brought him back to life and given meaning to his dreams. He must have accomplished a great feat, then forgotten it, because the very fates had intervened to gift her to him.

Someday he would find the words to explain that had she been the most impoverished lady in the kingdom, he would have paid his entire fortune to have her, and then counted himself prosperous.

She was his fortune. *She* was his destiny. Indeed, he held his very future in his arms.

THANK YOU FOR READING!

I hope you enjoyed reading *She Owns the Knight*. If so, *Bewitching the Knight* is next in the series and I've written more medieval stories in *The Ghosts of Culloden Moor* series.

For information about future books, please visit www.DianeDarcy.com to sign up for my mailing list.

BOOKS IN A KNIGHT'S TALE SERIES

Series page on Amazon

Fairy Tale Romance

She's Just Right

The Princess Problem

Beauty and the Beach

The Texas Sisters

Steal His Heart

Christmas Novella

The Christmas Star

Stand Alone Stories

Serendipity

A Penny for Your Thoughts

How to Rewrite a Love Letter

Historical Western Romance: Rachel

How Miss West Was Won

Montana Gold

Regency Romance

P.S. I Loathe You

~

Cozy Mysteries

Murder Ties the Knot

Murder Misses the Mark

Murder Kicks the Bucket

EXCERPT FROM BEWITCHING THE KNIGHT

In Medieval Scotland, if she dresses, talks, and curses like a witch...

Archaeologist Dr. Samantha Ryan has figured out where The Scottish Crown is hidden—an artifact that went missing over 750 years ago. Now she just needs to beat her lying, cheating competitor to the Highlands and find it first. When a struggle ensues, they travel back in time to medieval Scotland where, unfortunately, the villagers think she's a witch, tie her up, and start gathering wood for a bonfire. Thinking to play on their superstitions so she can save herself, she curses them all. Not her best idea yet.

...it's time to gather firewood!

Laird Ian MacGregor is a dead man walking. It's only a matter of time before one of the many attempts on his life will succeed. When he is informed the villagers are burning another witch, he is enraged and determined to save the hapless woman. Unfortunately, the foolish female doesn't know when to keep her mouth shut. Ian rescues her anyway, ensuring any headway he'd made toward earning the villagers' trust is shattered. Locking her up only makes his people fear the witch in possession of his tower—a witch determined to steal the crown entrusted to him. While trying to find a murderer, keep King Alexander's crown safe, and control the unruly woman who may indeed be gifted with foresight, he finds himself wondering—now that he's caught her, how does he keep her?

Past and present are about to ignite.

When modern meets medieval, can there be a happily ever after?

~

Scotland, 1239

Ian fought for all he was worth. At eight, he was big for his age— sturdy as a pack horse, his mother liked to say—and he bit, scratched, and kicked, earning a cuff on the side of his head hard enough to fell him to his knees. But at last he was free.

"Mother!" He glanced wildly about, searching through legs, skirts, and feet, seeking a green gown as hard hands clamped on his arms, his shoulders, pulling him back. *"Mum!"*

"Ian! Go inside, love! Go with Brodrick!"

The desperation in his mother's voice spurred him to greater fury, and a kick to the knee of one of the men holding him resulted in a loosened grip as the man cursed and stumbled back. A bite to the fingers of the hand on his upper arm and he was free again.

Ian snaked through the crowd and it only took a few moments to find his mum in the crowd's center. He squirmed around one of the men restraining her and wrapped both arms tightly about her waist.

"Oh, Ian. No, son. You cannot be here." She kissed the top of his head, and struggled against the men holding her fast. "You need to stay with Joan and Brodrick. Please, dearest, can you not do this for me?"

"*Nae.*" He screamed the word. "I'll not leave ye." Rough hands grabbed him by the waist and pulled. He tightened his grasp around his mother and wouldn't let go. Fingers bit into his stomach, digging, stretching skin, hurting, and he cried out.

His mother struggled in earnest, her black braid swinging forward to fall against his face. "Do not hurt him! Do not touch him! I will talk to my son."

The slap across her face startled Ian enough to loosen his grip so he could look up at her, and he was immediately torn away. He glanced between the adults, men he'd known his entire life, clutching and pushing at his mother. How could they have turned on them? *"Let go of her! Let go! I'll bash you!"*

Clawing at the fingers holding him did no good, so he turned and bit the fleshy forearm of the man gripping him.

The man let out a yell, released Ian, and backhanded his face. "Filthy witch's get."

The force and pain felled Ian to the ground, but when the man reached for him again, Ian scooted and scrambled between the legs of the men and women gathered around. He turned and crawled, kicked the hand that grabbed his foot, and when he reached his mother, latched onto the leg of one of the men holding her, and bit with all his might.

The man screamed, jerked his leg, hauled back to deliver a kick, and suddenly Ian's mother was there, covering him with her body, protecting him with arms wrapped tight about him. "Leave him be." Tears fell hot against his neck. *"Let him alone!"*

Now that Ian was engulfed in his mother's arms, in her scent, he started to sob, the fear of the last moments giving way, burning through him.

"There, there, lad." Her English accent was strong now, sharp with emotion, and Ian wondered if the clan had turned on her because of her *otherness*. He'd heard the whispers. Knew some despised her. She knelt in the dirt with him, clasping him tightly as if she'd never let him go. He was eight, not a baby anymore, but right now he was exactly where he needed to be. She started to rock him. "There, there, little man." He couldn't help the sobs that burst from him, nor the ones that followed, threatening to overwhelm.

"Do not let her contaminate the child with her wickedness." The voice, the new priest come to village this past fortnight, sent ice and fiery hatred through Ian's veins. When harsh hands pulled and lifted them both, Ian clung with everything in him, clutching his mother as she clasped him in return. A blow to her back unbalanced them both and numbed his hands and another attacker jerked him away as she tried to cling. He thrust his fingers out as far as they'd reach. "Mum! Mum! Dinna touch her. *I'll kill you if you touch her!*"

"You see? Already, she taints the child."

His mother sobbed as she reached for him but her arms were captured and jerked behind her back. She drew a deep breath. *"Joan!"* His mother screamed for her friend and neighbor. "Take my son. Take him from here. I do not wish him to see this. Please keep him safe. Please keep him well, I beg you. He's yours now."

"No! Mum, no!"

Strong arms enclosed Ian as he was passed to Brodrick, Joan's burly husband, and his mother dragged in another direction as Brodrick shouldered his way through the crowd, clasping Ian tight, restraining his thrashing legs in a firm hold. Joan was suddenly there, fear stark on her pale face, the whites of her eyes showing as she advanced with her husband toward their hut.

"Wait."

That voice again.

Brodrick stopped and turned and Ian finally got a clear view of the man standing on the back of a wagon, his fine red garment glowing bright in the afternoon sunlight, the large gold cross gleaming at his chest. When Ian first saw the man, the *priest*, he'd thought him a fine figure, tall, slim, and elegant, everything a man of God should be. Later, when the priest cut himself on an edge of rough stone and visited his mother for a poultice, the man had given Ian a spiders-down-his-shirt feeling as he'd touched his mother's hand and stared upon her.

Now he knew the man's true character. Could see clearly that, black heart and soul, the man was the devil himself.

"I wish the boy to watch. I wish him to see what happens to witches when they practice their craft in the world of decent God-fearing men."

"Liar! I'll kill you! My mother isna a—"

Brodrick's hard hand clamped tight over Ian's mouth, but it didn't stop Ian from glaring at the devil. He tried to convey that he may have fooled others, but not Ian. If it took the whole of his life, he'd find the man and send him back to the fiery pits from whence he'd sprung.

"He's just a boy, your worship," Brodrick said. "Big for his age, to be sure, but a boy nonetheless."

"He's old enough to understand murder, surely? And he's threatened to kill me, has he not? Bring him forward." He motioned to one of his men, a guard who pushed through the crowd to follow instructions.

"No!" Mum's voice rang out. *"Let him be!"*

Ian was grasped with hard hands but Brodrick wrenched away and gave the man his broad back.

"What is this?" The priest's voice was amused. "I'm unsurprised by the witch's defiance, but would you directly challenge a man of God? Do you wish to join the witch in the flames? Or perhaps it's your wife who has been spending too much time with her friend?"

"My wife is a God-fearing woman," Brodrick's voice was stark, overloud. "She is good wi' the young ones, that is all, and wouldna wish to see one scared or hurt."

"Release the boy."

Brodrick slowly loosened his hold on Ian and he ran toward his mother, but was quickly intercepted by one of the priest's men and thrown roughly over a shoulder.

"Bring him here."

"No." His mother screamed the word. "*What is wrong with you all? Let him go!*"

Ian was dumped on the ground and secured by two men, one of whom cupped his chin, urging his face upward, forcing him to stare into the triumphant eyes of the fiend himself.

"How can you do this? His mother's voice rang out. "Have I not tended your young? Healed your wounds? Dugan," her voice broke. "Remember when you injured your arm?"

The devil, still gazing into Ian's eyes, lifted both hands into the air. "He has her look. Dark hair, pretty features, and green eyes." He raised his voice. "Mayhap he is a witch in the making?"

"Laird MacGregor!" his mother sobbed. "He is your son. Your *blood*. Take him from here, Sinclair. *Please help him.*"

All eyes turned toward the laird, including Ian's. Whispers started. His son? What did she mean?

"Take him to England. To my family. Or I swear by all I hold sacred I will haunt you and your *wife*," she spat the last word, "for the rest of your short lives."

The laird's wife drew herself up. "She curses us. Did ye hear?"

"Burn her," the priest intoned. "Before she can do more damage. And burn her spawn, as well."

"Sinclair! *Do something.*"

The laird stepped forward. "Nae the boy."

"He has her eyes," the priest intoned.

"I say nay. Are not little children innocent before God?"

With cold fury in his eyes, the priest bowed his head. "As you wish, Laird. But I hope you will not live to regret your interference. But I insist the boy watch. As a warning against following in his mother's destructive path."

Ian's mother was wrestled and tied to the beam in the center of the village, already black from previous burnings. "I wish him taken to my family, do you hear?" One of the priest's men thrust a torch into the wood and straw.

Fire licked hungrily toward his mother.

Ian bucked against the guards as blooms of smoked filled the air. "*Noooo! Nooooo! Stop!*"

He met his mother's eyes, and she gazed upon him for a long moment, before smoke started to obscure his view. "*I love you, Ian. Never forget it.* Now close your eyes, my love. Look away." And then the fire reached for her and she screamed.

Ian, eyes and mouth wide, shrieked until he was hoarse, his vision blocked by tears and smoke as the minutes and horror dragged on. He clenched his eyes tight when he smelled her, burnt and quiet now, surely dead, gone from him forever. He collapsed, hanging limp and exhausted in the guard's grasp.

"You may take him from here," the priest said.

Ian, his body shaking, studied the man responsible for his mother's murder. He noted the clean clothes, the jewels, and the man's smug expression. Ian had truly thought him God's messenger when he'd first seen him, his finery so bright and impressive.

But with his figure silhouetted against the darkening sky, the fire's light dancing across his face, playing over the scratches his mother had marked upon his cheek the night before, how could his kinsmen not see the devil himself, masquerading as a man of God?

Brodrick collected Ian again, carried him like a babe, his face pressed to big man's neck as Ian lay limp and exhausted, looking over his shoulder. As they shuffled away, Ian, eyes burning hotly, watched the devil climb down from the wagon and stride away. When Ian was older and stronger, he vowed he'd send the demon back to his fiery home and rid this world of evil.

He swore it on his mother's body.

If you'd like to read more, please go here.

Printed in Great Britain
by Amazon

45740217R00225